全国高等教育英语专业规划系列教材

英美短篇小说阅读与赏析教程
British and American Short Stories: Reading and Teaching

主　编　李金云

编写人员　（按姓氏音序排列）

黄　晶　沈国环　王　杨

吴林凯　周红霞

苏州大学出版社

图书在版编目(CIP)数据

英美短篇小说阅读与赏析教程 = British and American Short Stories: Reading and Teaching / 李金云主编. — 苏州:苏州大学出版社,2021.11
全国高等教育英语专业规划系列教材
ISBN 978-7-5672-3754-4

Ⅰ.①英… Ⅱ.①李… Ⅲ.①短篇小说-文学欣赏-美国-高等学校-教材②短篇小说-文学欣赏-英国-高等学校-教材 Ⅳ.①I712.074②I561.074

中国版本图书馆 CIP 数据核字(2021)第 219978 号

| 书　　名：英美短篇小说阅读与赏析教程 |
| British and American Short Stories: Reading and Teaching |
| 主　　编：李金云 |
| 责任编辑：汤定军 |
| 策划编辑：汤定军 |
| 装帧设计：刘　俊 |
| 出版发行：苏州大学出版社(Soochow University Press) |
| 社　　址：苏州市十梓街1号　邮编:215006 |
| 印　　装：广东虎彩云印刷有限公司 |
| 网　　址：www.sudapress.com |
| E - mail：tangdingjun@suda.edu.cn |
| 邮购热线：0512-67480030 |
| 销售热线：0512-67481020 |
| 开　　本：700 mm×1 000 mm　1/16　印张:19.25　字数:300 千 |
| 版　　次：2021 年 11 月第 1 版 |
| 印　　次：2021 年 11 月第 1 次印刷 |
| 书　　号：ISBN 978-7-5672-3754-4 |
| 定　　价：68.00 元 |

凡购本社图书发现印装错误,请与本社联系调换。服务热线:0512-67481020

序 言

美国作家亨利·詹姆斯(Henry James)曾指出,与长篇小说相比,短篇小说更适合表现瞬息即逝的现代生活。长篇小说发源于18世纪,短篇小说于19世纪后半期在法国和俄国取得长足发展,法国有梅里美、莫泊桑等短篇小说家,俄国有果戈理、契诃夫等短篇小说家,他们确立了短篇小说的独立地位,并将之提高到一个前所未有的水平。莫泊桑和契诃夫的作品被认为是短篇小说的两种范式:前者具有明显的现实主义和自然主义特征,用客观中立、不带价值判断和感情色彩的方式叙述故事,结构严谨精巧,情节连贯完整;后者则带有明显的印象主义特征,通过一些生活琐事表现厚重复杂的主题,作品结构松散,情节留有空白。这两种范式对英国和美国的短篇小说都产生了深远影响。

受殖民历史影响,英国短篇小说融入大量海外元素,包括印度、非洲、远东等。史蒂文森(Robert Louis Stevenson)、吉卜林(Rudyard Kipling)、毛姆(William Somerset Maugham)、乔伊斯(James Joyce)等作家的短篇小说反映了海外殖民给白人殖民者、当地原住民等造成的影响。史蒂文森的短篇小说《马克海姆》("Markheim")中,主人公不甘穷困现状,意欲通过抢劫古董店而快速致富。吉卜林在短篇小说《园丁》("The Gardener")中描写了一位悲恸的母亲,她儿子在海外战场上去世,母亲辗转多时才找到儿子的坟墓。高尔斯华绥(John Galsworthy)的《补偿》("Compensation")中,海外度假地一位年轻的犹太小贩不辞辛苦地劳作,终于攒了一笔钱准备返乡结婚,却被一个小偷全部偷走了。毛姆的《患难之交》("A Friend in Need")揭示了英国驻日商人爱德华·伯顿的丑恶嘴脸,他阴险狡诈、工于心计,不动声色地将身陷窘境前来求职的穷远亲列尼·伯顿置于死地。

在审美上,英国作家们观察细致入微,通过一些环境和细节描写反映主人公细致入微的心理活动,具有契诃夫式的印象主义风格。乔伊斯的《阿拉比》("Araby")中,一个天真无邪的男孩出于对同学姐姐朦胧的爱情,前往充满异域风情的阿拉比集市为其购买礼物,却意外窥见成人世界里庸俗的爱情,这使得他异常痛苦和愤怒。在《马贩子的女儿》("The Horse Dealer's Daughter")中,作者劳伦斯(David Herbert Lawrence)通过景色描写和一连串动作刻画出一个生动的、性格刚烈的、勇敢追求爱情的马贩子女儿的形象,同时也反映了医生杰克·弗格森优柔寡断的性格。曼斯菲尔德(Katherine Mansfield)在《没有脾气的男人》("The Man Without a Temperament")中通过描写一对英国夫妇在法国度假时一天中的生活片段,运用象征主义的手法揭示了貌似幸福的婚姻中丈夫的压抑和苦闷。伍尔芙(Virginia Woolf)在《墙上的斑点》("The Mark on the Wall")中运用意识流手法,讲述了主人公偶然抬头看见墙上的斑点,她由斑点联想到钉痕、挂肖像的前任房客、一座古冢等,进而想到忧伤、白骨和考古……最后发现墙上的斑点不过是一只蜗牛。

  与英国短篇小说相比,美国短篇小说的发展更为充分,内容涉及侦探、哥特、种族主义、少数族裔、西进运动等多种元素。爱伦·坡(Edgar Allan Poe)的短篇小说确立了侦探小说和哥特恐怖小说的样式,影响十分深远。短篇小说《莫格街谋杀案》("The Murders in the Rue Morgue")是文学史上第一篇侦探小说,开启了侦探小说的先河。爱伦·坡经常通过描写怪诞离奇的故事映射个体意识及潜意识中的阴暗面,创作了许多脍炙人口的恐怖小说。《泄密的心》("The Tell — Tale Heart")中,爱伦·坡将奇异恐怖的哥特式氛围渲染到极致,揭示了一个精神分裂症患者无端杀人分尸,之后又向警方自首的异常心理。霍桑(Nathaniel Hawthorne)的《胎记》("The Birthmark")中,主人公阿尔默是一位雄心勃勃的科学家,他意欲将妻子脸颊上一块绯红色的手形胎记去除,他认为胎记象征着罪恶、伤悲和死亡。妻子服下丈夫配制的药水后,胎记马上消失了,但她因此失去性命。福克纳(William Faulkner)在《干旱的九月》("Dry September")中以冷静客观的笔触描写了美国南方根深蒂固的种族主义。已是不惑之年的白人贵族小姐明尼·库伯为吸引众人关注,捏造出被黑人威尔强暴的谣言。尽管有人认为威尔绝无可能去冒犯明尼,但是镇上的其他白人坚持认为应该相信明尼的话,最后一群白人暴徒私刑处死了无辜的威尔。马拉默德(Bernard Malamud)的《魔桶》("The Magic Barrel")具有浓厚的犹太性,主人公利奥·芬克尔是一名学业有成的犹太青年,即将出任拉比。为获取人们信任,他决定先成家再出任拉比。最后他爱上了妓女斯特拉,在救赎斯特拉的过程中芬克尔得以自救。纳博科夫(Vladimir Vladimirovich Nabokov)的《圣诞节》("Christmas")有着浓郁的俄国风情,主人公斯列普佐夫在圣诞节前失去唯一的儿子,悲痛万分。他来到儿子生前居住的房间,忆及儿子过往的点滴,心中万念俱灰。这时他意外地看见儿子生前收藏在陶罐里的蚕蛹破茧成蝶的过程,似乎儿子得到了重生,这使他又重新燃起生活的希望。

西进运动和小镇沉闷乏味的生活也是美国作家们着力描写的对象。马克·吐温(Mark Twain)的短篇小说《卡拉维拉斯县驰名的跳蛙》("The Notorious Frog of Calaveras County")运用颇具地方色彩的西部方言刻画了一个嗜赌如命的赌徒形象,反映出西部生活的沉闷与无聊,开启了"奇谈怪闻"(Tall Tale)的先河。安德森(Sherwood Anderson)的《手》("Hands")描写了中西部边远小镇上的一位怪人。主人公毕德鲍姆是一位教师,他有一双灵巧的手。他性格温和,对学生满腔热忱,但他无法用语言表达内心对学生的热爱,只好借助他纤细的手指,通过对孩子们轻柔的抚触表达自己的爱心,却被家长误认为是同性恋而被逐出学校。史坦贝克(John Steinbeck)的《菊花》("The Chrysanthemums")反映了枯燥烦闷的小镇生活对女主人公的压抑。女主人公是一位能干的主妇,却经常被丈夫忽视。她酷爱种植菊花,以此打发无聊的时光。一次,一位补锅匠上门招揽生意,洞悉女主人公的爱好后,他假装喜欢菊花,骗取了女主人公的好感,随后却将她送的菊花丢弃在路边。

南方文学是美国文学的一个重要组成部分。南方作家重视家庭、宗教和传统道德观念,注重反映白人和黑人之间的种族冲突。除上文提及的福克纳外,波特(Katherine Anne Porter)和奥康纳(Flannery O'Conner)也是著名的南方作家,他们发表了系列短篇小说。波特在《被遗弃的韦瑟罗尔奶奶》("The Jilting of Granny Weatherall")中运用意识流手法,描写了韦瑟罗尔奶奶生命垂危之际脑海中闪现的回忆片段,这些片段交织串起老奶奶的一生,反映了黑奴、农场、天主教等南方生活的主要内容。奥康纳的《好人难寻》("A Good Man Is Hard to Find")则通过血腥的暴力描写,反映了罪与非罪、神圣之爱与宗教救赎的主题,揭示出南方社会浓厚的天主教氛围。

在文体方面,美国短篇小说既有马克·吐温倡导的方言写作,也有海明威(Ernest Miller Hemingway)提出的新闻式极简主义写作。海明威的短篇小说《杀手》("The Killers")文字简洁,节奏较快。乔治的餐馆里进来两个杀手,他们商量着去谋杀一个人。充满正义感的餐馆服务生尼克飞速赶往这个人的住所,告诉了他这个消息,却发现他对此无动于衷。海明威将故事情节淡化至最低限度,并未交代杀手行凶的原因和受害人为什么无动于衷,这充分体现了"冰山原则"。

这些英美短篇小说犹如一个个钻石,闪烁着璀璨的光芒。它们表现了两个国家不同的社会风貌,体现了各自的文学传统,并成为世界文学的重要组成部分。卡夫卡说:"书必须是凿破我们心中冰封的海洋的一把斧头。"我们希望这本书也是"一把斧头",能给读者带来一定启发,能使读者对人生、社会、理想等有新的认知,同时能体验短篇小说和文学之美。

本书是武汉科技大学研究生教材建设项目的成果,同时也受到学校教务处教材项目的资助,既可以作为外国文学专业研究生教材和英语相关专业高年级本科生的文学课教材,也可以作为非英语专业本科生和研究生的课外读物。此外,本书也适用于广大英语爱好者和文学爱好者。

本书由编写组共同努力完成,其中 Unit 1、2、6、10、14、16 由李金云完成,Unit 3、13、17 由黄晶完成,Unit 4、5、12 由沈国环完成,Unit 7、8、15 由周红霞完成,Unit 9、18 由王杨完成,Unit 11 由吴林凯完成。李金云负责本书内容的选定与安排,并对全书内容做了审定和修改。苏州大学出版社汤定军先生对本书提出很多宝贵修改意见,在此一并感谢!

尽管我们很努力,但本书可能还会存在一些问题,真诚希望读者能给我们提出宝贵意见,以便我们能够继续修改完善!

Contents

Part A British Short Stories

Unit 1   Markheim   / *003*
Unit 2   The Gardener   / *026*
Unit 3   Compensation   / *041*
Unit 4   A Friend in Need   / *053*
Unit 5   The Celestial Omnibus   / *063*
Unit 6   Araby   / *088*
Unit 7   The Mark on the Wall   / *100*
Unit 8   The Horse Dealer's Daughter   / *113*
Unit 9   The Man Without a Temperament   / *137*

Part B American Short Stories

Unit 10   The Birthmark   / *159*
Unit 11   The Tell—Tale Heart   / *183*
Unit 12   The Notorious Frog of Calaveras County   / *193*
Unit 13   Hands   / *205*
Unit 14   Dry September   / *216*
Unit 15   The Killers   / *234*
Unit 16   Christmas   / *250*
Unit 17   The Chrysanthemums   / *262*
Unit 18   A Good Man Is Hard to Find   / *279*

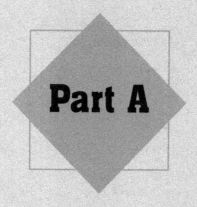

British Short Stories

Unit 1 Markheim

About the writer

　　罗伯特·路易斯·史蒂文森(Robert Louis Stevenson, 1850–1894),苏格兰作家、诗人、音乐家。1850年史蒂文森出生在苏格兰爱丁堡的一个工程师家庭,17岁进入爱丁堡大学,大学毕业后开始从事文学创作。史蒂文森一生共创作了13部小说、6部短篇小说集、4部诗集、3部散文集等,代表作品有《金银岛》(*Treasure Island*, 1883)、《化身博士》(*The Strange Case of Dr. Jekyll and Mr. Hyd*, 1886)、《绑架》(*Kidnapped*, 1886)、《一个孩子的诗歌花园》(*A Child's Garden of Verses*, 1885)等。

　　史蒂文森从小体弱多病,一生都在与病魔做斗争。尽管疾病缠身,但他热爱旅行和写作,足迹遍及英国、德国、意大利、太平洋诸岛国等,这为他之后的文学创作积累了宝贵素材。1879年,他远赴美国,与年长他10岁的范妮·奥斯本结婚。之后肺病日趋严重,他被迫带着妻子与义子劳埃德定居美国。1880年,他返回苏格兰,开始构思小说《金银岛》。1883年,《金银岛》正式出版,史蒂文森从此一跃成名、蜚声文坛。

　　史蒂文森的成名作《金银岛》是一部探险小说,讲述了主人公吉姆·霍金斯从海盗船长比尔那里偶然得到一张埋藏巨额财富的荒岛地形图,并在当地乡绅特里劳尼的支持下组织探险队前往金银岛寻宝的故事。寻宝途中,船上混入一伙海盗,海盗们意图夺船并独吞这笔财富。吉姆无意中得到这一消息,他配合特里劳尼同海盗们展开英勇机智的斗争,最后终于战胜海盗并找到宝藏。《金银岛》的故事主要以少年吉姆的角度展开,以孩童的口吻叙述了寻宝探险的整个历程,不仅充满着诱人的冒险气息,而且散发出浓厚的孩童情趣。斯蒂文森生活在19世纪资本主义的发展时期。新兴的资产阶级变本加厉地掠夺殖民地的资源,攫取巨大的商业利益。《金银岛》的情节在一定程度上展示了西方殖民者对殖民地的压榨,反映了当时的社会现状。史蒂文森借少年吉姆之口清晰地展现出欧洲资本主义走向帝国主义的发展历程,并在故事情节中流露出不满和讽刺。

《化身博士》是一部寓意深刻的经典讽刺悬疑小说,史蒂文森运用离奇非凡的笔法塑造了一个充满恐怖和奇幻的故事。主人公基杰尔博士是一名受人尊敬的科学家,为了释放自己身上邪恶的一面,他发明了一种药水,将自己变身为海德先生,通过这一身份纵情享乐。之后,分离出去的"恶"竟然变成一个独立的人格,到处作恶杀人。基杰尔在两种身份之间纠结,成为"双重人格"的象征。他深陷于名声与欲望、自我肯定与自我否定的矛盾之中,虽然试图消除内心的冲突,但最终还是在绝望与苦恼中自尽。小说探讨了人内心善恶相斗的问题,斯蒂文森在恐怖的氛围中探究人类的内心世界,将人的两面性展示在读者面前,意在告诫人们警惕心中邪恶、黑暗的一面。

德国诗人诺瓦利斯(Novalis)说:"疾病是丰富多彩生活的强大兴奋剂。"病痛造就了史蒂文森。他自幼患病,一生都在与病魔做斗争,但是他始终没有放弃自我,而是坚持创作。史蒂文森是19世纪英国新浪漫主义的重要代表作家,他的文笔细腻,语言流畅,故事新颖浪漫,作品寓意深刻,不仅吸引了成人读者,而且吸引了全世界众多儿童读者。

About the story

《马克海姆》是史蒂文森的经典短篇小说之一,收录于短篇小说集《快乐的男人们及其他故事》(*The Merry and Other Tales and Fable*, 1887)。一个下雨的圣诞节下午,36岁的主人公马克海姆来到一家古董店,假装在为一位女士挑选求婚礼物。然而,他真正的目的是谋杀店主,这样他就可以得到他的金钱和财物。马克海姆拒绝了店主给他推荐的古董镜子,当店主还在帮他找礼物时,马克海姆刺死了他。之后,在店里搜寻财物的过程中,马克海姆遇到一个似己非己的幽灵,在与幽灵的对话中,他决定放下屠刀,不再继续作恶。他原本可以杀死女仆后敛财逃逸,但他最终决定投案自首。

小说带有超现实主义色彩,谋杀店主后的故事情节大部分发生在马克海姆的脑海中,表现为马克海姆内心与自己的对话,展示了他激烈的内心冲突。小说的气氛阴森诡异,店里光线昏暗,蜡烛摇曳投射着奇怪的影子,镜子和油画看起来光怪陆离,时钟在昏暗中滴答作响。店外面雨水淅淅沥沥发出各种令人吃惊的声音，听起来像脚步声和回声。昏暗、阴雨的环境让马克海姆神经异常紧张，杀死店主之后他陷入极度恐惧和焦虑之中。

作案前，马克海姆害怕看到镜子，因为镜子会映射出他邪恶的灵魂。作案后，他忧心忡忡，觉得邻居和街上的人都发现了自己的罪行，内心充满不安和恐惧。同时，他仿佛又听到各种各样的声音，一幅幅恐怖的画面在他的脑海中浮现。"The sense that he was not alone grew upon him to the verge of madness. On every side he was haunted and begirt by presences. He heard them moving in the upper chambers; from the shop, he heard the dead man getting to his legs; and as he began with a great effort to mount the stairs, feet fled quietly before him and followed stealthily behind." 如果他不赶紧逃跑，就会立马被抓住。随着时间慢慢流逝，马克海姆的生命也在慢慢逝去，滴滴答答的钟声增加了紧张的气氛。因此，作案后不久他立即预见到犯罪结果，他将被警察带走，将面临审判和绞刑。作者将马克海姆的心理活动描写刻画得入木三分，主人公仿佛在与另一个自己对话，内心的善恶展露无遗。

该短篇采用第三人称叙事视角，主要通过马克海姆的内心活动推动小说的情节发展。小说将哥特小说的神秘元素与恐怖小说的罪恶巧妙地加以融合，通过语言和颇具有象征意义的意象渲染气氛，生动地描写了人物在特定情境中的特定心态，将现实描写与奇异的想象、丰富的象征、鲜明的意象、深刻的寓意和神秘的氛围等完美地结合在一起，以此烘托人物善与恶的心理之战。

《马克海姆》的主题与史蒂文森1886年发表的中篇小说《化身博士》相似，即人类灵魂中善与恶、向善与沉沦之间的斗争。《马克海姆》中，这种对个人美德和罪恶的分析通过一个模棱两可的幽灵来访者得以实现，多数评论家将其解释为马克海姆善良的化身。起初，马克海姆认为这个幽灵是撒旦，将帮助他进行另一场谋杀，以防止他被捕和定罪。然而，出人意料的是，马克海姆在与来访者的对话中最终寻求悔悟。马克海姆内心的愧疚促使他认罪伏法，向自己和他人忏悔，以此实现自我救赎。

许多评论家认为史蒂文森是英国现代短篇小说的先驱，《马克海姆》是他最著名的短篇小说之一。史蒂文森深受爱伦·坡的影响，在该短篇中，他完美地将阴暗、谋杀、幽灵等哥特元素与人物的内心冲突融合在一起，反映了人物双重人格之间的激烈争斗。小说结尾主人公善良道德的一面胜出，这意味着史蒂文森对人类还是持有信心的。

Markheim

"Yes," said the dealer, "our windfalls are of various kinds. Some customers are ignorant, and then I touch a dividend on my superior knowledge. Some are dishonest," and here he held up the candle, so that the light fell strongly on his visitor, "and in that case," he continued, "I profit by my virtue."

Markheim had but just entered from the daylight streets, and his eyes had not yet grown familiar with the mingled shine and darkness in the shop. At these pointed words, and before the near presence of the flame, he blinked painfully and looked aside.

The dealer chuckled. "You come to me on Christmas Day," he resumed, "when you know that I am alone in my house, put up my shutters, and make a point of refusing business. Well, you will have to pay for that; you will have to pay for my loss of time, when I should be balancing my books; you will have to pay, besides, for a kind of manner that I remark in you today very strongly. I am the essence of discretion, and ask no awkward questions; but when a customer cannot look me in the eye, he has to pay for it." The dealer once more chuckled; and then, changing to his usual business voice, though still with a note of irony, "You can give, as usual, a clear account of how you came into the possession of the object?" he continued. "Still your uncle's cabinet? A remarkable collector, sir!"

And the little pale, round-shouldered dealer stood almost on tiptoe, looking over the top of his gold spectacles, and nodding his head with every mark of disbelief. Markheim returned his gaze with one of infinite pity, and a touch of horror.

"This time," said he, "you are in error. I have not come to sell, but to buy. I have no curios① to dispose of; my uncle's cabinet is bare to the wainscot; even were it still intact, I have done well on the Stock Exchange, and should more likely add to it than otherwise, and my errand today is simplicity itself. I seek a Christmas present for a lady," he continued, waxing more fluent as he struck into the speech he had prepared; "and certainly I owe you every excuse for thus disturbing you upon so small a matter. But the thing was neglected yesterday; I must produce my little compliment at dinner; and, as you very well know, a rich marriage is not a thing to be neglected."

There followed a pause, during which the dealer seemed to weigh this statement incredulously. The ticking of many clocks among the curious lumber of the shop, and the faint rushing of the cabs in a near thoroughfare, filled up the interval of silence.

"Well, sir," said the dealer, "be it so. You are an old customer after all; and if, as you say, you have the chance of a good marriage, far be it from me to be an obstacle②. Here is a nice thing for a lady, now," he went on, "this hand glass—fifteenth century, warranted; comes from a good collection, too; but I reserve the name, in the interests of my customer, who was just like yourself, my dear sir, the nephew and sole heir of a remarkable collector."

The dealer, while he thus ran on in his dry and biting voice, had stooped to take the object from its place; and, as he had done so, a shock had passed through Markheim, a start both of hand and foot, a sudden leap of many tumultuous passions to the face. It passed as swiftly as it came, and left no trace beyond a certain trembling of the hand that now received the glass.

"A glass," he said hoarsely, and then paused, and repeated it more

---

① curios:curio 的复数,(常指收藏的)小件稀有物。
② far be it from me to be an obstacle:我绝不会成为障碍。

clearly. "A glass? For Christmas? Surely not?"

"And why not?" cried the dealer. "Why not a glass?"

Markheim was looking upon him with an indefinable expression. "You ask me why not?" he said. "Why, look here—look in it—look at yourself! Do you like to see it? No! Nor I—Nor any man."

The little man had jumped back when Markheim had so suddenly confronted him with the mirror; but now, perceiving there was nothing worse on hand, he chuckled. "Your future lady, sir, must be pretty hard favored," said he.

"I ask you," said Markheim, "for a Christmas present, and you give me this—this damned reminder of years and sins and follies—this hand-conscience! Did you mean it? Had you a thought in your mind? Tell me. It will be better for you if you do. Come, tell me about yourself. I hazard a guess now, that you are in secret a very charitable man?"

The dealer looked closely at his companion. It was very odd. Markheim did not appear to be laughing; there was something in his face like an eager sparkle of hope, but nothing of mirth.

"What are you driving at?" the dealer asked.

"Not charitable?" returned the other, gloomily. "Not charitable; not pious; not scrupulous; unloving, unbeloved; a hand to get money, a safe to keep it. Is that all? Dear God, man, is that all?"

"I will tell you what it is," began the dealer, with some sharpness, and then broke off again into a chuckle. "But I see this is a love match of yours, and you have been drinking the lady's health."

"Ah!" cried Markheim, with a strange curiosity. "Ah, have you been in love? Tell me about that."

"I!" cried the dealer. "I in love! I never had the time, nor have I the time today for all this nonsense. Will you take the glass?"

"Where is the hurry?" returned Markheim. "It is very pleasant to stand here talking; and life is so short and insecure that I would not hurry away from any pleasure—no, not even from so mild a one as this. We should rather cling, cling to what little we can get, like a man at a cliff's edge. Every second is a cliff, if you think upon it—a cliff a mile high—high enough, if we fall, to dash us out of every feature of humanity. Hence it is best to talk pleasantly. Let us talk of each other; why should we wear this mask? Let us be confidential. Who knows, we might become friends?"

"I have just one word to say to you," said the dealer. "Either make your purchase, or walk out of my shop."

"True, true," said Markheim. "Enough fooling. To business. Show me something else."

The dealer stooped once more, this time to replace the glass upon the shelf, his thin blond hair falling over his eyes as he did so. Markheim moved a little nearer, with one hand in the pocket of his great coat; he drew himself up and filled his lungs; at the same time many different emotions were depicted together on his face—terror, horror, and resolve, fascination, and a physical repulsion; and through a haggard① lift of his upper lip, his teeth looked out.

"This, perhaps, may suit," observed the dealer; and then, as he began to re-arise, Markheim bounded from behind upon his victim. The long, skewer-like dagger flashed and fell. The dealer struggled like a hen, striking his temple on the shelf, and then tumbled on the floor in a heap.

Time had some score of small voices in that shop, some stately and slow as was becoming to their great age, others garrulous and hurried. All these told out the seconds in an intricate chorus of tickings. Then the passage of a lad's feet, heavily running on the pavement, broke in upon these smaller voices and startled Markheim into the consciousness of his surroundings. He looked about him awfully. The candle stood on the counter, its flame solemnly wagging in a draught; and by that

---

① haggard: 疲惫的,憔悴的。

inconsiderable movement, the whole room was filled with noiseless bustle and kept heaving like a sea: the tall shadows nodding, the gross blots of darkness swelling and dwindling as with respiration, the faces of the portraits and the china gods changing and wavering like images in water. The inner door stood ajar, and peered into that leaguer of shadows with a long slit of daylight like a pointing finger.

From these fear-stricken rovings, Markheim's eyes returned to the body of his victim, where it lay both humped and sprawling, incredibly small and strangely meaner than in life. In these poor, miserly clothes, in that ungainly attitude, the dealer lay like so much sawdust. Markheim had feared to see it, and, lo! It was nothing. And yet, as he gazed, this bundle of old clothes and pool of blood began to find eloquent voices. There it must lie; there was none to work the cunning hinges or direct the miracle of locomotion—there it must lie till it was found. Found! Aye, and then? Then would this dead flesh lift up a cry that would ring over England, and fill the world with the echoes of pursuit. Aye, dead or not, this was still the enemy. "Time was that when the brains were out," he thought; and the first word struck into his mind. Time, now that the deed was accomplished—time, which had closed for the victim, had become instant and momentous for the slayer.

The thought was yet in his mind, when, first one and then another, with every variety of pace and voice—one deep as the bell from a cathedral turret, another ringing on its treble notes the prelude of a waltz—the clocks began to strike the hour of three in the afternoon.

The sudden outbreak of so many tongues in that dumb chamber staggered him. He began to bestir himself, going to and fro with the candle, beleaguered by moving shadows, and startled to the soul by chance reflections. In many rich mirrors, some of home designs, some from Venice or Amsterdam, he saw his face repeated and repeated, as it were an army of spies; his own eyes met and detected him; and the sound of his own steps, lightly as they fell, vexed the surrounding quiet. And still as he continued to fill his pockets, his mind accused him, with a sickening iteration, of the thousand faults of his design. He should have chosen a more quiet hour; he should have prepared an alibi; he should not have used a knife; he should have been more cautious, and only bound and gagged the dealer, and not killed him; he should have been more bold, and killed the servant also; he should have done all things otherwise; poignant regrets, weary, incessant toiling of the mind to change what was unchangeable, to plan what was now useless, to be the architect of the irrevocable past. Meanwhile, and behind all this activity, brute terrors, like the scurrying of rats① in a deserted attic, filled the more remote chambers of his brain with riot; the hand of the constable would fall heavy on his shoulder, and his nerves would jerk like a hooked fish; or he beheld, in galloping defile, the dock, the prison, the gallows, and the black coffin.

Terror of the people in the street sat down before his mind like a besieging army. It was impossible, he thought, but that some rumor of the struggle must have reached their ears and set on edge their curiosity; and now, in all the neighboring houses, he divined them sitting motionless and with uplifted ear—solitary people, condemned to spend Christmas dwelling alone on memories of the past, and now startlingly recalled from that tender exercise; happy family parties, struck into silence round the table, the mother still with raised finger: every degree and age and humor, but all, by their own hearths, prying and hearkening and weaving the rope that was to hang him. Sometimes it seemed to him he could not move too softly; the clink of the tall Bohemian goblets② rang out loudly like a bell; and alarmed by the bigness of the ticking, he was tempted to stop the clocks. And then, again, with a swift transition of his terrors, the very silence of the place

---

① the scurrying of rats: 仓促的老鼠。
② Bohemian goblets: 波希米亚高脚杯。

appeared a source of peril, and a thing to strike and freeze the passer-by; and he would step more boldly, and bustle aloud among the contents of the shop, and imitate, with elaborate bravado, the movements of a busy man at ease in his own house.

But he was now so pulled about by different alarms that, while one portion of his mind was still alert and cunning, another trembled on the brink of lunacy. One hallucination in particular took a strong hold on his credulity. The neighbor hearkening with white face beside his window, the passer-by arrested by a horrible surmise on the pavement—these could at worst suspect, they could not know; through the brick walls and shuttered windows only sounds could penetrate. But here, within the house, was he alone? He knew he was; he had watched the servant set forth sweethearting, in her poor best, "out for the day" written in every ribbon and smile. Yes, he was alone, of course; and yet, in the bulk of empty house about him, he could surely hear a stir of delicate footing—he was surely conscious, inexplicably conscious of some presence. Aye, surely; to every room and corner of the house his imagination followed it; and now it was a faceless thing, and yet had eyes to see with; and again it was a shadow of himself; and yet again behold the image of the dead dealer, reinspired with cunning and hatred.

At times, with a strong effort, he would glance at the open door which still seemed to repel his eyes. The house was tall, the skylight small and dirty, the day blind with fog; and the light that filtered down to the ground story was exceedingly faint, and showed dimly on the threshold of the shop. And yet, in that strip of doubtful brightness, did there not hang wavering a shadow?

Suddenly, from the street outside, a very jovial gentleman began to beat with a staff on the shop door, accompanying his blows with shouts and railleries in which the dealer was continually called upon by name. Markheim, smitten into ice, glanced at the dead man. But no! He lay quite still; he was fled away far beyond ear-shot of these blows and shoutings; he was sunk beneath seas of silence; and his name, which would once have caught his notice above the howling of a storm, had become an empty sound. And presently the jovial gentleman desisted from his knocking and departed.

Here was a broad hint to hurry what remained to be done, to get forth from this accusing neighborhood, to plunge into a bath of London multitudes, and to reach, on the other side of day, that haven of safety and apparent innocence—his bed. One visitor had come: at any moment another might follow and be more obstinate. To have done the deed, and yet not to reap the profit, would be too abhorrent a failure. The money, that was now Markheim's concern; and as a means to that, the keys.

He glanced over his shoulder at the open door, where the shadow was still lingering and shivering; and with no conscious repugnance of the mind, yet with a tremor of the belly, he drew near the body of his victim. The human character had quite departed. Like a suit half-stuffed with bran, the limbs lay scattered, the trunk doubled, on the floor; and yet the thing repelled him. Although so dingy and inconsiderable to the eye, he feared it might have more significance to the touch. He took the body by the shoulders, and turned it on its back. It was strangely light and supple, and the limbs, as if they had been broken, fell into the oddest postures. The face was robbed of all expression; but it was as pale as wax, and shockingly smeared with blood about one temple. That was, for Markheim, the one displeasing circumstance. It carried him back, upon the instant, to a certain fair day in a fishers' village: a gray day, a piping wind, a crowd upon the street, the blare of brasses, the booming of drums, the nasal voice of a ballad singer; and a boy going to and fro, buried over head in the crowd and divided between interest and fear, until, coming out upon the chief place of concourse, he beheld a booth and a great screen with pictures, dismally designed, garishly colored: Brownrigg with her apprentice; the

Mannings with their murdered guest; We are in the death grip of Thurtell, and a score besides of famous crimes. The thing was as clear as an illusion; he was once again that little boy; he was looking once again, and with the same sense of physical revolt, at these vile pictures; he was still stunned by the thumping of the drums. A bar of that day's music returned upon his memory; and at that, for the first time, a qualm came over him, a breath of nausea, a sudden weakness of the joints, which he must instantly resist and conquer.

He judged it more prudent to confront than to flee from these considerations; looking the more hardily in the dead face, bending his mind to realize the nature and greatness of his crime. So little a while ago that face had moved with every change of sentiment, that pale mouth had spoken, that body had been all on fire with governable energies; and now, and by his act, that piece of life had been arrested, as the horologist①, with interjected finger, arrests the beating of the clock. So he reasoned in vain; he could rise to no more remorseful consciousness; the same heart which had shuddered before the painted effigies of crime, looked on its reality unmoved. At best, he felt a gleam of pity for one who had been endowed in vain with all those faculties that can make the world a garden of enchantment, one who had never lived and who was now dead. But of penitence, no, not a tremor.

With that, shaking himself clear of these considerations, he found the keys and advanced toward the open door of the shop. Outside, it had begun to rain smartly; and the sound of the shower upon the roof had banished silence. Like some dripping cavern, the chambers of the house were haunted by an incessant echoing, which filled the ear and mingled with the ticking of the clocks. And, as Markheim approached the door, he seemed to hear, in answer to his own cautious tread, the steps of another

---

① horologist:钟表制造者。

foot withdrawing up the stair. The shadow still palpitated① loosely on the threshold. He threw a ton's weight of resolve upon his muscles, and drew back the door②.

The faint, foggy daylight glimmered dimly on the bare floor and stairs; on the bright suit of armor posted, halbert in hand, upon the landing; and on the dark wood carvings and framed pictures that hung against the yellow panels of the wainscot. So loud was the beating of the rain through all the house that, in Markheim's ears, it began to be distinguished into many different sounds. Footsteps and sighs, the tread of regiments marching in the distance, the chink of money in the counting, and the creaking of doors held stealthily ajar, appeared to mingle with the patter of the drops upon the cupola③ and the gushing of the water in the pipes. The sense that he was not alone grew upon him to the verge of madness. On every side he was haunted and begirt④ by presences. He heard them moving in the upper chambers; from the shop, he heard the dead man getting to his legs; and as he began with a great effort to mount the stairs, feet fled quietly before him and followed stealthily behind. If he were but deaf, he thought, how tranquilly he would possess his soul! And then again, and hearkening with ever fresh attention, he blessed himself for that unresting sense which held the outposts and stood a trusty sentinel upon his life. His head turned continually on his neck; his eyes, which seemed starting from their orbits, scouted on every side, and on every side were half rewarded as with the tail of something nameless vanishing. The four-and-twenty steps to the first floor

---

① palpitate: 急速跳动。
② He threw a ton's weight of resolve upon his muscles, and drew back the door: 他下了很大决心, 才将门拉回。此处, 马克海姆杀害店主后, 非常紧张, 即使是做把开着门拉回这个简单的动作, 他也需要下很大决心。
③ cupola: 圆屋顶。
④ begirt: begird 的过去分词和过去式。围绕, 包围。

were four-and-twenty agonies①.

On that first story the doors stood ajar, three of them like three ambushes, shaking his nerves like the throats of cannon. He could never again, he felt, be sufficiently immured and fortified from men's observing eyes; he longed to be home, girt in by walls, buried among bedclothes, and invisible to all but God. And at that thought he wondered a little, recollecting tales of other murderers and the fear they were said to entertain of heavenly avengers. It was not so, at least, with him. He feared the laws of nature, lest, in their callous and immutable procedure, they should preserve some damning evidence of his crime. He feared tenfold more, with a slavish, superstitious terror, some scission in the continuity of man's experience, some willful illegality of nature. He played a game of skill, depending on the rules, calculating consequence from cause; and what if nature, as the defeated tyrant overthrew the chessboard, should break the mold of their succession? The like had befallen Napoleon (so writers said) when the winter changed the time of its appearance. The like might befall Markheim: the solid walls might become transparent and reveal his doings like those of bees in a glass hive; the stout planks might yield under his foot like quicksands and detain him in their clutch; aye, and there were soberer accidents that might destroy him: if, for instance, the house should fall and imprison him beside the body of his victim; or the house next door should fly on fire, and the firemen invade him from all sides. These things he feared; and, in a sense, these things might be called the hands of God reached forth against sin. But about God himself he was at ease; his act was doubtless exceptional, but so were his excuses, which God knew; it was there, and not among men, that he felt sure of justice.

When he got safe into the drawing-room, and shut the door behind

---

① The four-and-twenty steps to the first floor were four-and-twenty agonies: 通向二楼的四二十级台阶是四十二种痛苦。此处，马克海姆惊慌失措，连做上台阶这种最简单的动作他都感觉非常痛苦。

him, he was aware of a respite from alarms. The room was quite dismantled, uncarpeted besides, and strewn with packing cases and incongruous furniture; several great pier glasses, in which he beheld himself at various angles, like an actor on a stage; many pictures, framed and unframed, standing, with their faces to the wall; a fine Sheraton sideboard, a cabinet of marquetry, and a great old bed, with tapestry hangings. The windows opened to the floor; but by great good fortune the lower part of the shutters had been closed, and this concealed him from the neighbors. Here, then, Markheim drew in a packing case before the cabinet, and began to search among the keys. It was a long business, for there were many; and it was irksome①, besides; for, after all, there might be nothing in the cabinet, and time was on the wing. But the closeness of the occupation sobered him. With the tail of his eye he saw the door—even glanced at it from time to time directly, like a besieged commander pleased to verify the good estate of his defenses. But in truth he was at peace. The rain falling in the street sounded natural and pleasant. Presently, on the other side, the notes of a piano were wakened to the music of a hymn, and the voices of many children took up the air and words. How stately, how comfortable was the melody! How fresh the youthful voices! Markheim gave ear to it smilingly, as he sorted out the keys; and his mind was thronged with answerable ideas and images; church-going children and the pealing of the high organ; children afield, bathers by the brookside, ramblers on the brambly common, kite-flyers in the windy and cloud-navigated sky; and then, at another cadence of the hymn, back again to church, and the somnolence of summer Sundays, and the high, genteel voice of the parson (which he smiled a little to recall), and the painted Jacobean tombs, and the dim lettering of the Ten Commandments in the chancel.

---

① irksome:使人烦恼的，令人生气的。

And as he sat thus, at once busy and absent, he was startled to his feet. A flash of ice, a flash of fire, a bursting gush of blood, went over him, and then he stood transfixed and thrilling. A step mounted the stair slowly and steadily, and presently a hand was laid upon the knob, and the lock clicked, and the door opened.

Fear held Markheim in a vise①. What to expect he knew not, whether the dead man walking, or the official ministers of human justice, or some chance witness blindly stumbling in to consign him to the gallows. But when a face was thrust into the aperture②, glanced round the room, looked at him, nodded and smiled as if in friendly recognition, and then withdrew again, and the door closed behind it, his fear broke loose from his control in a hoarse cry. At the sound of this the visitant returned.

"Did you call me?" he asked pleasantly, and with that he entered the room and closed the door behind him.

Markheim stood and gazed at him with all his eyes. Perhaps there was a film upon his sight, but the outlines of the newcomer seemed to change and waver like those of the idols in the wavering candlelight of the shop: and at times he thought he knew him; and at times he thought he bore a likeness to himself; and always, like a lump of living terror, there lay in his bosom the conviction that this thing was not of the earth and not of God.

And yet the creature had a strange air of the common-place, as he stood looking on Markheim with a smile; and when he added: "You are looking for the money, I believe?" It was in the tones of everyday politeness.

Markheim made no answer.

"I should warn you," resumed the other, "that the maid has left her sweetheart earlier than usual and will soon be here. If Mr. Markheim be found in this house, I need not describe to him the consequences."

---

① Fear held Markheim in a vise: 恐惧使马克海姆陷入困境。
② aperture: 小孔，缝隙。

"You know me?" cried the murderer.

The visitor smiled. "You have long been a favorite of mine," he said, "and I have long observed and often sought to help you."

"What are you?" cried Markheim, "The devil?"

"What I may be," returned the other, "cannot affect the service I propose to render you."

"It can," cried Markheim, "It does! Be helped by you? No, never; not by you! You do not know me yet; thank God, you do not know me!"

"I know you," replied the visitor, with a sort of kind severity or rather firmness. "I know you to the soul①."

"Know me!" cried Markheim. "Who can do so? My life is but a travesty and slander on myself. I have lived to belie my nature. All men do; all men are better than this disguise that grows about and stifles them. You see each dragged away by life, like one whom bravos have seized and muffled in a cloak. If they had their own control—if you could see their faces, they would be altogether different, they would shine out for heroes and saints! I am worse than most; myself is more overlaid; my excuse is known to me and God. But, had I the time, I could disclose myself." "To me?" inquired the visitor.

"To you before all," returned the murderer. "I supposed you were intelligent. I thought—since you exist—you would prove a reader of the heart. And yet you would propose to judge me by my acts! Think of it; my acts! I was born and I have lived in a land of giants; giants have dragged me by the wrists since I was born out of my mother—the giants of circumstance. And you would judge me by my acts! But can you not look within? Can you not understand that evil is hateful to me? Can you not see within me the clear writing of conscience, never blurred by any willful sophistry, although too often disregarded? Can you not read me for a thing that surely must be

---

① I know you to the soul:我非常了解你。

common as humanity—the unwilling sinner?"

"All this is very feelingly expressed," was the reply, "but it regards me not. These points of consistency are beyond my province, and I care not in the least by what compulsion you may have been dragged away, so as you are but carried in the right direction. But time flies; the servant delays, looking in the faces of the crowd and at the pictures on the hoardings, but still she keeps moving nearer; and remember, it is as if the gallows itself were striding toward you through the Christmas streets! Shall I help you—I, who know all? Shall I tell you where to find the money?" "For what price?" asked Markheim.

"I offer you the service for a Christmas gift," returned the other.

Markheim could not refrain from smiling with a kind of bitter triumph. "No," said he, "I will take nothing at your hands; if I were dying of thirst, and it was your hand that put the pitcher to my lips, I should find the courage to refuse. It may be credulous, but I will do nothing to commit myself to evil."

"I have no objection to a death-bed repentance," observed the visitant.

"Because you disbelieve their efficacy!" Markheim cried.

"I do not say so," returned the other, "but I look on these things from a different side, and when the life is done my interest falls. The man has lived to serve me, to spread black looks under color of religion, or to sow tares in the wheat field, as you do, in a course of weak compliance with desire. Now that he draws so near to his deliverance, he can add but one act of service—to repent, to die smiling, and thus to build up in confidence and hope the more timorous① of my surviving followers. I am not so hard a master. Try me. Accept my help. Please yourself in life as you have done hitherto; please yourself more amply, spread your elbows at the board; and

---

① timorous: 羞怯的，胆怯的。

when the night begins to fall and the curtains to be drawn, I tell you, for your greater comfort, that you will find it even easy to compound your quarrel with your conscience, and to make a truckling peace with God. I came but now from such a death-bed, and the room was full of sincere mourners, listening to the man's last words; and when I looked into that face, which had been set as a flint against mercy, I found it smiling with hope."

"And do you, then, suppose me such a creature?" asked Markheim. "Do you think I have no more generous aspirations than to sin, and sin, and sin, and, at last, sneak into heaven? My heart rises at the thought. Is this, then, your experience of mankind? Or is it because you find me with red hands that you presume such baseness? And is this crime of murder indeed so impious as to dry up the very springs of good?"

"Murder is to me no special category," replied the other. "All sins are murder, even as all life is war. I behold your race, like starving mariners on a raft, plucking crusts out of the hands of famine and feeding on each other's lives. I follow sins beyond the moment of their acting; I find in all that the last consequence is death; and to my eyes, the pretty maid who thwarts her mother with such taking graces on a question of a ball, drips no less visibly with human gore① than such a murderer as yourself. Do I say that I follow sins? I follow virtues also; they differ not by the thickness of a nail, they are both scythes② for the reaping angel of Death. Evil, for which I live, consists not in action but in character. The bad man is dear to me; not the bad act, whose fruits, if we could follow them far enough down the hurtling cataract of the ages, might yet be found more blessed than those of the rarest virtues. And it is not because you have killed a dealer, but because you are Markheim, that I offered to forward your escape."

"I will lay my heart open to you," answered Markheim. "This crime

---

① gore:(尤指在暴力情况下)伤口流出的血,凝固的血。
② scythes:长柄大镰刀。

on which you find me is my last. On my way to it I have learned many lessons; itself is a lesson, a momentous lesson. Hitherto I have been driven with revolt to what I would not; I was a bondslave to poverty, driven and scourged. There are robust virtues that can stand in these temptations; mine was not so: I had a thirst of pleasure. But today, and out of this deed, I pluck both warning and riches—both the power and a fresh resolve to be myself. I become in all things a free actor in the world; I begin to see myself all changed, these hands the agents of good, this heart at peace. Something comes over me out of the past; something of what I have dreamed on Sabbath evenings to the sound of the church organ, of what I forecast when I shed tears over noble books, or talked, an innocent child, with my mother. There lies my life; I have wandered a few years, but now I see once more my city of destination."

"You are to use this money on the Stock Exchange, I think?" remarked the visitor; "and there, if I mistake not, you have already lost some thousands?"

"Ah," said Markheim, "but this time I have a sure thing."

"This time, again, you will lose," replied the visitor, quietly.

"Ah, but I keep back the half!" cried Markheim.

"That also you will lose," said the other.

The sweat started upon Markheim's brow. "Well, then, what matter?" he exclaimed. "Say it be lost, say I am plunged again in poverty, shall one part of me, and that the worse, continue until the end to override the better? Evil and good run strong in me, hailing me both ways. I do not love the one thing. I love all. I can conceive great deeds, renunciations, martyrdoms; and though I be fallen to such a crime as murder, pity is no stranger to my thoughts. I pity the poor; who knows their trials better than myself? I pity and help them; I prize love, I love honest laughter; there is no good thing nor true thing on earth but I love it from my heart. And are my vices only to direct my life, and my virtues to lie without effect, like some passive lumber of the mind? Not so; good, also, is a spring of acts."

But the visitant raised his finger. "For six and thirty years that you have been in this world," said he, "through many changes of fortune and varieties of humor, I have watched you steadily fall. Fifteen years ago you would have started at a theft. Three years back you would have blenched at the name of murder. Is there any crime, is there any cruelty or meanness, from which you still recoil? —five years from now I shall detect you in the fact! Downward, downward lies your way; nor can anything but death avail to stop you."

"It is true," Markheim said huskily, "I have in some degree complied with evil. But it is so with all: the very saints, in the mere exercise of living, grow less dainty, and take on the tone of their surroundings."

"I will propound to you one simple question," said the other; "and as you answer, I shall read to you your moral horoscope. You have grown in many things more lax; possibly you do right to be so; and at any account, it is the same with all men. But granting that, are you in any one particular, however trifling, more difficult to please with your own conduct, or do you go in all things with a looser rein?"

"In any one?" repeated Markheim, with an anguish of consideration. "No," he added, with despair, "in none! I have gone down in all."

"Then," said the visitor, "content yourself with what you are, for you will never change; and the words of your part on this stage are irrevocably written down."

Markheim stood for a long while silent, and indeed it was the visitor who first broke the silence. "That being so," he said, "shall I show you the money?"

"And grace?" cried Markheim.

"Have you not tried it?" returned the other. "Two or three years ago, did I not see you on the platform of revival meetings, and was not your voice the loudest in the hymn?"

"It is true," said Markheim; "and I see clearly what remains for me by way of duty. I thank you for these lessons from my soul; my eyes are opened, and I behold myself at last for what I am."

At this moment, the sharp note of the door bell rang through the house; and the visitant, as though this were some concerted signal for which he had been waiting, changed at once in his demeanor.

"The maid!" he cried. "She has returned, as I forewarned you, and there is now before you one more difficult passage. Her master, you must say, is ill; you must let her in, with an assured but rather serious countenance—no smiles, no overacting, and I promise you success! Once the girl within, and the door closed, the same dexterity that has already rid you of the dealer will relieve you of this last danger in your path. Thenceforward you have the whole evening—the whole night, if needful—to ransack the treasures of the house and to make good your safety. This is help that comes to you with the mask of danger. Up!" he cried: "up, friend; your life hangs trembling in the scales: up, and act!"

Markheim steadily regarded his counselor. "If I be condemned to evil acts," he said, "there is still one door of freedom open—I can cease from action. If my life be an ill thing, I can lay it down. Though I be, as you say truly, at the beck of every small temptation, I can yet, by one decisive gesture, place myself beyond the reach of all. My love of good is damned to barrenness; it may, and let it be! But I have still my hatred of evil; and from that, to your galling disappointment, you shall see that I can draw both energy and courage."

The features of the visitor began to undergo a wonderful and lovely change: they brightened and softened with a tender triumph; and, even as they brightened, faded and dislimned. But Markheim did not pause to watch or understand the transformation. He opened the door and went downstairs very slowly, thinking to himself. His past went soberly before him; he beheld it as it was, ugly and strenuous like a dream, random as chance-medley—a scene of defeat. Life, as he thus reviewed it, tempted him no longer; but on the farther side he perceived a quiet haven for his bark. He paused in the passage, and looked into the shop, where the candle still burned by the dead body. It was strangely silent. Thoughts of the dealer swarmed into his mind, as he stood gazing. And then the bell once more broke out into impatient clamor.

He confronted the maid upon the threshold with something like a smile.

"You had better go for the police," said he: "I have killed your master."

Questions

1. Stevenson is heavily influenced by Allan Poe. "Markheim" is a typical Gothic story. What are the gothic factors in the story? And what are their functions?

2. The reason why Markheim murdered the dealer and usurped his money is that he intended to use this money on the Stock Exchange. To some degree, Stevenson reveals the connection between Capitalism and crime. Are there any other indications of this connection?

Further Readings

Stevenson's short stories are notable for psychological descriptions and human beings' inner sharp conflicts. The following are some of his important short stories.

1. "The Adventure of Prince Florizel and a Detective"(《弗罗利泽王子和侦探历险记》)
2. "Olalla"(《欧拉拉》)
3. "The Merry Man"(《快乐的人》)

Unit 2　The Gardener

About the writer

　　拉迪亚德·吉卜林（Rudyard Kipling，1865 – 1936），英国小说家、诗人，是第一位获得诺贝尔文学奖的英国作家。吉卜林一生共创作了 8 部诗集、4 部长篇小说、21 部短篇小说集，以及大量散文、随笔、游记等。吉卜林的一生与大英帝国紧密相连，其作品大都渗透着浓浓的帝国意识，被誉为"帝国诗人"。

　　吉卜林于 1865 年出生在印度孟买，6 岁时被送到英国接受教育，17 岁中学毕业后返回印度。他的父亲曾是孟买艺术学校的教师，后任拉合尔艺术学校的校长和博物馆馆长。父亲对吉卜林的影响很大，他的不少作品比如《基姆》(*Kim*, 1901)、《丛林之书续编》(*The Second Jungle Book*, 1895) 等都受到父亲的极大启发。吉卜林早年曾在印度从事新闻报道工作，这为他之后的文学创作奠定了基础。

　　吉卜林的文学创作主要包括两个阶段。第一阶段是从 19 世纪 80 年代末到 90 年代中期，作品主要描写英国人在印度的殖民生活及印度的风土人情，包括《山里的故事》(*Plain Tales from the Hills*, 1988)、《雪松下》(*Under the Deodars*, 1888)、《丛林之书》(*Jungle Book*, 1894)、《如此故事》(*Just So Stories*, 1902) 等。在这些作品中，吉卜林描绘了印度的自然风景以及英国士兵和官员的生活。他生动地描述了这些人不择手段的贪婪和不道德行为，斥责了殖民统治者的虚伪和残酷，同时也表达了对底层劳动人民的同情。

　　第二阶段是在 19 世纪 90 年代下半叶。在这个阶段，吉卜林扩大了作品的主题和人物的活动空间。这一时期的主要作品有《勇敢的船长们》(*Captains Courageous*, 1897)、《斯托基公司》(*Stalky & Co*, 1899)、《基姆》等。此外，这一时期他还出版了一些短篇小说集和诗集，包括《交通与发明》

(*Traffics and Discoveries*, 1904)、《各种各样的人》(*A Diversity of Creatures*, 1917)、《普克山的帕克》(*Puck of Pook's Hill*, 1906)等。

《基姆》是吉卜林创作的一部以印度为题材的作品，被认为是吉卜林最出色的长篇小说，吉卜林凭借该作品获得诺贝尔文学奖。小说主人公基姆是一个混迹于印度市井的白人男孩，他善于结交朋友，懂得各种人情世故。小说重点描写了基姆与一名远道而来的佛教喇嘛寻找箭河的故事。为了寻找传说中涤清罪恶的箭河，喇嘛出现在印度街头。在偷听了喇嘛与拉合尔博物馆白人馆长的谈话后，基姆直觉地喜欢上了喇嘛，决定要照料他的生活，并自告奋勇成为喇嘛的弟子。喇嘛也认为基姆是受命而来帮助他寻找那条河的弟子。于是，虔诚而单纯的僧人，狡黠而世故的男孩，就此踏上宿命般的冒险之旅。年长的喇嘛代表东方文化，年轻的基姆则代表西方文化。吉卜林以印度为背景，透过西方人之眼，一方面将东方世界的风土人情、生活习俗等描写得细致入微、流光溢彩，另一方面凸显了东西方文明的冲撞与融合。

吉卜林于1936年因脑出血在伦敦逝世，英国政府和各界名流为他举行了国葬，其骨灰被送往西敏斯特教堂"诗人角"。吉卜林的一生与大英帝国密不可分，他曾多次公开表明自己为帝国服务的决心和目的，这使得他的声名毁誉参半、备受争议。但是他新颖的想象、雄浑的思想和杰出的叙事才能，以及作品中拟人、象征和寓言的创造性运用使他的作品具有跨时代的魅力。

About the story

《园丁》是一个以第一次世界大战为题材的短篇小说，发表于1926年。小说的灵感源于吉卜林在1925年对法国鲁昂一处军人墓地的探访经历。该作品颂扬了爱的主题，表达了作者对社会偏见的控诉以及对下层劳动人民特别是女性悲惨遭遇的同情。小说讲述了主人公海伦·特里尔抚养私生子迈克长大成人，在儿子牺牲后去军人公墓寻找儿子坟墓的故事。表面上海伦·特里尔是一位中年老姑娘，抚养了她兄弟乔治·特里尔的儿子迈克，实际上迈克是她的私生子，迫于世俗偏见，海伦不得不隐藏这个秘密，将迈克称作她的侄子。后来，迈克在一战中阵亡，海伦悲痛欲绝。于是，海伦决定去寻找迈克的坟墓。在寻找坟墓的途中，她遇到了斯卡斯沃斯太太，和她的经历一样，这位太太也前去悼念自己的私生子。倾听了斯卡斯沃斯太太的经历后，海伦内心的枷锁随之被打开。最后，园丁指引着海伦向迈克的坟墓走去。

《园丁》中，儿时的迈克对自己的身世极为敏感，他很想知道为什么不能喊海伦妈妈。海伦告诉他，说自己只是他的姑妈。迈克是海伦的私生子，在当时的英国，女子有了私生子无疑会招致众人的鄙夷，遭到社会唾弃。为了隐藏自己的秘密，海伦将迈克说成是自己的侄子。海伦历尽艰辛，独自将迈克抚养长大。迈克本来可以获得奖学金去牛津大学深造，然而第一次世界大战爆发，他不得不从军，最后战死沙场。得知迈克在战争中死去，海伦悲痛欲绝，内疚更是加剧了她的悲伤。

小说中的斯卡斯沃斯太太同样也因不能公开追求爱情而深受其害，在长达九年零九个月的时间里，她压抑着内心的煎熬，隐藏自己和恋人的关系。然而她最终还是冲破世俗偏见，向海伦吐露了实情。她依靠自己的力量从自责的阴影中走了出来，获得心灵的解脱。受到斯卡斯沃斯太太的鼓舞，海伦最终在外界力量的帮助下勇敢地面对现实，正视自我，获得救赎。

小说名为《园丁》，但是通篇无过多笔墨描写园丁，而是围绕海伦展开。作者设置悬念，园丁仅在故事结尾才出现，可谓点睛之笔。"'Lieutenant Michael Turrell—my nephew', said Helen slowly and word for word, as she had many thousands of times in her life. The man lifted his eyes and looked at her with infinite compassion before he turned from the fresh-sown grass toward the naked black crosses. 'Come with me,' he said, "and I will show you where your son lies."通过园丁的话，读者才得以明白海伦和迈克之间的母子关系。在海伦的一生中，她遭受很多挫折，可是从未退缩，没有抱怨，正是她内心的坚强和博爱使她能够战胜灾难，独自将孩子抚养长大。因此，小说《园丁》无疑是对爱的颂歌，一个伟大的母亲形象顿时跃然纸上。

小说中，吉卜林运用现实主义的写作手法，通过细腻的笔触描写了迈克儿时不谙世事的天真与愤懑，展现了海伦隐忍半生的母爱与伤悲，描摹了斯卡斯沃斯太太瞬间爆发的倾诉欲望，凸显了园丁异于常人的洞察力和无限怜悯之心。小说中的园丁其实象征着上帝，他洞悉海伦的隐秘，并指引她来到儿子的墓前哀悼，使她完成了自己作为母亲的救赎。象征手法的运用使小说意蕴丰富，令人回味无穷。

The Gardener

Everyone in the village knew that Helen Turrell did her duty by all her world, and by none more honourably than by her only brother's unfortunate child. The village knew, too, that George Turrell had tried his family severely since early youth, and were not surprised to be told that, after many fresh starts given and thrown away, he, an Inspector of Indian Police, had entangled himself with the daughter of a retired non-commissioned officer, and had died of a fall from a horse a few weeks before his child was born.

Mercifully, George's father and mother were both dead, and though Helen, thirty-five and independent, might well have washed her hands of the whole disgraceful affair, she most nobly took charge, though she was, at the time, under threat of lung trouble which had driven her to the south of France. She arranged for the passage of the child and a nurse from Bombay, met them at Marseilles, nursed the baby through an attack of infantile dysentery① due to the carelessness of the nurse, whom she had to dismiss, and at last, thin and worn but triumphant, brought the boy late in the autumn, wholly restored, to her Hampshire home.

All these details were public property, for Helen was as open as the day, and held that scandals are only increased by hushing them up. She admitted that George had always been rather a black sheep, but things might have been much worse if the mother had insisted on her right to keep the boy. Luckily, it seemed that people of that class would do almost anything for money, and, as George had always turned to her in his scrapes, she felt herself justified—her friends agreed with her—in cutting the whole non-commissioned officer connection, and giving the child every

---

① infantile dysentery: 小儿痢疾。

advantage. A christening, by the Rector, under the name of Michael, was the first step. So far as she knew herself, she was not, she said, a child-lover, but, for all her faults, she had been very fond of George, and she pointed out that little Michael had his father's mouth to a line, which made something to build upon.

As a matter of fact, it was the Turrell forehead, broad, low, and well-shaped, with the widely spaces eyes beneath it, that Michael had most faithfully reproduced. His mouth was somewhat better cut than the family type. But Helen, who would concede nothing good to his mother's side, vowed he was a Turrell all over, and, there being no one to contradict, the likeness was established.

In a few years Michael took his place, as accepted as Helen had always been—fearless, philosophical, and fairly good-looking. At six, he wished to know why he could not call her "Mummy", as other boys called their mothers. She explained that she was only his auntie, and that aunties were not quite the same as mummies, but that, if it gave him pleasure, he might call her "Mummy" at bedtime, for a pet-name between themselves.

Michael kept his secret most loyally, but Helen, as usual, explained the fact to her friends; which when Michael heard, he raged.

"Why did you tell? Why did you tell?" came at the end of the storm.

"Because it's always best to tell the truth," Helen answered, her arm round him as he shook in his cot.

"All right, but when the troof's ugly I don't think it's nice."

"Don't you, dear?"

"No, I don't and"—she felt the small body stiffen—"now you've told, I won't call you 'Mummy' any more—not even at bedtimes."

"But isn't that rather unkind?" said Helen softly.

"I don't care! I don't care! You have hurt me in my insides and I'll hurt you back. I'll hurt you as long as I live!"

"Don't, oh, don't talk like that, dear! You don't know what—"

"I will! And when I'm dead I'll hurt you worse!"

"Thank goodness, I shall be dead long before you, darling."

"Huh! Emma says, 'Never know your luck'." (Michael had been talking to Helen's elderly, flat-faces maid.) "Lots of little boys die quite soon. So'll I. Then you'll see!"

Helen caught her breath and moved towards the door, but the wail of "Mummy! Mummy!" drew her back again, and the two wept together.

At ten years old, after two terms at a prep. school, something or somebody gave him the idea that his civil status was not quite regular. He attacked Helen on the subject, breaking down her stammered defences with the family directness.

"Don't believe a word of it," he said, cheerily, at the end. "People wouldn't have talked like they did if my people had been married. But don't you bother, Auntie. I've found out all about my sort in English Hist'ry and the Shakespeare bits. There was William the Conqueror to begin with, and—oh, heaps more, and they all got on first-rate. 'Twon't① make any difference to you, by being that—will it?"

"As if anything could—" she began.

"All right. We won't talk about it any more if it makes you cry." He never mentioned the thing again of his own will, but when, two years later, he skillfully managed to have measles② in the holidays, as his temperature went up to the appointed one hundred and four, he muttered of nothing else, till Helen's voice, piercing at last his delirium, reached him with assurance that nothing on earth or beyond could make any difference between them.

The terms at his public school and the wonderful Christmas, Easter, and Summer holidays followed each other, variegated③ and glorious as jewels on a string; and as jewels Helen treasured them. In due time Michael

---

① 'Twon't: it won't。
② measles:麻疹。
③ variegated:斑驳的,五花八门的。

developed his own interests, which ran their courses and gave way to others; but his interest in Helen was constant and increasing throughout. She repaid it with all that she had of affection or could command of counsel and money; and since Michael was no fool, the War took him just before what was like to have been a most promising career.

He was to have gone up to Oxford, with a scholarship, in October. At the end of August he was on the edge of joining the first holocaust of public-school boys who threw themselves into the Line; but the captain of his O.T.C., where he had been sergeant for nearly a year, headed him off and steered him directly to a commission in a battalion so new that half of it still wore the old Army red, and the other half was breeding meningitis① through living overcrowdedly in damp tents. Helen had been shocked at the idea of direct enlistment.

"But it's in the family," Michael laughed.

"You don't mean to tell me that you believed that story all this time?" said Helen. (Emma, her maid, had been dead now several years.) "I gave you my word of honour—and I give it again—that—that it's all right. It is indeed."

"Oh, that doesn't worry me. It never did," he replied valiantly. "What I meant was, I should have got into the show earlier if I'd enlisted—like my grandfather."

"Don't talk like that! Are you afraid of its ending so soon, then?"

"No such luck. You know what K. says."

"Yes. But my banker told me last Monday it couldn't possibly last beyond Christmas—for financial reasons."

"I hope he's right, but our Colonel—and he's a Regular—say it's going to be a long job."

Michael's battalion was fortunate in that, by some chance which meant

---

① meningitis: 脑膜炎。

several 'leaves', it was used for coast-defence among shallow trenches on the Norfolk coast; thence sent north to watch the mouth of a Scotch estuary, and, lastly, held for weeks on a baseless rumour of distant service. But, the very day that Michael was to have met Helen for four whole hours at a railway-junction up the line, it was hurled out, to help make good the wastage of Loos, and he had only just time to send her a wire of farewell.

In France luck again helped the battalion. It was put down near the Salient, where it led a meritorious and unexacting life, while the Somme was being manufactured; and enjoyed the peace of the Armenties and Laventie sectors when that battle began. Finding that it had sound views on protecting its own flanks and could dig, a prudent Commander stole it out of its own Division, under pretence of helping to lay telegraphs, and used it round Ypres at large.

A month later, and just after Michael had written Helen that there was noting special doing and therefore no need to worry, a shell-splinter dropping out of a wet dawn killed him at once. The next shell uprooted and laid down over the body what had been the foundation of a barn wall, so neatly that none but an expert would have guessed that anything unpleasant had happened.

By this time the village was old in experience of war, and, English fashion, had evolved a ritual to meet it. When the postmistress handed her seven-year-old daughter the official telegram to take to Miss Turrell, she observed to the Rector's gardener: "It's Miss Helen's turn now." He replied, thinking of his own son: "Well, he's lasted longer than some." The child herself came to the front-door weeping aloud, because Master Michael had often given her sweets. Helen, presently, found herself pulling down the house-blinds one after one with great care, and saying earnestly to each: "Missing *always* means dead." Then she took her place in the dreary procession that was impelled to go through an inevitable series of unprofitable emotions. The Rector, of course, preached hope end prophesied word, very soon, from a prison camp. Several friends, too, told her perfectly truthful tales, but always about other women, to whom, after months and months of silence, their missing had been miraculously restored. Other people urged her to communicate with infallible Secretaries of organizations who could communicate with benevolent neutrals, who could extract accurate information from the most secretive of Hun commandants. Helen did and wrote and signed everything that was suggested or put before her.

Once, on one of Michael's leaves, he had taken her over a munition factory, where she saw the progress of a shell from blank-iron to the all but finished article. It struck her at the time that the wretched thing was never left alone for a single second; and "I'm being manufactured into a bereaved next of kin", she told herself, as she prepared her documents.

In due course, when all the organizations had deeply or sincerely regretted their inability to trace, etc, something gave way within her and all sensations—save of thankfulness for the release—came to an end in blessed passivity. Michael had died and her world had stood still and she had been one with the full shock of that arrest. Now she was standing still and the world was going forward, but it did not concern her—in no way or relation did it touch her. She knew this by the ease with which she could slip Michael's name into talk and incline her head to the proper angle, at the proper murmur of sympathy.

In the blessed realization of that relief, the Armistice with all its bells broke over her and passed unheeded. At the end of another year she had overcome her physical loathing of the living and returned young, so that she could take them by the hand and almost sincerely wish them well. She had no interest in any aftermath, national or personal, of the war, but, moving at an immense distance, she sat on various relief committees and held strong views—she heard herself delivering them—about the site of the proposed village War Memorial.

Then there came to her, as next of kin, an official intimation, backed by a page of a letter to her in indelible pencil, a silver identity-disc and a watch, to the effect that the body of Lieutenant Michael Turrell had been found, identified, and re-interred in Hagenzeele Third Military Cemetery—the letter of the row and the grave's number in that row duly given.

So Helen found herself moved on to another process of the manufacture—to a world full of exultant or broken relatives, now strong in the certainty that there was an altar upon earth where they might lay their love. These soon told her, and by means of time-tables made clear, how easy it was and how little it interfered with life's affairs to go and see one's grave.

"So different", as the Rector's wife said, "if he'd been killed in Mesopotamia, or even Gallipoli."

The agony of being waked up to some sort of second life drove Helen across the Channel, where, in a new world of abbreviated titles, she learnt that Hagenzeele Third could be comfortably reached by an afternoon train which fitted in with the morning boat, and that there was a comfortable little hotel not three kilometres from Hagenzeele itself, where one could spend quite a comfortable night and see one's grave next morning. All this she had from a Central Authority who lived in a board and tar-paper shed on the skirts of a razed city of whirling lime-dust and blown papers.

"By the way", said he, "you know your grave, of course?"

"Yes, thank you", said Helen, and showed its row and number typed on Michael's own little typewriter. The officer would have checked it, out of one of his many books; but a large Lancashire woman thrust between them and bade him tell her where she might find her son, who had been corporal in the A.S.C. His proper name, she sobbed, was Anderson, but, coming of respectable folk, he had of course enlisted under the name of Smith; and had been killed at Dickiebush, in early 'Fifteen'. She had not his number nor did she know which of his two Christian names she might have used with his alias; but her Cook's tourist ticket expired at the end of Easter week, and if by then she could not find her child she should go mad. Whereupon she fell forward on Helen's breast; but the officer's wife came out quickly from a little bedroom behind the office, and the three of them lifted the woman on to the cot.

"They are often like this," said the officer's wife, loosening the tight bonnet-strings. "Yesterday she said he'd been killed at Hooge. Are you sure you know your grave? It makes such a difference."

"Yes, thank you," said Helen, and hurried out before the woman on the bed should begin to lament again.

Tea in a crowded mauve and blue striped wooden structure, with a false front, carried her still further into the nightmare. She paid her bill beside a stolid, plain-featured Englishwoman, who, hearing her inquire about the train to Hagenzeele, volunteered to come with her.

"I'm going to Hagenzeele myself," she explained. "Not to Hagenzeele Third; mine is Sugar Factory, but they call it La Rosie now. It's just south of Hagenzeele Three. Have you got your room at the hotel there?"

"Oh yes, thank you, I've wired."

"That's better. Sometimes the place is quite full, and at others there's hardly a soul. But they've put bathrooms into the old Lion d'Or—that's the hotel on the west side of Sugar Factory—and it draws off a lot of people, luckily."

"It's all new to me. This is the first time I've been over."

"Indeed! This is my ninth time since the Armistice. Not on my own account. I haven't lost anyone, thank God—but, like everyone else, I've lots of friends at home who have. Coming over as often as I do, I find it helps them to have someone just look at the place and tell them about it afterwards. And one can take photos for them, too. I get quite a list of commissions to execute." She laughed nervously and tapped her slung Kodak. "There are two or three to see at Sugar Factory this time, and plenty of others in the cemeteries all about. My system is to save them up, and arrange them, you know. And when I've got enough commissions for one area to make it worth while, I pop over and execute them. It *does* comfort people."

"I suppose so," Helen answered, shivering as they entered the little train.

"Of course it does. (Isn't lucky we've got windows-seats?) It must do or they wouldn't ask one to do it, would they? I've a list of quite twelve or fifteen commissions here,"—she tapped the Kodak again—"I must sort them out tonight. Oh, I forgot to ask you. What's yours?"

"My nephew," said Helen. "But I was very fond of him."

"Ah, yes! I sometimes wonder whether they know after death? What do you think?"

"Oh, I don't—I haven't dared to think much about that sort of thing", said Helen, almost lifting her hands to keep her off.

"Perhaps that's better," the woman answered. "The sense of loss must be enough, I expect. Well, I won't worry you any more."

Helen was grateful, but when they reached the hotel, Mrs. Scarsworth (they had exchanged names) insisted on dining at the same table with her, and after the meal, in the little, hideous salon full of low-voiced relatives, took Helen through her "commissions" with biographies of the dead, where she happened to know them, and sketches of their next of kin. Helen endured till nearly half-past nine, ere she fled to her room.

Almost at one there was a knock at her door and Mrs. Scarsworth entered; her hands, holding the dreadful list, clasped before her.

"Yes—yes—I know," she began. "You're sick of me, but I want to tell you something. You—you aren't married, are you? Then perhaps you won't ... But it doesn't matter. I've got to tell someone. I can't go on any longer like this."

"But please—" Mrs. Scarsworth had backed against the shut door, and her mouth worked dryly.

"In a minute," she said. "You—you know about these graves of mine I was telling you about downstairs, just now? They really are commissions. At least several of them are." Here eye wandered round the room. "What extraordinary wall-papers they have in Belgium, don't you think? ... Yes. I swear they are commissions. But there's one, d'you see, and—and he was more to me than anything else in the world. Do you understand?"

Helen nodded.

"More than anyone else. And, of course, he oughtn't to have been. He ought to have been nothing to me. But he was. He is. That's why I do the commissions, you see. That's all."

"But why do you tell me?" Helen asked desperately.

"Because I'm so tired of lying. Tired of lying—always lying—year in and year out. When I don't tell lies I've got to act 'em and I've got to think 'em, always. You don't know what that means. He was everything to me that he oughtn't to have been—the real thing—the only thing that ever happened to me in all my life; and I've had to pretend he wasn't. I've had to watch every word I said, and think out what lie I'd tell next, for years and years!"

"How many years?" Helen asked.

"Six years and four months before, and two and three-quarters after. I've gone to him eight times, since. Tomorrow I'll make the ninth, and—and I can't—I can't go to him again with nobody in the world knowing. I want to be honest with someone before I go. Do you understand? It doesn't matter about me. I was never truthful, even as a girl. But it isn't worthy of him. So—so I—I had to tell you. I can't keep it up any longer. Oh, I can't!"

Next morning Mrs Scarsworth left early on her round of commissions, and Helen walked alone to Hagenzeele Third. The place was still in the making, and stood some five or six feet above the metalled road, which it flanked for hundreds of yards. Culverts across a deep ditch served for entrances through the unfinished boundary wall. She climbed a few wooden-faced earthen steps and then met the entire crowded level of the thing in one held breath. She did not know that Hagenzeele Third counted twenty-one thousand dead already. All she saw was a merciless sea of black crosses, bearing little strips of stamped tin at all angles across their faces. She could distinguish no order or arrangement in their mass; nothing but a waist-high wilderness as of weeds stricken dead, rushing at her. She went forward, moved to the left and the right hopelessly, wondering by what guidance she should ever come to her own. A great distance away there was a line of whiteness. It proved to be a block of some two or three hundred graves whose headstones had already been set, whose flowers were planted out, and whose new-sown grass showed green. Here she could see clear-cut letters at the ends of the rows, and, referring to her slip, realized that it was not here she must look.

A man knelt behind a line of headstones—evidently a gardener, for he was firming a young plant in the soft earth. She went towards him, her paper in her hand. He rose at her approach and without prelude or salutation asked, "Who are you looking for?"

"Lieutenant Michael Turrell—my nephew," said Helen slowly and word for word, as she had many thousands of times in her life.

The man lifted his eyes and looked at her with infinite compassion before he turned from the fresh-sown grass toward the naked black crosses.

"Come with me," he said, "and I will show you where your son lies."

When Helen left the Cemetery she turned for a last look. In the distance she saw the man bending over his young plants; and she went away, supposing him to be the gardener.

Questions

1. Is the man who leads Helen to Michael's grave a real gardener? What does the last sentence of the story mean?

2. According to you, why is Mrs. Scarsworth eager to tell her secret to Helen, a total stranger?

Further Readings

Rudyard Kipling uses daily English and simple plots in his short stories. However, they are imbued with multiple-layered connotations and philosophical meanings. The following are some of his important short stories.

1. "The Man Who Would Be King"(《想做国王的人》)
2. "Tiger! Tiger!"(《老虎！老虎！》)
3. "Cupid's Arrows"(《爱神之箭》)

Unit 3 Compensation

About the writer

　　约翰·高尔斯华绥(John Galsworthy, 1867－1933)是20世纪英国批判现实主义小说家、戏剧家。在二十多年的创作生涯里,他创作了大量作品,包括3组三部曲小说、27部戏剧作品及多篇短篇小说、散文随笔和文学评论。他与韦尔斯(Herbert George Wells, 1866－1946)、阿诺德·贝内特(Enoch Arnold Bennett, 1867－1931)一起被称为爱德华时代的文学"三巨头"。他的作品多以19世纪末和20世纪初的英国社会为背景,描写英国社会各个阶层的真实生活,具有极高的文学价值。1929年,他接受英国政府功勋奖章。1932年,"因其卓越的描述艺术——这种艺术在《福尔赛世家》(The Forsyte Saga)中达到高峰",他荣获诺贝尔文学奖。

　　高尔斯华绥1867年出生于伦敦一个富裕的中产阶级家庭,父亲是知名律师,母亲是一位典型的贵族家庭妇女。高尔斯华绥1889年毕业于牛津大学,获得法律学位,后取得律师资格,但他本人对法律工作不感兴趣,借帮父亲管理海外公司的机会周游世界,其间与约瑟夫·康拉德相识,共同的文学爱好使他们成为一生的挚友。高尔斯华绥继承了维多利亚时代的文学传统,在情节发展、人物塑造、细节描写等方面遵循写实主义的创作原则,以细腻的笔法反映了英国社会从维多利亚时期向现代英国转变过程中的种种社会现实。

　　1906年,长篇小说《有产业的人》(The Man of Property)为他赢得巨大声誉,成为《福尔赛世家》系列长篇三部曲的开端。另外两部是《骑虎》(In Chancery, 1920)和《出租》(To Let, 1921)。三部曲描写福尔赛家族由兴到衰的过程。福尔赛家族19世纪初从农村来到城市,在英国工业发展和帝国的海外扩张中发迹。三部曲从三个年龄段塑造了索米斯这个典型的英国资产阶级人物形象,反映了英国维多利亚时代资产阶级的家庭生活及其演变,刻画了三代人的精神面貌,批判了"福尔赛主义"(Forsytism)——对财产无止境占有的私欲和用金钱衡量一切的财产意识。三部曲对资产阶级进行了犀利的讽刺,体现了作者的进步思想、人文精神和艺术手法,奠定了高尔斯华绥在英国文学界的地位。

此后高尔斯华绥又完成了两个三部曲:由《白猿》(The White Monkey, 1924)、《银匙》(The Silver Spoon, 1926)、《天鹅之歌》(Swan Song, 1928)和两部插曲组成的三部曲《现代喜剧》(Forsyte Saga: A Modern Comedy, 1929);由《女仆》(Maid in Waiting, 1931)、《开花的荒野》(Flowering Wilderness, 1932)和《河那边》(Over the River, 1933)组成的三部曲《尾声》(Forsyte Saga: End of the Chapter, 1933)。从《有产业的人》到《河那边》,高尔斯华绥的三组三部曲记录和体现了英国社会二十多年的变化和动荡,反映了时代的变迁,丰富和发展了 20 世纪初的现实主义小说。

高尔斯华绥一生共完成了 27 个剧本,剧作在英国国内一经推出便大受好评,热演不衰。《银烟盒:三幕喜剧》(The Silver Box, 1906)是高尔斯华绥创作的第一部完整的戏剧作品,一面世就受到评论界关注。该作将酒后盗窃行为安置在两个不同阶层的人物身上,通过鲜明的比较,揭露了资本主义社会"法律面前人人平等"这一谎言的本质。

高尔斯华绥还创作了大量短篇小说,他以现实主义为基调,融入大量心理描写,通过极具画面感的明暗对比引发读者共鸣。《品质》("Quality", 1911)描写优秀的传统手工技艺在廉价机器工业产品竞争下的绝望挣扎,流露出作者对老鞋匠诚信品质的崇敬之情。《苹果树》("The Apple Tree", 1918)讲述了一个动人的爱情悲剧,男女主人公在苹果树下相恋、定情又因阶级差异而分手,小说的写实手法与唯美倾向融合,十分感人。

高尔斯华绥十分重视艺术的社会和道德功用,认为艺术通过表现善与美可以推动社会改造和进步,"小说家应该通过性格的塑造而对人类伦理道德做出有益贡献"。他的小说运用写实手法,将情节发展和性格塑造有机结合,情节紧凑生动,叙述客观冷静,语言自然流畅,各种艺术手法交织使用,揭示了英国的社会现状。

About the story

《补偿》("Compensation", 1904)是短篇小说集《杂集》(A Motley,

1910)的第 7 篇,故事中有三个人物:故事听众"你"(谢尔顿,Sheldon)、故事叙述者"我"(费兰德,Ferrand)、故事主人公"他"(邱丘,Tchuk-Tchuk)。谢尔顿是一个周游欧洲的资产阶级青年,在比利时海滨度假胜地奥斯坦德遇到下层青年费兰德,听他讲述小商贩邱丘的故事,引发他对"世间万事有付出必有回报"的思考。

故事伊始,费兰德对谢尔顿"世间万事有付出必有回报"的观点提出质疑,并且讲述了阿尔及利亚犹太小商贩邱丘的真实故事。基于种族歧视等原因,邱丘谎称自己是意大利南部人,在度假季离开家乡到比利时的海滨度假胜地奥斯坦德,在海滩上向游客兜售劣质小饰品,希望借此能攒够钱回家和心爱的姑娘组成家庭,过上富裕的生活。他节衣缩食,努力工作,然而最后积蓄被盗,梦想破灭,失魂落魄地离开。

小说运用第一人称讲述故事,在继承现实主义传统的同时,借助自然主义的手法,刻画了一个在社会底层苦苦挣扎的小人物邱丘。小说运用大量细节描写,塑造了一个栩栩如生的形象,使邱丘这个人物显得格外真实可信。外形方面,邱丘是一个年轻的小伙子,眼睛又黑又亮,鼻梁高挺,有一头漂亮的小卷发,常穿着英国游客丢弃的法兰绒长裤、旧罩袍和圆礼帽,邱丘太瘦以至于这套组合怪异的服饰穿在他身上就像是一个套着麻袋的稻草人似的,但是邱丘毫不在意,因为这些衣服不花钱。邱丘将一日三餐压缩至勉强能维系生命的水平,一整天只吃不到半斤重的面包或面条,加上一丁点儿奶酪,偶尔吃一点肉肠就是大餐。

邱丘一方面拼命压缩生活开支,另一方面拼尽全力赚钱。他花掉所有本钱,在海滩上租了一个小摊位卖饰品——花哨的珊瑚饰品、意式搪瓷别针、赛璐珞小玩意儿。在费兰德眼里这些饰品与垃圾无二。邱丘带着满腔的热忱投入他的事业中,不论白天黑夜、日晒雨淋,都守着他的小摊,不愿意放过任何一个可能的顾客。聪明的邱丘总是笑脸迎客,把小饰品送到女顾客们(特别是妓女们)的面前,并且眼巴巴地看着她们,希望博得同情而卖掉货物。在费兰德眼中,邱丘是一个工作的奴隶,"nothing interested him; he despised all the world around him—the people, the sea, the amusements; they were ridiculous and foreign. He had his stall, and he lived to sell. He was like a man shut up in a box—with not a pleasure, not a sympathy, nothing wherewith to touch this strange world in which he found himself."。邱丘对卖东西赚钱之外的任何事物毫无兴趣,游客、海滩和娱乐项目在他看来既荒谬又怪异。

邱丘真的是一台只知赚钱的机器吗？事实并非如此，他如此拼命赚钱的动力恰恰是源自对生活的热爱。家乡贫穷落后，生计艰难。他有一个无时无刻不盼望着和他团聚的爱人，他梦想着攒上二三百英镑回乡，和心爱的姑娘过上富裕的生活。邱丘虽然努力工作，但是并没有积蓄，前一年攒下的钱被互助同乡会搜刮一空，以此换来旅游旺季海边的一个小摊位。为了早日达成心愿，他更加勤俭努力。

度假季转瞬即逝，游客们纷纷离去。傍晚时分，费兰德在小酒馆见到了邱丘，邱丘不仅自己花钱买酒喝，甚至还大方地给费兰德和另外三个意大利骗子买了酒。在酒精的刺激下，邱丘几个月来的谨小慎微和压抑的情绪得到释放，他侃侃而谈，心情欢畅，又唱又笑。在意大利人的激将下邱丘展示了他挣得的4 000法郎，使所有在场的人目瞪口呆。邱丘兴奋地打着响指，嚷着要回乡娶妻，此时的他完全不知厄运即将来临。第二天上午，费兰德在小酒馆见到了失魂落魄、伤心欲绝的邱丘。邱丘酒后睡得很沉，丧失了警惕，全部积蓄被盗，前途尽毁。由于他只是个不名一文的犹太人，警察也懒得理他。邱丘变卖了所有东西也没能凑够一张去布鲁塞尔的车票，只能徒步返回布鲁塞尔。

这个故事篇幅较短，是高尔斯华绥最发人深省的短篇小说之一，涉及种族、爱情、阶级、罪恶、人性等元素，真实展现了社会百态。作者在讽刺贫富差异较大的资本主义社会的同时，赞美了底层人物不屈不挠、希望凭借勤劳实现梦想的优秀品质。尽管小说围绕"付出与回报"的关系展开故事情节，反映的却是"是否应该对生活和人性保有信念"的问题。故事反映了多数人的生活状态：他们对生活充满信心，有着种种憧憬，即便有时努力付出却没有回报，但依然会坚持自己的理想并为之奋斗，这也是邱丘这个小人物身上的闪光点。

Compensation

If, as you say (said Ferrand), there is compensation in this life for everything, do tell me where it comes in here.①

---

① where it comes in here: it 指代上句的 compensation。如果依你所言，生活中万事有付出必有回报，请告诉我这个故事里的回报在哪儿。

Two years ago I was interpreter① to an hotel in Ostend②, and spent many hours on the Plage③ waiting for the steamers to bring sheep to my slaughter④. There was a young man about that year who had a stall of cheap jewellery; I don't know his name, for among us he was called Tchuk-Tchuk; but I knew him—for we interpreters know everybody. He came from Southern Italy and called himself an Italian, but by birth he was probably an Algerian Jew; an intelligent boy, who knew that, except in England, it is far from profitable to be a Jew in these days⑤. After seeing his nose and his beautiful head of frizzly hair, however, there was little more to be said on the subject⑥. His clothes had been given him by an English tourist—a pair of flannel trousers, an old frock coat, a bowler hat⑦. Incongruous? Yes, but think, how cheap! The only thing that looked natural to him was his tie; he had unsewn the ends and wore it without a collar. He was little and thin, which was not surprising, for all he ate a day was half a pound of bread, or its equivalent in macaroni, with a little piece of cheese, and on a feast day a bit of sausage. In those clothes, which were made for a fat man, he had the appearance of a scarecrow with a fine, large head. These "Italians" are the Chinese of the West. The conditions of life down there being impossible⑧, they are driven out like locusts or the old inhabitants of Central Asia—a regular invasion. In every country they have a

---

① interpreter：羊儿客，捎客，拉客仔。interpreter 前未加冠词，并非拼写或语法错误，而是作者还原 Ferrand 所说的话语。
② Ostend：奥斯坦德，比利时的西北部城市，属于西佛兰德省，著名旅游城市，海滨疗养地。
③ Plage：普拉格海滩，弗兰德斯海岸一连串海滩中的一个，由比利时近荷兰边境的海岸计起到法国北部与英国对望的地区，长约 100 千米。
④ sheep：指来此地度假的游客。slaughter 指酒店。Ferrand 把要住酒店的游客比喻成待宰的羔羊。
⑤ it is far from profitable to be a Jew in these days：近来犹太人的身份绝不是件好事。
⑥ subject：指 Tchuk-Tchuk 的身份问题。
⑦ a pair of flannel trousers, an old frock coat, a bowler hat：一条法兰绒长裤、一件旧罩袍和一顶圆礼帽。
⑧ The conditions of life down there being impossible：生活条件十分恶劣，让人难以忍受。

kind of Society which helps them to make a start. When once provided with organs, jewellery, or whatever their profession, they live on nothing, drink nothing, spend no money. Smoke? Yes, they smoke; but you have to give them the tobacco. Sometimes they bring their women; more often they come alone—they make money more quickly without. The end they have in view is to scrape together① a treasure of two or three hundred pounds and go back to Italy rich men. If you're accustomed to the Italian at home, it will astonish you to see how he works when he's out of his own country, and how provident he is—a regular Chinaman. Tchuk-Tchuk was alone, and he worked like a slave. He was at his stand, day in, day out; if the sun burned, if there was a gale; he was often wet through, but no one could pass without receiving a smile from his teeth and a hand stretched out with some gimcrack or other. He always tried to impress the women, with whom he did most of his business—especially the *cocotterie*②. Ah! how he looked at them with his great eyes! Temperamentally, I dare say, he was vicious enough; but, as you know, it costs money to be vicious, and he spent no money. His expenses were twopence a day for food and fourpence for his bed in a *café* full of other birds of his feather③—sixpence a day, three shillings and sixpence a week. No other sort of human creature can keep this up long. My minimum is tenpence, which is not a bed of roses④; but, then, I can't do without tobacco (to a man in extreme poverty a single vice is indispensable⑤). But these "Italians" do without even that. Tchuk-Tchuk sold; not very hard work, you say? Try it for half an hour; try and sell something good—and Tchuk-Tchuk's things were rubbish—flash coral

---

① scrape together:意大利人竭力省下每一分钱。
② cocotterie:法语,荡妇、妓女。
③ full of other birds of his feather:他的同类。
④ a bed of roses:舒适豪华的境况,常用作反语。
⑤ to a man in extreme poverty a single vice is indispensable:一个穷鬼在所难免会有点小毛病。

jewellery, Italian enamels made up into pins and brooches, celluloid gimcracks①. In the evenings I've often seen him doze off from sheer fatigue, but always with his eyes half-open, like a cat. His soul was in his stall; he watched everything—but only to sell his precious goods, for nothing interested him; he despised all the world around him—the people, the sea, the amusements; they were ridiculous and foreign. He had his stall, and he lived to sell. He was like a man shut up in a box—with not a pleasure, not a sympathy, nothing wherewith to touch this strange world in which he found himself②.

"I'm of the South," he would say to me, jerking his head at the sea; "it's hard there. Over there I got a girl. She wouldn't be sorry to see me again, not too sorry! Over there one starves; name of a Saint③" (he chose this form of oath, no doubt, because it sounded Christian), "it's hard there!"

I am not sentimental about Tchuk-Tchuk; he was an egoist to the bottom of his soul, but that did not in the least prevent his suffering for the want of his South, for the want of his sunshine, and his girl④—the greater the egoism the greater the suffering. He craved like a dumb animal; but, as he remarked, "Over there one starves!" Naturally he had not waited for that. He had his hopes. "Wait a bit!" he used to say. "Last year I was in Brussels. Bad business! At the end they take away all my money for the Society, and give me this stall. This is all right—I make some money this season."

---

① flash coral jewellery, Italian enamels made up into pins and brooches, celluloid gimcracks：花哨的珊瑚饰品，意式搪瓷别针，赛璐珞（塑料）的小玩意儿。说明邱丘售卖质量低劣、不值钱的东西。

② with not a pleasure, not a sympathy, nothing wherewith to touch this strange world in which he found himself：既没有快乐也没有同情，浑身上下没有一点东西跟这世界有关联。

③ name of a Saint：以圣人之名发誓，我说的是真话。

④ but that did not in the least prevent his suffering for the want of his South, for the want of his sunshine, and his girl：这一点也没让他免受对南方、阳光和女孩的思念之苦。

He had many clients among "women of morals"①, who had an eye for his beautiful head of hair, who know, too, that life is not all roses; and there was something pathetic in the persistency of Tchuk-Tchuk and the way his clothes hung about him like sacks; nor was he bad-looking, with his great black eyes and his slim, dirty hands.

One wet day I came on the Estacade② when hardly a soul was there. Tchuk-Tchuk had covered his stall with a piece of old tarpaulin. He was smoking a long cigar.

"Aha! Tchuk-Tchuk," I said, "smoking?"

"Yes," says he, "it's good!"

"Why not smoke every day, you miser③? It would comfort you when you're hungry."

He shook his head. "Costs money," says he. "This one cost me nothing. A kind of an individual gave it to me—a red-faced Englishman—said he couldn't smoke it. He knew nothing, the idiot—this is good, I tell you!"

But it was Tchuk-Tchuk who knew nothing—he had been too long without the means of knowledge. It was interesting to see the way he ate, drink, inhaled, and soaked up that rank cigar—a true revel of sensuality④.

The end of the season came, and all of us birds who prey on the visitors were getting ready to fly; but I stayed on, because I liked the place—the gay-coloured houses, the smell of fish in the port, the good air, the long green seas, the dunes; there's something of it all in my blood, and I'm always sorry to leave. But after the season is over—as Tchuk-Tchuk would say—"Name of a Saint—one starves over there!"

---

① women of morals: 行事放荡的女人, 妓女。
② Estacade: 防波堤栅。
③ you miser: 你这个守财奴。
④ It was interesting to see the way he ate, drink, inhaled, and soaked up that rank cigar—a true revel of sensuality: 他吃饭、喝水、吸烟、沉浸在那种劣质香烟中的样子真是有趣——那才是真正的纵情享受。

One evening, at the very end, when there were scarcely twenty visitors in the place, I went as usual to a certain *café* with two compartments, where everyone comes whose way of living is dubious—bullies, comedians, off-colour actresses, women of morals, "Turks", "Italians", "Greeks"—all such, in fact, as play the game of stealing—a regular rag-shop of cheats and gentlemen of industry①—very interesting people, with whom I am well acquainted. Nearly everyone had gone; so that evening there were but few of us in the restaurant, and in the inner room three Italians only. I passed into that.

Presently in came Tchuk-Tchuk, the first time I had ever seen him in a place where one could spend a little money. How thin he was, with his little body and his great head! One would have said he hadn't eaten for a week. A week? A year! Down he sat, and called for a bottle of wine; and at once he began to chatter and snap his fingers②.

"Ha, ha!" says one of the Italians; "look at Tchuk-Tchuk. What a nightingale he has become all of a sudden. Come, Tchuk-Tchuk, give us some of your wine, seeing you're in luck!"

Tchuk-Tchuk gave us of his wine, and ordered another bottle.

"Ho, ho!" says another Italian, "must have buried his family, this companion!" We drank—Tchuk-Tchuk faster than all. Do you know that sort of thirst, when you drink just to give you the feeling of having blood in the veins at all? Most people in that state can't stop—they drink themselves dead drunk③. Tchuk-Tchuk was not like that. He was careful, as always, looking to his future. Oh! He kept his heart in hand; but in such cases a

---

① where everyone comes whose way of living is dubious—bullies, comedians, off-colour actresses, women of morals, "Turks", "Italians", "Greeks"—all such, in fact, as play the game of stealing—a regular rag-shop of cheats and gentlemen of industry：这里每个人的日子都过得不太光彩——皮条客、搞笑艺人、过气女演员、放荡的妓女、"土耳其人""意大利人""希腊人"——诸如此类，事实上他们坑蒙拐骗———群人模狗样的骗子杂碎。

② chatter and snap his fingers：把手指捏得咔咔响。

③ they drink themselves dead drunk：他们喝得酩酊大醉。

little goes a long way①; he became cheerful—it doesn't take much to make an Italian cheerful who has been living for months on water and half-rations of bread and macaroni. It was evident, too, that he had reason to feel gay. He sang and laughed, and the other Italians sang and laughed with him. One of them said, "It seems our Tchuk-Tchuk has been doing good business. Come, Tchuk-Tchuk, tell us what you have made this season!"

But Tchuk-Tchuk only shook his head.

"Eh!" said the Italian, "the shy bird. It ought to be something good. As for me, comrades, honestly, five hundred francs is all I've made—not a centime more—and the half of that goes to the patron."②

And each of them began talking of his gains, except Tchuk-Tchuk, who showed his teeth, and kept silence③.

"Come, Tchuk-Tchuk," said one, "don't be a bandit—a little rankness!"④

"He won't beat my sixteen hundred!"⑤ said another.

"Name of a Saint!" said Tchuk-Tchuk suddenly, "What do you say to four thousand?"

But we all laughed.

"La, la!" said one, "He mocks us!"

Tchuk-Tchuk opened the front of his old frockcoat.

"Look!" he cried, and he pulled out four bills—each for a thousand francs. How we stared!

"See," said he, "what it is to be careful—I spend nothing—every cent is here! Now I go home—I get my girl; wish me good journey!" He set to

---

① he kept his heart in hand; but in such cases a little goes a long way:他一直控制着内心的渴望,但是这种情形下一丁点儿酒就让他忘乎所以。

② five hundred francs is all I've made—not a centime more—and the half of that goes to the patron:我就赚了五百法郎,一分多的都没有,还交了一半给保护人。

③ showed his teeth, and kept silence:一副欲言又止的样子。

④ don't be a bandit—a little rankness:别使坏——那就扫兴了。

⑤ He won't beat my sixteen hundred:他反正不会超过我的1600。

work again to snap his fingers.

We stayed some time and drank another bottle. Tchuk-Tchuk paying. When we parted nobody was helpless, only, as I say, Tchuk-Tchuk on the road to the stars, as one is after a six months' fast. The next morning I was drinking a "bock" in the same *café*, for there was nothing else to do, when all of a sudden who should come running in but this same Tchuk-Tchuk! Ah! But he was no longer on the road to the stars. He flung himself down at the table①, with his head between his hands, and the tears rolled down his cheeks.

"They've robbed me," he cried, "robbed me of every sou②; robbed me while I slept. I had it here, under my pillow; I slept on it; it's gone—every sou!" He beat his breast.

"Come, Tchuk-Tchuk," said I, "from under your pillow? That's not possible!"

"How do I know?" he groaned, "It's gone, I tell you—all my money, all my money. I was heavy with the wine—" All he could do was to repeat again and again: "All my money, all my money!"

"Have you been to the police?"

He had been to the police. I tried to console him, but without much effect, as you may imagine. The boy was beside himself③.

The police did nothing—why should they? If he had been a Rothschild④, it would have been different, but seeing he was only a poor devil of an Italian who had lost his all—!

Tchuk-Tchuk had sold his stall, his stock, everything he had, the day before, so he had not even the money for a ticket to Brussels. He was obliged to walk. He started—and to this day I see him starting, with his little

---

① He flung himself down at the table：他冲过来趴在桌上。
② sou：苏（法国旧时低值硬币）。
③ The boy was beside himself：这孩子疯疯癫癫的。
④ Rothschild：罗斯柴尔德家族，200多年来在欧洲有着巨大影响力的犹太银行家族。

hard hat on his beautiful black hair, and the unsewn ends of his tie. His face was like the face of the Devil thrown out of Eden!

What became of him I can not say, but I do not see too clearly in all this the compensation of which you have been speaking.

And Ferrand was silent.

Questions

1. A story generally depends much on its plot, which usually consists of exposition, complication, conflict, climax and denouement. Can you divide the plot of this story into five parts? If you can't, what is the course of this plot then? What does this plot course imply?

2. A story usually has multiple themes. What are the themes of this story?

Further Readings

John Galsworthy's short stories reflect the social life of the UK in the early 20th century. They are remarkable for their brilliant illustrations, psychological analysis and moral strength. The following are some of his important short stories.

1. "Quality" (《品质》)
2. "Courage" (《勇气》)
3. "Virtue" (《美德》)
4. "Evolution" (《进化》)

Unit 4　A Friend in Need

About the writer

　　威廉·萨默塞特·毛姆（William Somerset Maugham，1874–1965），英国著名小说家、剧作家和评论家。毛姆一生著作颇丰，先后出版 20 部长篇小说、31 部剧本、9 部短篇小说集、7 部随笔，被誉为"20 世纪最值得读的作家之一"。

　　毛姆出生于法国，自小口吃，性格比较敏感。9 岁时母亲因难产而死，他被送回英国，与陌生的伯父一家生活在一起。尽管伯父一家热情友善，但他还是有寄人篱下之感，这在他的作品《人性的枷锁》(Of Human Bondage, 1915) 中有所体现。毛姆一生历经维多利亚时代后半期和两次世界大战，其作品全面反映了英国这一时期的社会变迁和民众的心理变化。创作风格方面，他深受法国自然主义影响，常以真实人物为创作原型，将事实与虚构交织在一起，以第一人称视角，向读者娓娓讲述一个又一个精彩的故事。

　　《人性的枷锁》是毛姆以早年生活经历为原型而创作的一部自传体成长小说。主人公菲利普一出生即面临着残酷的人生和命运：足部天生畸形，周围人常以异样眼光盯着他，由于 9 岁丧母他不得不寄人篱下与伯父一家生活在一起。所有这一切使得他敏感又自卑。之后，在疼爱他的伯母的安排下，他前往德国海德堡研究哲学，开始认真思考人生的意义。

　　《月亮和六便士》(The Moon and Sixpence, 1919) 是毛姆以法国印象派画家高更 (Paul Gauguin, 1848–1903) 为原型而创作的一部小说。金融界成功人士思特里克兰德一天突然放弃如日中天的事业和看起来幸福美满的家庭，跑到巴黎学习绘画。之后，他前往南太平洋塔西提岛写生，虽然忍受着物质上的贫穷和麻风病的折磨，但他创作出辉煌的艺术杰作。小说中，叙事者"我"作为故事讲述者，以好奇、不带情感和道德判断的口吻，向读者呈现主人公对道德、社会、生活及艺术追求的取舍,同时也迫使读者审视自己的生活与追求。

《刀锋》(The Razor's Edge, 1944)被认为是毛姆最好的作品,出版的第一个月,在美国便卖出50万本。"如同刀锋险峻不易跨越,救赎之路难走,能成功的人寥寥无几",这句来自印度经典《奥义书》的话,既是作品的题记,也是其主旨。《刀锋》围绕着主人公莱瑞和他有关的几个人物展开,每个人物都在寻找自己的救赎之路。莱瑞作为飞行员曾参与第一次世界大战,在一次空战中,战友舍弃自己的生命为他赢得了生机,活下来的莱瑞开始思考生命的意义和存在的价值。面对没有受过战争影响并沉浸于物欲中的美国人,他的思考显得格格不入。于是,他离开美国,开始游历世界,在印度他接触并阅读了《奥义书》。受该书启发,他明白了生命的真谛,得到了精神的救赎。

毛姆还是一个出色的短篇小说家,共创作了150余篇短篇小说。其短篇的突出特征在于:主题上聚焦人性的复杂,尤其是人性中恶的一面;叙事视角上采用第一人称叙事,叙事者作为故事的听众或者参与者,将听到的故事转述给读者;叙事结构上采用倒叙、插叙等方法,往往在故事开头即交代故事结局,然后逐渐铺开导致这一结局的原因;写作手法上常采用反讽,描写主要人物的表里不一,讽刺、揭露人性的弱点或人性的阴暗面。毛姆常会在短篇小说开篇发表一些议论,在下文以浅显语言讲述一个故事,来印证这些议论。因此,阅读他的短篇小说,理解开篇的议论往往是关键所在。

About the story

《患难之交》短小精悍,讲述了外表和善、内心恶毒的商人爱德华·伯顿拒绝前来求助的远亲列尼·伯顿并置他于死地的故事。在这个故事里,毛姆告诫读者,不能仅凭一个人的外表或别人的评价来判断他的善恶,否则可能会像故事中的列尼·伯顿一样,以悲剧结束。

在《患难之交》开篇,毛姆以第一人称"我"的叙事视角,与读者分享人们以貌识人的经验和叙事者"我"的困惑,引发读者共鸣。接着,设置一个悬念以引起读者的兴趣:"我对他感兴趣,是因为他着实让我大吃一惊。如果这故事不是从他亲口说出,我是怎么也不会相信他居然干得出那样的事儿来的。正因为他的外貌举止都显示他是我认定的一类,那事儿才更让我瞠目。"爱德华·伯顿究竟做了什么事,让"我"大吃一惊?

毛姆很清楚读者的心理活动：如果仅仅基于外貌评判一个人并不准确，那么纳入周围人的评价及其所在的家庭环境等因素后，评判会准确吗？比如，"我"运用许多积极的词汇，全方位塑造了一个似乎与人为善、积极正面的形象：爱德华身材矮小、体格瘦弱，年龄在60岁左右，举止与其年龄和地位相符。爱德华·伯顿桥牌打得不错，在社交圈很受欢迎；他的家庭和睦友爱。爱德华给人留下最突出的印象是温柔善良，对同胞有爱心，有人格魅力，能激起别人对他的保护欲。但是，毛姆想要告诉读者的是，认识一个人，远不止如此简单。人性异常复杂，不能仅从其外表和周围环境加以识别，还需要根据其所作所为判断。

毛姆让爱德华本人讲述自己的所作所为，只有这样才能让读者们信服。爱德华讲述的故事非常简单：身无分文、无半技之长且身体状况欠佳的列尼前来寻求帮助，他没有拒绝，却提出一个似乎是让列尼知难而退的条件——如果列尼能够从神户的盐田俱乐部下水，游过水流湍急的灯塔，并成功抵达对岸，那么就给他一个工作机会。走投无路的列尼只好答应了这个条件，却被淹死了。故事伊始，爱德华对"我"坦言，面对35岁却依然一事无成的列尼时，他感到幸灾乐祸。故事结尾，面对"我"的疑问，"When you made him that offer of a job, did you know he'd be drowned?"时，他的反应竟然是"Well, I hadn't got a vacancy in my office at the moment."。"我"以旁观者身份，详细记录下爱德华讲故事时心安理得的语气，让读者感受到看起来弱小善良的爱德华内心是多么阴暗和冷酷无情。

在《患难之交》里，共有两次叙事视角的转换，提醒读者故事叙述者身份的变化。第一次以"Burton sipped his gin fizz"提醒读者，由此处开始故事的讲述者由"我"（第一人称）回忆性叙事视角转换到爱德华，由他亲口讲述自己给他人落井下石的故事。第二次发生在爱德华讲完故事之后，叙事视角又转到"我"的第一人称叙事视角。视角转换表明，这个故事不是叙事者"我"编造出来的，而是爱德华亲口讲述的。毛姆以反讽的手法，通过刻画爱德华表面连"苍蝇都不忍伤害"实际上虚伪冷酷的商人形象，一方面讽刺了他的表里不一，揭示了人性的阴暗与复杂，另一方面也嘲讽人们（当然也包括作者自己）在判断他人善恶上的自以为是，以达到警示和教育的目的。

A Friend in Need

For thirty years now I have been studying my fellow-men. I do not know very much about them. I should certainly hesitate to engage a servant on his face, and yet I suppose it is on the face that for the most part we judge the persons we meet. We draw our conclusions from the shape of the jaw, the look in the eyes, the contour of the mouth. I wonder if we are more often right than wrong. Why novels and plays are so often untrue to life is because their authors, perhaps of necessity, make their characters all of a piece①. They cannot afford to make them self-contradictory, for then they become incomprehensible, and yet self-contradictory is what most of us are. We are a haphazard bundle of inconsistent qualities②. In books on logic they will tell you that it is absurd to say that yellow is tubular or gratitude heavier than air; but in that mixture of incongruities that makes up the self yellow may very well be a horse and cart and gratitude the middle of next week. I shrug my shoulders when people tell me that their first impressions of a person are always right. I think they must have small insight or great vanity. For my own part I find that the longer I know people the more they puzzle me; my oldest friends are just those of whom I can say that I don't know the first thing about them③.

These reflections have occurred to me because I read in this morning's paper that Edward Hyde Burton had died at Kobe④. He was a merchant and he had been in business in Japan for many years. I knew him very little, but he interested me because once he gave me a great surprise. Unless I had heard the story from his own lips I should never have believed that he was capable of such an action. It⑤ was more startling because both in appearance and manner he suggested a very definite type. Here if ever was

---

① all of a piece: 表里如一。
② We are a haphazard bundle of inconsistent qualities: 我们就是矛盾品性的偶然组合体。
③ I don't know the first thing about them: 我对他们一无所知。
④ Kobe: (日本)神户。
⑤ it 指前一句中的 such an action。作者在这里没有交代是什么行为,勾起了读者急切往下读的兴趣。事实上,下文整个故事就是在交代 such an action 的始末。

a man all of a piece①. He was a tiny little fellow, not much more than five feet four in height, and very slender, with white hair, a red face much wrinkled, and blue eyes. I suppose he was about sixty when I knew him. He was always neatly and quietly dressed in accordance with his age and station.

Though his offices were in Kobe, Burton often came down to Yokohama②. I happened on one occasion to be spending a few days there, waiting for a ship, and I was introduced to him at the British Club. We played bridge together. He played a good game and a generous one. He did not talk very much, either then or later when we were having drinks, but what he said was sensible. He had a quiet, dry humour③. He seemed to be popular at the club and afterwards, when he had gone, they described him as one of the best. It happened that we were both staying at the Grand Hotel and next day he asked me to dine with him. I met his wife, fat, elderly, and smiling, and his two daughters. It was evidently a united and affectionate family. I think the chief thing that struck me about Burton was his kindliness. There was something very pleasing in his mild blue eyes. His voice was gentle; you could not imagine that he could possibly raise it in anger; his smile was benign. Here was a man who attracted you because you felt in him a real love for his fellows. He had charm. But there was nothing mawkish in him: he liked his game of cards and his cocktail, he could tell with point a good and spicy story, and in his youth he had been something of an athlete. He was a rich man and he had made every penny himself. I suppose one thing that made you like him was that he was so small and frail; he aroused your instincts of protection. You felt that he could not bear to hurt a fly.

One afternoon I was sitting in the lounge of the Grand Hotel. This was

---

① Here if ever was a man all of a piece: 要说有人表里如一，那就是他了。
② Yokohama: (日本) 横滨。
③ dry humour: 冷幽默。

before the earthquake① and they had leather arm-chairs there. From the windows you had a spacious view of the harbour with its crowded traffic. There were great liners on their way to Vancouver and San Francisco or to Europe by way of Shanghai, Hong-Kong, and Singapore; there were tramps of all nations, battered and sea-worn, junks with their high sterns and great coloured sails, and innumerable sampans. It was a busy, exhilarating scene, and yet, I know not why, restful to the spirit. Here was romance and it seemed that you had but to stretch out your hand to touch it.

Burton came into the lounge presently and caught sight of me. He seated himself in the chair next to mine.

"What do you say to a little drink?"

He clapped his hands for a boy and ordered two gin fizzes. As the boy brought them a man passed along the street outside and seeing me waved his hand.

"Do you know Turner?" said Burton as I nodded a greeting.

"I've met him at the club. I'm told he's a remittance man②."

"Yes, I believe he is. We have a good many here."

"He plays bridge well."

"They generally do. There was a fellow here last year, oddly enough a namesake of mine③, who was the best bridge player I ever met. I suppose you never came across him in London. Lenny Burton he called himself. I believe he'd belonged to some very good clubs."

"No, I don't believe I remember the name."

"He was quite a remarkable player. He seemed to have an instinct about the cards. It was uncanny. I used to play with him a lot. He was in Kobe for some time."

---

① the earthquake: 1923 年发生的关东大地震,震级为 7.9 级。横滨为重灾区之一,所有的外国使馆都在这次地震中倒塌。

② remittance man: 侨居在国外依靠国内汇款生活的人,或者靠家里寄钱生活的人。

③ a namesake of mine: 与我同姓的人,指的是下文中的 Lenny Burton。

Burton sipped his gin fizz.

"It's rather a funny story," he said. "He wasn't a bad chap. I liked him. He was always well-dressed and smart-looking. He was handsome in a way with curly hair and pink-and-white cheeks. Women thought a lot of him. There was no harm in him, you know, he was only wild. Of course he drank too much. Those sort of fellows always do. A bit of money used to come in for him once a quarter and he made a bit more by card-playing. He won a good deal of mine, I know that."

Burton gave a kindly chuckle. I knew from my own experience that he could lose money at bridge with a good grace. He stroked his shaven chin with his thin hand; the veins stood out on it and it was almost transparent.

"I suppose that is why he came to me when he went broke, that and the fact that he was a namesake of mine. He came to see me in my office one day and asked me for a job. I was rather surprised. He told me that there was no more money coming from home and he wanted to work. I asked him how old he was."

"Thirty-five," he said.

"And what have you been doing hitherto?" I asked him.

"Well, nothing very much, he said. I couldn't help laughing.

"I'm afraid I can't do anything for you just yet," I said. "Come back and see me in another thirty-five years, and I'll see what I can do."

"He didn't move. He went rather pale. He hesitated for a moment and then he told me that he had had bad luck at cards for some time. He hadn't been willing to stick to bridge, he'd been playing poker, and he'd got trimmed. He hadn't a penny. He'd pawned everything he had. He couldn't pay his hotel bill and they wouldn't give him any more credit. He was down and out[①]. If he couldn't get something to do he'd have to commit suicide."

"I looked at him for a bit. I could see now that he was all to pieces.

---

① down and out:穷困潦倒，一无所有。

He'd been drinking more than usual and he looked fifty. The girls wouldn't have thought so much of him if they'd seen him then."

"Well, isn't there anything you can do except play cards?" I asked him.

"I can swim," he said.

"Swim!"

"I could hardly believe my ears; it seemed such an insane answer to give."

"I swam for my university."

"I got some glimmering of what he was driving at①. I've known too many men who were little tin gods② at their university to be impressed by it."

"I was a pretty good swimmer myself when I was a young man," I said.

"Suddenly I had an idea."

Pausing in his story, Burton turned to me.

"Do you know Kobe?" he asked.

"No," I said, "I passed through it once, but I only spent a night there."

"Then you don't know the Shioya Club. When I was a young man I swam from there round the beacon and landed at the creek of Tarumi. It's over three miles and it's rather difficult on account of the currents round the beacon③. Well, I told my young namesake about it and I said to him that if he'd do it I'd give him a job."

"I could see he was rather taken aback."

"You say you're a swimmer," I said.

---

① I got some glimmering of what he was driving at：我大致明白他说的是什么意思。
② little tin gods：自命不凡的人。
③ it's rather difficult on account of the currents round the beacon：由于灯塔四周的水流，要游过去相当困难。

"I'm not in very good condition," he answered.

"I didn't say anything. I shrugged my shoulders. He looked at me for a moment and then he nodded."

"All right," he said, "When do you want me to do it?"

"I looked at my watch. It was just after ten."

"The swim shouldn't take you much over an hour and a quarter. I'll drive round to the creek at half past twelve and meet you. I'll take you back to the club to dress and then we'll have lunch together."

"Done," he said.

"We shook hands. I wished him good luck and he left me. I had a lot of work to do that morning and I only just managed to get to the creek at Tarumi at half past twelve. But I needn't have hurried; he never turned up."

"Did he funk it at the last moment?" I asked.

"No, he didn't funk it. He started all right. But of course he'd ruined his constitution by drink and dissipation. The currents round the beacon were more than he could manage. We didn't get the body for about three days."

I didn't say anything for a moment or two. I was a trifle shocked. Then I asked Burton a question.

"When you made him that offer of a job, did you know he'd be drowned?"

He gave a little mild chuckle and he looked at me with those kind and candid blue eyes of his. He rubbed his chin with his hand.

"Well, I hadn't got a vacancy in my office at the moment."

Questions

1. According to Edward Burton, why did Lenny Burton come to him for help? In your opinion, why did Lenny Burton ask help from Edward Burton?

2. Why did Edward Burton ask Lenny Burton to swim the 3-mile-long journey even if he had no vacancy in his office?

3. Why did Edward Burton think that Lenny Burton's story was funny?

Further Readings

Maugham is renowned both for his novels and short stories. His stories often probe into complicated human nature, which is expounded by different characters that he depicts in great detail with the skill of irony. The following are some of his stories which explores the hypocrisies and evils of human nature just as "A friend in Need" does.

1. "The Luncheon"(《午餐》)
2. "Appearance and Reality"(《外表与现实》)
3. "The Treasure"(《宝贝》)
4. "Lord Mountdrago"(《蒙特拉古勋爵》)

Unit 5　The Celestial Omnibus

About the writer

E. M. 福斯特(Edward Morgan Forster, 1879－1970)，英国著名小说家、文学评论家，发表6部长篇小说、2部短篇小说集和一些文学评论散文。福斯特在其小说创作中批判性地探讨了英国工业革命后资本主义高度发展所造成的人际关系异化，在英国乃至世界文坛产生了深远影响，为英国批判现实主义文学的杰出代表。

福斯特1879年出生于英国伦敦，2岁时父亲患肺病去世。1897年，福斯特进入剑桥大学国王学院，攻读历史和希腊文学，初步形成了关于个性自由的人文主义思想。福斯特先后两次在印度待过较长时间，对英国的殖民统治及印度的文化有着深刻的思考，这为他的经典著作《印度之行》(A Passage to India, 1924)准备了丰富素材。

福斯特的小说常采用跨文化视角，批判性地审视英国文化的局限性，以及英国人面对异国文化时的傲慢与偏见。他认为异域文化、风景及生活在那片土地上的人有助于英国人更好地认识自己，以便克服工业化带来的精神空虚和帝国扩张带来的盲目自大。例如，《天使不敢涉足的地方》(Where Angels Fear to Tread, 1905)和《看得见风景的房间》(A Room with a View, 1908)均以意大利为场景展开故事，表现了英国中产阶级和意大利人之间的差异：前者礼仪烦琐、令人窒息，后者却质朴自然、生机勃勃。福斯特最杰出的作品《印度之行》同样采用跨文化视角，探讨了殖民者与被殖民者两个群体、两种文化之间的关系问题。小说以印度为背景，展示了英国人和印度人之间的各种矛盾，描写了英国人和印度人迥异的民族心理和文化立场。

1910年，福斯特发表小说《霍华德别墅》(Howards End)，反映了爱德华时代的英国社会现状。小说围绕三个家庭展开。施莱格尔三姐弟住在伦敦一个公馆内,过着传统的英国中上层社会的生活,代表当时英国的文化生活。威尔科克斯一家住在霍华德别墅,靠在非洲的投资买地、农场经营以及在英国的商业公司大发其财,代表当时的物质生活。伦纳德·巴斯特一家则挣扎在中下层社会的边缘,代表着当时英国社会的多数普通家庭。小说探讨了不同社会群体之间消除矛盾产生"联结"的可能性。

福斯特的文学评论著作《小说面面观》(Aspects of the Novel, 1927)是他1927年春季应剑桥大学三一学院之邀所做讲座的汇编。他的8次讲座,一次比一次反响热烈,为他在文学界和文学评论界赢得巨大声望,奠定了其著名评论家的地位。他一改大众对文学批评学究式的刻板印象,以谈话方式结合大量作家和作品,带领听众走进小说的神奇世界。他系统阐述了小说的故事、人物、情节、模式、节奏等诸多构成要素,以及它们之间的关系,展示了小说作为一个有机整体的魅力。《小说面面观》成为20世纪英国小说艺术的经典理论著作。

福斯特作品最明显的特征在于大量运用象征和对比手法。他的6部小说中有4部小说的题目来自经典诗行,具有丰富的象征意义。象征手法赋予常见的场景或者物品深刻的内涵,让读者从不同的角度解读作品的主题,并通过他们的解读赋予作品新的生命。对比手法能够清楚展现不同群体迥异的认知,让读者明白小说矛盾冲突的各个主体,使他们在阅读过程中跟随不同主体或妥协调和,或冲突对立,从而实现他所说的小说"触动人们心灵的目的"。

About the story

E. M. 福斯特的短篇小说《天国驿车》("The Celestial Omnibus")发表于1908年,讲述了一个小男孩和一个成年人登上天国驿车的故事。小男孩出于好奇,在家对面按照诗人雪莱留下的路牌标记,登上天国驿车。不曾想这真的是一辆通往天国的驿车,在天国里他见到了古希腊神话和其他文学作品里的人物和美景。回家后小男孩急切地将这一切告诉父母,想把他们也带到那里,却遭到嘲笑和惩罚。父母还请当地最博学的邦斯先生帮忙去除他心中的幻想。为了证实小男孩所到过的地方只不过是他的幻想,邦斯先生陪着小男孩一起登上了天国驿车。然而,从上车的那一刻起,邦斯先生不停地用他那世俗的知识和标准判断他所见到的一切。当驿车抵达目的地后,小男孩跳下车见到的依然是那个美丽的世界,而邦斯先生跳下车却什么也没有看到,只能掉入无底的深渊。

《天国驿车》里有很多超自然事件:马车不留痕迹地进出小巷;马车在只有 20 码长的巷子里笔直前行直达天国;赶车人是已经死了几百年的作家;小男孩在一个由各种文学人物和神话传说组成的世界里快乐地玩耍。在《天国驿车》里,小男孩尚处于对这个世界懵懂无知、充满好奇的年龄阶段,虽然无法想象马车怎么进出小巷,虽然怀疑海报上内容的真实性,但是他选择了求证的态度,并且一旦见到马车的存在就深信不疑。以邦斯先生为代表的成年人熟知自然法则和社会法则,他们听到或者经历这些超自然事件时表示出绝对的怀疑。

小男孩和以邦斯先生为代表的成年人对超自然事件有着截然不同的反应,这使得小说呈现出价值观的二元对立。借用这种对比手法,福斯特直观地表达了他对文学和艺术的态度:文学艺术不是个人向上攀爬的工具,而是个人心灵修养的源泉。《天国驿车》里,对小男孩而言,文学作品或者故事里的人和物,包括他们的创造者,和现实世界里的人和物一样,都是鲜活的。他只是凭直觉和感官相信他所见到的和听到的一切,它们没有幻想和真实之分,也没有过去和现在之别,当然人们之间更无高下之异。例如,他两次坐上天国驿车,关注的都是马车夫本人,而不是马车夫的身份。对他来说,他更喜欢活泼有趣的马车夫托马斯·布朗,而不是严肃沉闷的丹德。所以,他的世界是单纯快乐的。

对以邦斯先生为代表的成年人来说,阅读和收藏文学作品的目的在于炫耀自己的学识和品位。例如,在故事第一部分,拥有众多社会头衔的邦斯先生到小男孩家做客时,很诧异小男孩居然没有听说过诗人雪莱。听到小男孩的妈妈说他们家有两本雪莱的诗集时,他马上骄傲地说"我有七本"。此处,拥有作家作品数量的多少反映了一个人的话语权和社会地位的高低。邦斯先生需要的不是文学内容的丰富与深刻,而是他家书房里装订精美的书籍给他装点门面。这让他远离了文学的审美功能,使他不能够像小男孩那样成为文学中的诗行,"all these words that only rhymed before, now that I've come back they're me",并体会到"艺术真理的灵光"(glimmer of Artistic Truth)。邦斯先生对待文学作品的态度代表了当时社会上很典型的实用主义态度:将文学阅读看作获取社会地位的一种手段。

福斯特创作的时代大体是大英帝国的黄金时代,人们使用各种手段获取社会财富，而文学也成为众多手段中的一种。在《天国驿车》里，福斯特借助但丁告诫邦斯先生的话来告诫人们，"诗歌是一种精神，崇拜诗歌的人必须相信它的精神和它传达的真理"。只有这样，人们才能像小男孩那样登上由作家驾驶的文学马车，进入文学的世界；否则，人们会像邦斯先生那样，以文学为手段追逐功名利禄，停止对艺术之美的追求，这无异于心灵的死亡。

The Celestial Omnibus

I

The boy who resided at Agathox Lodge, 28, Buckingham Park Road, Surbiton, had often been puzzled by the old sign-post that stood almost opposite. He asked his mother about it, and she replied that it was a joke, and not a very nice one, which had been made many years back by some naughty young men, and that the police ought to remove it. For there were two strange things about this sign-post: firstly, it pointed up a blank alley, and, secondly, it had painted on it in faded characters, the words, "To Heaven".

"What kind of young men were they?" he asked.

"I think your father told me that one of them wrote verses, and was expelled from the University and came to grief① in other ways. Still, it was a long time ago. You must ask your father about it. He will say the same as I do, that it was put up as a joke."

"So it doesn't mean anything at all?"

She sent him upstairs to put on his best things②, for the Bonses were coming to tea, and he was to hand the cake-stand③.

It struck him, as he wrenched on his tightening trousers, that he might

---

① came to grief：倒霉，吃苦头，受挫。
② put on his best things：穿上他最好的衣服。
③ he was to hand the cake-stand：cake-stand 本意是指烘烤蛋糕的托盘或者架子，这里指蛋糕，即男孩要给他们端上蛋糕。

do worse than ask Mr. Bons about the sign-post. His father, though very kind, always laughed at him—shrieked with laughter whenever he or any other child asked a question or spoke. But Mr. Bons was serious as well as kind. He had a beautiful house and lent one books; he was a churchwarden, and a candidate for the County Council; he had donated to the Free Library enormously, he presided over the Literary Society, and had Members of Parliament to stop with him—in short, he was probably the wisest person alive.

Yet even Mr. Bons could only say that the sign-post was a joke—the joke of a person named Shelley.

"Of course!" cried the mother, "I told you so, dear. That was the name."

"Had you never heard of Shelley①?" asked Mr. Bons.

"No," said the boy, and hung his head.

"But is there no Shelley② in the house?"

"Why, yes!" exclaimed the lady, in much agitation. "Dear Mr. Bons, we aren't such Philistines③ as that. Two at the least. One a wedding present, and the other, smaller print, in one of the spare rooms."

"I believe we have seven Shelleys," said Mr. Bons, with a slow smile. Then he brushed the cake crumbs off his stomach, and, together with his daughter, rose to go.

The boy, obeying a wink from his mother, saw them all the way to the garden gate④, and when they had gone he did not at once return to the house, but gazed for a little up and down Buckingham Park Road.

His parents lived at the right end of it. After No. 39 the quality of the

---

① Shelly:英国诗人雪莱(Percy Bysshe Shelly, 1792 – 1822)。
② 此处指 Shelly 的作品。
③ Philistines:腓力斯汀人。有考证显示古希腊文明的衰亡与他们的入侵有关。后来该词逐渐有了"鄙视艺术的人""野蛮人""粗俗的人""文化修养低的人"等含义。
④ saw them all the way to the garden gate:把他们一直送到花园门口。

houses dropped very suddenly, and 64 had not even a separate servants' entrance①. But at the present moment the whole road looked rather pretty, for the sun had just set in splendor, and the inequalities of rent were drowned in a saffron afterglow. Small birds twittered, and the breadwinners' train shrieked musically down through the cutting②—that wonderful cutting which has drawn to itself the whole beauty out of Surbiton, and clad itself, like any Alpine valley, with the glory of the fir and the silver birch and the primrose③. It was this cutting that had first stirred desires within the boy— desires for something just a little different, he knew not what desires that would return whenever things were sunlit, as they were this evening, running up and down inside him, up and down, up and down, till he would feel quite unusual all over, and as likely as not would want to cry. This evening he was even sillier, for he slipped across the road towards the sign-post and began to run up the blank alley.

The alley runs between high walls—the walls of the gardens of "Ivanhoe" and "Belle Vista" respectively. It smells a little all the way, and is scarcely twenty yards long, including the turn at the end. So not unnaturally the boy soon came to a standstill. "I'd like to kick that Shelley," he exclaimed, and glanced idly at a piece of paper which was pasted on the wall. Rather an odd piece of paper, and he read it carefully before he turned back. This is what he read:

S. AND C. R. C. C.

Alteration in Service.

Owing to lack of patronage the Company are regretfully compelled to

---

① 64 had not even a separate servants' entrance:64号甚至都没有单独的仆人出入的边门。

② cutting:(开凿的)铁路。

③ the breadwinners' train shrieked musically down through the cutting—that wonderful cutting which has drawn to itself the whole beauty out of Surbiton, and clad itself, like any Alpine valley, with the glory of the fir and the silver birch and the primrose:养家糊口的人乘坐的火车,发出悦耳的叫声一路远去。这条神奇的铁路是赛比顿最美的地方,它就好像是长有冷杉、白桦和报春花的阿尔卑斯山美丽的深谷。

suspend the hourly service, and to retain only the

Sunrise and Sunset Omnibuses,

which will run as usual. It is to be hoped that the public will patronize an arrangement which is intended for their convenience. As an extra inducement, the Company will, for the first time, now issue

Return Tickets!

(available one day only), which may be obtained of the driver. Passengers are again reminded that no tickets are issued at the other end, and that no complaints in this connection will receive consideration from the Company. Nor will the Company be responsible for any negligence or stupidity on the part of Passengers, nor for Hailstorms, Lightning, Loss of Tickets, nor for any Act of God①.

For the Direction.

Now he had never seen this notice before, nor could he imagine where the omnibus went to. S. of course was for Surbiton, and R. C. C. meant Road Car Company. But what was the meaning of the other C. ? Coombe and Maiden, perhaps, of possibly "City". Yet it could not hope to compete with the South-Western. The whole thing, the boy reflected, was run on hopelessly unbusiness-like lines. Why no tickets from the other end? And what an hour to start! Then he realized that unless the notice was a hoax, an omnibus must have been starting just as he was wishing the Bonses good-bye. He peered at the ground through the gathering dusk, and there he saw what might or might not be the marks of wheels. Yet nothing had come out of the alley. And he had never seen an omnibus at any time in the Buckingham Park Road. No: it must be a hoax, like the sign-posts, like the fairy tales, like the dreams upon which he would wake suddenly in the

---

① Nor will the Company be responsible for any negligence or stupidity on the part of Passengers, nor for Hailstorms, Lightning, Loss of Tickets, nor for any Act of God:因乘客的疏忽、愚蠢或者冰雹、闪电、遗失票据或者上帝的任何行为而造成的损失,本公司概不负责。

night. And with a sigh he stepped from the alley—right into the arms of his father.

　　Oh, how his father laughed! "Poor, poor Popsey①!" he cried. "Diddums!② Diddums! Diddums think he'd walky-palky up to Evvink!" And his mother, also convulsed with laughter, appeared on the steps of Agathox Lodge. "Don't, Bob!" she gasped. "Don't be so naughty! Oh, you'll kill me! ③ Oh, leave the boy alone!" But all that evening the joke was kept up. The father implored to be taken too. Was it a very tiring walk? Need one wipe one's shoes on the door-mat? And the boy went to bed feeling faint and sore, and thankful for only one thing—that he had not said a word about the omnibus. It was a hoax, yet through his dreams it grew more and more real, and the streets of Surbiton, through which he saw it driving, seemed instead to become hoaxes and shadows. And very early in the morning he woke with a cry, for he had had a glimpse of its destination. He struck a match, and its light fell not only on his watch but also on his calendar, so that he knew it to be half-an-hour to sunrise. It was pitch dark④, for the fog had come down from London in the night, and all Surbiton was wrapped in its embraces. Yet he sprang out and dressed himself, for he was determined to settle once for all which was real: the omnibus or the streets. "I shall be a fool one way or the other," he thought, "until I know." Soon he was shivering in the road under the gas lamp that guarded the entrance to the alley. To enter the alley itself required some courage. Not only was it horribly dark, but he now realized that it was an impossible terminus for an omnibus. If it had not been for a

---

　　① Popsey:这个名字并不是男孩的名字,而是人们通常给自己的狗狗起的名字,在这里是父亲对儿子亲昵的称呼。
　　② diddums:小可怜,小乖乖(对他人孩子般或者幼稚的行为所表示的一种看似同情的表达)。
　　③ Oh, you'll kill me:笑死我了(妈妈也觉得孩子的言行很幼稚,再加上爸爸的嘲讽)。
　　④ pitch dark:漆黑。

policeman, whom he heard approaching through the fog, he would never have made the attempt. The next moment he had made the attempt and failed. Nothing. Nothing but a blank alley and a very silly boy gaping at its dirty floor. It was a hoax. "I'll tell papa and mamma," he decided. "I deserve it. I deserve that they should know. I am too silly to be alive." And he went back to the gate of Agathox Lodge. There he remembered that his watch was fast. The sun was not risen; it would not rise for two minutes. "Give the bus every chance," he thought cynically, and returned into the alley.

But the omnibus was there.

II

It had two horses, whose sides were still smoking from their journey, and its two great lamps shone through the fog against the alley's walls, changing their cobwebs and moss into tissues of fairyland. The driver was huddled up in a cape. He faced the blank wall, and how he had managed to drive in so neatly and so silently was one of the many things that the boy never discovered. Nor could he imagine how ever he would drive out.

"Please," his voice quavered through the foul brown air[①], "Please, is that an omnibus?"

"Omnibus est," said the driver, without turning round. There was a moment's silence. The policeman passed, coughing, by the entrance of the alley. The boy crouched in the shadow, for he did not want to be found out. He was pretty sure, too, that it was a Pirate; nothing else, he reasoned, would go from such odd places and at such odd hours.

"About when do you start?" He tried to sound nonchalant.

"At sunrise."

"How far do you go?"

---

① the foul brown air: 这里指伦敦的空气质量较差,散发着臭味,雾呈现出棕色。

"The whole way."

"And can I have a return ticket which will bring me all the way back?"

"You can."

"Do you know, I half think I'll come." The driver made no answer. The sun must have risen, for he unhitched the brake. And scarcely had the boy jumped in before the omnibus was off.

How? Did it turn? There was no room. Did it go forward? There was a blank wall. Yet it was moving—moving at a stately pace through the fog, which had turned from brown to yellow. The thought of warm bed and warmer breakfast made the boy feel faint. He wished he had not come. His parents would not have approved. He would have gone back to them if the weather had not made it impossible. The solitude was terrible; he was the only passenger. And the omnibus, though well-built, was cold and somewhat musty. He drew his coat round him, and in so doing chanced to feel his pocket. It was empty. He had forgotten his purse.

"Stop!" he shouted. "Stop!" And then, being of a polite disposition, he glanced up at the painted notice-board so that he might call the driver by name. "Mr. Browne! stop; O, do please stop!" Mr. Browne did not stop, but he opened a little window and looked in at the boy. His face was a surprise, so kind it was and modest. "Mr. Browne, I've left my purse behind. I've not got a penny. I can't pay for the ticket. Will you take my watch, please? I am in the most awful hole①."

"Tickets on this line," said the driver, "whether single or return, can be purchased by coinage from no terrene mint②. And a chronometer, though it had solaced the vigils of Charlemagne③, or measured the slumbers

---

① in the most awful hole:太尴尬了。
② terrene mint:俗世的造币厂。
③ Charlemagne:(公元742年—公元814年),查理曼大帝,建立了囊括西欧大部分地区的查理曼帝国。

of Laura①, can acquire by no mutation the double-cake that charms the fangless Cerberus② of Heaven!" So saying, he handed in the necessary ticket, and, while the boy said "Thank you," continued: "Titular pretensions, I know it well, are vanity. Yet they merit no censure when uttered on a laughing lip, and in an homonymous world are in some sort useful, since they do serve to distinguish one Jack from his fellow. Remember me, therefore, as Sir Thomas Browne③."

"Are you a Sir? Oh, sorry!" He had heard of these gentlemen drivers. "It is good of you about the ticket. But if you go on at this rate, however does your bus pay?"

"It does not pay. It was not intended to pay. Many are the faults of my equipage; it is compounded too curiously of foreign woods; its cushions tickle erudition rather than promote repose④; and my horses are nourished not on the evergreen pastures of the moment, but on the dried bents and clovers of Latinity⑤. But that it pays! —that error at all events was never intended and never attained⑥."

"Sorry again," said the boy rather hopelessly. Sir Thomas looked sad,

---

① Laura: 可能是指意大利著名的十四行诗诗人彼特拉克(Francesco Petrarca)的恋人劳拉。

② The fangless Cerberus of Heaven: 古希腊罗马神话中地狱的看门犬 Cerberus, 有3个头, 身上缠绕着毒蛇, 非常凶猛可怕。当这三个头经常为抢夺食物打架时, Cerberus 就会放松对冥界大门的守卫。古希腊神话中的女子 Psyche, 为了见到自己的爱人 Eros, 曾以含有催眠药的蛋糕吸引 Cerberus 的注意力使其吃下昏睡而得以进出冥界, 这是她完成的爱神交给她的任务之一。古希腊人有在死者的棺材里放蜜饼的习俗, 估计与这个神话有关, 可能是希望亲人能够躲过 Cerberus 的守卫而回到人间。但是, 在此文中, 作者有意将其改为无牙的天堂守门犬。

③ Sir Thomas Browne: 托马斯·布朗(1605—1682), 英国医生、作家、哲学家。

④ its cushions tickle erudition rather than promote repose: 它的坐垫是激发人做学问的, 而不是让人享受的。

⑤ my horses are nourished not on the evergreen pastures of the moment, but on the dried, bents and clovers of Latinity: 我的马吃的可不是当下长青的牧草, 而是古罗马的干草和三叶草。

⑥ But that it pays! —that error at all events was never intended and never attained: 不过还是赚了, 因为它从来都不是故意犯错的, 而且也从来没有犯过错。

fearing that, even for a moment, he had been the cause of sadness①. He invited the boy to come up and sit beside him on the box, and together they journeyed on through the fog, which was now changing from yellow to white②. There were no houses by the road; so it must be either Putney Heath or Wimbledon Common③.

"Have you been a driver always?"

"I was a physician once."

"But why did you stop? Weren't you good?"

"As a healer of bodies I had scant success, and several score of my patients preceded me. But as a healer of the spirit I have succeeded beyond my hopes and my deserts. For though my draughts were not better nor subtler than those of other men, yet, by reason of the cunning goblets wherein I offered them, the queasy soul was ofttimes tempted to sip and be refreshed④."

"The queasy soul," he murmured; "if the sun sets with trees in front of it, and you suddenly come strange all over, is that a queasy soul?"

"Have you felt that?"

"Why yes."

After a pause he told the boy a little, a very little, about the journey's end. But they did not chatter much, for the boy, when he liked a person, would as soon sit silent in his company as speak, and this, he discovered, was also the mind of Sir Thomas Browne and of many others with whom he was to be acquainted. He heard, however, about the young man Shelley,

---

① Thomas 担心自己说的话可能太高深，孩子听不懂，当孩子说"抱歉"的时候，Thomas 就觉得是自己的原因。

② 雾的颜色变化，从棕色到黄色再到白色，表明他们来到了一个越来越干净的地方。

③ Putney Heath 和 Wimbledon Common 是伦敦西南部大片开阔的地区，占地大约 4.6 平方公里。

④ For though my draughts were not better nor subtler than those of other men, yet, by reason of the cunning goblets wherein I offered them, the queasy soul was ofttimes tempted to sip and be refreshed：尽管我的药水并不比他人的强或者微妙，然而，因为我给精巧的酒杯里倒入药水，不安的灵魂总是忍不住要去吸吮，然后得到放松。

who was now quite a famous person, with a carriage of his own, and about some of the other drivers who are in the service of the Company. Meanwhile the light grew stronger, though the fog did not disperse. It was now more like mist than fog, and at times would travel quickly across them, as if it was part of a cloud. They had been ascending, too, in a most puzzling way; for over two hours the horses had been pulling against the collar, and even if it were Richmond Hill① they ought to have been at the top long ago. Perhaps it was Epsom②, or even the North Downs③; yet the air seemed keener than that which blows on either④. And as to the name of their destination, Sir Thomas Browne was silent.

Crash!

"Thunder, by Jove⑤!" said the boy, "and not so far off either. Listen to the echoes! It's more like mountains." He thought, not very vividly, of his father and mother. He saw them sitting down to sausages and listening to the storm. He saw his own empty place. Then there would be questions, alarms, theories, jokes, consolations. They would expect him back at lunch. To lunch he would not come, nor to tea, but he would be in for dinner, and so his day's truancy would be over. If he had had his purse he would have bought them presents—not that he should have known what to get them.

Crash! The peal and the lightning came together. The cloud quivered as if it were alive, and torn streamers of mist rushed past. "Are you afraid?" asked Sir Thomas Browne.

---

① Richmond Hill: 位于伦敦西郊的小镇 Richmond,有着英格兰唯一受议会法案保护的景色。Walter Scott 曾称赞其周围景色是 unrivalled landscape(无与伦比的景色)。

② Epsom: 伦敦南部郊区的一个小镇。

③ the North Downs: 和 the South Downs 一起都是英格兰南部的两条著名的徒步旅行线路。在此地名中,down 和 hill 的意思差不多。

④ the air seemed keener than that which blows on either: 然而这里的风似乎比那两个地方的风更为寒冷刺骨。

⑤ Jove 是罗马主神 Jupiter 的名字, by Jove 相当于 my God,表示惊讶、赞同、高兴、失望等。

"What is there to be afraid of? Is it much farther?" The horses of the omnibus stopped just as a ball of fire burst up and exploded with a ringing noise that was deafening but clear, like the noise of a blacksmith's forge. All the cloud was shattered.

"Oh, listen, Sir Thomas Browne! No, I mean look; we shall get a view at last. No, I mean listen; that sounds like a rainbow!"

The noise had died into the faintest murmur, beneath which another murmur grew, spreading stealthily, steadily, in a curve that widened but did not vary. And in widening curves a rainbow was spreading from the horses' feet into the dissolving mists.

"But how beautiful! What colours! Where will it stop? It is more like the rainbows you can tread on. More like dreams."

The colour and the sound grew together. The rainbow spanned an enormous gulf. Clouds rushed under it and were pierced by it, and still it grew, reaching forward, conquering the darkness, until it touched something that seemed more solid than a cloud.

The boy stood up. "What is that out there?" he called. "What does it rest on, out at that other end?" In the morning sunshine a precipice shone forth beyond the gulf. A precipice—or was it a castle? The horses moved. They set their feet upon the rainbow.

"Oh, look!" the boy shouted. "Oh, listen! Those caves—or are they gateways? Oh, look between those cliffs at those ledges. I see people! I see trees!"

"Look also below," whispered Sir Thomas Browne. "Neglect not the diviner Acheron①." The boy looked below, past the flames of the rainbow that licked against their wheels. The gulf also had cleared, and in its depths there flowed an everlasting river. One sunbeam entered and struck a green

---

① Acheron: 古希腊神话中的冥河 Styx 的一个支流，冥王 Hades 的船夫卡戎将死者的魂灵运渡此河，进入冥界。

pool, and as they passed over he saw three maidens rise to the surface of the pool, singing, and playing with something that glistened like a ring.

"You down in the water—" he called. They answered,

"You up on the bridge—" There was a burst of music. "You up on the bridge, good luck to you. Truth in the depth, truth on the height."

"You down in the water, what are you doing?"

Sir Thomas Browne replied: "They sport in the mancipiary possession of their gold"①; and the omnibus arrived.

III

The boy was in disgrace. He sat locked up in the nursery of Agathox Lodge, learning poetry for a punishment. His father had said, "My boy! I can pardon anything but untruthfulness," and had caned him, saying at each stroke, "There is *no* omnibus, *no* driver, *no* bridge, *no* mountain; you are a *truant*, *guttersnipe*, a *liar*." His father could be very stern at times. His mother had begged him to say he was sorry. But he could not say that. It was the greatest day of his life, in spite of the caning, and the poetry at the end of it. He had returned punctually at sunset—driven not by Sir Thomas Browne, but by a maiden lady who was full of quiet fun. They had talked of omnibuses and also of barouche landaus②. How far away her gentle voice seemed now! Yet it was scarcely three hours since he had left her up the alley.

His mother called through the door. "Dear, you are to come down and to bring your poetry with you." He came down, and found that Mr. Bons was in the smoking-room with his father. It had been a dinner party.

"Here is the great traveler!" said his father grimly. "Here is the young gentleman who drives in an omnibus over rainbows, while young ladies sing

---

① They sport in the mancipary possession of their gold:她们手上摆弄着金子。
② barouche landaus:敞篷四轮马车,顶部可以折叠,非常适合夏季乡村出游。

to him." Pleased with his wit, he laughed.

"After all," said Mr. Bons, smiling, "there is something a little like it in Wagner①. It is odd how, in quite illiterate minds, you will find glimmers of Artistic Truth. The case interests me. Let me plead for the culprit. We have all romanced in our time, haven't we?"

"Hear how kind Mr. Bons is," said his mother, while his father said, "Very well. Let him say his Poem, and that will do. He is going away to my sister on Tuesday, and she will cure him of this alley-slopering." (Laughter.) "Say your Poem."

The boy began. "'Standing aloof in giant ignorance.'"②

His father laughed again—roared. "One for you, my son! 'Standing aloof in giant ignorance!' I never knew these poets talked sense. Just describes you. Here, Bons, you go in for poetry. Put him through it, will you, while I fetch up the whisky?"

"Yes, give me the Keats③," said Mr. Bons. "Let him say his Keats to me."

So for a few moments the wise man and the ignorant boy were left alone in the smoking-room.

"'Standing aloof in giant ignorance, of thee I dream and of the Cyclades④, as one who sits ashore and longs perchance to visit—'"

"Quite right. To visit what?"

"'To visit dolphin coral in deep seas,'" said the boy, and burst into tears.

"Come, come! Why do you cry?"

---

① 此处指德国音乐家、剧作家、评论家和哲学家理查德·瓦格纳(Richard Wagner, 1813－1883)。

② 小男孩此处背诵的诗歌来自 John Keats 的十四行诗 "To Homer" 中的第一行。在此处特别应景,在成年人眼里,小男孩即是无知。然而在福斯特眼里,成人不相信小孩的话,或者忘记了曾经充满幻想的自己,又何尝不是无知呢。

③ the Keats:此处指济慈的诗集。

④ the Cyclades:希腊爱琴海基克拉迪群岛。

"Because—because all these words that only rhymed before, now that I've come back they're me①."

Mr. Bons laid the Keats down. The case was more interesting than he had expected.

"*You*?" he exclaimed, "This sonnet, *you*?"

"Yes—and look further on: 'Aye, on the shores of darkness there is light, and precipices show untrodden green.' It is so, sir. All these things are true."

"I never doubted it," said Mr. Bons, with closed eyes.

"You—then you believe me? You believe in the omnibus and the driver and the storm and that return ticket I got for nothing and—"

"Tut, tut!② No more of your yarns, my boy. I meant that I never doubted the essential truth of Poetry. Some day, when you read more, you will understand what I mean."

"But Mr. Bons, it is so. There is light upon the shores of darkness. I have seen it coming. Light and a wind."

"Nonsense," said Mr. Bons.

"If I had stopped! They tempted me. They told me to give up my ticket—for you cannot come back if you lose your ticket. They called from the river for it, and indeed I was tempted, for I have never been so happy as among those precipices. But I thought of my mother and father, and that I must fetch them. Yet they will not come, though the road starts opposite our house. It has all happened as the people up there warned me, and Mr. Bons has disbelieved me like everyone else. I have been caned. I shall never see that mountain again."

"What's that about me?" said Mr. Bons, sitting up in his chair very suddenly.

---

① all these words that only rhymed before, now that I've come back they're me: 这儿句以前只是押韵的诗歌而已, 而现在, 在我回来后, 它们说的就是我。

② Tut, tut: 表示不赞成的咂嘴声。

"I told them about you, and how clever you were, and how many books you had, and they said, 'Mr. Bons will certainly disbelieve you.'"

"Stuff and nonsense, my young friend. You grow impertinent. I—well—I will settle the matter. Not a word to your father. I will cure you. To morrow evening I will myself call here to take you for a walk, and at sunset we will go up this alley opposite and hunt for your omnibus, you silly little boy."

His face grew serious, for the boy was not disconcerted, but leapt about the room singing, "Joy! Joy! I told them you would believe me. We will drive together over the rainbow. I told them that you would come." After all, could there be anything in the story? Wagner? Keats? Shelley? Sir Thomas Browne? Certainly the case was interesting.

And on the morrow evening, though it was pouring with rain, Mr. Bons did not omit to call at Agathox Lodge. The boy was ready, bubbling with excitement, and skipping about in a way that rather vexed the President of the Literary Society①. They took a turn down Buckingham Park Road, and then—having seen that no one was watching them—slipped up the alley. Naturally enough (for the sun was setting) they ran straight against the omnibus.

"Good heavens!" exclaimed Mr. Bons. "Good gracious heavens!"

It was not the omnibus in which the boy had driven first, nor yet that in which he had returned. There were three horses—black, gray, and white, the gray being the finest. The driver, who turned round at the mention of goodness and of heaven, was a sallow man with terrifying jaws and sunken eyes. Mr. Bons, on seeing him, gave a cry as if of recognition, and began to tremble violently. The boy jumped in.

"Is it possible?" cried Mr. Bons. "Is the impossible possible?"

"Sir; come in, sir. It is such a fine omnibus. Oh, here is his name—

---

① the President of the Literary Society: 即 Mr. Bons, 他是文学协会的主席。

Dan some one①."

Mr. Bons sprang in, too. A blast of wind immediately slammed the omnibus door, and the shock jerked down all the omnibus blinds, which were very weak on their springs.

"Dan ... Show me. Good gracious heavens! We're moving."

"Hooray!" said the boy. Mr. Bons became flustered. He had not intended to be kidnapped. He could not find the door-handle, nor push up the blinds. The omnibus was quite dark, and by the time he had struck a match, night had come on outside also. They were moving rapidly.

"A strange, a memorable adventure," he said, surveying the interior of the omnibus, which was large, roomy, and constructed with extreme regularity, every part exactly answering to every other part. Over the door (the handle of which was outside) was written, "Lasciate ogni baldanza voi che entrate"②—at least, that was what was written, but Mr. Bons said that it was Lashy arty something, and that baldanza was a mistake for speranza. His voice sounded as if he was in church. Meanwhile, the boy called to the cadaverous③ driver for two return tickets. They were handed in without a word. Mr. Bons covered his face with his hand and again trembled. "Do you know who that is!" he whispered, when the little window had shut upon them. "It is the impossible."

"Well, I don't like him as much as Sir Thomas Browne, though I shouldn't be surprised if he had even more in him④."

"More in him?" He stamped irritably. "By accident you have made the greatest discovery of the century, and all you can say is that there is more in

---

① Dan some one：小男孩不认识但丁的全名 Dante Alighieri，因而只能以 some one 代替。
② Lasciate ogni baldanza voi che entrate：拉丁语，出自但丁的《神曲》，该句被刻在地狱的门上，意思是"进来的人，放弃一切希望吧"。
③ cadaverous：面容枯槁的。
④ he had even more in him：他本事更大。

this man. Do you remember those vellum books① in my library, stamped with red lilies? This—sit still, I bring you stupendous news! —this is the man who wrote them②."

The boy sat quite still. "I wonder if we shall see Mrs. Gamp③?" he asked, after a civil pause.

"Mrs. —?"

"Mrs. Gamp and Mrs. Harris. I like Mrs. Harris. I came upon them quite suddenly. Mrs. Gamp's bandboxes have moved over the rainbow so badly. All the bottoms have fallen out, and two of the pippins off her bedstead tumbled into the stream."

"Out there sits the man who wrote my vellum books!" thundered Mr. Bons, "and you talk to me of Dickens and of Mrs. Gamp?"

"I know Mrs. Gamp so well," he apologized. "I could not help being glad to see her. I recognized her voice. She was telling Mrs. Harris about Mrs. Prig."

"Did you spend the whole day in her elevating company?"

"Oh, no. I raced. I met a man who took me out beyond to a race-course. You run, and there are dolphins out at sea."

"Indeed. Do you remember the man's name?"

"Achilles④. No; he was later. Tom Jones⑤."

Mr. Bons sighed heavily. "Well, my lad, you have made a miserable mess of it. Think of a cultured person with your opportunities! A cultured person would have known all these characters and known what to have said

---

① vellum books：牛皮纸或者羊皮纸书（极为珍贵或者重要的书）。

② this is the man who wrote them：这个赶车人就是写了那些书的人（即赶车人为但丁）。

③ Mrs. Gamp 和下文中的 Mrs. Harris, Mrs. Prig：狄更斯小说 *Martin Chuzzlewit* 中的人物。

④ Achilles：古希腊神话人物阿喀琉斯，出生时母亲将他的脚跟提着，浸入冥河水中，因此他除了脚部外，全身其他地方都是刀枪不入，任何武器都伤害不了他。在特洛伊战争中，他因脚后跟被阿波罗射中而死，因而习语 Achilles' heel 意为"致命弱点"。

⑤ Tom Jones：亨利·菲尔丁（Henry Fielding, 1707–1754）的同名小说 *Tom Jones* 的主人公。

to each. He would not have wasted his time with a Mrs. Gamp or a Tom Jones. The creations of Homer, of Shakespeare, and of Him who drives us now, would alone have contented him. He would not have raced. He would have asked intelligent questions."

"But, Mr. Bons," said the boy humbly, "you will be a cultured person. I told them so."

"True, true, and I beg you not to disgrace me when we arrive. No gossiping. No running. Keep close to my side, and never speak to these Immortals unless they speak to you. Yes, and give me the return tickets. You will be losing them." The boy surrendered the tickets, but felt a little sore. After all, he had found the way to this place. It was hard first to be disbelieved and then to be lectured. Meanwhile, the rain had stopped, and moonlight crept into the omnibus through the cracks in the blinds.

"But how is there to be a rainbow?" cried the boy.

"You distract me," snapped Mr. Bons. "I wish to meditate on beauty. I wish to goodness I was with a reverent and sympathetic person." The lad bit his lip. He made a hundred good resolutions. He would imitate Mr. Bons all the visit. He would not laugh, or run, or sing, or do any of the vulgar things that must have disgusted his new friends last time. He would be very careful to pronounce their names properly, and to remember who knew whom. Achilles did not know Tom Jones—at least, so Mr. Bons said. The Duchess of Malfi① was older than Mrs. Gamp—at least, so Mr. Bons said. He would be self-conscious, reticent, and prim. He would never say he liked anyone. Yet when the wind flew up at a chance touch of his head, all these good resolutions went to the winds②, for the omnibus had reached the summit of a moonlit hill, and there was the chasm, and there, across it, stood the old precipices, dreaming, with their feet in the everlasting river.

---

① the Duchess of Malfi：英国剧作家约翰·韦伯斯特（John Webster, 1580－1634）同名戏剧 *The Duchess of Malfi* 中的人物。

② all these good resolutions went to the winds：所有这些决心都被抛到脑后了。

He exclaimed, "The mountain! Listen to the new tune in the water! Look at the camp fires in the ravines," and Mr. Bons, after a hasty glance, retorted, "Water? Camp fires? Ridiculous rubbish. Hold your tongue. There is nothing at all." Yet, under his eyes, a rainbow formed, compounded not of sunlight and storm, but of moonlight and the spray of the river. The three horses put their feet upon it. He thought it the finest rainbow he had seen, but did not dare to say so, since Mr. Bons said that nothing was there. He leant out—the window had opened—and sang the tune that rose from the sleeping waters.

"The prelude to Rhinegold①?" said Mr. Bons suddenly. "Who taught you these leit motifs?" He, too, looked out of the window. Then he behaved very oddly. He gave a choking cry, and fell back on to the omnibus floor. He writhed and kicked. His face was green.

"Does the bridge make you dizzy?" the boy asked.

"Dizzy!" gasped Mr. Bons. "I want to go back. Tell the driver." But the driver shook his head. "We are nearly there," said the boy, "They are asleep. Shall I call? They will be so pleased to see you, for I have prepared them."

Mr. Bons moaned. They moved over the lunar rainbow, which ever and ever broke away behind their wheels. How still the night was! Who would be sentry at the Gate?

"I am coming," he shouted, again forgetting the hundred resolutions. "I am returning—I, the boy."

"The boy is returning," cried a voice to other voices, who repeated, "The boy is returning."

"I am bringing Mr. Bons with me."

Silence.

---

① the prelude to Rhinegold：德国音乐家 Richard Wagner 所创作的音乐剧 *The Rhinegold* 的序曲。

"I should have said Mr. Bons is bringing me with him."

Profound silence.

"Who stands sentry?"

"Achilles."

And on the rocky causeway, close to the springing of the rainbow bridge, he saw a young man who carried a wonderful shield.

"Mr. Bons, it is Achilles, armed."

"I want to go back," said Mr. Bons. The last fragment of the rainbow melted, the wheels sang upon the living rock, the door of the omnibus burst open. Out leapt the boy—he could not resist—and sprang to meet the warrior, who, stooping suddenly, caught him on his shield.

"Achilles!" he cried, "Let me get down, for I am ignorant and vulgar, and I must wait for that Mr. Bons of whom I told you yesterday." But Achilles raised him aloft. He crouched on the wonderful shield, on heroes and burning cities, on vineyards graven in gold, on every dear passion, every joy, on the entire image of the Mountain that he had discovered, encircled, like it, with an everlasting stream. "No, no," he protested, "I am not worthy. It is Mr. Bons who must be up here."

But Mr. Bons was whimpering, and Achilles trumpeted and cried, "Stand upright upon my shield!"

"Sir, I did not mean to stand! Something made me stand. Sir, why do you delay? Here is only the great Achilles, whom you knew."

Mr. Bons screamed, "I see no one. I see nothing. I want to go back." Then he cried to the driver, "Save me! Let me stop in your chariot. I have honored you. I have quoted you. I have bound you in vellum. Take me back to my world."

The driver replied, "I am the means and not the end. I am the food and not the life. Stand by yourself, as that boy has stood. I cannot save you. For poetry is a spirit; and they that would worship it must worship in spirit and in truth."

Mr. Bons—he could not resist—crawled out of the beautiful omnibus. His face appeared, gaping horribly. His hands followed, one gripping the step, the other beating the air. Now his shoulders emerged, his chest, his stomach. With a shriek of "I see London", he fell—fell against the hard, moonlit rock, fell into it as if it were water, fell through it, vanished, and was seen by the boy no more.

"Where have you fallen to, Mr. Bons? Here is a procession arriving to honour you with music and torches. Here come the men and women whose names you know. The mountain is awake, the river is awake, over the racecourse the sea is awaking those dolphins, and it is all for you. They want you—"

There was the touch of fresh leaves on his forehead. Some one had crowned him.

TELOS[①]

From the *Kingston Gazette*, *Surbiton Times*, and *Paynes Park Observer*.

The body of Mr. Septimus Bons has been found in a shockingly mutilated condition in the vicinity of the Bermondsey gas-works. The deceased's pockets contained a sovereign-purse, a silver cigar-case, a bijou[②] pronouncing dictionary, and a couple of omnibus tickets. The unfortunate gentleman had apparently been hurled from a considerable height. Foul play is suspected, and a thorough investigation is pending by the authorities.

Questions

1. What fantasies can you find in this story? And what do these fantasies imply in your opinion?

---

① TELOS:希腊语,表示"终极目的",此处指小男孩代表着文学最终要达到的境界。
② bijou:小巧的。

2. Why was the little boy crowned TELOS?

3. Symbolism was a late-nineteenth-century art movement of French and Belgian origin, using symbols which suggest a connection between the ordinary sense of reality and a moral or spiritual order. Can you find any symbols in this story and what do these symbols imply?

Further Readings

The following four short stories are collected with "The Celestial Omnibus" in a short story collection by E. M. Forster. All these stories explore and express his fantasies about escape from the discouraging reality.

1. "Other Kingdom"（《异界》）
2. "The Other Side of the Hedge"（《树篱的另一边》）
3. "The Road from Colonus"（《始于科娄纳斯之路》）
4. "The Story of a Panic"（《惊恐记》）

Unit 6　Araby

About the writer

詹姆斯·乔伊斯（James Joyce, 1882 –1941）是西方现代文学史上一位举足轻重的人物，他在作品中大量运用意识流手法，细致入微地刻画了人物的心理活动，对英国文学乃至世界文学均产生了极其深刻的影响，其代表作《尤利西斯》(*Ulysses*, 1922) 被视为现代主义小说的典范之作。

乔伊斯1882年出生于爱尔兰都柏林一个具有浓厚天主教和民族主义氛围的家庭，小时候家庭相当富裕，但后来家道中落。他自小在教会学校接受了严格的宗教教育。学生时代，他曾一度热衷于天主教，但后来逐渐反感教会，在都柏林大学读书期间，他阅读了大量天主教会的禁书，并最终决定从事文学创作。大学毕业后，他离开爱尔兰远赴欧洲大陆，在法国、意大利、瑞士等国家旅居，直至去世。乔伊斯的生活并不安逸，始终为贫穷所困扰，晚年患有严重眼疾，常为出版自己的作品四处求人。

乔伊斯对自己的创作精益求精，一生只写了3部小说、1部短篇小说集、2部诗集和1部戏剧。小说与短篇小说的故事背景均为爱尔兰尤其是都柏林，围绕爱尔兰人和他们的生活展开。1914年，乔伊斯出版了短篇小说集《都柏林人》(*Dubliners*)。《都柏林人》共包括15个短篇小说，前三个故事以自传形式讲述了一个不知名的小男孩从童年到青年的成长过程，接下来的七个故事都围绕成人的生活展开，再接下来四个故事则是关于社会生活，最后一个故事《死者》是全书的归纳和总结。这15个短篇都展示了"可爱而肮脏的都柏林"的一个方面，涉及道德、政治、精神等方面。

1916年，乔伊斯的第一部长篇小说《一位青年艺术家的画像》(*A Portrait of the Artist as a Young Man*) 出版。这部小说有着浓厚的自然主义色彩，描述了主人公痛苦的生活经历和最后艺术与精神上的解放。小说主人公是中产阶级男孩史蒂芬·德达拉斯,故事从他的幼年时期讲起,一直到 20 年后他离开爱尔兰。乔伊斯在这部小说里开始使用意识流手法,生动地展现了主人公瞬息万变的心理活动。

乔伊斯的代表作《尤利西斯》非常奇特,它缺乏传统小说的所有要素,没有故事,没有情节,几乎没有动作,也没有鲜明的人物形象。《尤利西斯》只写了一个人在都柏林一天之内(1904 年 6 月 16 日)的生活。小说只有 3 个主要角色:爱尔兰犹太人利奥普尔德·布鲁姆、他的妻子莫莉·布鲁姆以及史蒂芬·德达拉斯,也即《一位青年艺术家的画像》中的主人公。小说分为 18 章,分别与一天内的 18 个小时相对应。小说中,这一天内发生的事情极为琐碎,毫无意义,甚至非常陈腐。但在这平庸的表面下隐藏着 3 个人物的意识流,反映了他们内心的思想活动及心情变化。《尤利西斯》构成了一幅现代荒原的画像,这里的现代人被画成粗俗、猥琐的动物,他们思想肮脏,萎靡不振,在衰败的世界里徒然寻求精神食粮。小说大量使用意识流手法,引用了历史、文学、宗教及地理方面的各种典故。小说的语言丰富多彩,夹杂着成语、双关语、文字游戏等。

乔伊斯花费 17 年时间创作了他的最后一部重要著作《芬尼根的觉醒》(Finnegans Wake, 1939)。在这部百科全书式的作品中,乔伊斯意欲将整个人类历史都包罗到一夜之梦中。在梦中,没有自我意识的逻辑,没有整齐有序的关联,没有固定的价值观,没有时空的局限,所有过去、现在和将来的情景都涌入脑海。

乔伊斯认为,一个艺术家若想在艺术与洞察力上登峰造极,就应像上帝一样超脱物外,以完全客观的视角看待事物;同时,他必须有意识地控制创作进程,并尽可能不将个人的性格与情感掺入作品中;他还应是一个洞悉一切的人,直接写出角色的心理活动,或者让角色以独白形式道出内心深处的想法。乔伊斯运用许多不完整、短促、支离破碎的语句和措辞,展现了小说人物思想意识的怪异多变、闪烁不定及杂乱无章。

About the story

《阿拉比》("Araby")是小说集《都柏林人》的第三篇,可被视为乔伊斯童年经历和情绪之写照。故事中的"我"是个天真无邪的男孩,他出于对朦胧爱情和理想本能的追求,渴望到具有异国浪漫情调的阿拉比集市为自己心爱的姑娘"曼根的姐姐"买件礼物,但是他身无分文。经过漫长焦急的等待后,叔叔回来了,拿到了叔叔给的钱后,男孩终于费尽周折赶到集市,却发现那里很快就要关门。他什么也没有买到,只看到两个男人在和一个女人调情。他感到痛苦和愤怒,虚荣心受到极大嘲弄。

故事中"我"住在一条衰败僻静的街上,街上有座房子里曾住过一位神父,房中只留下几本破旧的小说,院子里一株灌木下丢着一个自行车打气筒。他们在这"古老"的角落里玩耍,灰坑和马厩传出的气味使人回想起过去,使主人公"我"着迷的是同伴曼根的姐姐。每天早晨他都望着她家的大门等候她的出现,然后跑出去假装无意间碰见她。每星期六他都随婶婶上街买东西,替婶婶捧着大包小包闯过闹市。在祈祷时他会不自觉地提到她的名字,眼里噙满泪水,心头热浪翻腾。然而,他并未留心她的长相,他只注意到了她行走时裙子的摆动和头发的甩动,以及灯光下雪白的脖颈、闪亮的头发、搭在栏杆上的小手,还有那衬裙的白边。

这些看似无关紧要的、琐碎的描写在故事中发挥着极其重要的作用,让读者看到了主人公的内心世界。故事中"我"虽然出生于小职员家庭,居住在一条破旧的街上,却想象自己生活在中世纪,是一位历史传奇中的骑士,而曼根的姐姐就是他愿意为之献身的情人。她是如此圣洁,就像圣母玛利亚一样。这一想象深深烙着爱尔兰天主教传统文化的印记,男孩将幼稚的童恋与中世纪宗教的豪侠之风结合在一起。当他心中的淑女随便提及不能去阿拉比集市时,他马上作答:"如果我去,我一定带样东西回来给你。"这成了他庄严的承诺。

星期六一整天他都魂不守舍,心急如焚地等待傍晚降临,叔叔却忘记按时归来。叔叔到家时已经很晚。他拿着叔叔给的钱赶到集市时,集市即将关门。他走到一家店铺前,店门口一位年轻的女店员正在和两个年轻人调情。他模模糊糊地听见了他们的对话:"啊,我从未说过这样的话!""啊,你说过!""啊,我没说过!""她说过那话吧?""对,我听她说过。""啊,你瞎说!"这就是现实世界,这就是现实的谈情说爱,粗俗无聊。这与他幻想的世界,与他梦中的爱情相差甚远。他感到悲愤,他美丽的幻想被冷酷的现实彻底粉碎了。

小说中最后一段的描写与男孩之前赶赴阿拉比集市时热切憧憬、激动渴望的情绪形成鲜明对比。从他缓慢的动作、任凭硬币在口袋里叮当作响也不理会等一系列表现,读者感受到男孩沮丧落寞、懊恼失望的心理。因为男孩突然感到这番无聊的对话就是对他浪漫主义爱情理想的无情嘲弄，刹那间他清醒地意识到自己的困境：随着对阿拉比集市美好幻想的彻底破灭，心中近乎宗教般神圣的爱情突然崩溃，他觉得自己只是"被虚荣驱使的一个动物"。他回到现实世界并开始重新审视周围的一切，并产生了"精神顿悟"——在残酷的现实社会中无法实现自己的理想。

　　故事中的"精神顿悟"并不突兀，而是一步一步营造出来的。首先，乔伊斯以细腻的笔触着力描写男孩所生活的北里奇蒙德街阴暗闭塞的环境，男孩所居住的房子曾住过一位已故牧师，形容词 musty, waste, littered, useless 等的使用营造出败落荒凉的背景氛围。接着，对都柏林夜幕降临时的情景进行描绘，同样采用 sombre, feeble, muddy, dark dripping 等形容词，又一次渲染了黑暗单调、死寂而令人窒息的氛围。可这样枯燥而刻板的现实并不能遏制男孩心中的憧憬和梦想，同伴曼根的姐姐给他的生活带来生机，任何外在环境的不和谐都不能抹去她那神圣的光环。当有一天女孩主动和他开口说话时，"The light from the lamp opposite our door caught the white curve of her neck, lit up her hair that rested there and, falling, lit up the hand upon the railing. It fell over one side of her dress and caught the white border of a petticoat, just visible as she stood at ease."。乔伊斯对曼根的姐姐采取光、影、色交相辉映的虚写手法，勾勒出男孩内心所崇拜的虚幻偶像，暗示着爱情对象的虚无，揭示了理想和现实的巨大反差，为小说结尾处的"精神顿捂"做了层层铺垫。

Araby

　　North Richmond Street[①], being blind, was a quiet street except at the hour when the Christian Brothers' School set the boys free. An uninhabited house of two storeys stood at the blind end, detached from its neighbors in a square ground. The other houses of the street, conscious of decent lives within them, gazed at one another with brown imperturbable faces.

---

　　① North Richmond Street：乔伊斯一家于1894年搬到都柏林的北里奇蒙德街17号。离他们家几步之遥有一个天主教宗教团体组织——基督兄弟学校，乔伊斯早年在这所学校待了很短一段时间。本篇中主人公的家与作者的老家在细节上完全一致。

The former tenant of our house, a priest, had died in the back drawing-room. Air, musty from having been long enclosed, hung in all the rooms, and the waste room behind the kitchen was littered with old useless papers. Among these I found a few paper-covered books①, the pages of which were curled and damp: *The Abbot*② by Walter Scott③, *The Devout Communicant*④ and *The Memoirs of Vidocq*⑤. I liked the last best because its leaves were yellow. The wild garden behind the house contained a central apple tree and a few straggling bushes under one of which I found the late tenant's rusty bicycle pump. He had been a very charitable priest; in his will he had left all his money to institutions and the furniture of his house to his sister.

When the short days of winter came dusk fell before we had well eaten our dinners. When we met in the street the houses had grown sombre. The space of sky above us was the colour of everchanging violet and towards it the lamps of the street lifted their feeble lanterns. The cold air stung us and we played till our bodies glowed⑥. Our shouts echoed in the silent street. The career of our play brought us through the dark muddy lanes behind the houses where we ran the gantlet of the rough tribes⑦ from the cottages, to the back doors of the dark dripping gardens where odours arose from the ashpits, to the dark odorous stables where a coachman smoothed and combed the horse or shook music from the buckled harness⑧. When we returned to the street light from the kitchen windows had filled the areas. If my uncle was seen turning the corner we hid in the shadow until we had

---

① I found a few paper-covered books：我翻到几本平装书。
② The Abbot：一部关于苏格兰玛丽女王的历史小说。
③ Walter Scott：瓦尔特·司各特（1771—1832），苏格兰诗人和小说家。
④ The Devout Communicant：一本天主教的宗教手册。
⑤ The Memoirs of Vidocq：维多克（Vidocq，1775－1857）的一本回忆录。此人具有传奇经历，他当过兵，做过小偷，曾是法国著名侦探，后成为一名私家侦探。
⑥ The cold air stung us and we played till our bodies glowed：寒气刺骨，我们不停地玩耍，直至身体暖和起来。
⑦ we ran the gauntlet of the rough tribes：我们玩野蛮部落的游戏。
⑧ shook music from the buckled harness：摆弄扣好的马具而发出悦耳的响声。

seen him safely housed①. Or if Mangan's sister came out on the doorstep to call her brother in to his tea, we watched her from our shadow peer up and down the street②. We waited to see whether she would remain or go in and if she remained, we left our shadow and walked up to Mangan's steps resignedly. She was waiting for us, and her figure defined by the light from the half-opened door. Her brother always teased her before he obeyed and I stood by the railings looking at her. Her dress swung as she moved her body and the soft rope of her hair tossed from side to side.

Every morning I lay on the floor in the front parlour watching her door. The blind was pulled down to within an inch of the sash so that I could not be seen③. When she came out on the doorstep my heart leaped. I ran to the hall, seized my books and followed her. I kept her brown figure always in my eye and when we came near the point at which our ways diverged I quickened my pace and passed her. This happened morning after morning. I had never spoken to her except for a few casual words and yet her name was like a summon④ to all my foolish blood.

Her image accompanied me even in places the most hostile to romance. On Saturday evenings when my aunt went marketing I had to go to carry some of the parcels. We walked through the flaring streets, jostled by drunken men and bargaining women, amid the curses of laborers, the shrill litanies of shop boys⑤ who stood on guard by the barrels of pigs' cheeks, the nasal chanting⑥ of street singers who sang a *come-all-you* about

---

① until we had seen him safely housed: 直到他走进屋子, 诸事平安为止。
② we watched her from our shadow peer up and down the street: 我们从暗影里看她眺望街的两头。
③ The blind was pulled down to within an inch of the sash so that I could not be seen: 我总是把百叶窗帘拉下来, 只留不到一英寸的缝隙, 那样别人就看不见我了。
④ summon: 召唤。女孩的名字就是对他热情的召唤, 其幼稚痴情可见一斑。
⑤ the shrill litanies of shop-boys: 店伙计的尖声叫卖。
⑥ the nasal chanting: 带着鼻音的哼唱声。

O'Donovan Rossa① or a ballad about the troubles in our native land. These noises converged in a single sensation of life for me: I imagined that I bore my chalice safely through a throng of foes②. Her name sprang to my lips at moments in strange prayers and praises which I myself did not understand. My eyes were often full of tears (I could not tell why) and at times a flood from my heart seemed to pour itself out into my bosom. I thought little of the future. I did not know whether I would ever speak to her or not or, if I spoke to her, how I could tell her of my confused adoration. But my body was like a harp and her words and gestures were like fingers running upon the wires.

    One evening I went into the back drawing-room in which the priest had died. It was a dark rainy evening and there was no sound in the house. Through one of the broken panes I heard the rain impinge upon the earth, the fine incessant needles of water playing in the sodden beds③. Some distant lamp or lighted window gleamed below me. I was thankful that I could see so little. All my senses seemed to desire to veil themselves and, feeling that I was about to slip from them④, I pressed the palms of my hands together until they trembled, murmuring: "O love! O love!" many times.

    At last she spoke to me. When she addressed the first words to me I was so confused that I did not know what to answer. She asked me was I going to Araby⑤. I forget whether I answered yes or no. It would be a splendid bazaar, and she said she would love to go.

---

    ① a come-all-you about O'Donovan rossa: 一首关于奥多诺万·罗莎的流行歌曲。come-all-you 意为"街头民谣",题目往往取自歌的第一句。这首民谣讲的是 19 世纪爱尔兰民族主义者 Jeremiah Donovan 的故事,人们称她为 O'Donovan Rossa。

    ② I bore my chalice safely through a throng of foes: 我捧着圣杯黯然穿过敌群。男孩想象自己是一位骑士。

    ③ the fine incessant needles of water playing in the sodden beds: 针一般的毛毛细雨落在潮湿的花坛上。

    ④ feeling that I was about to slip from them: 我感到就要失去知觉。them 指前句的 senses。

    ⑤ Araby: 阿拉比集市。Araby 一词亦指 1894 年 5 月 14 至 19 日在都柏林举行的一次集会,在"官方文献"中被描述为"盛大的东方庆典"。

"And why can't you?" I asked.

While she spoke she turned a silver bracelet round and round her wrist. She could not go, she said, because there would be a retreat that week in her convent①. Her brother and two other boys were fighting for their caps and I was alone at the railings. She held one of the spikes, bowing her head towards me. The light from the lamp opposite our door caught the white curve of her neck, lit up the hair that rested there and, falling, lit up the hand upon the railing. It fell over one side of her dress and caught the white border of a petticoat, just visible as she stood at ease.

"It's well for you," she said.

"If I go," I said, "I will bring you something."

What innumerable follies laid waste my waking and sleeping thoughts② after that evening! I wished to annihilate the tedious intervening days. I chafed against the work of school. At night in my bedroom and by day in the classroom her image came between me and the page I strove to read. The syllables of the word *Araby* were called to me through the silence in which my soul luxuriated and cast an eastern enchantment over me③. I asked for leave to go to the bazaar on Saturday night. My aunt was surprised and hoped it was not some freemason affair④. I answered few questions in class. I watched my master's face pass from amiability to sternness; he hoped I was not beginning to idle. I could not call my wandering thoughts together. I had hardly any patience with the serious work of life which, now that it stood between me and my desire, seemed to me child's play, ugly monotonous child's play.

---

① there would be a retreat that week in her convent: 本周她上学的修道院有一次静修。retreat 为一种宗教活动，要求在一段时间内远离日常生活，过隐居的日子。

② What innumerable follies laid waste my waking and sleeping thoughts: 多少荒唐的念头使我日夜不安。

③ cast an eastern enchantment over me: 让我像中了东方的魔法一样。

④ it was not some freemason affair: 不是干什么秘密帮会的勾当。freemason affair 是欧洲古老的秘密反天主教团体。

On Saturday morning I reminded my uncle that I wished to go to the bazaar in the evening. He was fussing at the hallstand, looking for the hatbrush, and answered me curtly:

"Yes, boy, I know."

As he was in the hall I could not go into the front parlour and lie at the window. I felt the house in bad humour and walked slowly towards the school. The air was pitilessly raw and already my heart misgave me.

When I came home to dinner my uncle had not yet been home. Still it was early. I sat staring at the clock for some time and, when its ticking began to irritate me, I left the room. I mounted the staircase and gained the upper part of the house. The high cold empty gloomy rooms liberated me and I went from room to room singing. From the front window I saw my companions playing below in the street. Their cries reached me weakened and indistinct and, leaning my forehead against the cool glass, I looked over at the dark house where she lived. I may have stood there for an hour seeing nothing but the brown-clad figure cast by my imagination, touched discreetly by the lamplight at the curved neck, at the hand upon the railings and at the border below the dress.

When I came downstairs again I found Mrs. Mercer sitting at the fire. She was an old garrulous woman, a pawnbroker's widow, who collected used stamps for some pious purpose. I had to endure the gossip of the teatable. The meal was prolonged beyond an hour and still my uncle did not come. Mrs. Mercer stood up to go: she was sorry she couldn't wait any longer, but it was after eight o'clock and she did not like to be out late, as the night air was bad for her. When she had gone I began to walk up and down the room, clenching my fists. My aunt said:

"I'm afraid you may put off your bazaar for this night of Our Lord①."

At nine o'clock I heard my uncle's latchkey in the halldoor. I heard him

---

① you may put off your bazaar for this night of Our Lord: 也许你该推迟去集市的日子,因为今晚是主的礼拜六夜晚。

talking to himself and heard the hallstand rocking when it had received the weight of his overcoat. I could interpret these signs. When he was midway through his dinner I asked him to give me the money to go to the bazaar. He had forgotten.

"The people are in bed and after their first sleep now," he said.

I did not smile. My aunt said to him energetically:

"Can't you give him the money and let him go? You've kept him late enough as it is."

My uncle said he was very sorry he had forgotten. He said he believed in the old saying: "All work and no play makes Jack a dull boy." He asked me where I was going and when I had told him a second time he asked me did I know "The Arab's Farewell to His Steed"①. When I left the kitchen he was about to recite the opening lines of the piece to my aunt.

I held a florin tightly in my hand as I strode down Buckingham Street towards the station. The sight of the streets thronged with buyers and glaring with gas recalled to me the purpose of my journey. I took my seat in a third class carriage of a deserted train. After an intolerable delay the train moved out of the station slowly. It crept onward among ruinous houses and over the twinkling river. At Westland Row Station a crowd of people pressed to the carriage doors; but the porters moved them back, saying that it was a special train for the bazaar. I remained alone in the bare carriage. In a few minutes the train drew up beside an improvised wooden platform. I passed out on to the road and saw by the lighted dial of a clock that it was ten minutes to ten. In front of me was a large building which displayed the magical name.

I could not find any sixpenny entrance and, fearing that the bazaar would be closed, I passed in quickly through a turnstile, handing a shilling to a weary-looking man. I found myself in a big hall girdled at half its height

---

① The Arab's Farewell to His Steed:《阿拉伯人告别他的骏马》是卡罗琳·诺顿（Caroline Norton）写的一首曾轰动一时的伤感诗。

by a gallery. Nearly all the stalls were closed and the greater part of the hall was in darkness. I recognized a silence like that which pervades a church after a service. I walked into the centre of the bazaar timidly. A few people were gathered about the stalls which were still open. Before a curtain over which the words *Café Chantant*① were written in coloured lamps, two men were counting money on a salver. I listened to the fall of the coins.

Remembering with difficulty why I had come I went over to one of the stalls and examined porcelain vases and flowered tea-sets. At the door of the stall a young lady was talking and laughing with two young gentlemen. I remarked their English accents and listened vaguely to their conversation.

"O, I never said such a thing!"

"O, but you did!"

"O, but I didn't!"

"Didn't she say that?"

"Yes. I heard her."

"O, there's a ... fib!"

Observing me the young lady came over and asked me did I wish to buy anything. The tone of her voice was not encouraging; she seemed to have spoken to me out of a sense of duty. I looked humbly at the great jars that stood like eastern guards at either side of the dark entrance to the stall and murmured:

"No, thank you."

The young lady changed the position of one of the vases and went back to the two young men. They began to talk of the same subject. Once or twice the young lady glanced at me over her shoulder.

I lingered before her stall, though I knew my stay was useless, to make my interest in her wares seem the more real. Then I turned away slowly and walked down the middle of the bazaar. I allowed the two pennies to fall

---

① Café Chantant: 20 世纪初很流行的一种音乐咖啡店。

against the six-pence in my pocket. I heard a voice call from one end of the gallery that the light was out. The upper part of the hall was now completely dark.

Gazing up into the darkness I saw myself as a creature driven and derided by vanity; and my eyes burned with anguish and anger.

Questions

1. What images does the author use in this short story? What roles do these images play in plot development and characterization?

2. Bildungsroman(成长小说) started in Germany at the end of the 18th century. It usually describes the protagonist's spiritual, moral and psychological experiences from childhood to adulthood. Most Bildungsroman has two plots: the protagonist undergoes some psychological imbalance due to a variety of setbacks, and he reestablishes his psychological balance after some struggle. In a broad sense, Bildungsroman also includes those anti-Bildungsroman (anti-growth novels), in which protagonists fail to reestablish their psychological balance, but end up in suicide or madness. Does this short story belong to Bildungsroman? Why or why not?

Further Readings

James Joyce's short stories are famous for their simple plots and philosophical meanings. The following are some of his important short stories.

1. "The Dead" (《死者》)
2. "An Encounter" (《偶遇》)
3. "A Painful Case" (《痛心的往事》)
4. "Eveline"《伊夫琳》

Unit 7　The Mark on the Wall

About the writer

弗吉尼亚·伍尔芙(Virginia Woolf, 1882 – 1941)是英国小说家、文学批评家,是意识流文学代表作家,被誉为 20 世纪现代主义和女性主义的先锋。其主要作品包括《达洛维夫人》(Mrs. Dalloway, 1925)、《到灯塔去》(To the Lighthouse, 1927)等。

伍尔芙1882 年出生于英国伦敦,父亲是知名的学者和传记作家。弗吉尼亚自幼体弱,靠阅读父亲藏书而自学成才。1906 年,她迁居伦敦的文化区布鲁姆斯伯里,后来成为著名的布鲁姆斯伯里文学团体(Bloomsburg Group)的核心人物,并与其中一名成员作家伦纳德·伍尔芙(Leonard Woolf, 1880 –1969)结婚。詹姆斯·乔伊斯的小说《尤利西斯》和亨利·伯格森(Henry Bergson, 1859 –1941)的直觉主义哲学对她产生了重要影响。从小说《雅各的房间》(Jacob's Room, 1920)开始,伍尔芙尝试意识流创作方法,着重揭示人物的内心活动。

《达洛维夫人》基于出色的意识流手法为伍尔芙赢得广泛赞誉。小说将所有事件都压缩在从上午 9 点到次日凌晨短短 15 个小时之内,记述这段时间内一位伦敦上层社会妇女达洛维夫人的心理活动。她在为晚会买花的途中想到了年轻时的恋人彼得,而刚从印度回来的彼得也正是在那天拜访了她。与此平行的叙述是关于塞·史密斯的故事,他在第一次世界大战中受爆炸惊吓而患上了精神病,在同一天去看心理医生。小说结尾,达洛维夫人的晚会将小说中提到的大部分人连接起来,尤其是当心理医生提及史密斯跳楼自杀时,虽然达洛维夫人与史密斯从未谋面,两人的身世与性格也迥异,但他们对生活中出现或潜在的恐惧所做出的反应却不无相似之处。

两年后,伍尔芙发表了小说《到灯塔去》。小说展现了主人公拉姆齐一家到灯塔去的经历,通过拉姆齐夫妇探讨了人的本性。拉姆齐先生是一位哲学家,他性格孤僻,过于强调理性和逻辑,他的夫人则是一位通情达理的贤妻良母,她温柔体贴,善解人意,感情丰富。拉姆齐夫妇代表象征着理性与情感、客观世界与精神世界的对立与冲突。《到灯塔去》叙事艺术独特,作者通过意识流在交织叙事中实现视角频繁转换,突出人物意识,进一步加深了读者对人物内心活动与真实感情的体会和理解。

伍尔芙在小说《海浪》(*The Waves*, 1931)中进行了与传统小说完全不同的大胆改革,将意识流手法运用到极致,尽量减少小说中的情节、对话和对外部事物的描写,集中展示了人物瞬息万变的内心世界。小说通过 6 个人物的内心独白或意识流动的"波浪"表现出他们的经历,探讨在"自我遭到压抑和抹杀的机械"时代人们是否能够保持精神的独立。

伍尔芙认为现实主义的创作方法刻意追求逼真而表现外部世界,不能深入人物内心展现其无意识活动。她极度推崇乔伊斯等"偏重精神"的作家们,因为他们致力于表现人物丰富广阔的精神世界。伍尔芙对叙事技巧进行了大胆探索,运用了意识流手法,使得小说的时间呈现碎片化,将过去、现在和未来并置。此外,伍尔芙在作品中通过大量的象征手法进入人物意识的深层,揭示了人物心理活动的多变性和含混性,赋予作品多层意蕴。伍尔芙探索了第一次世界大战前后和两次世界大战这段动荡时期英国中上层阶级人们的精神世界,把意识流小说推向高峰,对之后的英国文学乃至世界文学产生了十分深远的影响。

About the story

《墙上的斑点》("The Mark on the Wall")是伍尔芙于 1919 年发表的短篇小说。小说主要讲述了主人公偶然抬头看见墙上的一个斑点,由此引发意识的飘逸流动,产生一系列遐想。主人公由斑点联想到钉痕、挂肖像的前任房客,由对斑点的疑惑联想到生命的神秘、思想的含混性和人类的无知,由斑点的形状联想到一座古冢,进而想到忧伤、白骨和考古……最后发现墙上的斑点不过是一只蜗牛。

《墙上的斑点》中除了主人公外没有其他人物,也没有任何故事情节,通篇都是主人公的思想过程。叙述者"我"想到自己与多数英国人一样偏爱忧伤,想到草地下埋着白骨,想到古物收藏家及与附近牧师的通信,最后想到博物馆里陈设的各类器具。叙述者接着又回到斑点,设想假如斑点是一枚钉到墙里已有 200 年的巨大的旧钉子的钉头,直到现在,由于一代又一代女仆的耐心擦拭,才得以露到油漆外面,这样做又能得到些什么呢? 是否会得到知识呢? 于是叙述者的思绪便被引向了知识层面的问题。这个世界要是没有教授、没有专家、没有警察面孔的管家,会是一个十分可爱的世界。接下来,叙述者又从自己构想的没有尊卑秩序的乌托邦的大同世界回到现实之中,清醒地认识到:"… for who will ever be able to lift a finger against Whitaker's Table of Precedency? The Archbishop of Canterbury is followed by the Lord High Chancellor; the Lord High Chancellor is followed by the Archbishop of York. Everybody follows somebody, such is the philosophy of Whitaker; and the great thing is to know who follows whom."。

  作为物件,作为具体的东西和人身外的世界,斑点代表着一种现实感。接着,叙述者又从赞赏衣柜联想到木头,并认为"木头是一件值得加以思索的愉快的事物"。叙述者的思绪流动,由"木头—树—树木生长的草地、森林、小河边",到"树下的母牛—被树木点染的小河里逆流而上的鱼群—河床上的水甲虫"等。然而,这种联想的跳跃之快,如同电影画面一个又一个快速闪过,以至于叙述者本人也难以使之定格、凝固。叙述者"我"的思绪像脱缰的野马,处于失控状态,因而产生障碍,使"我"思后而不能想前了。"我想到什么地方啦? 是怎么样想到这里的呢? 一棵树? 一条河? 丘陵草原地带? 惠特克年鉴? 盛开水仙花的原野? 我什么也记不起来了。一切在转动、在下沉、在滑开去、在消失……事物陷进了大动荡之中。"枯燥的生活和残酷的战争将叙事者的思绪拉回到现实中,终止了"我"的各种联想和思想"冒险",那个墙上的斑点原来只是一只蜗牛。

  在结构方面,《墙上的斑点》表现的是叙事者"我"的内心活动,记录了"我"不停流动的思绪。故事结构看似杂乱无章,实则是以斑点为中心引发的丰富联想,是以心理活动为框架的辐射型结构。这是伍尔芙独特的叙事试验,也是其对传统小说结构的创新。《墙上的斑点》是意识流的代表作。叙述者"我"的每一次思绪漫游如同幻觉般天马行空,跳跃式地向前跃进,一件事与一件事之间,一个对象与另一个对象之间,既无必然的联系,也无偶然的关联,甚至也没有必要的过渡。它基本上撇开了现实中客观存在物与外在的东西,除了偶尔回到斑点这一依托物之外,几乎完全任由人物意识自在地、任意地流动。伍尔芙让读者看到,人的主观意识极为丰富,将墙上的斑点做一个稍微不同的假设，就会引出无穷多的缤纷思绪。伍尔芙对人物精神世界浓墨重彩的描写，对客观外界大刀阔斧的弃绝，使她将人物意识流的动感与美感表现到了极致，这也是该短篇小说最具特色的地方。

The Mark on the Wall

PERHAPS IT WAS the middle of January in the present year that I first looked up and saw the mark on the wall. In order to fix a date it is necessary to remember what one saw. So now I think of the fire; the steady film of yellow light upon the page of my book; the three chrysanthemums in the round glass bowl on the mantelpiece. Yes, it must have been the winter time, and we had just finished our tea, for I remember that I was smoking a cigarette when I looked up and saw the mark on the wall for the first time. I looked up through the smoke of my cigarette and my eye lodged for a moment upon the burning coals, and that old fancy of the crimson flag flapping from the castle tower came into my mind, and I thought of the cavalcade of red knights riding up the side of the black rock. Rather to my relief the sight of the mark interrupted the fancy, for it is an old fancy, an automatic fancy, made as a child perhaps. The mark was a small round mark, black upon the white wall, about six or seven inches above the mantelpiece.

How readily our thoughts swarm upon a new object, lifting it a little way, as ants carry a blade of straw so feverishly, and then leave it ... If that mark was made by a nail, it can't have been for a picture, it must have been for a miniature—the miniature of a lady with white powdered curls, powder-dusted cheeks, and lips like red carnations. A fraud of course, for the people who had this house before us would have chosen pictures in that way—an old picture for an old room. That is the sort of people they were—very interesting people, and I think of them so often, in such queer places, because one will never see them again, never know what happened next.

They wanted to leave this house because they wanted to change their style of furniture, so he said, and he was in process of saying that in his opinion art should have ideas behind it when we were torn asunder, as one is torn from the old lady about to pour out tea and the young man about to hit the tennis ball in the back garden of the suburban villa as one rushes past in the train.

But as for that mark, I'm not sure about it; I don't believe it was made by a nail after all; it's too big, too round, for that. I might get up, but if I got up and looked at it, ten to one I shouldn't be able to say for certain; because once a thing's done, no one ever knows how it happened. Oh! dear me, the mystery of life; the inaccuracy of thought! The ignorance of humanity! To show how very little control of our possessions we have—what an accidental affair this living is after all our civilization—let me just count over a few of the things lost in one lifetime, beginning, for that seems always the most mysterious of losses—what cat would gnaw, what rat would nibble—three pale blue canisters of book-binding tools? Then there were the bird cages, the iron hoops, the steel skates, the Queen Anne① coal-scuttle②, the bagatelle③ board, the hand organ—all gone, and jewels, too. Opals and emeralds, they lie about the roots of turnips. What a scraping paring affair it is to be sure! The wonder is that I've any clothes on my back, that I sit surrounded by solid furniture at this moment. Why, if one wants to compare life to anything, one must liken it to being blown through the Tube④ at fifty miles an hour—landing at the other end without a single hairpin in one's hair! Shot out at the feet of God entirely naked! Tumbling head over heels in the asphodel meadows⑤ like brown paper

---

① the Queen Anne：18 世纪早期（安妮女王时期）流行于英国家庭的家具特有的简单曲线和弯腿家具风格。
② coal-scuttle：煤斗。
③ bagatelle：巴格代拉桌球游戏。
④ the Tube：伦敦地铁。
⑤ the asphodel meadows：天堂（希腊神话中，百合花是生长在极乐世界里的）。

parcels pitched down a shoot in the post office! With one's hair flying back like the tail of a race-horse. Yes, that seems to express the rapidity of life, the perpetual waste and repair; all so casual, all so haphazard ...

But after life. The slow pulling down of thick green stalks so that the cup of the flower, as it turns over, deluges one with purple and red light. Why, after all, should one not be born there as one is born here, helpless, speechless, unable to focus one's eyesight, groping at the roots of the grass, at the toes of the Giants? As for saying which are trees, and which are men and women, or whether there are such things, that one won't be in a condition to do for fifty years or so. There will be nothing but spaces of light and dark, intersected by thick stalks, and rather higher up perhaps, rose-shaped blots of an indistinct colour—dim pinks and blues—which will, as time goes on, become more definite, become—I don't know what ...

And yet that mark on the wall is not a hole at all. It may even be caused by some round black substance, such as a small rose leaf, left over from the summer, and I, not being a very vigilant housekeeper—look at the dust on the mantelpiece, for example, the dust which, so they say, buried Troy① three times over, only fragments of pots utterly refusing annihilation, as one can believe.

The tree outside the window taps very gently on the pane ... I want to think quietly, calmly, spaciously, never to be interrupted, never to have to rise from my chair, to slip easily from one thing to another, without any sense of hostility, or obstacle. I want to sink deeper and deeper, away from the surface, with its hard separate facts. To steady myself, let me catch hold of the first idea that passes ... Shakespeare ... Well, he will do as well as another. A man who sat himself solidly in an arm-chair, and looked into the fire, so—A shower of ideas fell perpetually from some very high Heaven down through his mind. He leant his forehead on his hand, and people,

---

① Troy:特洛伊(荷马史诗《伊利亚特》中的传说城址)。

looking in through the open door—for this scene is supposed to take place on a summer's evening—But how dull this is, this historical fiction! It doesn't interest me at all. I wish I could hit upon a pleasant track of thought, a track indirectly reflecting credit upon myself, for those are the pleasantest thoughts, and very frequent even in the minds of modest mouse-coloured people, who believe genuinely that they dislike to hear their own praises. They are not thoughts directly praising oneself; that is the beauty of them; they are thoughts like this:

"And then I came into the room. They were discussing botany. I said how I'd seen a flower growing on a dust heap on the site of an old house in Kingsway①. The seed, I said, must have been sown in the reign of Charles the First②. What flowers grew in the reign of Charles the First?" I asked—(but I don't remember the answer). Tall flowers with purple tassels to them perhaps. And so it goes on. All the time I'm dressing up the figure of myself in my own mind, lovingly, stealthily, not openly adoring it, for if I did that, I should catch myself out, and stretch my hand at once for a book in self-protection. Indeed, it is curious how instinctively one protects the image of oneself from idolatry or any other handling that could make it ridiculous, or too unlike the original to be believed in any longer. Or is it not so very curious after all? It is a matter of great importance. Suppose the looking glass smashes, the image disappears, and the romantic figure with the green of forest depths all about it is there no longer, but only that shell of a person which is seen by other people—what an airless, shallow, bald, prominent world it becomes! A world not to be lived in. As we face each other in omnibuses and underground railways we are looking into the mirror; that accounts for the vagueness, the gleam of glassiness, in our eyes. And the novelists in future will realize more and more the importance

---

① Kingsway: 伦敦市区一街名。
② Charles the First: 英国国王查尔斯一世(1600—1649)于 1625—1649 年间统治英国,在英国革命期间被处决。

of these reflections, for of course there is not one reflection but an almost infinite number; those are the depths they will explore, those the phantoms they will pursue, leaving the description of reality more and more out of their stories, taking a knowledge of it for granted, as the Greeks did and Shakespeare perhaps—but these generalizations are very worthless. The military sound of the word is enough. It recalls leading articles, cabinet ministers—a whole class of things indeed which as a child one thought the thing itself, the standard thing, the real thing, from which one could not depart save at the risk of nameless damnation. Generalizations bring back somehow Sunday in London, Sunday afternoon walks, Sunday luncheons, and also ways of speaking of the dead, clothes, and habits—like the habit of sitting all together in one room until a certain hour, although nobody liked it. There was a rule for everything. The rule for tablecloths at that particular period was that they should be made of tapestry with little yellow compartments marked upon them, such as you may see in photographs of the carpets in the corridors of the royal palaces. Tablecloths of a different kind were not real tablecloths. How shocking, and yet how wonderful it was to discover that these real things, Sunday luncheons, Sunday walks, country houses, and tablecloths were not entirely real, were indeed half phantoms, and the damnation which visited the disbeliever in them was only a sense of illegitimate freedom. What now takes the place of those things I wonder, those real standard things? Men perhaps, should you be a woman; the masculine point of view which governs our lives, which sets the standard, which establishes Whitaker's Table of Precedency①, which has become, I suppose, since the war half a phantom to many men and women, which soon, one may hope, will be laughed into the dustbin

---

① Whitaker's Table of Precedency: 刊发在 *Whitaker's Almanack* 上的（头衔阶层）优先列表。

where the phantoms go, the mahogany sideboards and the Landseer① prints, Gods and Devils, Hell and so forth, leaving us all with an intoxicating sense of illegitimate freedom—if freedom exists ...

In certain lights that mark on the wall seems actually to project from the wall. Nor is it entirely circular. I cannot be sure, but it seems to cast a perceptible shadow, suggesting that if I ran my finger down that strip of the wall it would, at a certain point, mount and descend a small tumulus, a smooth tumulus like those barrows② on the South Downs③ which are, they say, either tombs or camps. Of the two I should prefer them to be tombs, desiring melancholy like most English people, and finding it natural at the end of a walk to think of the bones stretched beneath the turf ... There must be some book about it. Some antiquary must have dug up those bones and given them a name ... What sort of a man is an antiquary, I wonder? Retired Colonels for the most part, I dare say, leading parties of aged labourers to the top here, examining clods of earth and stone, and getting into correspondence with the neighbouring clergy, which, being opened at breakfast time, gives them a feeling of importance, and the comparison of arrow-heads necessitates cross-country journeys to the county towns, an agreeable necessity both to them and to their elderly wives, who wish to make plum jam or to clean out the study, and have every reason for keeping that great question of the camp or the tomb in perpetual suspension, while the Colonel himself feels agreeably philosophic in accumulating evidence on both sides of the question. It is true that he does finally incline to believe in the camp; and, being opposed, indites a pamphlet which he is about to read at the quarterly meeting of the local society when a stroke lays him low, and his last conscious thoughts are not of wife or child, but of the

---

① Landseer:兰西尔(Sir Edwin Henry Landseer, 1802–1873),英国画家。他描摹的动物画,尤其是马、狗和雄鹿,在维多利亚时代的家庭中很常见。
② barrows:古坟。
③ the South Downs:英格兰东南部系列低矮山丘。

camp and that arrowhead there, which is now in the case at the local museum, together with the foot of a Chinese murderess, a handful of Elizabethan nails, a great many Tudor① clay pipes, a piece of Roman pottery, and the wine-glass that Nelson② drank out of—proving I really don't know what.

No, no, nothing is proved, nothing is known. And if I were to get up at this very moment and ascertain that the mark on the wall is really—what shall we say?—the head of a gigantic old nail, driven in two hundred years ago, which has now, owing to the patient attrition of many generations of housemaids, revealed its head above the coat of paint, and is taking its first view of modern life in the sight of a white-walled fire-lit room, what should I gain?—knowledge? Matter for further speculation? I can think sitting still as well as standing up. And what is knowledge? What are our learned men save the descendants of witches and hermits who crouched in caves and in woods brewing herbs, interrogating shrew-mice and writing down the language of the stars? And the less we honour them as our superstitions dwindle and our respect for beauty and health of mind increases ... Yes, one could imagine a very pleasant world. A quiet, spacious world, with the flowers so red and blue in the open fields. A world without professors or specialists or house-keepers with the profiles of policemen, a world which one could slice with one's thought as a fish slices the water with his fin, grazing the stems of the water-lilies, hanging suspended over nests of white sea eggs ... How peaceful it is down here, rooted in the centre of the world and gazing up through the grey waters, with their sudden gleams of light, and their reflections—if it were not for *Whitaker's Almanack*③—if it were not

---

① Tudor:流行于整个都铎王朝(15世纪)的英国建筑风格,外观可见用石膏和砖块填充的木材框架。
② Nelson:Horatio Nelson(1758-1805),英国海军上将。
③ *Whitaker's Almanack*:《惠特克年鉴》。该年鉴是由英国出版家约瑟夫·惠特克(Joseph Whitaker, 1820-1895)于1868年创刊,被誉为英国最好的年鉴和微型百科全书。其收录的内容上至天文,下至地理,旁及世界各国的基本情况和科学知识。

for the Table of Precedency!

I must jump up and see for myself what that mark on the wall really is— a nail, a rose-leaf, a crack in the wood?

Here is nature once more at her old game of self-preservation. This train of thought, she perceives, is threatening mere waste of energy, even some collision with reality, for who will ever be able to lift a finger against Whitaker's Table of Precedency? The Archbishop of Canterbury is followed by the Lord High Chancellor①; the Lord High Chancellor is followed by the Archbishop of York②. Everybody follows somebody, such is the philosophy of Whitaker; and the great thing is to know who follows whom. Whitaker knows, and let that, so Nature counsels, comfort you, instead of enraging you; and if you can't be comforted, if you must shatter this hour of peace, think of the mark on the wall.

I understand Nature's game—her prompting to take action as a way of ending any thought that threatens to excite or to pain. Hence, I suppose, comes our slight contempt for men of action—men, we assume, who don't think. Still, there's no harm in putting a full stop to one's disagreeable thoughts by looking at a mark on the wall.

Indeed, now that I have fixed my eyes upon it, I feel that I have grasped a plank in the sea; I feel a satisfying sense of reality which at once turns the two Archbishops and the Lord High Chancellor to the shadows of shades. Here is something definite, something real. Thus, waking from a midnight dream of horror, one hastily turns on the light and lies quiescent, worshipping the chest of drawers, worshipping solidity, worshipping reality, worshipping the impersonal world which is a proof of some existence other than ours. That is what one wants to be sure of … Wood is a pleasant thing to think about. It comes from a tree; and trees grow, and we don't know

---

① the Lord High Chancellor:最高议长,掌控司法权,主持上议院。
② the Archbishop of York:约克(英格兰北部的教区)大主教。

how they grow. For years and years they grow, without paying any attention to us, in meadows, in forests, and by the side of rivers—all things one likes to think about. The cows swish their tails beneath them on hot afternoons; they paint rivers so green that when a moorhen dives one expects to see its feathers all green when it comes up again. I like to think of the fish balanced against the stream like flags blown out; and of water-beetles slowly raising domes of mud upon the bed of the river. I like to think of the tree itself: first the close dry sensation of being wood; then the grinding of the storm; then the slow, delicious ooze of sap. I like to think of it, too, on winter's nights standing in the empty field with all leaves close-furled, nothing tender exposed to the iron bullets of the moon, a naked mast upon an earth that goes tumbling, tumbling, all night long. The song of birds must sound very loud and strange in June; and how cold the feet of insects must feel upon it, as they make laborious progresses up the creases of the bark, or sun themselves upon the thin green awning of the leaves, and look straight in front of them with diamond-cut red eyes ... One by one the fibres snap beneath the immense cold pressure of the earth, then the last storm comes and, falling, the highest branches drive deep into the ground again. Even so, life isn't done with; there are a million patient, watchful lives still for a tree, all over the world, in bedrooms, in ships, on the pavement, lining rooms, where men and women sit after tea, smoking cigarettes. It is full of peaceful thoughts, happy thoughts, this tree. I should like to take each one separately—but something is getting in the way ... Where was I? What has it all been about? A tree? A river? The Downs①? *Whitaker's Almanack*? The fields of asphodel? I can't remember a thing. Everything's moving, falling, slipping, vanishing ... There is a vast upheaval of matter. Someone is standing over me and saying—

"I'm going out to buy a newspaper."

---

① The Downs:肯特郡东海岸附近的一部分海域。

"Yes?"

"Though it's no good buying newspapers ... Nothing ever happens. Curse this war; God damn this war! ... All the same, I don't see why we should have a snail on our wall."

Ah, the mark on the wall! It was a snail.

Questions

1. After several pages of digressions on history, reality, society, art, writing, and life itself, the story concludes with the identification that the mark is actually a snail. How do you react to this revelation? Do you expect such a closure?

2. Discuss the issue of verb tense in the story. Except for the first paragraph and the last line/paragraph where Woolf uses the past tense, the whole story is told in the present tense. What special effect is achieved by this shift of tense?

Further Readings

Virginia Woolf's short stories are innovative and experimental, especially characteristic of stream-of-consciousness and feminism. The following are some of her important short stories.

1. "Moments of Being" (《存在的瞬间》)
2. "A Haunted House" (《幽灵之屋》)
3. "The New Dress" (《新裙子》)
4. "Monday or Tuesday" (《星期一或星期二》)

Unit 8 The Horse Dealer's Daughter

About the writer

戴维·赫伯特·劳伦斯(David Herbert Lawrence,1885 – 1930)是英国现实主义小说家、诗人和批评家。他的作品主要以英格兰中部诺丁汉郡一带的矿区村为背景,描绘了工业化和机器文明时代人们精神上和道德上发生的异化。劳伦斯认为,工业革命的主要危害在于压抑和歪曲了人的自然本性,特别是爱与性的本能,破坏了人与人之间的和谐关系。劳伦斯将社会批判和心理探索结合起来,形成其小说创作的主要特色。

劳伦斯1885年出生于诺丁汉郡一个贫穷的煤矿工人家庭,父亲是矿工,酗酒成瘾,母亲是小学教师,酷爱读书,文化水平较高。父母之间常因为家庭琐事摩擦不断,这对青少年时期的劳伦斯产生了重要影响,在之后的创作中劳伦斯经常涉及家庭矛盾对儿童心理造成的不良后果。劳伦斯一生著作颇丰,包括10部长篇小说、11部短篇小说集、4部戏剧、10部诗集、4部散文集、5部理论论著、3部游记和大量书信。

1913年发表的小说《儿子与情人》(Sons and Lovers)带有较大自传性成分,反映了劳伦斯青年时期的经历。小说描述了保罗·莫瑞尔与三位女性即他母亲、米利安和克拉拉的关系,阐述了理智与情感的激烈冲突。于保罗而言,母亲是理性的化身,代表着名利;初恋女友米利安是灵魂伴侣,代表着纯洁;情人克拉拉则是发泄的工具,代表着享受。劳伦斯试图在保罗身上体现完美的人性:努力奋斗以争取社会的认可,同时又压抑自己的天性;注重精神追求,同时也享受人生的乐趣。保罗体现了作者劳伦斯对工业时代完整人性的探索,保罗经历的失败、挫折和痛苦反映出劳伦斯在严峻的社会现实面前、在理智与情感的对立中表现出的无助与迷茫。

1915年劳伦斯出版了小说《虹》(The Rainbow)。小说大胆地探索了有关性和爱的心理问题,以家族史方式展开,叙述了自耕农布莱文一家三代人的经历与变迁。第一代人莉迪亚和汤姆的生活带有田园诗色彩,但同时预示着古老的农业文明即将结束。第二代人威尔和安娜的冲突最终导致双方在婚姻中都未获得满足感,他们精神苦闷,目光呆滞,反映了工业社会对人性的异化。第三代人厄休拉与安东、厄休拉与伯基的探索具有积极的社会意义,表达了人们对和谐美好生活的渴望和追求。

劳伦斯在《虹》的续篇——《恋爱中的女人》(Women in Love, 1920)中继续鞭挞现代工业文明的危害,并尝试以多种手法表现作品人物的性心理和无意识。《恋爱中的女人》描写了两种男女关系:一种是杰拉尔德和古德伦之间营造的毁灭性爱情,另一种是伯金和厄秀拉之间构建的建设性爱情。劳伦斯试图运用自己理想主义者的视角,探索一种理想的男女两性关系,在他看来只有通过健康的男女关系,英国才能从萎靡中解脱出来。

劳伦斯的创作深受西方现代心理学和哲学影响,揭露了工业文明如何摧残以性心理为中心的自然本性,主张以人的自然本性的全面复苏来克服工业社会的弊病。劳伦斯是英国文学史上最有影响力也最具争议的作家之一,其文学创作的价值主要在于对工业革命后英国社会现状和人性堕落腐化的揭露、对两性关系的重新思考,以及对建构和谐两性关系的主张。

About the story

短篇小说《马贩子的女儿》("The Horse Dealer's Daughter")发表于1916年。故事发生地是英国工业革命时期的乡村小镇,这里冰冷的机器代替了和煦的自然,人们承受着社会变迁带来的科技进步之苦,社会风气日渐衰败,人们道德沦丧。27岁的未婚女人梅布尔双亲俱丧,家道中落,她为了三个兄弟辛苦操劳长达十年,不仅没有得到他们的爱怜和庇护,反而在家庭即将破产之际被他们驱逐。她决定在祭奠过母亲之后自杀,后被医生杰克·弗格森救起,最终收获美好爱情。

故事伊始,阴郁的氛围笼罩着马贩子一家:已故的马贩子约瑟夫·佩文那所昔日风光无限的大宅子现今已是人去楼空、一片萧条,女儿梅布尔和她的三个兄弟对这种潦倒境况深感痛苦和无奈,他们坐在餐桌旁开着那毫无结果的家庭会议。佩文死后留给这四兄妹的是一个烂摊子和数不清的债务。三个兄弟软弱无能,家事只能由能干的梅布尔苦苦地硬撑着。几个月过去了,家境每况愈下,她的努力无济于事。

一天,三个兄弟决定离开那所大宅各奔前程。35 岁的大哥乔一副满不在乎的样子,因为他很"侥幸","Luckily he was engaged to a woman as old as himself, and therefore her father, who was steward of a neighboring estate, would provide him with a job."。33 岁的二哥弗莱德善于谋划,他总是盛气凌人,意图安排梅布尔去姐姐家借住。22 岁的马尔科姆是家里最小的,听闻弗莱德对梅布尔的数落,他洋洋自得,并表示如果他是梅布尔,就去接受培训以便将来成为一名护士。虽然梅布尔告诉他们,姐姐并不欢迎她,但是三人的态度并未改变,仍然对其严加逼迫,并警告说如果她不去,下周三她就得去睡马路。兄弟三人无情无义,都想摆脱梅布尔,不想给她任何帮助。正是兄弟三人的冷酷导致了梅布尔对生活的绝望。

梅布尔此时另有打算,祭扫完母亲的墓之后,她便径直走向她家宅院下面一个深水池中。她怪异的行为始终在医生杰克的注视之下,在池水浸没她的那一刻,他虽不会游泳却跨进池塘,冒着生命危险将她救回岸上。苏醒后的梅布尔在确认是杰克帮自己脱下湿衣物而裹上毛毯后,本能地认为医生爱上了自己,并一再追问"You love me. I know you love me, I know."。此时,杰克只是呆呆地站立着,他感觉到灵魂在被一点一点地溶化掉。一方面就医生职业而言,杰克一心想的是救护病人,即使面对梅布尔裸露的身体也无任何私心杂念;另一方面,他又震慑于梅布尔的举止,不愿再用任何否定的方式重新把她推向死亡。杰克的内心深处展开了一场激烈的战斗:"理性的自我"告诉他,接受梅布尔的爱是对医生神圣职责的玷污;"潜意识的自我"却正在敦促他接受这份爱情。最终,杰克接受了这份爱情。

杰克拯救了梅布尔的生命,随后梅布尔完成了她对杰克的拯救。之前,杰克过着浑浑噩噩的生活,整日辗转于多个矿区,机械地履行作为医生的职责,生活沉闷而乏味。和梅布尔相爱后,他感觉自己身上的活力似乎又恢复了,觉得从烦闷焦躁的日常生活中获得了解脱,重新发现了生活的意义。

故事在人物的理性意识和肉体冲动的相互冲撞下圆满结尾,这正是作者劳伦斯所期望的人类摆脱工业文明枷锁后的和谐生活画面。在《马贩子的女儿》中,劳伦斯也批判了社会中无处不在的男性至上现象,表达了对女性不幸遭遇的同情,肯定了女性为争取平等和自由的斗争,赞扬了女性意识的觉醒,更昭示了男女之爱的意义——拯救,拯救不仅是对个人灵魂的救赎,更是恢复世界秩序、重现人间温暖的有效力量。

The Horse Dealer's Daughter

"Well, Mabel, and what are you going to do with yourself?" asked Joe, with foolish flippancy. He felt quite safe himself. Without listening for an answer, he turned aside, worked a grain of tobacco to the tip of his tongue, and spat it out. He did not care about anything, since he felt safe himself.

The three brothers and the sister sat round the desolate breakfast-table, attempting some sort of desultory consultation. The morning's post had given the final tap to the family fortunes, and all was over. The dreary dining-room itself, with its heavy mahogany① furniture, looked as if it were waiting to be done away with. But the consultation amounted to nothing. There was a strange air of ineffectuality about the three men, as they sprawled at table, smoking and reflecting vaguely on their own condition. The girl was alone, a rather short, sullen-looking young woman of twenty-seven. She did not share the same life as her brothers. She would have been good-looking, save for the impressive fixity of her face, "bull-dog"②, as her brothers called it.

There was a confused tramping of horses' feet outside. The three men all sprawled round in their chairs to watch. Beyond the dark holly bushes that separated the strip of lawn from the high-road, they could see a cavalcade of shire horses③ swinging out of their own yard, being taken for exercise. This was the last time. These were the last horses that would go through their hands. The young men watched with critical, callous look. They were all frightened at the collapse of their lives, and the sense of disaster in which they were involved left them no inner freedom.

---

① mahogany: 桃花心木,热带产之坚硬红木,尤用于制作家具。
② bull-dog: 斗牛狗,一种头大毛短、身体结实的猛犬。
③ shire horse: 英格兰中部的大挽马。

Yet they were three fine, well-set fellows enough. Joe, the eldest, was a man of thirty-five, broad and handsome in a hot flushed way. His face was red, he twisted his black moustache over a thick finger, and his eyes were shallow and restless. He had a sensual way of uncovering his teeth when he laughed, and his bearing was stupid. Now he watched the horses with a glazed look of helplessness in his eyes, a certain stupor of downfall.

The great drought-horses swung past. They were tied head to tail, four of them, and they heaved along to where a lane branched off from the highroad, planting their great roofs flouting in the fine black mud, swinging their great rounded haunches sumptously, and trotting a few sudden steps as they were led into the lane, round the corner. Every movement showed a massive, slumberous strength, and a stupidity which held them in subjection. The groom at the head looked back, jerking the leading rope. And the cavalcade moved out of sight up the lane, the tail of the last horse, bobbed up tight and stiff, held out taut from the swinging great haunches as they rocked behind the hedges in a motion-like sleep.

Joe watched with glazed hopeless eyes. The horses were almost like his own body to him. He felt he was done for now. Luckily he was engaged to a woman as old as himself, and therefore her father, who was steward of a neighbouring estate, would provide him with a job. He would marry and go into harness. His life was over, and he would be a subject animal now.

He turned uneasily aside, the retreating steps of the horses echoing in his ears. Then, with foolish restlessness, he reached for the scraps of bacon-rind from the plates, and making a faint whistling sound, flung them to the terrier that lay against the fender. He watched the dog swallow them and waited till the creature looked into his eyes. Then a faint grin came on his face, and in a high, foolish voice he said:

"You won't get much more bacon, shall you, you little b-?"

The dog faintly and dismally wagged its tail, then lowered its haunches, circled round, and lay down again.

There was another hopeless silence at the table. Joe sprawled uneasily in his seat, not willing to go till the family conclave was dissolved. Fred Henry, the second brother, was erect, clean-limbed①, alert. He had watched the passing of the horses with more *sang-froid*②. If he was an animal, like Joe, he was an animal which controls, not one which is controlled. He was master of any horse, and he carried himself with a well-tempered air of mastery. But he was not master of the situation of life. He pushed his coarse brown moustache upwards, off his lip, and glanced irritably at his sister, who sat impassive and inscrutable.

"You'll go and stop with Lucy for a bit, shan't you?" he asked. The girl did not answer.

"I don't see what else you can do," persisted Fred Henry.

"Go as a skivvy③," Joe interpolated laconically.

The girl did not move a muscle.

"If I was her, I should go in for training for a nurse," said Malcolm, the youngest of them all. He was the baby of the family, a young man of twenty-two, with a fresh, jaunty museau④.

But Mabel did not take any notice of him. They had talked at her and round her for so many years, that she hardly heard them at all.

The marble clock on the mantel piece softly chimed the half-hour, and the dog rose uneasily from the hearth-rug and looked at the party at the breakfast-table. But still they sat on in ineffectual conclave.

"Oh, all right," said Joe suddenly, apropos of nothing⑤. "I'll get a move on."

He pushed back his chair, straddled his knees with a downward jerk, to get them free, in horsey fashion, and went to the fire. Still, he did not go

---

① clean-limbed：四肢匀称。
② sang-froid：(法语)冷血；此处指超然、冷静、沉着。
③ skivvy：专做清洗打杂粗活的女用人。
④ museau：(四肢动物的)口鼻部分；(俚语，贬义)此处指人脸。
⑤ apropos of nothing：无缘无故地。

out of the room; he was curious to know what the others would do or say. He began to charge his pipe, looking down at the dog and saying in a high affected voice:

"Going wi' me? Going wi' me are ter? Tha'rt goin' further than tha counts on just now, dost hear?"①

The dog faintly wagged its tail, the man stuck out his jaw and covered his pipe with his hands, and puffed intently, losing himself in the tobacco, looking down all the while at the dog with an absent brown eye. The dog looked up at him in mournful distrust. Joe stood with his knees stuck out, in real horsey fashion.

"Have you had a letter from Lucy?" Fred Henry asked of his sister.

"Last week," came the neutral reply.

"And what does she say?"

There was no answer.

"Does she ask you to go and stop there?" persisted Fred Henry.

"She says I can if I like."

"Well, then, you'd better. Tell her you'll come on Monday."

This was received in silence.

"That's what you'll do then, is it?" said Fred Henry, in some exasperation.

But she made no answer. There was a silence of futility and irritation in the room. Malcolm grinned fatuously.

"You'll have to make up your mind between now and next Wednesday," said Joe loudly, "or else find your lodgings on the kerbstone."

The face of the young woman darkened, but she sat on immutable.

"Here's Jack Fergusson!" exclaimed Malcolm, who was looking aimlessly out of the window.

---

① "Going wi' me? …, dost hear?":"跟我一起走吗? 跟我一起走,是吗? 这儿没什么指望了,听到没有?"

"Where?" exclaimed Joe loudly.

"Just gone past."

"Coming in?"

Malcolm craned his neck to see the gate.

"Yes," he said.

There was a silence. Mabel sat on like one condemned, at the head of the table. Then a whistle was heard from the kitchen. The dog got up and barked sharply. Joe opened the door and shouted:

"Come on."

After a moment a young man entered. He was muffled in overcoat and a purple woollen scarf, and his tweed cap, which he did not remove, was pulled down on his head. He was of medium height, his face was rather long and pale, and his eyes looked tired.

"Hello, Jack! Well, Jack!" exclaimed Malcolm and Joe. Fred Henry merely said: "Jack."

"What's doing?" asked the newcomer, evidently addressing Fred Henry.

"Same. We've got to be out by Wednesday. Got a cold?"

"I have—got it bad, too."

"Why don't you stop in?"

"Me stop in? When I can't stand on my legs, perhaps I shall have a chance." The young man spoke huskily. He had a slight Scotch accent.

"It's a knock-out①, isn't it," said Joe, boisterously, "if a doctor goes round croaking with a cold. Looks bad for the patients, doesn't it?"

The young doctor looked at him slowly.

"Anything the matter with you then?" he asked sarcastically.

"Not as I know of. Damn your eyes, I hope not. Why?"

"I thought you were very concerned about the patients, wondered if

---

① knock-out: 给人留下深刻印象的事物。

you might be one yourself."

"Damn it, no, I've never been a patient to no flaming doctor, and hope I never shall be," returned Joe.

At this point Mabel rose from the table, and they all seemed to become aware of their existence. She began putting the dishes together. The young doctor looked at her, but did not address her. He had not greeted her. She went out the room with the tray, her face impassive and unchanged.

"When are you off then, all of you?" asked the doctor.

"I'm catching the eleven-forty," replied Malcolm. "Are you goin' down wi' th' trap, Joe?"

"Yes, I've told you I'm going down wi' th' trap, haven't I?"

"We'd better be getting in then. So long, Jack, if I don't see you before I go," said Malcolm, shaking hands.

He went out, followed by Joe, who seemed to have his tail between his legs.

"Well, this is the devil's own①," exclaimed the doctor, when he was left alone with Fred Henry. "Going before Wednesday, are you?"

"That's the orders," replied the other.

"Where, to Northampton?"

"That's it."

"The devil!" exclaimed Fergusson, with quiet chagrin②.

And there was silence between the two.

"All settled up, are you?" asked Fergusson.

"About."

There was another pause.

"Well, I shall miss yer, Freddy, boy," said the young doctor.

"And I shall miss thee, Jack," returned the other.

"Miss you like hell," mused the doctor.

---

① the devil's own: 非同小可。
② chagrin: 懊恼。

Fred Henry turned aside. There was nothing to say. Mabel came in again, to finish clearing the table.

"What are you going to do, then, Miss Pervin?" asked Fergusson. "Going to your sister's, are you?"

Mabel looked at him with her steady, dangerous eyes, that always made him uncomfortable, unsettling his superficial ease.

"No," she said.

"Well, what in the name of fortune are you going to do? Say what you mean to do," cried Fred Henry, with futile intensity.

But she only averted her head, and continued her work. She folded the white table-cloth, and put on the chenille cloth.

"The sulkiest bitch that ever trod!" muttered her brother.

But she finished her task with perfectly impassive face. The young doctor watching her interestedly all the while. Then she went out.

Fred Henry stared after her, clenching his lips, his blue eyes fixing in sharp antagonism, as he made a grimace of sour exasperation.

"You could bray her into bits, and that's all you'd get out of her," he said, in a small, narrowed tone.

The doctor smiled faintly.

"What's she going to do, then?" he asked.

"Strike me if I know!" returned the other.

There was a pause. Then the doctor stirred.

"I'll be seeing you to night, shall I?" he said to his friend.

"Ay—where's it to be? Are we going over to Jessdale?"

"I don't know. I've got such a cold on me. I'll come round to the 'Moon and Stars'①, anyway."

"Let Lizzie and May miss their night for once, eh?"

"That's it—if I feel as I do now."

---

① Moon and Stars: 酒吧名。

"All's one—"

The two young men went through the passage and down to the back door together. The house was large, but it was servantless now, and desolate. At the back was a small bricked house-yard and beyond that a big square, gravelled fine and red, and having stables on two sides. Sloping, dank, winter-dark fields stretched away on the open sides. But the stables were empty. Joseph Pervin, the father of the family, had been a man of no education, who had become a fairly large horse-dealer. The stables had been full of horses, there was a great turmoil and come-and-go of horses and of dealers and grooms. Then the kitchen was full of servants. But of late things has declined. The old man had married a second time, to retrieve his fortunes. Now he was dead and everything was gone to the dogs①, there was nothing but debt and threatening.

For months, Mabel had been servantless in the big house, keeping the home together in penury for her ineffectual brothers. She had kept house for ten years. But previously it was with unstinted means②. Then, however brutal and coarse everything was, the sense of money had kept her proud, confident. The men might be foul-mouthed, the women in the kitchens might have bad reputations, and her brothers might have illegitimate children. But so long as there was money, the girl felt herself established, and brutally proud, reserved.

No company came to the house, save dealers and coarse men. Mabel had no associates of her own sex, after her sister went away. But she did not mind. She went regularly to church, she attended to her father. And she lived in the memory of her mother, who had died when she was fourteen, and whom she had loved. She had loved her father, too, in a different way, depending upon him, and feeling secure in him, until at the age of

---

① go to the dogs:(俚语)急剧恶化,潦倒。
② unstinted means:不受限制的,不遗余力的。

fifty-four he married again. And then she had set hard against him. Now he had died and left them all hopelessly in debt.

She had suffered badly during the period of poverty. Nothing, however, could shake the curious, sullen, animal pride that dominated each member of the family. Now, for Mabel, the end had come. Still she would not cast about① her. She would follow her own way just the same. She would always hold the keys of her own situation. Mindless and persistent, she endured from day to day. Why should she think? Why should she answer anybody? It was enough that this was the end, and there was no way out. She need not pass any more darkly along the main street of the small town, avoiding every eye. She need not pass any more darkly along the main street of the small town, avoiding every eye. She need not demean herself any more, going into the shops and buying the cheapest food. This was at an end. She thought of nobody, not even herself. Mindless and persistent, she seemed in a sort of ecstasy to be coming nearer to her fulfilment, her own glorification, approaching her dead mother, who was glorified.

In the afternoon she took a little bag, with shears and sponge and a small scrubbing-brush, and went out. It was a grey, wintry day, with saddened, dark green fields and an atmosphere blackened by the smoke of foundries not far off. She went quickly, darkly along the causeway, heeding nobody, through the town to the churchyard.

There she always felt secure, as if no one could see her, although as a matter of fact she was exposed to the stare of everyone who passed along the churchyard wall. Nevertheless, once under the shadow of the great looming church, among the graves, she felt immune from the world, reserved within the thick churchyard wall as in another country.

Carefully she clipped the grass from the grave, and arranged the pinky

---

① cast about/around (for sth.): 寻觅(某事物)。

white, small chrysanthemums in the tin cross. When this was done, she took an empty jar from a neighbouring grave, brought water, and carefully, most scrupulously sponged the marble headstone and the coping-stone.

It gave her sincere satisfaction to do this. She felt in immediate contact with the world of her mother. She took minute pains, went through the park in a state bordering on pure happiness, as if in performing this task she came into a subtle, intimate connection with her mother. For the life she followed here in the world was far less real than the world of death she inherited from her mother.

The doctor's house was just by the church. Fergusson, being a mere hired assistant, was slave to the country-side. As he hurried now to attend to the out-patients in the surgery, glancing across the graveyard with his quick eye, he saw the girl at task at the grave. She seemed so intent and remote; it was looking into another world. Some mystical element was touched in him. He slowed down as he walked, watching her as if spellbound[①].

She lifted her eyes, feeling him looking. Their eyes met. And each looked again at once, each feeling, in some way, found out by the other. He lifted his cap and passed on down the road. There remained distinct in consciousness, like a vision, the memory of her face, lifted from the tombstone in the churchyard, and looking at him with slow, large, portentous eyes. It was portentous, her face. It seemed to mesmerise him. There was a heavy power in her eyes which laid hold of his whole being, as if he had drunk some powerful drug. He had been feeling weak and done before. Now the life came back into him, he felt delivered from his own fretted, daily self.

He finished his duties at the surgery as quickly as might be, hastily filling up the bottles of the waiting people with cheap drugs. Then, in

---

① spellbound: 入迷的, 被魔咒镇住的。

perpetual haste, he set off again to visit several cases in another part of his round, before tea time. At all times he preferred to walk if he could, but particularly, when he was not well. He fancied the motion restored him.

The afternoon was falling. It was grey, deadened, and wintry, with a slow, moist, heavy coldness sinking in and deadening all the faculties. But why should he think or notice? He hastily climbed the hill and turned across the dark green fields, following the black cinder-track①. In the distance, across a shallow dip in the country, the small town was clustered like smouldering ash, a tower, a spire, a heap of low, raw, extinct houses. And on the nearest fringe of the town, sloping into the dip, was Oldmeadow, the Pervins' house. He could see the stables and the outbuildings distinctly, as they lay towards him on the slope. Well, he would not go there many more times! Another resource would be lost to him, another place gone: the only company he cared for in the alien, ugly little town he was losing. Nothing but work, drudgery, constant hastening from dwelling to dwelling among the colliers and the iron-workers. It wore him out, but at the same time he had a craving for it. It was a stimulant to him to be in the bones of the working people, moving, as it were, through the innermost body of their life. His nerves were excited and gratified. He could come so near, into the very lives of the rough, inarticulate, powerfully emotional men and women. He grumbled, he said he hated the hellish hole. But as a matter of fact it excited him, the contact with the rough, strongly-feeling people was a stimulant applied direct to his nerves.

Below Oldmeadow, in the green, shallow, soddened hollow of fields, lay a square, deep pond. Roving across the landscape, the doctor's quick eye detected a figure in black passing through the gate of the field, down towards the pond. He looked again. It would be Mabel Pervin. His mind suddenly became alive and attentive.

---

① cinder-track: 煤渣路。

Why was she going down there? He pulled up on the path on the slope above, and stood staring. He could just make sure of the small black figure moving in the hollow of the failing day. He seemed to see her in the midst of such obscurity, that he was like a clairvoyant①, seeing rather with the mind's eye that with ordinary sight. Yet he could see her positively enough, whilst he kept his eye attentive. He felt, if he looked away from her, in the thick, ugly falling dusk, he would lose her altogether.

He followed her minutely as she moved, direct and intent, like something transmitted rather than stirring in voluntary activity, straight down the field towards the pond. There she stood on the bank for a moment. She never raised her head. Then she waded slowly into the water.

He stood motionless as the small black figure walked slowly and deliberately towards the centre of the pond, very slowly, gradually moving deeper into the motionless water, and still moving forward as the water got up to her breast. Then he could see her no more in the dusk of the dead afternoon.

"There!" he exclaimed. "Would you believe it?"

And he hastened straight down, running over the wet, soddened fields, pushing through the hedges, down into the depression of callous wintry obscurity. It took him several minutes to come to the pond. He stood on the bank, breathing heavily. He could see nothing. His eyes seemed to penetrate the dead water. Yes, perhaps that was the dark shadow of her black clothing beneath the surface of water.

He slowly ventured into the pond. The bottom was deep, soft clay, he sank in, and the water clasped dead cold round his legs. As he stirred he could smell the cold, rotten clay that fouled up into the water. It was objectionable in his lungs. Still, repelled and yet not heeding, he moved deeper into the pond. The cold water rose over his thighs, over his loins,

---

① clairvoyant: 有超人视力的人。

upon his abdomen. The lower part of body was all sunk in the hideous cold element. And the bottom was so deeply soft and uncertain, he was afraid of pitching with his mouth underneath. He could not swim, and was afraid.

He crouched a little, spreading his hands under the water and moving them round, trying to feel for her. The dead cold pond swayed upon his chest. He moved again, a little deeper, and again, with his hands underneath, he felt all around under the water. And he touched her clothing. But it evaded his fingers. He made a desperate effort to grasp it.

And so doing he lost his balance and went under, horribly, suffocating in the foul earthy water, struggling madly for a few moments. At last, after what seemed an eternity, he got his footing, rose again into the air and looked around. He gasped, and knew he was in the world. Then he looked at the water. She had risen near him. He grasped her clothing, and drawing her nearer, turned to take his way to land again.

He went very slowly, carefully, absorbed in the slow process. He rose higher, climbing out of the pond. The water was now only about his legs; he was thankful, full of relief to be out of the clutches of the pond. He lifted her and staggered on to the bank, out of the horror of wet, grey clay.

He laid her down on the bank. She was quite unconscious and running with water. He made the water come from her mouth; he worked to restore her. He did not have to work very long before he could feel the breathing begin again in her; she was breathing heavily naturally. He worked a little longer. He could feel her live beneath his hands; she was coming back. He wiped her face, wrapped her in his overcoat, looked round into the dim, dark grey world, then lifted her and staggered down the bank and across the fields.

It seemed an unthinkably long way, and his burden so heavy, he felt he would never get to the house. But at last he was in the stable-yard, and then in the house-yard. He opened the door and went into the house. In the kitchen he laid her down on the hearth-rug and called. The house was empty. But the fire was burning in the grate.

Then again he kneeled to attend to her. She was breathing regularly, her eyes wide open and as if conscious, but there seemed something missing in her look. She was conscious in herself, but unconscious of her surroundings.

He ran upstairs, took blankets from a bed and put them before the fire to warm. Then he removed her saturated, earthy-smelling clothing, rubbed her dry with a towel, and wrapped her naked in the blankets. Then he went into the dining-room, to look for spirits. There was a little whisky. He drank a gulp himself, and put some into her mouth.

The effect was instantaneous. She looked full into his face, as if she had been seeing him for some time, and yet had only just become conscious of him.

"Dr. Fergusson?" she said.

"What?" he answered.

He was divesting himself of his coat, intending to find some dry clothing upstairs. He could not bear the smell of the dead, clayey water, and he was mortally afraid for his own health.

"What did I do?" she asked.

"Walked into the pond," he replied. He had begun to shudder like one sick, and could hardly attend to her. Her eyes remained full on him; he seemed to be going dark in his mind, looking back at her helplessly. The shuddering became quieter in him; his life came back to him, dark and unknowing, but strong again.

"Was I out of my mind?" she asked, while her eyes were fixed on him all the time.

"Maybe, for the moment," he replied. He felt quiet, because his strength had come back. The strange fretful strain had left him.

"Am I out of my mind now?" she asked.

"Are you?" he reflected a moment. "No," he answered truthfully, "I don't see that you are." He turned his face aside. He was afraid now, because he felt dazed, and felt dimly that her power was stronger than his, in this issue. And she continued to look at him fixedly all the time. "Can you tell me where I shall find some dry things to put on?" he asked.

"Did you dive into the pond for me?" she asked.

"No," he answered. "I walked in. But I went in overhead as well."

There was silence for a moment. He hesitated. He very much wanted to go upstairs to get into dry clothing. But there was another desire in him. And she seemed to hold him. His will seemed to have gone to sleep, and left him, standing there slack before her. But he felt warm inside himself. He did not shudder at all, though his clothes were sodden on him.

"Why did you?" she asked.

"Because I didn't want you to do such a foolish thing," he said.

"It wasn't foolish," she said, still gazing at him as she lay on the floor, with a sofa cushion under her head. "It was the right thing to do. I knew best, then."

"I'll go and shift these wet things," he said. But still he had not the power to move out of her presence, until she sent him. It was as if she had the life of his body in her hands, and he could not extricate himself. Or perhaps he did not want to.

Suddenly she sat up. Then she became aware of her own immediate condition. She felt the blankets about her, she knew her own limbs. For a moment it seemed as if her reason were going. She looked round, with wild eye, as if seeking something. He stood still with fear. She saw her clothing lying scattered.

"Who undressed me?" she asked, her eyes resting full and inevitable on his face.

"I did," he replied, "to bring you round."

For some moments she sat and gazed at him awfully, her lips parted.

"Do you love me, then?" she asked.

He only stood and stared at her, fascinated. His soul seemed to melt.

She shuffled forward on her knees, and put her arms round him, round his legs, as he stood there, pressing her breasts against his knees and thighs, clutching him with strange, convulsive certainty, pressing his thighs against her, drawing him to her face, her throat, as she looked up at him with flaring, humble eyes and transfiguration, triumphant in first possession.

"You love me," she murmured, in strange transport①, yearning and triumphant and confident. "You love me. I know you love me, I know."

And she was passionately kissing his knees, through the wet clothing, passionately and indiscriminately kissing his knees, his legs, as if unaware of everything.

He looked down at the tangled wet hair, the wild, bare, animal shoulders. He was amazed, bewildered and afraid. He had never thought of loving her. He had never wanted to love her. When he rescued her and restored her, he was a doctor, and she was a patient. He had had no single personal thought of her. Nay②, this introduction of the personal element was very distasteful to him, a violation of his professional honour. It was horrible to have her there embracing his knees. It was horrible. He revolted from it, violently. And yet—and yet—he had not the power to break away.

She looked at him again, with the same supplication of powerful love, and that same transcendent, frightening light of triumph. In view of the delicate flame which seemed to come from her face like a light, he was powerless. And yet he had never intended to love her. He had never intended. And something stubborn in him could not give way.

"You love me," she repeated, in a murmur of deep, rhapsodic③ assurance. "You love me."

Her hands were drawing him, drawing him down to her. He was

---

① transport:激动,狂喜。
② Nay:不止于此。
③ rhapsodic:狂热的,兴高采烈的。

afraid, even a little horrified. For he had, really, no intention of loving her. Yet her hands were drawing him towards her. He put out his hand quickly to steady himself, and grasped her bare shoulder. He had no intention of loving her: his whole will was against his yielding. It was horrible. And yet wonderful was the touch of her shoulders, beautiful the shining of her face. Was she perhaps mad? He had a horror of yielding to her. Yet something in him ached also.

  He had been staring away at the door, away from her. But his hand remained on her shoulder. She had gone suddenly very still. He looked down at her. Her eyes were now wide with fear, with doubt; the light was dying from her face; a shadow of terrible greyness was returning. He could not bear the touch of her eyes' question upon him, and the look of death behind the question.

  With an inward groan he gave way, and let his heart yield towards her. A sudden gentle smile came on his face. And her eyes, which never left his face, slowly, slowly filled with tears. He watched the strange water rise in her eyes, like some slow fountain coming up. And his heart seemed to burn and melt away in his breast.

  He could not bear to look at her any more. He dropped on his knees and caught her head. with his arms and pressed her face against his throat. She was very still. His heart, which seemed to have broken, was burning with a kind of agony in his breast. And he felt her slow, hot tears wetting his throat. But he could not move.

  He felt the hot tears wet his neck and the hollows of his neck, and he remained motionless, suspended through one of man's eternities. Only now it had become indispensable to him to have her face pressed close to him; he could never let her go again. He could never let her head go away from the close crutch of his arm. He wanted to remain like that forever, with his heart hurting him in a pain that was also life to him. Without knowing, he was looking down on her damp, soft brown hair.

Then, as it were suddenly, he smelt the horrid stagnant smell of that water. And at the same moment she drew away from him and looked at him. Her eyes were wistful and unfathomable. He was afraid of them, and he fell to kissing her, not knowing what he was doing. He wanted her eyes not to have that terrible, wistful, unfathomable look.

When she turned her face to him again, a faint delicate flush was glowing, and there was again dawning that terrible shining of joy in her eyes, which really terrified him, and yet which he now wanted to see, because he feared the look of doubt still more.

"You love me?" she said, rather faltering.

"Yes." The word cost him a painful effort. Not because it wasn't true. But because it was too newly true. The saying seemed to tear open again his newly-torn heart. And he hardly wanted it to be true, even now.

She lifted her face to him, and he bent forward and kissed her on the mouth, gently, with the one kiss that is an eternal pledge. And as he kissed her his heart strained again in his breast. He never intended to love her. But now it was over. He had crossed over the gulf to her, and all that he had left behind had shrivelled and become void.

After the kiss, her eyes again slowly filled with tears. She sat still, away from him, with her face drooped aside, and her hands folded in her lap. The tears fell very slowly. There was complete silence. He too sat there motionless and silent on the hearth-rug. The strange pain of his heart that was broken seemed to consume him. That he should love her? That this was love! That he should be ripped open in this way! Him, a doctor! How they would all jeer if they knew! It was agony to him to think they might know.

In the curious naked pain of the thought he looked again to her. She was sitting there drooped into a muse. He saw a tear fall, and his heart flared hot. He saw for the first time that one of her shoulders was quite uncovered, one arm bare, he could see one of her small breasts; dimly, because it had become almost dark in the room.

"Why are you crying?" he asked, in an altered voice.

She looked up at him, and behind her tears the consciousness of her situation for the first time brought a dark look of shame to her eyes.

"I'm not crying, really," she said, watching him, half-frightened.

He reached his hand, and softly closed it on her bare arm.

"I love you! I love you!" he said in a soft, low vibrating voice, unlike himself.

She shrank, and dropped her head. The soft, penetrating grip of his hand on her arm distressed her. She looked up at him.

"I want to go," she said. "I want to go and get you some dry things."

"Why?" he said. "I'm all right."

"But I want to go," she said. "And I want you to change your things."

He released her arm, and she wrapped herself in the blanket, looking at him rather frightened. And still she did not rise.

"Kiss me," she said wistfully.

He kissed her, but briefly, half in anger.

Then, after a second, she rose nervously, all mixed up in the blanket. He watched her in her confusion as she tried to extricate herself and wrap herself up so that she could walk. He watched her relentlessly, as she knew. And as she went, the blanket trailing, and he saw a glimpse of her feet and her white leg, he tried to remember her as she was when he had wrapped her up in the blanket. But then he didn't want to remember, because she had been nothing to him then, and his nature revolted from remembering her as she was when she was nothing to him.

A tumbling, muffled noise from within the dark house startled him. Then he heard her voice: "There are clothes." He rose and went to the foot of the stairs, and gathered up the garments she had thrown down. Then he came back to the fire, to rub himself down and dress. He grinned at his own appearance when he had finished.

The fire was sinking, so he put on coal. The house was now quite dark, save for the light of a street-lamp that shone in faintly from beyond the holly trees. He lit the gas with matches he found on the mantelpiece. Then he emptied the pockets of his own clothes, and threw all his wet things in a heap into the scullery. After which he gathered up her sodden clothes, gently, and put them in a separate heap on the copper-top in the scullery.

It was six o'clock on the clock. His own watch had stopped. He ought to go back to the surgery. He waited, and still she did not come down. So he went to the foot of the stairs and called:

"I shall have to go."

Almost immediately he heard her coming down. She had on her best dress of black voile, and her hair was tidy, but still damp. She looked at him—and in spite of herself, smiled.

"I don't like you in those clothes," she said.

"Do I look a sight?" he answered.

They were shy of one another.

"I'll make you some tea," she said.

"No, I must go."

"Must you?" And she looked at him again with the wide, strained, doubtful eyes. And again, from the pain of his breast, he knew how he loved her. He went and bent to kiss her, gently, passionately, with his heart's painful kiss.

"And my hair smells so horrible," she murmured in distraction. "And I'm so awful, I'm so awful! Oh no, I'm too awful." And she broke into bitter, heart-broken sobbing. "You can't want to love me. I'm horrible."

"Don't be silly, don't be silly," he said, trying to comfort her, kissing her, holding her in his arms. "I want you. I want to marry you. We're going to be married, quickly, quickly—tomorrow if I can."

But she only sobbed terribly, and cried:

"I feel awful. I feel awful. I feel I'm horrible to you."

"No, I want you, I want you," was all he answered, blindly, with that terrible intonation which frightened her almost more than her horror lest he should not want her.

Questions

1. In what ways does the opening scene at the Pervin house help us understand Mabel and the events that follow?

2. What kind of person is Mabel? Does she undergo some transformations in the story?

3. What do the "pond" and "water" symbolize in the story? How does this symbolism contribute to the theme of the story?

Further Readings

D. H. Lawrence's explorations of the dark strata of unconsciousness and his disclosure of the dark side of industrialization place him unarguably among the greatest writers of his age. Some of his best known short stories are:

1. "Odour of Chrysanthemums"(《菊香》)

2. "The Prussian Officer"(《普鲁士军官》)

3. "The Fox"(《狐》)

4. "The Virgin and the Gypsy"(《处女与吉卜赛人》)

5. "The Women Who Rode Away"(《骑马出走的女人》)

Unit 9　The Man Without a Temperament

About the writer

凯瑟琳·曼斯菲尔德(Katherine Mansfield, 1888 – 1923)是英国短篇小说家。她为短篇小说创作开辟了新的途径,在短篇小说创作中完美演绎了现代主义写作技巧与手法。曼斯菲尔德在短篇小说领域取得了乔伊斯与伍尔夫在长篇小说领域所取得的成就。

曼斯菲尔德1888年出生于新西兰首都惠灵顿,父亲是一位成功的银行家,在惠灵顿社交界享有很高威望。1903年,父亲将她送至伦敦皇后学院(Queen's College)深造。1906年,曼斯菲尔德结业后回到新西兰。1908年,为了在文学方面获得更好发展,曼斯菲尔德重返伦敦,开始了职业写作生涯。1918年她与批评家约翰·米德尔顿·默里(John Middleton Murry, 1889 –1957)结婚。1923年,曼斯菲尔德因肺结核逝世于法国枫丹白露,年仅34岁。

在短暂的一生中,曼斯菲尔德共创作了93篇短篇小说,这些作品被陆续收录于几部短篇小说集中。1911年,曼斯菲尔德出版第一部短篇小说集《在德国公寓》(In a German Pension),反响良好。《幸福集》(Bliss and Other Stories, 1920)与《园会集》(The Garden Party and Other Stories, 1922)两部小说集则正式奠定了曼斯菲尔德在英国文坛的地位。此外还有默里整理出版的小说集《鸽巢集》(The Dove's Nest and Others Stories, 1923)、《稚气集》(Something Childish and Other Stories, 1924)等。

曼斯菲尔德被称为"英国的契诃夫",其早期作品的风格与契诃夫的现实主义短篇小说相似。短篇小说集《在德国公寓》中的8个短篇小说均存在明显的对契诃夫短篇小说的模仿痕迹。与契诃夫一样,曼斯菲尔德在这些作品中并不追求离奇曲折的情节,而是从看似平凡的小处着手,着重描写婚姻带给女性的屈辱与压抑,以及婢仆的悲惨生活。

1917年,她创作完成著名的短篇小说《序曲》("Prelude")。这部作品在内容方面挖掘了新西兰的乡土文化与田园情趣,表现了作家对新西兰家乡的美好回忆。在形式方面,《序曲》采取了一种介于诗歌与散文之间的小说形式。故事共分12个部分,每一部分讲述一个生活片段,整个故事由这一系列生活片段与联想串联而成,各片段之间则通过象征性物体或行为的不断重现而得以衔接。在这部作品中,曼斯菲尔德创造了一种新的小说形式,形成自己独特的创作风格,她将之命名为"序曲体"。这种新型小说形式采取一种自然展开、完全开放的结构,采用多重叙述视角,巧妙剪贴一个个片段。曼斯菲尔德也由此实现了从现实主义文学继承者到现代主义文学开拓者的转变。

曼斯菲尔德短篇小说创作的一个显著特征是无情节结构。传统短篇小说以情节取胜,而她的作品摆脱了情节的束缚,或刻意淡化情节,或采用无情节结构。其短篇小说的另一个特征是对意识流技巧的运用。曼斯菲尔德摒弃了传统短篇小说对"钟表时间"的依赖,取而代之的是人物的"心理时间",她多采用一天或一夜的框架模式,通过描写人物的意识活动构建一个交错凌乱的时空。同时,她运用大量的象征暗示与内心独白深入探求小说人物的精神世界,表现人物的孤立、沮丧与幻灭。此外,曼斯菲尔德擅长细节描写,通过精心选择有意义的细节来刻画人物,表现人物之间复杂微妙的关系。语言方面,曼斯菲尔德的作品措辞讲究,用词精当。她仔细斟酌每个句子的长短、音调,以及各个段落的起伏,使文字能够与作品主题及情境气氛相契合,从而令原本就充满抒情意味的作品回荡着散文诗般的旋律。

About the story

短篇小说《没有脾气的男人》("The Man Without a Temperament")带有明显的自传性质。1919年9月,曼斯菲尔德因肺病去意大利疗养。12月16日,默里收到她几封诉苦的信,遂前往意大利探望她,陪她住到次年1月2日。这次短暂的相聚并未修复两人之间日益加深的裂痕。1920年1月10日晚,曼斯菲尔德在身体与精神都十分虚弱的情况下构思出了这个短篇小说。故事讲述了一对英国夫妇在法国度假时一天中的生活片段。罗伯特陪伴患有严重心脏病的妻子来到法国海滨的一座别墅公寓疗养,他对妻子关怀备至、百依百顺,内心却深感压抑与痛苦。

《没有脾气的男人》是曼斯菲尔德编织最为紧密、艺术成就最高的作品之一。该小说多处运用了意识流写作手法,最典型的例子是穿插于故事中的三段回忆。第一次回忆源于一封信件。吉妮开心地读着朋友的来信,信中提及一场大雪。这让罗伯特想起了他和妻子在伦敦家中的生活。那是一个清晨,雪下了整整一夜,厚厚的积雪让吉妮兴奋不已,她轻快地跑下楼梯,请求丈夫带家中的小猫去欣赏它有生以来的第一场雪。第二次回忆发生于罗伯特独自外出散步期间。一个深秋下午,他冒着风雨赶回了家,刚好来得及在晚餐前洗个澡,换身衣服。吉妮坐在客厅的炉火旁和他打招呼,晚餐已经准备好了,来访的朋友们快活地说笑着。第三次回忆是医生如实告知他吉妮的病情,以及吉妮请求他陪自己出国养病。叙述时空的不停转换与主人公意识的不断跳跃展现了作者高超的叙事技巧。

小说也多次运用了象征主义写作手法。作品中最重要的象征是罗伯特小指上的那枚印章戒指。作者多次描写罗伯特转动印章戒指这一细节。故事开篇便写到罗伯特"转着小指上那沉甸甸的印章戒指",这一动作在接下来的情节中又出现了三次,而在故事的结尾处则是吉妮转动着丈夫的戒指。罗伯特不停地转动戒指,似乎是想要取下戒指、摆脱婚姻,又似乎是在提醒自己要牢记作为丈夫的责任与义务。戒指象征着妻子的疾病对罗伯特的束缚与囚困。同样具有此种象征意义的还有环境描写。酒店内部两棵枝叶折断的棕榈树"活像两个老乞丐";花园里的"每一片叶子、每一朵花都摊开了,一动不动,好像精疲力竭了";酒店外贫民区的道路"又窄又脏,两边是破旧的高房屋";深谷下的河床已经干涸,"遍地是小破房子,石质阳台已经坍毁"……破败老旧及毫无生气的景象与吉妮的病情相互映照,似乎象征着她每况愈下的身体状态。

此外,小说人物的姓名也富有深意。首先,罗伯特的姓氏塞尔斯拜(Salesby)如果颠倒一下顺序就成了 by Sales,这暗示着他为了金钱与富家小姐结合,从而卖掉了自己,成为一个百依百顺的"没有脾气的男人"。其次,妻子吉妮并不像作者所描述的那样无条件地爱着丈夫。在罗伯特的第一段回忆中,吉妮一大早下楼吃早餐,关心的不是丈夫,而是小猫;在第二段回忆中,她只顾着与朋友聊天,却将刚赶回家的丈夫撇在一边;在第三段回忆中,她坚持要丈夫陪自己出国养病,她说:"你是一切。你是面包和酒。"再次,作者将闪电比作一只不断挣扎着的受伤的小鸟,而这正是罗伯特本人的写照。最后,吉妮转动丈夫小指上的印章戒指,意在反复提醒他的地位和他所应承担的义务。

　　小说结尾意味深长，罗伯特起床帮吉妮打死了帐子里的一只蚊子。被妻子问及是否介意陪她出国养病时，罗伯特只是弯下身，亲吻了妻子，然后低声说了一句"Rot!" rot 为多义词，意为"腐烂，变质"和"废话，胡说"。罗伯特究竟何意？这给读者留下了解读的空间。

The Man Without a Temperament

　　He stood at the hall door turning the ring, turning the heavy signet ring① upon his little finger while his glance travelled coolly, deliberately, over the round tables and basket chairs scattered about the glassed-in veranda②. He pursed his lips—he might have been going to whistle—but he did not whistle—only turned the ring—turned the ring on his pink, freshly washed hands.

　　Over in the corner sat the Two Topknots③, drinking a decoction they always drank at this hour—something whitish, greyish, in glasses, with little husks floating on the top—and rooting in a tin full of paper shavings for pieces of speckled biscuit, which they broke, dropped into the glasses and fished for with spoons. Their two coils of knitting④, like two snakes, slumbered beside the tray.

　　The American Woman sat where she always sat against the glass wall, in the shadow of a great creeping thing with wide open purple eyes that pressed—that flattened itself against the glass, hungrily watching her. And she knoo⑤ it was there—she knoo it was looking at her just that way. She played up to it; she gave herself little airs⑥. Sometimes she even pointed at

---

① signet ring：印章戒指。
② the glassed-in veranda：玻璃游廊。
③ the Two Topknots：两个梳着顶髻的女人。
④ coils of knitting：毛线团。
⑤ knoo：knew。
⑥ gave herself little airs：有些装腔作势。

it, crying: "Isn't that the most terrible thing you've ever seen! Isn't that ghoulish!" It was on the other side of the veranda, after all ... and besides it couldn't touch her, could it, Klaymongso①? She was an American Woman, wasn't she, Klaymongso, and she'd just go right away to her Consul. Klaymongso, curled in her lap, with her torn antique brocade bag, a grubby handkerchief, and a pile of letters from home on top of him, sneezed for reply.

The other tables were empty. A glance passed between the American and the Topknots. She gave a foreign little shrug; they waved an understanding biscuit. But he saw nothing. Now he was still, now from his eyes you saw he listened. "Hoo-e-zip-zoo-oo!" sounded the lift. The iron cage clanged open. Light dragging steps sounded across the hall, coming towards him. A hand, like a leaf, fell on his shoulder. A soft voice said: "Let's go and sit over there—where we can see the drive. The trees are so lovely." And he moved forward with the hand still on his shoulder, and the light, dragging steps beside his. He pulled out a chair and she sank into it, slowly, leaning her head against the back, her arms falling along the sides.

"Won't you bring the other up closer? It's such miles away." But he did not move.

"Where's your shawl?" he asked.

"Oh!" She gave a little groan of dismay. "How silly I am. I've left it upstairs on the bed. Never mind. Please don't go for it. I shan't want it. I know I shan't."

"You'd better have it." And he turned and swiftly crossed the veranda into the dim hall with its scarlet plush and gilt furniture—conjuror's furniture—its Notice of Services at the English Church, its green baize board with the unclaimed letters climbing the black lattice, huge "Presentation" clock that struck the hours at the half-hours, bundles of sticks and umbrellas

---

① Klaymongso:此处为狗的名字。

and sunshades in the clasp of a brown wooden bear, past the two crippled palms, two ancient beggars① at the foot of the staircase, up the marble stairs three at a time, past the life-size group on the landing of two stout peasant children with their marble pinnies full of marble grapes, and along the corridor, with its piled-up wreckage of old tin boxes, leather trunks, canvas holdalls, to their room.

The servant girl was in their room, singing loudly while she emptied soapy water into a pail. The windows were open wide, the shutters put back, and the light glared in. She had thrown the carpets and the big white pillows over the balcony rails; the nets were looped up from the beds; on the writing-table there stood a pan of fluff and match-ends. When she saw him her small, impudent eyes snapped and her singing changed to humming. But he gave no sign. His eyes searched the glaring room. Where the devil was the shawl!

"Vous desirez, Monsieur?"② mocked the servant girl.

No answer. He had seen it. He strode across the room, grabbed the grey cobweb and went out, banging the door. The servant girl's voice at its loudest and shrillest followed him along the corridor.

"Oh, there you are. What happened? What kept you? The tea's here, you see. I've just sent Antonio off for the hot water. Isn't it extraordinary? I must have told him about it sixty times at least, and still he doesn't bring it. Thank you. That's very nice. One does just feel the air when one bends forward."

"Thanks." He took his tea and sat down in the other chair. "No, nothing to eat."

"Oh, do! Just one, you had so little at lunch and it's hours before dinner."

Her shawl dropped off as she bent forward to hand him the biscuits. He

---

① two ancient beggars: 指前文提到的两棵棕榈树。
② "Vous desirez, Monsieur?": (法语)您要什么吗, 先生?

took one and put it in his saucer.

"Oh, those trees along the drive," she cried. "I could look at them for ever. They are like the most exquisite huge ferns. And you see that one with the grey-silver bark and the clusters of cream-coloured flowers, I pulled down a head of them yesterday to smell, and the scent"—she shut her eyes at the memory and her voice thinned away, faint, airy—"was like freshly ground nutmegs." A little pause. She turned to him and smiled. "You do know what nutmegs smell like—do you Robert?"

And he smiled back at her. "Now how am I going to prove to you that I do?"

Back came Antonio with not only the hot water—with letters on a salver and three rolls of paper.

"Oh, the post! Oh, how lovely! Oh, Robert, they mustn't be all for you! Have they just come, Antonio?" Her thin hands flew up and hovered over the letters that Antonio offered her, bending forward.

"Just this moment, Signora," grinned Antonio. "I took—a them from the postman myself. I made—a the postman give them for me."

"Noble Antonio!" laughed she. "There—those are mine, Robert; the rest are yours."

Antonio wheeled sharply, stiffened, the grin went out of his face. His striped linen jacket and his flat gleaming fringe made him look like a wooden doll.

Mr. Salesby put the letters into his pocket; the papers lay on the table. He turned the ring, turned the signet ring on his little finger and stared in front of him, blinking, vacant.

But she—with her teacup in one hand, the sheets of thin paper in the other, her head tilted back, her lips open, a brush of bright colour on her cheek-bones, sipped, sipped, drank ... drank.

"From Lottie," came her soft murmur. "Poor dear ... such trouble ... left foot. She thought ... neuritis ... Doctor Blyth ... flat foot ... massage. So many robins this year ... maid most satisfactory ... Indian Colonel ... every grain of rice separate ... very heavy fall of snow." And her wide lighted eyes looked up from the letter. "Snow, Robert! Think of it!" And she touched the little dark violets pinned on her thin bosom and went back to the letter.

... Snow. Snow in London. Millie with the early morning cup of tea. "There's been a terrible fall of snow in the night, sir." "Oh, has there, Millie?" The curtains ring apart, letting in the pale, reluctant light. He raises himself in the bed; he catches a glimpse of the solid houses opposite framed in white, of their window boxes full of great sprays of white coral①... In the bathroom—overlooking the back garden. Snow—heavy snow over everything. The lawn is covered with a wavy pattern of cat's paws; there is a thick, thick icing on the garden table; the withered pods of the laburnum tree are white tassels; only here and there in the ivy is a dark leaf showing ... Warming his back at the dining-room fire, the paper drying over a chair. Millie with the bacon. "Oh, if you please, Sir, there's two little boys come as will do the steps and front② for a shilling, shall I let them?" ... And then flying lightly, lightly down the stairs—Jinnie. "Oh, Robert, isn't it wonderful! Oh, what a pity it has to melt. Where's the pussy-wee③?" "I'll get him from Millie." ... "Millie, you might just hand me up the kitten if you've got him down there." "Very good, sir." He feels the little beating heart under his hand. "Come on, old chap, your missus wants you." "Oh, Robert, do show him the snow—his first snow. Shall I open the window and give him a little piece on his paw to hold? ..."

"Well, that's very satisfactory on the whole—very. Poor Lottie! Darling Anne! How I only wish I could send them something of this," she cried, waving her letters at the brilliant, dazzling garden. "More tea, Robert?

---

① sprays of white coral: 白珊瑚枝。
② do the steps and front: 清扫台阶上及门前的积雪。
③ pussy-wee: 小猫咪。

Robert dear, more tea?"

"No, thanks, no. It was very good," he drawled.

"Well, mine wasn't. Mine was just like chopped hay. Oh, here comes the Honeymoon Couple."

Half striding, half running, carrying a basket between them and rods and lines, they came up the drive, up the shallow steps.

"My! have you been out fishing?" cried the American Woman. They were out of breath, they panted: "Yes, yes, we have been out in a little boat all day. We have caught seven. Four are good to eat. But three we shall give away. To the children."

Mrs. Salesby turned her chair to look; the Topknots laid the snakes down. They were a very dark young couple—black hair, olive skin, brilliant eyes and teeth. He was dressed "English fashion" in a flannel jacket, white trousers and shoes. Round his neck he wore a silk scarf; his head, with his hair brushed back, was bare. And he kept mopping his forehead, rubbing his hands with a brilliant handkerchief. Her white skirt had a patch of wet; her neck and throat were stained a deep pink. When she lifted her arms big half-hoops of perspiration showed under her arm-pits; her hair clung in wet curls to her cheeks. She looked as though her young husband had been dipping her in the sea and fishing her out again to dry in the sun and then—in with her again—all day.

"Would Klaymongso like a fish?" they cried. Their laughing voices charged with excitement beat against the glassed-in veranda like birds and a strange, saltish smell came from the basket.

"You will sleep well tonight," said a Topknot, picking her ear with a knitting needle while the other Topknot smiled and nodded.

The Honeymoon Couple looked at each other. A great wave seemed to go over them. They gasped, gulped, staggered a little and then came up laughing—laughing.

"We cannot go upstairs; we are too tired. We must have tea just as we are. Here—coffee. No—tea. No—coffee. Tea—coffee, Antonio!" Mrs. Salesby turned.

"Robert! Robert!" Where was he? He wasn't there. Oh, there he was at the other end of the veranda, with his back turned, smoking a cigarette. "Robert, shall we go for our little turn?"

"Right." He stumped the cigarette into an ash-tray and sauntered over, his eyes on the ground. "Will you be warm enough?"

"Oh, quite."

"Sure?"

"Well," she put her hand on his arm, "perhaps"—and gave his arm the faintest pressure—"it's not upstairs, it's only in the hall—perhaps you'd get me my cape. Hanging up."

He came back with it and she bent her small head while he dropped it on her shoulders. Then, very stiff, he offered her his arm. She bowed sweetly to the people of the veranda while he just covered a yawn, and they went down the steps together.

"Vous avez voo ca!"① said the American Woman.

"He is not a man," said the Two Topknots, "He is an ox②. I say to my sister in the morning and at night when we are in bed, I tell her—No man is he, but an ox!"

Wheeling, tumbling, swooping, the laughter of the Honeymoon Couple dashed against the glass of the veranda.

The sun was still high. Every leaf, every flower in the garden lay open, motionless, as if exhausted, and a sweet, rich, rank smell filled the quivering air. Out of the thick, fleshy leaves of a cactus there rose an aloe stem loaded with pale flowers that looked as though they had been cut out of butter; light flashed upon the lifted spears of the palms; over a bed of

---

① Vous avez voo ca！：（原文为蹩脚的法语）你有这个！
② ox：被阉割的公牛。

scarlet waxen flowers some black insects "zoom-zoomed"; a great, gaudy creeper, orange splashed with jet, sprawled against the wall.

"I don't need my cape after all," said she. "It's really too warm." So he took it off and carried it over his arm. "Let us go down this path here. I feel so well today—marvellously better. Good heavens—look at those children! And to think it's November!"

In a corner of the garden there were two brimming tubs of water. Three little girls, having thoughtfully taken off their drawers and hung them on a bush, their skirts clasped to their waists, were standing in the tubs and tramping up and down. They screamed; their hair fell over their faces; they splashed one another. But suddenly, the smallest, who had a tub to herself, glanced up and saw who was looking. For a moment she seemed overcome with terror, then clumsily she struggled and strained out of her tub, and still holding her clothes above her waist, "The Englishman! The Englishman!" she shrieked and fled away to hide. Shrieking and screaming the other two followed her. In a moment they were gone; in a moment there was nothing but the two brimming tubs and their little drawers on the bush.

"How—very—extraordinary!" said she. "What made them so frightened? Surely they were much too young to ..." She looked up at him. She thought he looked pale—but wonderfully handsome with that great tropical tree behind him with its long, spiked thorns.

For a moment he did not answer. Then he met her glance, and smiling his slow smile, "Très rum!"① said he.

Très rum! Oh, she felt quite faint. Oh, why should she love him so much just because he said a thing like that. Très rum! That was Robert all over. Nobody else but Robert could ever say such a thing. To be so wonderful, so brilliant, so learned, and then to say in that queer, boyish voice ... She could have wept.

---

① Très rum!: (法语)非常离奇!

"You know you're very absurd, sometimes," said she.

"I am," he answered. And they walked on.

But she was tired. She had had enough. She did not want to walk any more.

"Leave me here and go for a little constitutional①, won't you? I'll be in one of these long chairs. What a good thing you've got my cape; you won't have to go upstairs for a rug. Thank you, Robert, I shall look at that delicious heliotrope … You won't be gone long?"

"No—no. You don't mind being left?"

"Silly! I want you to go. I can't expect you to drag after your invalid wife every minute … How long will you be?"

He took out his watch. "It's just after half-past four. I'll be back at a quarter-past five."

"Back at a quarter-past five," she repeated, and she lay still in the long chair and folded her hands.

He turned away. Suddenly he was back again. "Look here, would you like my watch?" And he dangled it before her.

"Oh!" She caught her breath. "Very, very much." And she clasped the watch, the warm watch, the darling watch in her fingers. "Now go quickly."

The gates of the Pension Villa Excelsior② were open wide, jammed open against some bold geraniums. Stooping a little, staring straight ahead, walking swiftly, he passed through them and began climbing the hill that wound behind the town like a great rope looping the villas together. The dust lay thick. A carriage came bowling along driving towards the Excelsior. In it sat the General and the Countess; they had been for his daily airing③. Mr. Salesby stepped to one side but the dust beat up, thick, white, stifling

---

① constitutional: 保健散步。
② Pension Villa Excelsior: 埃克塞尔西奥别墅公寓。
③ his daily airing: 将军每天都出去兜风。

like wool. The Countess just had time to nudge the General.

"There he goes," she said spitefully.

But the General gave a loud caw and refused to look.

"It is the Englishman," said the driver, turning round and smiling. And the Countess threw up her hands and nodded so amiably that he spat with satisfaction and gave the stumbling horse a cut①.

On—on—past the finest villas in the town, magnificent palaces, palaces worth coming any distance to see, past the public gardens with the carved grottoes and statues and stone animals drinking at the fountain, into a poorer quarter. Here the road ran narrow and foul between high lean houses, the ground floors of which were scooped and hollowed into stables and carpenters' shops. At a fountain ahead of him two old hags were beating linen②. As he passed them they squatted back on their haunches, stared, and then their "A-hak-kak-kak!" with the slap, slap, of the stone on the linen sounded after him.

He reached the top of the hill; he turned a corner and the town was hidden. Down he looked into a deep valley with a dried-up river bed at the bottom. This side and that was covered with small dilapidated houses that had broken stone verandas where the fruit lay drying, tomato lanes in the garden and from the gates to the doors a trellis of vines. The late sunlight, deep, golden, lay in the cup of the valley; there was a smell of charcoal in the air. In the gardens the men were cutting grapes. He watched a man standing in the greenish shade, raising up, holding a black cluster in one hand, taking the knife from his belt, cutting, laying the bunch in a flat boat-shaped basket. The man worked leisurely, silently, taking hundreds of years over the job. On the hedges on the other side of the road there were grapes small as berries, growing among the stones. He leaned against a wall, filled

---

① gave the stumbling horse a cut:给了那匹打着趔趄的马一鞭子。
② two old hags were beating linen:两个丑老婆子正在捶打亚麻布。

his pipe, put a match to it …

Leaned across a gate, turned up the collar of his mackintosh. It was going to rain. It didn't matter; he was prepared for it. You didn't expect anything else in November. He looked over the bare field. From the corner by the gate there came the smell of swedes, a great stack of them, wet, rank coloured. Two men passed walking towards the straggling village. "Good day!" "Good day!" By Jove! he had to hurry if he was going to catch that train home. Over the gate, across a field, over the stile, into the lane, swinging along in the drifting rain and dusk … Just home in time for a bath and a change before supper … In the drawing-room, Jinnie is sitting pretty nearly in the fire. "Oh, Robert, I didn't hear you come in. Did you have a good time? How nice you smell! A present?" "Some bits of blackberry I picked for you. Pretty colour." "Oh, lovely, Robert! Dennis and Beaty are coming to supper." Supper—cold beef, potatoes in their jackets①, claret, household bread. They are gay—everybody's laughing. "Oh, we all know Robert," says Dennis, breathing on his eyeglasses and polishing them. "By the way, Dennis, I picked up a very jolly little edition of …"

A clock struck. He wheeled sharply. What time was it. Five? A quarter past? Back, back the way he came. As he passed through the gates he saw her on the look-out. She got up, waved and slowly she came to meet him, dragging the heavy cape. In her hand she carried a spray of heliotrope.

"You're late," she cried gaily. "You're three minutes late. Here's your watch; it's been very good while you were away. Did you have a nice time? Was it lovely? Tell me. Where did you go?"

"I say—put this on," he said, taking the cape from her. "Yes, I will. Yes, it's getting chilly. Shall we go up to our room?"

When they reached the lift she was coughing. He frowned.

---

① potatoes in their jackets: 带皮的马铃薯。

"It's nothing. I haven't been out too late. Don't be cross." She sat down on one of the red plush chairs while he rang and rang, and then, getting no answer, kept his finger on the bell.

"Oh, Robert, do you think you ought to?"

"Ought to what?"

The door of the salon opened. "What is that? Who is making that noise?" sounded from within. Klaymongso began to yelp. "Caw! Caw! Caw!" came from the General. A Topknot darted out with one hand to her ear, opened the staff door, "Mr. Queet! Mr. Queet!" she bawled. That brought the manager up at a run.

"Is that you ringing the bell, Mr. Salesby? Do you want the lift? Very good, sir. I'll take you up myself. Antonio wouldn't have been a minute; he was just taking off his apron—" And having ushered them in, the oily manager went to the door of the salon. "Very sorry you should have been troubled, ladies and gentlemen." Salesby stood in the cage, sucking in his cheeks, staring at the ceiling and turning the ring, turning the signet ring on his little finger ...

Arrived in their room he went swiftly over to the washstand, shook the bottle, poured her out a dose① and brought it across.

"Sit down. Drink it. And don't talk." And he stood over her while she obeyed. Then he took the glass, rinsed it and put it back in its case. "Would you like a cushion?"

"No, I'm quite all right. Come over here. Sit down by me just a minute, will you, Robert? Ah, that's very nice." She turned and thrust the piece of heliotrope in the lapel of his coat. "That," she said, "is most becoming." And then she leaned her head against his shoulder and he put his arm round her.

"Robert—" her voice like a sigh—like a breath.

---

① poured her out a dose: 为她倒出一份药水。

"Yes—"

They sat there for a long while. The sky flamed, paled; the two white beds were like two ships ... At last he heard the servant girl running along the corridor with the hot-water cans, and gently he released her and turned on the light.

"Oh, what time is it? Oh, what a heavenly evening. Oh, Robert, I was thinking while you were away this afternoon ..."

They were the last couple to enter the dining-room. The Countess was there with her lorgnette and her fan, the General was there with his special chair and the air cushion and the small rug over his knees. The American Woman was there showing Klaymongso a copy of the *Saturday Evening Post* ... "We're having a feast of reason and a flow of soul①." The Two Topknots were there feeling over the peaches and the pears in their dish of fruit and putting aside all they considered unripe or overripe to show to the manager, and the Honeymoon Couple leaned across the table, whispering, trying not to burst out laughing.

Mr. Queet, in everyday clothes and white canvas shoes, served the soup, and Antonio, in full evening dress, handed it round.

"No," said the American Woman, "take it away, Antonio. We can't eat soup. We can't eat anything mushy, can we, Klaymongso?"

"Take them back and fill them to the rim!" said the Topknots, and they turned and watched while Antonio delivered the message.

"What is it? Rice? Is it cooked?" The Countess peered through her lorgnette. "Mr. Queet, the General can have some of this soup if it is cooked."

"Very good, Countess."

The Honeymoon Couple had their fish instead.

---

① having a feast of reason and a flow of soul：享受一桌理性的筵席与一场灵魂的交流。

"Give me that one. That's the one I caught. No, it's not. Yes, it is. No, it's not. Well, it's looking at me with its eye, so it must be. Tee! Hee! Hee!" Their feet were locked together under the table.

"Robert, you're not eating again. Is anything the matter?"

"No. Off food①, that's all."

"Oh, what a bother. There are eggs and spinach coming. You don't like spinach, do you? I must tell them in future ..."

An egg and mashed potatoes for the General.

"Mr. Queet! Mr. Queet!"

"Yes, Countess."

"The General's egg's too hard again."

"Caw! Caw! Caw!"

"Very sorry, Countess. Shall I have you another cooked, General?"

They are the first to leave the dining-room. She rises, gathering her shawl and he stands aside, waiting for her to pass, turning the ring, turning the signet ring on his little finger. In the hall Mr. Queet hovers. "I thought you might not want to wait for the lift. Antonio's just serving the finger bowls②. And I'm sorry the bell won't ring. It's out of order. I can't think what's happened."

"Oh, I do hope ..." from her.

"Get in," says he.

Mr. Queet steps after them and slams the door ...

"Robert, do you mind if I go to bed very soon? Won't you go down to the salon or out into the garden? Or perhaps you might smoke a cigar on the balcony. It's lovely out there. And I like cigar smoke. I always did. But if you'd rather ..."

"No, I'll sit here."

He takes a chair and sits on the balcony. He hears her moving about in

---

① Off food:没胃口。
② finger bowls:(餐桌上供客人就餐后清洗手指用的)洗指碗。

the room, lightly, lightly, moving and rustling. Then she comes over to him. "Good night, Robert."

"Good night." He takes her hand and kisses the palm. "Don't catch cold."

The sky is the colour of jade. There are a great many stars; an enormous white moon hangs over the garden. Far away lightning flutters—flutters like a wing—flutters like a broken bird that tries to fly and sinks again and again struggles.

The lights from the salon shine across the garden path and there is the sound of a piano. And once the American Woman, opening the French window to let Klaymongso into the garden, cries: "Have you seen this moon?" But nobody answers.

He gets very cold sitting there, staring at the balcony rail. Finally he comes inside. The moon—the room is painted white with moonlight. The light trembles in the mirrors; the two beds seem to float. She is asleep. He sees her through the nets, half sitting, banked up with pillows, her white hands crossed on the sheet, her white cheeks, her fair hair pressed against the pillow, are silvered over[1]. He undresses quickly, stealthily and gets into bed. Lying there, his hands clasped behind his head …

In his study. Late summer. The virginia creeper just on the turn[2]…

"Well, my dear chap, that's the whole story. That's the long and the short of it. If she can't cut away for the next two years and give a decent climate a chance she don't stand a dog's—h'm—show[3]. Better be frank about these things." "Oh, certainly …" "And hang it all[4], old man, what's to prevent you going with her? It isn't as though you've got a regular

---

[1] are silvered over: 整个儿被镀上了一层银。
[2] The virginia creeper just on the turn: 五叶地锦的叶子正在变色。
[3] If she can't cut away for the next two years and give a decent climate a chance she don't stand a dog's—h'm—show: 如果她不能马上离开两年, 到气候适宜的地方去, 那她就绝无可能恢复健康了。
[4] hang it all: 见鬼。

job like us wage earners. You can do what you do wherever you are—" "Two years." "Yes, I should give it two years. You'll have no trouble about letting this house, you know. As a matter of fact ..."

He is with her. "Robert, the awful thing is—I suppose it's my illness—I simply feel I could not go alone. You see—you're everything. You're bread and wine, Robert, bread and wine. Oh, my darling—what am I saying? Of course I could, of course I won't take you away ..."

He hears her stirring. Does she want something?

"Boogles?"

Good Lord! She is talking in her sleep. They haven't used that name for years.

"Boogles. Are you awake?"

"Yes, do you want anything?"

"Oh, I'm going to be a bother. I'm so sorry. Do you mind? There's a wretched mosquito inside my net—I can hear him singing. Would you catch him? I don't want to move because of my heart."

"No, don't move. Stay where you are." He switches on the light, lifts the net. "Where is the little beggar? Have you spotted him?"

"Yes, there, over by the corner. Oh, I do feel such a fiend to have dragged you out of bed. Do you mind dreadfully?"

"No, of course not." For a moment he hovers① in his blue and white pyjamas. Then, "Got him," he said.

"Oh, good. Was he a juicy one②?"

"Beastly." He went over to the washstand and dipped his fingers in water. "Are you all right now? Shall I switch off the light?"

"Yes, please. No. Boogles! Come back here a moment. Sit down by me. Give me your hand." She turns his signet ring. "Why weren't you asleep? Boogles, listen. Come closer. I sometimes wonder—do you mind awfully being out here with me?"

---

① hover: 这里指来回折腾打蚊子。
② a juicy one: 一只吸饱了血的蚊子。

He bends down. He kisses her. He tucks her in①. He smooths the pillow.

"Rot!" he whispers.

Questions

1. How does Katherine Mansfield present Mr. Salesby to the reader?
2. How do you interpret the ending of the story?

Further Readings

Katherine Mansfield's short stories are famous for their plotless structure and symbolism. The following are some of her important short stories.

1. "Bliss"(《幸福》)
2. "At the Bay"(《在海湾》)
3. "The Garden Party"(《园会》)

---

① He tucks her in:他为她掖好被子。

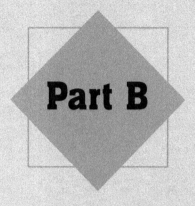

American Short Stories

Unit 10　The Birthmark

About the writer

　　纳撒尼尔·霍桑（Nathaniel Hawthorne，1804 –1864）是美国19世纪的浪漫主义小说家，擅长在作品中对人物心理进行全方位的分析和展示，奠定了心理分析小说的基础。霍桑的代表作是长篇小说《红字》(*The Scarlet Letter*, 1850)，其短篇小说的代表作有《小伙子古德蒙·布朗》("Young Goodman Brown", 1935)、《胎记》("The Birthmark", 1843)、《牧师的黑面纱》("The Minister's Black Veil", 1832)等。

　　霍桑1804年出生于马萨诸塞州萨勒姆镇一个具有浓厚清教主义氛围的破落贵族家庭。1821年，他进入缅因州的博多因学院学习，大学期间开始写作。1839年，霍桑任职波士顿海关，有了稳定的收入，同时积累了丰富的创作素材。之后，霍桑创作出一系列令人惊叹的作品，包括长篇小说《红字》、《带有七个尖角的房子》(*The House of the Seven Gables*, 1851)、《福谷传奇》(*The Blithedale Romance*, 1852)、《玉石雕像》(*The Marble Faun*, 1860)，以及短篇小说集《故事新编》(*Twice-told Tales*, 1837)、《古宅青苔》(*Mosses from an Old Manse*, 1846)等。

　　短篇小说《牧师的黑面纱》较好地体现了霍桑的创作主题。故事中，倍受教民爱戴的胡珀牧师突然在脸上蒙上黑纱，并坚决不许克拉克神父摘去。黑面纱具有双重象征意义：一方面，黑面纱完全掩盖了牧师的面目，但并未影响他的视力，反而使一切蒙上一层黑影。在牧师看来，好像到处充满了罪恶。另一方面，在人们看来，牧师脸上的黑面纱象征着牧师的罪恶，要么是他玩弄了良家少女，要么是他杀死了挚友或情人。霍桑借由这种意义含混的象征手法表达了自己的观点：人人皆有罪，罪恶与人类如影随行。

　　长篇小说《红字》是美国浪漫主义小说的代表作，同时也开启了美国心理分析小说的先河。小说讲述了一个发生在殖民时期新英格兰的爱情悲剧,女主人公海丝特·白兰嫁给了医生奇灵渥斯,可他们之间没有爱情。之后,白兰与牧师丁梅斯代尔相恋并生下女儿珠儿。因触犯通奸罪,白兰被责罚戴上标志"通奸"的红色"A"字示众。但白兰始终拒绝说出孩子的父亲是谁。奇灵渥斯发誓报仇,之后他发现丁梅斯代尔是珠儿的父亲,就对牧师进行了长期的心理折磨。牧师不堪忍受内心的煎熬,心力交瘁而死。小说中,红字"A"是贯穿全书的主线,具有多重象征意义。最初,"A"字表示通奸罪(adultery)。之后,白兰带着珠儿住到远离萨勒姆镇的林中小屋,靠做针线活为生,并把多余的收入用于救济他人,此时"A"字意味着"能干"(able)、"令人敬佩的"(adorable)、"天使"(angel)等。小说凸显了霍桑的"原罪"思想:无论是白兰、奇灵渥斯、丁梅斯代尔,还是刑台前的普通看客,几乎每个人都是有罪的。尽管人人生而有罪,但人们可以通过善行和忏悔洗刷罪恶,获得救赎。

尽管霍桑家庭生活美满,但他在思想上经常沉浸于孤寂之中。霍桑的作品往往不会描写他周围的人和事,而是带有一种神秘和超自然的色彩,给读者带来虚实难辨、似小说又似寓言的独特审美感受。霍桑以"传奇"(romance)一词阐述自己的创作理念,他认为,"传奇作为艺术创作,必须严格遵守艺术法则,如果背离人性的真实,同样是不可原谅的罪过"。由此可知,尽管霍桑的作品远离现实生活,却深刻地揭露了人性的阴暗面,引起了读者的共鸣。

About the story

短篇小说《胎记》收录于《古宅青苔》,反映了霍桑的科技观。男主人公阿尔默是一位科学家,他娶了一位漂亮的女子乔治亚娜为妻。一天,阿尔默突然发现妻子的脸颊上有一块绯红色的小手形状的胎记。乔治亚娜将之视为天使在她脸上留下的印记,认为这是自己的迷人之处。但在阿尔默看来,这象征着罪恶、伤悲、衰败和死亡。于是他千方百计要将它去除,以使妻子成为他眼中完美无瑕的人。通过一次次科学实验,他终于配置出可以消除胎记的药。妻子服下后,胎记逐渐消失,但最终失去了性命。

小说中,阿尔默是一位成功的科学家,他有自己的实验室和助手,藏有大量自然科学书籍,做过很多成功实验,甚至制造了能延长人寿命的神奇药水。

他似乎与上帝一样无所不能。在实验室取得成功后,他转而追求爱情,迎娶了美丽的乔治亚娜。他深爱自己的妻子,却对她脸上的一小块胎记耿耿于怀,认为它破坏了妻子的完美。他对胎记的嫌恶与日剧增,胎记甚至成为他生活的主宰。清晨,他睁开眼睛后首先看到的就是这个胎记;傍晚,坐在壁炉前,借着火光他偷偷地打量着妻子的脸;就连梦里面他都能梦见这个可怕的胎记,他梦见自己亲手切掉了已经深入妻子心脏的那只小手形状的胎记。

阿尔默对胎记的恐惧已经远超对妻子的爱,胎记给他们的生活蒙上了厚厚的阴影。每当发觉阿尔默在盯着自己的脸时,乔治亚娜就会因为恐惧而不由自主地颤抖,她的脸色霎时变得异常苍白,绯红色的胎记益发醒目。"Georgiana soon learned to shudder at his gaze. It needed but a glance with the peculiar expression that his face often wore to change the roses of her cheek into a deathlike paleness, amid which the crimson hand was brought strongly out, like a bass-relief of ruby on the whitest marble."无奈之下,乔治亚娜请求丈夫不惜一切风险用科学手段去除这个胎记,否则两人都会疯掉。对此,阿尔默兴奋不已,认为自己完全有能力将造物主不完美的作品变得完美无瑕,他将取得巨大成功。

小说凸显了男权社会中丈夫对妻子的支配权。阿尔默不仅是世俗意义上的丈夫,同时也是上帝和造物主,他要重新塑造出一个完全符合自己要求的女性。乔治亚娜是被男权社会成功规训的妻子,她完全屈从于丈夫的意志。尽管她认为胎记是天使留在她脸上的标记,增添了自己的魅力,却最终顺从丈夫的看法,将之视为罪恶和瑕疵,并鼓励丈夫研制可以去除胎记的药水,声称自己将不顾一切喝下这个药水,"I shall quaff whatever draught you bring me; but it will be on the same principle that would induce me to take a dose of poison if offered by your hand."。甚至在丈夫提醒她喝下药水会有危险时,她激动地喊道:"Danger? There is but one danger—that this horrible stigma shall be left upon my cheek!"

除该短篇外,霍桑也在《拉伯西尼医生的女儿》("Rappaccini's Daughter",1846)中反映了自己对科技的看法。阿尔默和拉伯西尼医生对科技极度热衷,妄图通过科学实验改变自然规律,最终却都以爱人或亲人的无谓牺牲作为代价。通过这些作品,霍桑对科技高速发展的美国社会提出了警示,提醒人们不要盲目崇拜科学,不要无止境地滥用科学技术,而是应该热爱自然、尊重自然。

叙事方面，霍桑在《胎记》中成功地运用了象征主义手法，赋予胎记十分丰富的内涵。一方面，胎记象征着人与自然、人与造物主的联结；另一方面，胎记也象征着人的原罪，罪恶是人的天性。阿尔默不断膨胀的科学欲望使他认为科学无所不能，认为自己可以通过科学控制自然，而乔治亚娜对丈夫的盲从使得她成为丈夫欲望的牺牲品。

The Birthmark

In the latter part of the last century[①] there lived a man of science, an eminent proficient in every branch of natural philosophy, who not long before our story opens had made experience of a spiritual affinity more attractive than any chemical one. He had left his laboratory to the care of an assistant, cleared his fine countenance from the furnace smoke, washed the stain of acids from his fingers, and persuaded a beautiful woman to become his wife. In those days when the comparatively recent discovery of electricity and other kindred mysteries of Nature seemed to open paths into the region of miracle, it was not unusual for the love of science to rival the love of woman in its depth and absorbing energy. The higher intellect, the imagination, the spirit, and even the heart might all find their congenial aliment in pursuits which, as some of their ardent votaries believed, would ascend from one step of powerful intelligence to another, until the philosopher should lay his hand on the secret of creative force and perhaps make new worlds for himself. We know not whether Aylmer possessed this degree of faith in man's ultimate control over Nature. He had devoted himself, however, too unreservedly to scientific studies ever to be weaned from them by any second passion. His love for his young wife might prove the stronger of the two; but it could only be by intertwining itself with his love of science, and uniting the strength of the latter to his own.

---

① the latter part of the last century：指 18 世纪下半叶。

Such a union accordingly took place, and was attended with truly remarkable consequences and a deeply impressive moral. One day, very soon after their marriage, Aylmer sat gazing at his wife with a trouble in his countenance that grew stronger until he spoke.

"Georgiana," said he, "has it never occurred to you that the mark upon your cheek might be removed?"

"No, indeed," said she, smiling; but perceiving the seriousness of his manner, she blushed deeply. "To tell you the truth it has been so often called a charm that I was simple enough to imagine it might be so."

"Ah, upon another face perhaps it might," replied her husband; "but never on yours. No, dearest Georgiana, you came so nearly perfect from the hand of Nature that this slightest possible defect, which we hesitate whether to term a defect or a beauty, shocks me, as being the visible mark of earthly imperfection."

"Shocks you, my husband!" cried Georgiana, deeply hurt; at first reddening with momentary anger, but then bursting into tears. "Then why did you take me from my mother's side? You cannot love what shocks you!"

To explain this conversation it must be mentioned that in the centre of Georgiana's left cheek there was a singular mark, deeply interwoven, as it were, with the texture and substance of her face. In the usual state of her complexion— a healthy though delicate bloom—the mark wore a tint of deeper crimson, which imperfectly defined its shape amid the surrounding rosiness. When she blushed it gradually became more indistinct, and finally vanished amid the triumphant rush of blood that bathed the whole cheek with its brilliant glow. But if any shifting motion caused her to turn pale there was the mark again, a crimson stain upon the snow, in what Aylmer sometimes deemed an almost fearful distinctness. Its shape bore not a little similarity to the human hand, though of the smallest pygmy size. Georgiana's lovers were wont to say that some fairy at her birth hour had laid her tiny hand upon the infant's cheek, and left this impress there in token of the magic endowments that were to give her such sway over all hearts. Many a desperate swain① would have risked life for the privilege of pressing his lips to the mysterious hand. It must not be concealed, however, that the impression wrought by this fairy sign manual varied exceedingly, according to the difference of temperament in the beholders. Some fastidious persons—but they were exclusively of her own sex— affirmed that the bloody hand, as they chose to call it, quite destroyed the effect of Georgiana's beauty, and rendered her countenance even hideous. But it would be as reasonable to say that one of those small blue stains which sometimes occur in the purest statuary marble would convert the Eve of Powers to a monster. Masculine observers, if the birthmark did not heighten their admiration, contented themselves with wishing it away, that the world might possess one living specimen of ideal loveliness without the semblance of a flaw. After his marriage,—for he thought little or nothing of the matter before—Aylmer discovered that this was the case with himself.

Had she been less beautiful,—if Envy's self could have found aught else to sneer at—he might have felt his affection heightened by the prettiness of this mimic hand, now vaguely portrayed, now lost, now stealing forth again and glimmering to and fro with every pulse of emotion that throbbed within her heart; but seeing her otherwise so perfect, he found this one defect grow more and more intolerable with every moment of their united lives. It was the fatal flaw of humanity which Nature, in one shape or another, stamps ineffaceably on all her productions, either to imply that they are temporary and finite, or that their perfection must be wrought by toil and pain. The crimson hand expressed the ineludible gripe in which mortality clutches the highest and purest of earthly mould, degrading them into kindred with the lowest, and even with the very brutes, like whom their

---

① swain：情郎，求爱者。

visible frames return to dust. In this manner, selecting it as the symbol of his wife's liability to sin, sorrow, decay, and death, Aylmer's sombre imagination was not long in rendering the birthmark a frightful object, causing him more trouble and horror than ever Georgiana's beauty, whether of soul or sense, had given him delight.

At all the seasons which should have been their happiest, he invariably and without intending it, nay, in spite of a purpose to the contrary, reverted to this one disastrous topic. Trifling as it at first appeared, it so connected itself with innumerable trains of thought and modes of feeling that it became the central point of all. With the morning twilight Aylmer opened his eyes upon his wife's face and recognized the symbol of imperfection; and when they sat together at the evening hearth his eyes wandered stealthily to her cheek, and beheld, flickering with the blaze of the wood fire, the spectral hand that wrote mortality where he would fain have worshipped. Georgiana soon learned to shudder at his gaze. It needed but a glance with the peculiar expression that his face often wore to change the roses of her cheek into a deathlike paleness, amid which the crimson hand was brought strongly out, like a bass-relief① of ruby on the whitest marble.

Late one night when the lights were growing dim, so as hardly to betray the stain on the poor wife's cheek, she herself, for the first time, voluntarily took up the subject.

"Do you remember, my dear Aylmer," said she, with a feeble attempt at a smile, "have you any recollection of a dream last night about this odious hand?"

"None! None whatever!" replied Aylmer, starting; but then he added, in a dry, cold tone, affected for the sake of concealing the real depth of his emotion, "I might well dream of it; for before I fell asleep it had taken a pretty firm hold of my fancy." "And you did dream of it?"

---

① bass-relief: 浅浮雕, 雕塑艺术之一。

continued Georgiana, hastily; for she dreaded lest a gush of tears should interrupt what she had to say. "A terrible dream! I wonder that you can forget it. Is it possible to forget this one expression? 'It is in her heart now; we must have it out!' Reflect, my husband; for by all means I would have you recall that dream."

The mind is in a sad state when Sleep, the all-involving, cannot confine her spectres within the dim region of her sway, but suffers them to break forth, affrighting this actual life with secrets that perchance belong to a deeper one. Aylmer now remembered his dream. He had fancied himself with his servant Aminadab, attempting an operation for the removal of the birthmark; but the deeper went the knife, the deeper sank the hand, until at length its tiny grasp appeared to have caught hold of Georgiana's heart; whence, however, her husband was inexorably resolved to cut or wrench it away.

When the dream had shaped itself perfectly in his memory, Aylmer sat in his wife's presence with a guilty feeling. Truth often finds its way to the mind close muffled in robes of sleep①, and then speaks with uncompromising directness of matters in regard to which we practise an unconscious self-deception during our waking moments. Until now he had not been aware of the tyrannizing influence acquired by one idea over his mind, and of the lengths which he might find in his heart to go for the sake of giving himself peace.

"Aylmer," resumed Georgiana, solemnly, "I know not what may be the cost to both of us to rid me of this fatal birthmark. Perhaps its removal may cause cureless deformity; or it may be the stain goes as deep as life itself. Again: do we know that there is a possibility, on any terms, of unclasping the firm gripe of this little hand which was laid upon me before I came into the world?"

---

① robes of sleep:一语双关，既指睡袍，又意味着睡眠对意识的桎梏。

"Dearest Georgiana, I have spent much thought upon the subject," hastily interrupted Aylmer. "I am convinced of the perfect practicability of its removal."

"If there be the remotest possibility of it," continued Georgiana, "let the attempt be made at whatever risk. Danger is nothing to me; for life, while this hateful mark makes me the object of your horror and disgust,— life is a burden which I would fling down with joy. Either remove this dreadful hand, or take my wretched life! You have deep science. All the world bears witness of it. You have achieved great wonders. Cannot you remove this little, little mark, which I cover with the tips of two small fingers? Is this beyond your power, for the sake of your own peace, and to save your poor wife from madness?"

"Noblest, dearest, tenderest wife," cried Aylmer, rapturously, "doubt not my power. I have already given this matter the deepest thought— thought which might almost have enlightened me to create a being less perfect than yourself. Georgiana, you have led me deeper than ever into the heart of science. I feel myself fully competent to render this dear cheek as faultless as its fellow①; and then, most beloved, what will be my triumph when I shall have corrected what Nature left imperfect in her fairest work! Even Pygmalion, when his sculptured woman assumed life, felt not greater ecstasy than mine will be."

"It is resolved, then," said Georgiana, faintly smiling. "And, Aylmer, spare me not, though you should find the birthmark take refuge in my heart at last."

Her husband tenderly kissed her cheek—her right cheek—not that which bore the impress of the crimson hand.

The next day Aylmer apprised his wife of a plan that he had formed whereby he might have opportunity for the intense thought and constant

---

① its fellow: 指乔治亚娜另一边没有胎记的脸颊。

watchfulness which the proposed operation would require; while Georgiana, likewise, would enjoy the perfect repose essential to its success. They were to seclude themselves in the extensive apartments occupied by Aylmer as a laboratory, and where, during his toilsome youth, he had made discoveries in the elemental powers of Nature that had roused the admiration of all the learned societies in Europe. Seated calmly in this laboratory, the pale philosopher had investigated the secrets of the highest cloud region and of the profoundest mines; he had satisfied himself of the causes that kindled and kept alive the fires of the volcano; and had explained the mystery of fountains, and how it is that they gush forth, some so bright and pure, and others with such rich medicinal virtues, from the dark bosom of the earth. Here, too, at an earlier period, he had studied the wonders of the human frame, and attempted to fathom the very process by which Nature assimilates all her precious influences from earth and air, and from the spiritual world, to create and foster man, her masterpiece. The latter pursuit, however, Aylmer had long laid aside in unwilling recognition of the truth—against which all seekers sooner or later stumble—that our great creative Mother, while she amuses us with apparently working in the broadest sunshine, is yet severely careful to keep her own secrets, and, in spite of her pretended openness, shows us nothing but results. She permits us, indeed, to mar, but seldom to mend, and, like a jealous patentee, on no account to make. Now, however, Aylmer resumed these half-forgotten investigations; not, of course, with such hopes or wishes as first suggested them; but because they involved much physiological truth and lay in the path of his proposed scheme for the treatment of Georgiana.

As he led her over the threshold of the laboratory, Georgiana was cold and tremulous. Aylmer looked cheerfully into her face, with intent to reassure her, but was so startled with the intense glow of the birthmark upon the whiteness of her cheek that he could not restrain a strong convulsive shudder. His wife fainted.

"Aminadab! Aminadab!" shouted Aylmer, stamping violently on the floor.

Forthwith there issued from an inner apartment a man of low stature, but bulky frame, with shaggy hair hanging about his visage, which was grimed with the vapors of the furnace. This personage had been Aylmer's underworker during his whole scientific career, and was admirably fitted for that office by his great mechanical readiness, and the skill with which, while incapable of comprehending a single principle, he executed all the details of his master's experiments. With his vast strength, his shaggy hair, his smoky aspect, and the indescribable earthiness that incrusted him, he seemed to represent man's physical nature; while Aylmer's slender figure, and pale, intellectual face, were no less apt a type of the spiritual element.

"Throw open the door of the boudoir, Aminadab," said Aylmer, "and burn a pastil."

"Yes, master," answered Aminadab, looking intently at the lifeless form of Georgiana; and then he muttered to himself, "If she were my wife, I'd never part with that birthmark."

When Georgiana recovered consciousness she found herself breathing an atmosphere of penetrating fragrance, the gentle potency of which had recalled her from her deathlike faintness. The scene around her looked like enchantment. Aylmer had converted those smoky, dingy, sombre rooms, where he had spent his brightest years in recondite pursuits, into a series of beautiful apartments not unfit to be the secluded abode of a lovely woman. The walls were hung with gorgeous curtains, which imparted the combination of grandeur and grace that no other species of adornment can achieve; and as they fell from the ceiling to the floor, their rich and ponderous folds, concealing all angles and straight lines, appeared to shut in the scene from infinite space. For aught Georgiana knew, it might be a pavilion among the clouds. And Aylmer, excluding the sunshine, which would have interfered with his chemical processes, had supplied its place with perfumed lamps, emitting flames of various hue, but all uniting in a soft, impurpled radiance. He now knelt by his wife's side, watching her earnestly, but without alarm; for he was confident in his science, and felt that he could draw a magic circle round her within which no evil might intrude.

"Where am I? Ah, I remember," said Georgiana, faintly; and she placed her hand over her cheek to hide the terrible mark from her husband's eyes.

"Fear not, dearest!" exclaimed he. "Do not shrink from me! Believe me, Georgiana. I even rejoice in this single imperfection, since it will be such a rapture to remove it."

"Oh, spare me!" sadly replied his wife. "Pray do not look at it again. I never can forget that convulsive shudder."

In order to soothe Georgiana, and, as it were, to release her mind from the burden of actual things, Aylmer now put in practice some of the light and playful secrets which science had taught him among its profounder lore. Airy figures, absolutely bodiless ideas, and forms of unsubstantial beauty came and danced before her, imprinting their momentary footsteps on beams of light. Though she had some indistinct idea of the method of these optical phenomena, still the illusion was almost perfect enough to warrant the belief that her husband possessed sway over the spiritual world. Then again, when she felt a wish to look forth from her seclusion, immediately, as if her thoughts were answered, the procession of external existence flitted across a screen. The scenery and the figures of actual life were perfectly represented, but with that bewitching, yet indescribable difference which always makes a picture, an image, or a shadow so much more attractive than the original. When wearied of this, Aylmer bade her cast, her eyes upon a vessel containing a quantity of earth. She did so, with little interest at first; but was soon startled to perceive the germ of a plant shooting upward from the soil. Then came the slender stalk; the leaves gradually unfolded themselves; and amid them was a perfect and lovely flower.

"It is magical!" cried Georgiana. "I dare not touch it."

"Nay, pluck it," answered Aylmer, "pluck it, and inhale its brief perfume while you may. The flower will wither in a few moments and leave nothing save its brown seed vessels; but thence may be perpetuated a race as ephemeral as itself."

But Georgiana had no sooner touched the flower than the whole plant suffered a blight, its leaves turning coal-black as if by the agency of fire.

"There was too powerful a stimulus," said Aylmer, thoughtfully.

To make up for this abortive experiment, he proposed to take her portrait by a scientific process of his own invention. It was to be effected by rays of light striking upon a polished plate of metal. Georgiana assented; but, on looking at the result, was affrighted to find the features of the portrait blurred and indefinable; while the minute figure of a hand appeared where the cheek should have been. Aylmer snatched the metallic plate and threw it into a jar of corrosive acid. Soon, however, he forgot these mortifying failures. In the intervals of study and chemical experiment he came to her flushed and exhausted, but seemed invigorated by her presence, and spoke in glowing language of the resources of his art. He gave a history of the long dynasty of the alchemists, who spent so many ages in quest of the universal solvent by which the golden principle might be elicited from all things vile and base. Aylmer appeared to believe that, by the plainest scientific logic, it was altogether within the limits of possibility to discover this long-sought medium; "but," he added, "a philosopher who should go deep enough to acquire the power would attain too lofty a wisdom to stoop to the exercise of it." Not less singular were his opinions in regard to the elixir vitae[①]. He more than intimated that it was at his option to concoct a liquid that should prolong life for years, perhaps interminably;

---

① elixir vitae: 长生不老药。

but that it would produce a discord in Nature which all the world, and chiefly the quaffer① of the immortal nostrum, would find cause to curse.

"Aylmer, are you in earnest?" asked Georgiana, looking at him with amazement and fear. "It is terrible to possess such power, or even to dream of possessing it."

"Oh, do not tremble, my love," said her husband. "I would not wrong either you or myself by working such inharmonious effects upon our lives; but I would have you consider how trifling, in comparison, is the skill requisite to remove this little hand."

At the mention of the birthmark, Georgiana, as usual, shrank as if a redhot iron had touched her cheek.

Again Aylmer applied himself to his labors. She could hear his voice in the distant furnace room giving directions to Aminadab, whose harsh, uncouth, misshapen tones were audible in response, more like the grunt or growl of a brute than human speech. After hours of absence, Aylmer reappeared and proposed that she should now examine his cabinet of chemical products and natural treasures of the earth. Among the former he showed her a small vial, in which, he remarked, was contained a gentle yet most powerful fragrance, capable of impregnating all the breezes that blow across a kingdom. They were of inestimable value, the contents of that little vial; and, as he said so, he threw some of the perfume into the air and filled the room with piercing and invigorating delight.

"And what is this?" asked Georgiana, pointing to a small crystal globe containing a gold-colored liquid. "It is so beautiful to the eye that I could imagine it the elixir of life."

"In one sense it is," replied Aylmer; "or, rather, the elixir of immortality. It is the most precious poison that ever was concocted in this world. By its aid I could apportion the lifetime of any mortal at whom you

---

① quaffer: 痛饮。

might point your finger. The strength of the dose would determine whether he were to linger out years, or drop dead in the midst of a breath. No king on his guarded throne could keep his life if I, in my private station, should deem that the welfare of millions justified me in depriving him of it."

"Why do you keep such a terrific drug?" inquired Georgiana in horror.

"Do not mistrust me, dearest," said her husband, smiling; "its virtuous potency is yet greater than its harmful one. But see! Here is a powerful cosmetic. With a few drops of this in a vase of water, freckles may be washed away as easily as the hands are cleansed. A stronger infusion would take the blood out of the cheek, and leave the rosiest beauty a pale ghost."

"Is it with this lotion that you intend to bathe my cheek?" asked Georgiana, anxiously. "Oh, no," hastily replied her husband; "this is merely superficial. Your case demands a remedy that shall go deeper."

In his interviews with Georgiana, Aylmer generally made minute inquiries as to her sensations and whether the confinement of the rooms and the temperature of the atmosphere agreed with her. These questions had such a particular drift that Georgiana began to conjecture that she was already subjected to certain physical influences, either breathed in with the fragrant air or taken with her food. She fancied likewise, but it might be altogether fancy, that there was a stirring up of her system—a strange, indefinite sensation creeping through her veins, and tingling, half painfully, half pleasurably, at her heart. Still, whenever she dared to look into the mirror, there she beheld herself pale as a white rose and with the crimson birthmark stamped upon her cheek. Not even Aylmer now hated it so much as she.

To dispel the tedium of the hours which her husband found it necessary to devote to the processes of combination and analysis, Georgiana turned over the volumes of his scientific library. In many dark old tomes she met with chapters full of romance and poetry. They were the works of philosophers of the middle ages, such as Albertus Magnus①, Cornelius Agrippa②, Paracelsus③, and the famous friar who created the prophetic Brazen Head. All these antique naturalists stood in advance of their centuries, yet were imbued with some of their credulity, and therefore were believed, and perhaps imagined themselves to have acquired from the investigation of Nature a power above Nature, and from physics a sway over the spiritual world. Hardly less curious and imaginative were the early volumes of the Transactions of the Royal Society, in which the members, knowing little of the limits of natural possibility, were continually recording wonders or proposing methods whereby wonders might be wrought.

But to Georgiana the most engrossing volume was a large folio from her husband's own hand, in which he had recorded every experiment of his scientific career, its original aim, the methods adopted for its development, and its final success or failure, with the circumstances to which either event was attributable. The book, in truth, was both the history and emblem of his ardent, ambitious, imaginative, yet practical and laborious life. He handled physical details as if there were nothing beyond them; yet spiritualized them all, and redeemed himself from materialism by his strong and eager aspiration towards the infinite. In his grasp the veriest clod of earth assumed a soul. Georgiana, as she read, reverenced Aylmer and loved him more profoundly than ever, but with a less entire dependence on his judgment than heretofore. Much as he had accomplished, she could not but observe that his most splendid successes were almost invariably failures, if compared with the ideal at which he aimed. His brightest diamonds were the merest pebbles, and felt to be so by himself, in comparison with the inestimable gems which lay hidden beyond his reach. The volume, rich

---

① Albertus Magnus:艾伯塔斯·马格努斯(1193/1206—1280),德国化学家、炼金术师。他成功地分离了金和银,并著有《炼金术》一书。

② Cornelius Agrippa:科尼利厄斯·阿格里帕(1486—1535),德国中世纪神学家、魔法师、占星师和炼金术师。

③ Paracelsus:帕拉塞尔苏斯(1493—1541),瑞士中世纪医生、炼金术士、植物学家。

with achievements that had won renown for its author, was yet as melancholy a record as ever mortal hand had penned. It was the sad confession and continual exemplification of the shortcomings of the composite man, the spirit burdened with clay and working in matter, and of the despair that assails the higher nature at finding itself so miserably thwarted by the earthly part. Perhaps every man of genius in whatever sphere might recognize the image of his own experience in Aylmer's journal.

So deeply did these reflections affect Georgiana that she laid her face upon the open volume and burst into tears. In this situation she was found by her husband.

"It is dangerous to read in a sorcerer's books," said he with a smile, though his countenance was uneasy and displeased. "Georgiana, there are pages in that volume which I can scarcely glance over and keep my senses. Take heed lest it prove as detrimental to you."

"It has made me worship you more than ever," said she.

"Ah, wait for this one success," rejoined he, "then worship me if you will. I shall deem myself hardly unworthy of it. But come, I have sought you for the luxury of your voice. Sing to me, dearest."

So she poured out the liquid music of her voice to quench the thirst of his spirit. He then took his leave with a boyish exuberance of gayety, assuring her that her seclusion would endure but a little longer, and that the result was already certain. Scarcely had he departed when Georgiana felt irresistibly impelled to follow him. She had forgotten to inform Aylmer of a symptom which for two or three hours past had begun to excite her attention. It was a sensation in the fatal birthmark, not painful, but which induced a restlessness throughout her system. Hastening after her husband, she intruded for the first time into the laboratory.

The first thing that struck her eye was the furnace, that hot and feverish worker, with the intense glow of its fire, which by the quantities of soot clustered above it seemed to have been burning for ages. There was a distilling apparatus in full operation. Around the room were retorts, tubes, cylinders, crucibles, and other apparatus of chemical research. An electrical machine stood ready for immediate use. The atmosphere felt oppressively close, and was tainted with gaseous odors which had been tormented forth by the processes of science. The severe and homely simplicity of the apartment, with its naked walls and brick pavement, looked strange, accustomed as Georgiana had become to the fantastic elegance of her boudoir. But what chiefly, indeed almost solely, drew her attention, was the aspect of Aylmer himself.

He was pale as death, anxious and absorbed, and hung over the furnace as if it depended upon his utmost watchfulness whether the liquid which it was distilling should be the draught of immortal happiness or misery. How different from the sanguine and joyous mien that he had assumed for Georgiana's encouragement!

"Carefully now, Aminadab; carefully, thou human machine; carefully, thou man of clay!" muttered Aylmer, more to himself than his assistant. "Now, if there be a thought too much or too little, it is all over."

"Ho! Ho!" mumbled Aminadab. "Look, master! Look!"

Aylmer raised his eyes hastily, and at first reddened, then grew paler than ever, on beholding Georgiana. He rushed towards her and seized her arm with a gripe that left the print of his fingers upon it.

"Why do you come hither? Have you no trust in your husband?" cried he, impetuously. "Would you throw the blight of that fatal birthmark over my labors? It is not well done. Go, prying woman, go!"

"Nay, Aylmer," said Georgiana with the firmness of which she possessed no stinted endowment, "it is not you that have a right to complain. You mistrust your wife; you have concealed the anxiety with which you watch the development of this experiment. Think not so unworthily of me, my husband. Tell me all the risk we run, and fear not that I shall shrink; for my share in it is far less than your own."

"No, no, Georgiana!" said Aylmer, impatiently, "it must not be."

"I submit," replied she calmly. "And, Aylmer, I shall quaff whatever draught you bring me; but it will be on the same principle that would induce me to take a dose of poison if offered by your hand."

"My noble wife," said Aylmer, deeply moved, "I knew not the height and depth of your nature until now. Nothing shall be concealed. Know, then, that this crimson hand, superficial as it seems, has clutched its grasp into your being with a strength of which I had no previous conception. I have already administered agents powerful enough to do aught except to change your entire physical system. Only one thing remains to be tried. If that fail us we are ruined."

"Why did you hesitate to tell me this?" asked she.

"Because, Georgiana," said Aylmer, in a low voice, "there is danger."

"Danger? There is but one danger—that this horrible stigma shall be left upon my cheek!" cried Georgiana. "Remove it, remove it, whatever be the cost, or we shall both go mad!"

"Heaven knows your words are too true," said Aylmer, sadly. "And now, dearest, return to your boudoir. In a little while all will be tested."

He conducted her back and took leave of her with a solemn tenderness which spoke far more than his words how much was now at stake. After his departure Georgiana became rapt in musings. She considered the character of Aylmer, and did it completer justice than at any previous moment. Her heart exulted, while it trembled, at his honorable love—so pure and lofty that it would accept nothing less than perfection nor miserably make itself contented with an earthlier nature than he had dreamed of. She felt how much more precious was such a sentiment than that meaner kind which would have borne with the imperfection for her sake, and have been guilty of treason to holy love by degrading its perfect idea to the level of the actual; and with her whole spirit she prayed that, for a single moment, she might satisfy his highest and deepest conception. Longer than one moment she well knew it could not be; for his spirit was ever on the march, ever ascending, and each instant required something that was beyond the scope of the instant before.

The sound of her husband's footsteps aroused her. He bore a crystal goblet containing a liquor colorless as water, but bright enough to be the draught of immortality. Aylmer was pale; but it seemed rather the consequence of a highly-wrought state of mind and tension of spirit than of fear or doubt.

"The concoction of the draught has been perfect," said he, in answer to Georgiana's look. "Unless all my science have deceived me, it cannot fail."

"Save on your account, my dearest Aylmer," observed his wife, "I might wish to put off this birthmark of mortality by relinquishing mortality itself in preference to any other mode. Life is but a sad possession to those who have attained precisely the degree of moral advancement at which I stand. Were I weaker and blinder it might be happiness. Were I stronger, it might be endured hopefully. But, being what I find myself, methinks① I am of all mortals the most fit to die."

"You are fit for heaven without tasting death!" replied her husband. "But why do we speak of dying? The draught cannot fail. Behold its effect upon this plant."

On the window seat there stood a geranium diseased with yellow blotches, which had overspread all its leaves. Aylmer poured a small quantity of the liquid upon the soil in which it grew. In a little time, when the roots of the plant had taken up the moisture, the unsightly blotches began to be extinguished in a living verdure.

---

① methinks:我想,我认为。

"There needed no proof," said Georgiana, quietly. "Give me the goblet, I joyfully stake all upon your word."

"Drink, then, thou lofty creature!" exclaimed Aylmer, with fervid admiration. "There is no taint of imperfection on thy spirit. Thy sensible frame, too, shall soon be all perfect."

She quaffed the liquid and returned the goblet to his hand.

"It is grateful," said she with a placid smile. "Methinks it is like water from a heavenly fountain; for it contains I know not what of unobtrusive fragrance and deliciousness. It allays a feverish thirst that had parched me for many days. Now, dearest, let me sleep. My earthly senses are closing over my spirit like the leaves around the heart of a rose at sunset."

She spoke the last words with a gentle reluctance, as if it required almost more energy than she could command to pronounce the faint and lingering syllables. Scarcely had they loitered through her lips ere she was lost in slumber. Aylmer sat by her side, watching her aspect with the emotions proper to a man the whole value of whose existence was involved in the process now to be tested. Mingled with this mood, however, was the philosophic investigation characteristic of the man of science. Not the minutest symptom escaped him. A heightened flush of the cheek, a slight irregularity of breath, a quiver of the eyelid, a hardly perceptible tremor through the frame—such were the details which, as the moments passed, he wrote down in his folio volume. Intense thought had set its stamp upon every previous page of that volume, but the thoughts of years were all concentrated upon the last.

While thus employed, he failed not to gaze often at the fatal hand, and not without a shudder. Yet once, by a strange and unaccountable impulse he pressed it with his lips. His spirit recoiled, however, in the very act, and Georgiana, out of the midst of her deep sleep, moved uneasily and murmured as if in remonstrance. Again Aylmer resumed his watch. Nor was it without avail. The crimson hand, which at first had been strongly visible upon the marble paleness of Georgiana's cheek, now grew more faintly outlined. She remained not less pale than ever; but the birthmark with every breath that came and went, lost somewhat of its former distinctness. Its presence had been awful; its departure was more awful still. Watch the stain of the rainbow fading out the sky, and you will know how that mysterious symbol passed away.

"By Heaven! It is well-nigh gone!" said Aylmer to himself, in almost irrepressible ecstasy. "I can scarcely trace it now. Success! Success! And now it is like the faintest rose color. The lightest flush of blood across her cheek would overcome it. But she is so pale!"

He drew aside the window curtain and suffered the light of natural day to fall into the room and rest upon her cheek. At the same time he heard a gross, hoarse chuckle, which he had long known as his servant Aminadab's expression of delight.

"Ah, clod! Ah, earthly mass!" cried Aylmer, laughing in a sort of frenzy, "You have served me well! Matter and spirit—earth and heaven— have both done their part in this! Laugh, thing of the senses! You have earned the right to laugh."

These exclamations broke Georgiana's sleep. She slowly unclosed her eyes and gazed into the mirror which her husband had arranged for that purpose. A faint smile flitted over her lips when she recognized how barely perceptible was now that crimson hand which had once blazed forth with such disastrous brilliancy as to scare away all their happiness. But then her eyes sought Aylmer's face with a trouble and anxiety that he could by no means account for.

"My poor Aylmer!" murmured she.

"Poor? Nay, richest, happiest, most favored!" exclaimed he. "My peerless bride, it is successful! You are perfect!"

"My poor Aylmer," she repeated, with a more than human tenderness, "you have aimed loftily; you have done nobly. Do not repent that with so high and pure a feeling, you have rejected the best the earth could offer. Aylmer, dearest Aylmer, I am dying!"

Alas! It was too true! The fatal hand had grappled with the mystery of life, and was the bond by which an angelic spirit kept itself in union with a mortal frame. As the last crimson tint of the birthmark—that sole token of human imperfection—faded from her cheek, the parting breath of the now perfect woman passed into the atmosphere, and her soul, lingering a moment near her husband, took its heavenward flight. Then a hoarse, chuckling laugh was heard again! Thus ever does the gross fatality of earth exult in its invariable triumph over the immortal essence which, in this dim sphere of half development, demands the completeness of a higher state. Yet, had Alymer reached a profounder wisdom, he need not thus have flung away the happiness which would have woven his mortal life of the selfsame texture with the celestial. The momentary circumstance was too strong for him; he failed to look beyond the shadowy scope of time, and, living once for all in eternity, to find the perfect future in the present.

Questions

1. Why is Aylmer determined to remove the birthmark?

2. Hawthorne's works do not directly depict contemporary life and the people and events around it, but are usually set in 17th-century Puritan New England, with a vague background of time and place. Thus, the works are imbued with a color of mystery, giving people a sense of fiction and fable. That's why Hawthorne called his works romance. In this short story, how does the author use the technique "romance"?

Further Readings

Nathaniel Hawthorne's works are famous for their characterization and psychological description. The following are some of his important short stories.

1. "The Minister's Black Veil" (《牧师的黑面纱》)
2. "Young Goodman Brown" (《小伙子古德蒙·布朗》)
3. "Wakefield" (《威客菲尔德》)
4. "Rappaccini's Daughter" (《拉伯西尼医生的女儿》)

Unit 11　The Tell—Tale Heart

About the writer

　　埃德加·爱伦·坡(Edgar Allan Poe, 1809 – 1849)是美国文学史上一位影响深远的小说家、诗人和文学评论家。作为黑色浪漫主义(Dark Romanticism)的代表人物之一，爱伦·坡擅长渲染奇异恐怖的哥特式氛围，经常通过描写怪诞离奇的故事映射个体意识及潜意识中的阴暗面，被誉为哥特小说、推理小说和科幻小说的先驱。

　　爱伦·坡 1809 年出生于美国波士顿。坡年幼时父母双亡，后被弗吉尼亚州的爱伦夫妇收养。坡很早就展现出了文学方面的天赋，然而养父执意将坡培养成一名商人，两人的矛盾在坡成年后逐渐爆发，最终迫使坡离家出走。1827 年，他出版了第一部作品《帖木儿及其他诗歌》(*Tamerlane and Other Poems*)。坡后来成功进入西点军校，但因故意抗命而被开除，随后他迁往巴尔的摩与姨妈和表妹同住。1836 年，坡与快满 14 岁的表妹弗吉尼亚(Virginia)结婚，他通过撰写小说、诗歌及书评勉强维持生计。

　　1836—1845 年可谓是坡的创作鼎盛期。这一时期，他出版了《丽姬娅》("Ligeia", 1838)、《厄舍大厦的倒塌》("The Fall of the House of Usher", 1839)、《莫格街谋杀案》("The Murders in the Rue Morgue", 1841)等近 70 个短篇小说。《莫格街谋杀案》讲述了发生在巴黎莫格街上的一桩残忍离奇的凶杀案。一对母女准备睡觉时被残忍杀害，但其财物并未丢失。有证人证实死者遇害身亡时还有其他人在案发现场，但没人能听懂他的语言。坡在描述案情时不断设置悬念，并使小说中的侦探杜宾按照蛛丝马迹追根溯源，最终确认凶手是一只大猩猩。《莫格街谋杀案》塑造了一个料事如神、智力超凡的侦探形象，他通过严谨的证据收集和逻辑分析逐步揭开事实真相。这种推理叙事模式深刻影响了后世的许多推理小说家。

坡也创作了许多脍炙人口的恐怖小说。在短篇小说《一桶白葡萄酒》（"The Cask of Amontillado"，1846）中，坡将奇异恐怖的哥特式氛围渲染到极致，通过对蒙特利瑟精心设计的复仇过程的描写映射出个体意识及潜意识中的黑暗面。小说中，弗图纳多是一位对葡萄酒颇具鉴赏力的贵族，他性格直爽，热情友善，但有时争强好胜，言辞不够谨慎。不知何故，他得罪了蒙特利瑟。蒙特利瑟工于心计、阴险狡诈，他发誓要报复。在狂欢节的傍晚，他以鉴赏葡萄酒为由，将喝得醉醺醺的弗图纳多骗至自家的酒窖里，并成功地激起了弗图纳多的好胜心，最终将弗图纳多领到酒窖深处，并将他活埋。

坡在诗歌方面也颇有建树，他于1845年发表了诗歌《乌鸦》（"The Raven"）。《乌鸦》中，坡巧妙运用文字的暗喻与诗歌的韵律，讲述了一名男子失去爱人后与乌鸦邂逅交谈的凄美故事。表面上看，男子因爱人逝世悲痛万分，但细细深究不难发现，诗歌中刻画的情感已远远超越纯粹的爱恋之情与哀悼之情，而是包含着悲伤、哀痛、绝望等永恒的人类情感。

坡认为，无论是小说还是诗歌的创作都必须讲究效果的统一，作品中每个词句都必须为设置好的效果服务。因此，坡的作品通常结构紧凑、文风简洁，几乎每个细节都蕴含着丰富寓意。此外，坡坚信小说要紧扣读者的心弦，使读者能够切身感受精心设计的艺术效果。为此，坡青睐于创作短篇小说，擅长通过短小精悍的故事情节与哥特式的恐怖氛围调动读者的感知体验。坡独树一帜的创作理念对美国文学乃至世界文学产生了深远的影响。

About the story

《泄密的心》（"The Tell—Tale Heart"）是坡1843年发表的短篇小说，称得上是坡创作的恐怖小说中的佳作。小说以第一人称自述的形式展开，"我"自述了杀害邻居老人并将其肢解的全过程。老人有一只灰蓝色的眼睛，这只眼睛如同鹰眼一般，似乎能够洞察一切，这使"我"倍感恼火。于是，"我"决定杀死老人，彻底摆脱这只眼睛。在接连七天的午夜时分，"我"偷偷潜入老人家中，寻找下手的机会。但老人双眼紧闭，这使得我无法下手，因为让我恼火的不是老人，而是他那只"邪恶的眼睛"。第八天夜晚，老人发现了"我"的潜入，他睁开眼睛，在极度恐惧中被"我"残忍杀害。"我"将老人的尸体肢解并藏在木板下，警察上门盘问时，"我"依然谈笑自如。然而，尽管老人已经死亡，"我"却能听到他的心跳声。老人可怕的心跳声最终使"我"彻底崩溃，

"我"将真相全盘脱出,至此,故事戛然而止。

小说中"我"自认神经过敏,但不承认自己发疯。随着故事的不断推进,一个心理状态间于正常与失常之间的恐怖形象跃然纸上。"我"清晰地知道自己的所作所为,精心布置了一切,在仔细观察八天后才动手杀害老人,如此看来,"我"似乎确实没有发疯。但"我"杀害老人的动机又过于荒谬,仅仅因为一只眼睛就意图将老人置于死地。小说关于疯癫的心理刻画与细致入微的环境描写凸显了恐怖氛围,坡巧妙运用夸张和暗喻的手法描述了"我"彻底异化的内心世界,映射出现实生活中人们不断异化的精神状态。

《泄密的心》中,坡并未明确"我"精神异化的具体原因,但在有限的篇幅中做出了诸多暗示。最为明显的线索便是老人那只逼疯"我"的眼睛。不难看出,"我"想要摆脱的束缚是老人的凝视,而并非老人本身。或许,老人的"鹰眼"能够洞察一切,已然构成一种独特的凝视系统,监视着"我"的一举一动并对"我"展开规训。"我"在长期的凝视下精神失常,最终采取极端措施进行反抗。

小说中另一个需要关注的重点则是这颗"泄密的心"。显然,"泄密的心"指的是老人的心脏,这颗心脏在老人死后依然砰砰作响,诉说着"我"的秘密。"我"与警察交谈时,老人的心跳声骤然响起且越来越响,最终彻底击垮了"我":"Anything was more tolerable than this derision! I could bear those hypocritical smiles no longer! I felt that I must scream or die!—and now—again!—hark! Louder! Louder! Louder! Louder!"这颗可怕的心既讲述了"我"杀害老人的秘密,也揭开了"我"异化的精神状态。老人已经死去多时,他的心脏显然不可能再次跳动,那这阵可怕的心跳声究竟缘何而来?实际上,在小说开头,坡就已经给出暗示:神经过敏的"我"听觉异常敏锐,甚至能听见天堂和地狱中的声音。或许,老人可怕的心跳声来自天堂或地狱,是精神异化的"我"难以解开的心结。

《泄密的心》体现了坡的创作理念。该短篇结构紧凑、字字珠玑,几乎所有词句都在为特定的恐怖效果服务。小说在色彩描写、场景布置、心理刻画等方面都营造了恐怖美学的效果。色彩描写上,小说选用诡异神秘的黑作为主色调,黑乎乎的提灯、难见五指的房间都弥漫着一种神秘的氛围。场景布置上,小说大部分情节发生在一座古老矮楼里,矮楼中老旧的地板、木质的门闩、闭合的百叶窗都带给读者一种沉闷感,进而营造出场景上的恐怖氛围。声音与场景的配合下,人物心理的刻画完成了恐怖效果的升华,达成了效果的统一。小说中,不只"我"异化的精神状态令人毛骨悚然,老人死亡前感到的恐惧也令人不寒而栗。这种恐惧不断被放大,带给读者异常独特的体验。

The Tell—Tale Heart

TRUE! —NERVOUS①—VERY, VERY dreadfully nervous I had been and am; but why will you say that I am mad? The disease had sharpened my senses—not destroyed—not dulled them. Above all was the sense of hearing acute. I heard all things in the heaven and in the earth. I heard many things in hell. How, then, am I mad? Hearken②! And observe how healthily—how calmly I can tell you the whole story.

It is impossible to say how first the idea entered my brain; but once conceived, it haunted me day and night③. Object there was none. Passion there was none. I loved the old man. He had never wronged me. He had never given me insult. For his gold I had no desire. I think it was his eye! Yes, it was this! One of his eyes resembled that of a vulture④—a pale blue eye, with a film over it. Whenever it fell upon me, my blood ran cold; and so by degrees—very gradually—I made up my mind to take the life of the old man, and thus rid myself of the eye for ever.

Now this is the point. You fancy me mad. Madmen know nothing. But you should have seen me. You should have seen how wisely I proceeded—with what caution—with what foresight—with what dissimulation I went to work! I was never kinder to the old man than during the whole week before I killed him. And every night, about midnight, I turned the latch of his door and opened it—oh, so gently! And then, when I had made an opening

---

① nervous:神经过敏。"我"杀人后神经过敏,以至于能够听见天堂和地狱中的声音。
② hearken:仔细听好。
③ It is impossible to say how first the idea entered my brain; but once conceived, it haunted me day and night:现在已没法说清当初那个念头是怎样钻进我的脑子,但它一旦钻入,就日日夜夜纠缠着我。
④ vulture:兀鹰,鸟类中的捕食者。此处是一个隐喻,喻指老人构成一种外在的威胁。

sufficient for my head, I put in a dark lantern, all closed, closed, so that no light shone out, and then I thrust in my head. Oh, you would have laughed to see how cunningly I thrust it in! I moved it slowly—very, very slowly, so that I might not disturb the old man's sleep. It took me an hour to place my whole head within the opening so far that I could see him as he lay upon his bed. Ha!—would a madman have been so wise as this? And then, when my head was well in the room, I undid the lantern cautiously—oh, so cautiously—cautiously (for the hinges creaked①)—I undid it just so much that a single thin ray fell upon the vulture eye. And this I did for seven long nights—every night just at midnight—but I found the eye always closed; and so it was impossible to do the work; for it was not the old man who vexed me, but his Evil Eye. And every morning, when the day broke, I went boldly into the chamber, and spoke courageously to him, calling him by name in a hearty tone, and inquiring how he had passed the night. So you see he would have been a very profound old man, indeed, to suspect that every night, just at twelve, I looked in upon him while he slept.

Upon the eighth night I was more than usually cautious in opening the door. A watch's minute hand moves more quickly than did mine. Never before that night had I felt the extent of my own powers—of my sagacity. I could scarcely contain my feelings of triumph. To think that there I was, opening the door, little by little, and he not even to dream of my secret deeds or thoughts. I fairly chuckled at the idea; and perhaps he heard me; for he moved on the bed suddenly, as if startled. Now you may think that I drew back—but no. His room was as black as pitch with the thick darkness (for the shutters were close fastened, through fear of robbers), and so I knew that he could not see the opening of the door, and I kept pushing it on steadily, steadily.

I kept quite still and said nothing. For a whole hour I did not move a

---

① for the hinges creaked：因为灯罩轴嘎吱作响。

muscle, and in the meantime I did not hear him lie down. He was still sitting up in the bed listening;—just as I have done, night after night, hearkening to the death watches① in the wall.

Presently I heard a slight groan, and I knew it was the groan of mortal terror. It was not a groan of pain or of grief—oh, no! —it was the low stifled sound that arises from the bottom of the soul when overcharged with awe. I knew the sound well. Many a night, just at midnight, when all the world slept, it has welled up from my own bosom, deepening, with its dreadful echo, the terrors that distracted me. I say I knew it well. I knew what the old man felt, and pitied him, although I chuckled at heart. I knew that he had been lying awake ever since the first slight noise, when he had turned in the bed. His fears had been ever since growing upon him. He had been trying to fancy them causeless, but could not. He had been saying to himself—"It is nothing but the wind in the chimney—it is only a mouse crossing the floor", or "it is merely a cricket which has made a single chirp". Yes, he has been trying to comfort himself with these suppositions; but he had found all in vain. All in vain; because Death, in approaching him, had stalked with his black shadow before him, and enveloped the victim. And it was the mournful influence of the unperceived shadow that caused him to feel—although he neither saw nor heard—to feel the presence of my head within the room.

When I had waited a long time, very patiently, without hearing him lie down, I resolved to open a little—a very, very little crevice in the lantern. So I opened it—you cannot imagine how stealthily, stealthily—until, at length, a single dim ray, like the thread of the spider, shot from out the crevice and full upon the vulture eye.

It was open—wide, wide open—and I grew furious as I gazed upon it. I saw it with perfect distinctness—all a dull blue, with a hideous veil over it

---

① death watches:报死虫,一种独眼的害虫。

that chilled the very marrow in my bones; but I could see nothing else of the old man's face or person: for I had directed the ray as if by instinct, precisely upon the damned spot①.

And now have I not told you that what you mistake for madness is but over—acuteness of the senses?—now, I say, there came to my ears a low, dull, quick sound, such as a watch makes when enveloped in cotton. I knew that sound well too. It was the beating of the old man's heart. It increased my fury, as the beating of a drum stimulates the soldier into courage.

But even yet I refrained and kept still. I scarcely breathed. I held the lantern motionless. I tried how steadily I could maintain the ray upon the eye. Meantime the hellish tattoo of the heart increased②. It grew quicker and quicker, and louder and louder every instant. The old man's terror must have been extreme! It grew louder, I say, louder every moment!—do you mark me well? I have told you that I am nervous: so I am. And now at the dead hour of the night, amid the dreadful silence of that old house, so strange a noise as this excited me to uncontrollable terror. Yet, for some minutes longer I refrained and stood still. But the beating grew louder, louder! I thought the heart must burst. And now a new anxiety seized me—the sound would be heard by a neighbor! The old man's hour had come③! With a loud yell, I threw open the lantern and leaped into the room. He shrieked once—once only. In an instant I dragged him to the floor, and pulled the heavy bed over him. I then smiled gaily, to find the deed so far done. But, for many minutes, the heart beat on with a muffled sound. This, however, did not vex me; it would not be heard through the wall. At length it ceased. The old man was dead. I removed the bed and examined

---

① the damned spot: 该死的蓝点, 此处指老人蓝灰色的眼睛。
② Meantime the hellish tattoo of the heart increased: 与此同时, 他可怕的心跳声不断加快。
③ The old man's hour had come: 这个老人的死期终于到了。

the corpse. Yes, he was stone, stone dead. I placed my hand upon the heart and held it there many minutes. There was no pulsation. He was stone dead. His eye would trouble me no more.

If still you think me mad, you will think so no longer when I describe the wise precautions I took for the concealment of the body. The night waned, and I worked hastily, but in silence. First of all I dismembered the corpse. I cut off the head and the arms and the legs.

I then took up three planks from the flooring of the chamber, and deposited all between the scantlings①. I then replaced the boards so cleverly, so cunningly, that no human eye—not even his—could have detected any thing wrong. There was nothing to wash out—no stain of any kind—no blood—spot whatever. I had been too wary for that. A tub had caught all—ha! Ha!

When I had made an end of these labors, it was four o'clock—still dark as midnight. As the bell sounded the hour, there came a knocking at the street door. I went down to open it with a light heart,—for what had I now to fear? There entered three men, who introduced themselves, with perfect suavity, as officers of the police. A shriek had been heard by a neighbor during the night; suspicion of foul play② had been aroused; information had been lodged at the police office, and they (the officers) had been deputed to search the premises.

I smiled,—for what had I to fear? I bade the gentlemen welcome. The shriek, I said, was my own in a dream. The old man, I mentioned, was absent in the country. I took my visitors all over the house. I bade them search—search well. I led them, at length, to his chamber. I showed them his treasures, secure, undisturbed. In the enthusiasm of my confidence, I

---

① I then took up three planks from the flooring of the chamber, and deposited all between the scantlings:接着我撬开卧室地板上的三块木板,把肢解开的尸体全塞进木缝之间。

② foul play:恶事凶行。

brought chairs into the room, and desired them here to rest from their fatigues, while I myself, in the wild audacity of my perfect triumph, placed my own seat upon the very spot beneath which reposed the corpse of the victim.

The officers were satisfied. My manner had convinced them. I was singularly at ease. They sat, and while I answered cheerily, they chatted familiar things. But, ere long, I felt myself getting pale and wished them gone. My head ached, and I fancied a ringing in my ears: but still they sat and still chatted. The ringing became more distinct:—it continued and became more distinct: I talked more freely to get rid of the feeling: but it continued and gained definitiveness—until, at length, I found that the noise was not within my ears.

No doubt I now grew very pale;—but I talked more fluently, and with a heightened voice. Yet the sound increased—and what could I do? It was a low, dull, quick sound—much such a sound as a watch makes when enveloped in cotton. I gasped for breath—and yet the officers heard it not. I talked more quickly—more vehemently; but the noise steadily increased. I arose and argued about trifles, in a high key and with violent gesticulations, but the noise steadily increased. Why would they not be gone? I paced the floor to and fro with heavy strides, as if excited to fury by the observation of the men—but the noise steadily increased. Oh God! What could I do? I foamed—I raved—I swore! I swung the chair upon which I had been sitting, and grated it upon the boards, but the noise arose over all and continually increased, it grew louder—louder—louder! And still the men chatted pleasantly, and smiled. Was it possible they heard not? Almighty God!—no, no! They heard!—they suspected!—they knew!—they were making a mockery of my horror!—this I thought, and this I think. But any thing was better than this agony! Any thing was more tolerable than this derision! I could bear those hypocritical smiles no longer! I felt that I must scream or die!—and now—again!—hark! Louder! Louder! Louder! Louder!—

"Villains!" I shrieked, "dissemble no more①! I admit the deed! —tear up the planks! —here, here! —it is the beating of his hideous heart!"

Questions

1. What narrative perspective does the author employ in this short story? What role does this narrative perspective play in building terrible atmosphere?

2. Edgar Allan Poe had an important influence on world literature. His achievement is mainly attributed to his creative ideas, the core of which is the "effect" theory that he repeatedly emphasized. Poe insisted that each sentence should be created for specific purposes. And every sentence, even every word in a short story should be created for the same purpose. In this short story, how does Poe achieve the "effect"?

Further Readings

Edgar Allan Poe's stories are famous for their horrible plots and philosophical meanings. The following are some of his important short stories.

1. "Ligeia" (《丽姬娅》)
2. "The Fall of the House of Usher" (《厄舍大厦的倒塌》)
3. "The Black Cat" (《黑猫》)

---

① dissemble no more: 别再装聋作哑。

Unit 12　The Notorious Frog of Calaveras County

About the writer

马克·吐温(Mark Twain, 1835 – 1910)是美国现实主义作家,其原名为塞缪尔·兰亨·克莱门斯(Samuel Langhorne Clemens),"马克·吐温"是他的笔名,意谓水深两浔(1 浔约 1.8 米),这是轮船安全航行的必要条件。马克·吐温曾在密西西比河上当领航员,这段经历给他之后的创作产生了一定的影响。他一生作品众多,以小说创作为主,还创作了大量游记和评论。马克·吐温是19世纪美国批判现实主义文学的主要奠基人之一,确立了美国文学的本土色彩,被福克纳称为"美国文学之父"。

1835 年,马克·吐温出生在密苏里州佛罗里达小镇。11 岁时,父亲去世,他只好辍学,打起了零工,开始自谋生活。他先后做过印刷所学徒、报童、排字工人、水手、淘金工人、记者等,广泛的生活阅历让他见识了各色各样的人,听说过种种奇闻怪谈(tall tales),这让他的作品带有浓厚的地方特色并开创了美国的"地方文学"(regionalism)先河。

马克·吐温的部分作品以青少年题材为主,最具代表性的是《汤姆·索亚历险记》(*Adventures of Tom Sawyer*, 1876)和《哈克贝利·费恩历险记》(*Adventures of Huckleberry Finn*, 1884)。《汤姆·索亚历险记》围绕密西西比河岸小镇圣彼得堡的顽童汤姆·索亚的冒险故事展开。汤姆·索亚和好友哈克在墓地玩耍时,目睹了镇上恶棍印第安·乔杀害鲁滨孙医生后打晕好人穆夫并嫁祸于他的全过程。之后,经过一番激烈的思想斗争,汤姆终于勇敢地站出来,指证了凶手。《哈克贝里·费恩历险记》讲述了哈克贝里·费恩的冒险故事。在被收养后,哈克无法忍受文明社会的约束及酒鬼养父的虐待,逃到一座小岛,遇到逃亡的黑奴吉姆。受南方蓄奴观念和法律的影响,哈克觉得不应该帮助吉姆,但在密西西比河上的漂流生活中,他逐渐被吉姆的善良无私感动,最终帮助吉姆获得自由。海明威对此评价为"全部美国现代文学起始于马克·吐温的一本叫《哈克贝里·费恩》的书"。

马克·吐温通过天马行空的想象、幽默的故事情节以及原汁原味的方言,展现了一个纯真美好、丰富多彩、生气勃勃的没有受到"文明教化"的孩子世界,与尔虞我诈、单调乏味、死气沉沉的成人世界形成了鲜明对比,体现了他对现实社会强烈的讽刺与批判。在马克·吐温看来,儿童有着善良正直的天性,不受传统、习俗等条条框框的束缚,他们是点亮黑暗社会的希望。例如,《王子与贫儿》(The Prince and the Pauper, 1880)讲述了互换身份的王子爱德华与贫儿汤姆各自的传奇经历。不谙世事的王子流落到民间,了解民众疾苦;聪明的贫儿汤姆在代理国王期间废除了苛捐杂税和严酷刑罚,使整个国家气象一新。

马克·吐温创造性地挪用了他早年听闻的各种离奇荒诞故事,使之成为作品的有机组成部分,赋予作品人物鲜明的个性特征和幽默色彩。奇闻怪谈作为美国民间口述文学的一种类型,采用夸张的手法,讲述历史上某个真实的时刻、某个超越常人的或真实或虚构的人物非同一般的经历,其矛盾冲突常以某种幽默方式解决。奇闻怪谈所具有的口语体、离奇夸张、幽默等特征构成了其作品的基本特征。不仅如此,荒诞故事本身也是他作品的基本叙事结构和技巧。一个接一个的奇闻怪谈推动着他的作品情节的发展。《卡拉维拉斯县驰名的跳蛙》("The Notorious Frog of Calaveras County")就是这样一个以奇闻怪谈为核心内容的经典短篇小说。

About the story

1865年,马克·吐温发表短篇小说《卡拉维拉斯县驰名的跳蛙》(以下简称《跳蛙》),他以独特的叙事技巧、幽默夸张的故事内容、生动丰富的本土语言及严肃的批判主题让"整个纽约大笑",该短篇使他成为"太平洋沿岸狂野的幽默家"。

《跳蛙》主要讲述了嗜赌成性的吉姆·斯迈利无所不赌的4个小故事,惟妙惟肖地刻画了一个丧失理性的赌徒形象。第一个故事是赌人。吉姆·斯迈利拿牧师沃克病重的妻子打赌,"出两块五,赌她好不了"。第二个故事是赌马。他的一匹看起来浑身都是毛病的母马总能骗取大家让它先跑几百码赛程的机会,并在比赛的最后取胜。第三个故事是斗狗。同母马一样,吉姆·斯迈利的小狗装可怜骗过了人们的眼睛,误导他们一再加大赌注,为吉姆·斯迈利赢了很多钱。第四个故事是跳蛙比赛。吉姆·斯迈利花了大力气训练出来的能力超凡的跳蛙居然败给了他给外乡人抓的一只普通青蛙,原因是外乡人趁吉姆·斯迈利去抓青蛙时给他的跳蛙肚子里塞满了铅珠。这4个看似零散的荒诞小故事共同刻画了西部淘金世界里投机主义者之间的尔虞我诈。

《跳蛙》里的奇闻怪谈不仅表现在吉姆·斯迈利无所不赌的赌鬼形象和他的怪异幽默的赌博故事,也体现在故事叙述者西蒙·威勒超出常人的絮絮叨叨和作者"我"在如洪水倾泻而下的絮叨中无处可逃的窘境。"我"被西蒙·威勒堵在墙角,听他唠叨了好久,最后不得不瞅准机会,落荒而逃。

《跳蛙》里,"我"的故事采用框架叙事结构,处于小说首尾部分。赌鬼吉姆·斯迈利的故事采用嵌入式叙事结构,嵌入到"我"的故事框架内,使之成为故事内的故事。这种框架-嵌入式叙事结构的优势在于,在不同叙事框架内,作者可以赋予叙事主体独立的人物形象。在《跳蛙》里,处于框架叙事中的"我"语言正式,与西蒙·威勒的对话均采用间接引语,显示出"我"对当地的疏离感和居高临下的优越感。处于嵌入式叙事结构里的人物,无论是叙事主体西蒙·威勒还是嵌入故事里的主人公吉姆·斯迈利,使用的都是非正式的、不合英语语法规范的方言,且全部采用直接引语。借助语言手段,作者一方面继承了奇闻怪谈这一民间文学的口述传统,忠实地反映了西部拓荒世界的语言特色,让人物栩栩如生地呈现在读者面前,另一方面通过两种语体的鲜明对比,展示了东部与西部的对立。

《跳蛙》中,马克·吐温不仅讽刺批判了以赌徒吉姆·斯迈利为代表的机会主义者对金钱毫无道德底线的追求,也讽刺了美国政客的才疏学浅、坑蒙拐骗的丑恶嘴脸,表达了他对美国政治生活的失望。例如,他有意将劣狗取名为安德鲁·杰克逊,将跳蛙取名为丹尼尔·韦伯斯特。这两个名字实有其人,分别是民主党和共和党的领导人。他把安德鲁·杰克逊比喻为斗狗,辅之以看似表扬实则挖苦的语言,"那可是只好狗,那个安德鲁·杰克逊要是活着,一准会出名,胚子好,又聪明"。同样,通过将跳蛙命名为丹尼尔·韦伯斯特,作者展现了一个表面聪明实则自负愚蠢的政客形象。

马克·吐温通过别具一格的叙事方法和活灵活现的地方语言,对他在西部听到的关于赌鬼的奇闻轶事进行加工和改编,将它们重现在《跳蛙》里。奇闻轶事本身所具有的奇趣，加上马克·吐温对生活的体验与观察，以及他对社会时政的关心，使得《跳蛙》故事情节妙趣横生，人物刻画惟妙惟肖，主题批判入木三分。

The Notorious Frog of Calaveras County

In compliance with the request of a friend of mine, who wrote me from the East, I called on good-natured, garrulous old Simon Wheeler, and inquired after my friend's friend, Leonidas W. Smiley①, as requested to do, and I hereunto② append the result. I have a lurking suspicion that Leonidas W. Smiley is a myth; that my friend never knew such a personage; and that he only conjectured that if I asked old Wheeler about him, it would remind him of his infamous Jim Smiley, and he would go to work and bore me to death with some exasperating reminiscence of him as long and as tedious as it should be useless to me. If that was the design, it succeeded③.

I found Simon Wheeler dozing comfortably by the barroom stove of the dilapidated tavern in the decayed mining camp of Angel's, and I noticed that he was fat and baldheaded, and had an expression of winning gentleness and simplicity upon his tranquil countenance④. He roused up, and gave me good day. I told him that a friend of mine had commissioned me to make some inquiries about a cherished companion of his boyhood named Leonidas W. Smiley—Rev. Leonidas W. Smiley, a young minister of the Gospel, who he had heard was at one time a resident of Angel's Camp. I added that if Mr. Wheeler could tell me anything about this Rev.

---

① 即下文第二段中的 Rev. Leonidas W. Smiley, Rev. 为 Reverend, 是对牧师的尊称, 他和故事的主人公赌棍 Jim Smiley 同姓。"我"怀疑朋友设计捉弄我, 是因为 Smiley 这个姓肯定会让 Simon Wheeler 想起赌棍 Jim Smiley。由此可知, Simon Wheeler 一定对很多人讲了 Jim Smiley 的故事。

② hereunto: 于是, 于此（非常正式的用语）。

③ If that was the design, it succeeded: 如果这一切是他设计的, 那么他成功了。

④ he was fat and baldheaded, and had an expression of winning gentleness and simplicity upon his tranquil countenance: 他体胖头秃, 面容平易近人, 朴实祥和。

Leonidas W. Smiley, I would feel under many obligations to him①.

Simon Wheeler backed me into a corner and blockaded me there with his chair, and then sat down and reeled off the monotonous narrative which follows this paragraph②. He never smiled, he never frowned, he never changed his voice from the gentle-flowing key to which he tuned his initial sentence, he never betrayed the slightest suspicion of enthusiasm; but all through the interminable narrative there ran a vein of impressive earnestness and sincerity, which showed me plainly that, so far from his imagining that there was anything ridiculous or funny about his story, he regarded it as a really important matter, and admired its two heroes as men of transcendent genius in finesse③. I let him go on in his own way, and never interrupted him once.

Rev. Leonidas W. H'm, Reverend Le—well, there was a feller④ here once by the name of Jim Smiley, in the winter of '49—or maybe it was the spring of '50—I don't recollect exactly, somehow, though what makes me think it was one or the other is because I remember the big flume warn't⑤ finished when he first come to the camp; but anyway, he was the curiousest⑥ man about always betting on anything that turned up you ever see, if he could get anybody to bet on the other side; and if he couldn't he'd change sides. Any way that suited the other man would suit him—any way just so's he got a bet, he was satisfied. But still he was lucky, uncommon lucky; he most always come out winner. He was always ready and laying for a chance; there couldn't be no solit'ry thing⑦ mentioned but

---

① I would feel under many obligations to him:(非正式)我对他不胜感激。
② Simon Wheeler backed me into a corner and blockaded me there with his chair, and then sat down and reeled off the monotonous narrative which follows this paragraph:Simon Wheeler 把我逼退到墙角,拿椅子把我堵在那儿,坐下来,一说起下面这个故事就没个停。
③ transcendent genius in finesse:超凡的天才。finesse 意为"手段,手腕,策略"。
④ feller:(口语)家伙。
⑤ warn't:(方言)相当于 wasn't 或者 weren't。
⑥ curiousest:most curious。
⑦ no solit'ry thing: no solitary thing,任何东西他都可以拿来打赌。

that feller'd offer to bet on it, and take any side you please, as I was just telling you. If there was a horse-race, you'd find him flush or you'd find him busted at the end of it; if there was a dog-fight, he'd bet on it; if there was a cat-fight, he'd bet on it; if there was a chicken-fight, he'd bet on it; why, if there was two birds setting on a fence, he would bet you which one would fly first; or if there was a camp-meeting, he would be there reg'lar to bet on Parson Walker, which he judged to be the best exhorter about here, and so he was too, and a good man. If he even see a straddle-bug start to go anywheres, he would bet you how long it would take him to get to—to wherever he was going to, and if you took him up, he would foller① that straddle-bug to Mexico but what he would find out where he was bound for and how long he was on the road. Lots of the boys here has seen that Smiley, and can tell you about him. Why, it never made no difference to him—he'd bet on any thing—the dangdest feller. Parson Walker's wife laid very sick once, for a good while, and it seemed as if they warn't going to save her; but one morning he come in, and Smiley up and asked him how she was, and he said she was considerable better—thank the Lord for his inf'nite② mercy—and coming on so smart that with the blessing of Prov'dence③ she'd get well yet; and Smiley, before he thought, says, "Well, I'll resk two-and-a-half she don't anyway④."

"Thish-yer Smiley had a mare—the boys called her the fifteen-minute nag⑤, but that was only in fun, you know, because of course she was faster than that—and he used to win money on that horse, for all she was so slow and always had the asthma, or the distemper, or the consumption, or something of that kind. They used to give her two or three hundred yards'

---

① foller: follow,（口语）跟随。
② inf'nite: infinite。
③ Prov'dence: Providence, 天意、天命、上帝。
④ I'll resk two-and-a-half she don't anyway: resk 为 risk。这句话的意思是"我押二块五,赌她好不了"。
⑤ nag: 老马或驽马。

start, and then pass her under way; but always at the fag end①of the race she'd get excited and desperate like, and come cavorting and straddling up, and scattering her legs around limber, sometimes in the air, and sometimes out to one side among the fences, and kicking up m-o-r-e dust and raising m-o-r-e racket with her coughing and sneezing and blowing her nose—and always fetch up② at the stand just about a neck ahead, as near as you could cipher it down."

And he had a little small bull-pup③, that to look at him you'd think he warn't worth a cent but to set around and look ornery and lay for a chance to steal something. But as soon as money was up on him he was a different dog; his under-jaw'd begin to stick out like the fo'castle④ of a steamboat, and his teeth would uncover and shine like the furnaces. And a dog might tackle him and bully-rag him, and bite him, and throw him over his shoulder two or three times, and Andrew Jackson⑤—which was the name of the pup-Andrew Jackson would never let on but what he was satisfied, and hadn't expected nothing else—and the bets being doubled and doubled on the other side all the time, till the money was all up; and then all of a sudden he would grab that other dog jest⑥ by the j'int⑦ of his hind leg and freeze to it—not chaw, you understand, but only just grip and hang on till they throwed up the sponge⑧, if it was a year. Smiley always come out winner on that pup, till he harnessed a dog once that didn't have no hind legs, because they'd been sawed off in a circular saw, and when the thing had gone along far enough, and the money was all up, and he come to

---

① fag end:本意是指"烟蒂,烟头",此处指比赛快到终点的一段路程。
② fetch up:(非正式)意外到达。
③ bull-pup:斗牛狗,该狗的名字叫 Andrew Jackson,他以美国第 7 任总统的名字命名这只狗。
④ fo'castle:forecastle,指船前甲板下面的部分,水手舱。
⑤ Andrew Jackson:美国民主党人,第 7 任美国总统,因其恒心与毅力,有"老胡桃木"之称。也因其对印第安人的搬迁政策,有"印第安人杀手"的称号。
⑥ jest:just。
⑦ j'int:joint。
⑧ throwed up the sponge:threw up the sponge,(俚语)认输。

make a snatch for his pet holt①, he see in a minute how he'd been imposed on, and how the other dog had him in the door②, so to speak, and he peared③ surprised, and then he looked sorter④ discouraged-like, and didn't try no more to win the fight, and so he got shucked out bad⑤. He give Smiley a look, as much as to say his heart was broke, and it was his fault, for putting up a dog that hadn't no hind legs for him to take holt of⑥, which was his main dependence in a fight, and then he limped off a piece and laid down and died. It was a good pup, was that Andrew Jackson, and would have made a name for hisself⑦ if he'd lived, for the stuff was in him and he had genius—I know it, because he hadn't no opportunities to speak of, and it don't stand to reason that a dog could make such a fight as he could under them⑧ circumstances if he hadn't no talent⑨. It always makes me feel sorry when I think of that last fight of his'n⑩, and the way it turned out.

Well, thish-yer Smiley had rat-terriers, and chicken cocks, and tomcats and all them kind of things, till you couldn't rest, and you couldn't fetch nothing for him to bet on but he'd match you⑪. He ketched⑫ a frog one day, and took him home, and said he cal'klated to edercate him⑬; and so he never done nothing for three months but set in his back yard and learn

---

① holt: hold; he come to make a snatch for his pet holt: 张嘴去咬它惯常喜欢咬的部位（后腿）。
② had him in the door: (口语) 字面意思是把某人堵在屋里，引申为难住某人。
③ peared: appeared。
④ sorter: sort of。
⑤ he got shucked out bad: he got shocked out bad, 他吓坏了。
⑥ take holt of: take hold of。
⑦ made a name for hisself: made a name for himself, 出名。
⑧ them: those。
⑨ he hadn't no opportunities to speak of, and it don't stand to reason that a dog could make such a fight as he could under them circumstances if he hadn't no talent: 它有的是机会证明这一点；再说了，如果它不行，那它怎么赢了那么多场？这说不通啊。
⑩ his'n: (俚语) his own。
⑪ you couldn't fetch nothing for him to bet on but he'd match you: 相当于 you could fetch anything for him to bet on but he'd match you, 不论你拿什么去和他赌，他都会和你赌的。
⑫ ketched: catch 的非标准读音与过去式形式，应为 caught。
⑬ he cal'klated to edercate him: he calculated to educate him, 他寻思着好好训练一下它。

that frog to jump. And you bet you he did learn him, too. He'd give him a little punch behind, and the next minute you'd see that frog whirling in the air like a doughnut—see him turn one summerset①, or maybe a couple, if he got a good start, and come down flat-footed and all right, like a cat. He got him up so in the matter of ketching flies, and kep' him in practice so constant, that he'd nail a fly every time as fur as he could see him. Smiley said all a frog wanted was education, and he could do most anything—and I believe him. Why, I've seen him set Dan'l Webster② down here on this floor—Dan'l Webster was the name of the frog-and sing out, 'Flies, Dan'l, flies!' and quicker'n③ you could wink he'd spring straight up and snake a fly off'n the counter there, and flop down on the floor ag'in as solid as a gob of mud, and fall to scratching the side of his head with his hind foot as indifferent as if he hadn't no idea he'd been doin' any more'n any frog might do. You never see a frog so modest and straight for'ard as he was, for all he was so gifted. And when it come to fair and square jumping on a dead level, he could get over more ground at one straddle than any animal of his breed you ever see. Jumping on a dead level was his strong suit④, you understand; and when it come to that, Smiley would ante up money on him as long as he had a red⑤. Smiley was monstrous proud of his frog, and well he might be, for fellers that had traveled and been everywheres all said he laid over any frog that ever they see.

Well, Smiley kep' the beast in a little lattice box, and he used to fetch him down-town sometimes and lay for a bet. One day a feller—a stranger in

---

① summerset:应为 somersault,(翻)跟头。
② Dan'l Webster Daniel Webster (1782 – 1852),美国著名的政治家、法学家和律师,曾三次担任美国国务卿,一生政治观点灵活多变。此处以他的名字来命名跳蛙,具有讽刺意义。
③ quicker'n:quicker than。小说下文中其他类似比较级后带 'n 都表示 than 的意思。
④ jumping on a dead level was his strong suit:立定跳高是它的强项。
⑤ Smiley would ante up money on him as long as he had a red:ante up money on sth.,(俚语),在……上下大赌注;had a red,(俚语)发脾气,气性大,在这里应该是指青蛙斗志高昂。这句话的意思是:只要它士气高,Smiley 就会下大赌注。

the camp, he was—come acrost① him with his box, and says:

"What might it be that you've got in the box?"

"And Smiley says, sorter indifferent-like, 'It might be a parrot, or it might be a canary, maybe, but it ain't—it's only just a frog.'"

"And the feller took it, and looked at it careful, and turned it round this way and that, and says, 'H'm—so 'tis. Well, what's he good for?'"

"'Well,' Smiley says, easy and careless, 'he's good enough for one thing, I should judge—he can outjump any frog in Calaveras County.'"

"The feller took the box again, and took another long, particular look, and give it back to Smiley, and says, very deliberate, 'Well,' he says, 'I don't see no p'ints② about that frog that's any better'n any other frog.'"

"'Maybe you don't,' Smiley says. 'Maybe you understand frogs and maybe you don't understand 'em; maybe you've had experience, and maybe you ain't only a amature③, as it were. Anyways, I've got my opinion, and I'll resk forty dollars that he can outjump any frog in Calaveras County.'"

"And the feller studied a minute, and then says, kinder sad-like, 'Well, I'm only a stranger here, and I ain't got no frog; but if I had a frog, I'd bet you.'"

"And then Smiley says, 'That's all right—that's all right—if you'll hold my box a minute, I'll go and get you a frog.'" And so the feller took the box, and put up his forty dollars along with Smiley's, and set down to wait.

So he set there a good while thinking and thinking to himself, and then he got the frog out and prized his mouth open and took a teaspoon and filled him full of quail-shot—filled him pretty near up to his chin—and set him on the floor. Smiley he went to the swamp and slopped around in the mud for a long time, and finally he ketched a frog, and fetched him in, and give

---

① acrost: across。
② p'ints: points。
③ you ain't only a amature: 你只不过是个业余的或者新手而已。

him to this feller, and says: "Now, if you're ready, set him alongside of Dan'l, with his fore paws just even with Dan'l's, and I'll give the word." Then he says, "One—two—three—git!" and him and the feller touched up the frogs from behind, and the new frog hopped off lively, but Dan'l give a heave, and hysted up his shoulders①—so—like a Frenchman, but it warn't no use—he couldn't budge; he was planted as solid as a church, and he couldn't no more stir than if he was anchored out. Smiley was a good deal surprised, and he was disgusted too, but he didn't have no idea what the matter was, of course.

The feller took the money and started away; and when he was going out at the door, he sorter jerked his thumb over his shoulder—so—at Dan'l, and said again, very deliberate, "Well," he said, "I don't see no p'ints about that frog that's any better'n any other frog."

"Smiley he stood scratching his head and looking down at Dan'l a long time, and at last he says, 'I do wonder what in the nation that frog throw'd off for—I wonder if there ain't something the matter with him—he 'pears to look mighty baggy, somehow.' And he ketched Dan'l by the nap of the neck, and hefted him②, and says, 'Why blame my cats if he don't weigh five pound!' and turned him upside down and he belched out a double handful of shot. And then he see how it was, and he was the maddest man—he set the frog down and took out after the feller, but he never ketched him. And—"

[Here Simon Wheeler heard his name called from the front yard, and got up to see what was wanted.] And turning to me as he moved away, he said, "Just set where you are, stranger, and rest easy—I ain't going to be gone a second."

But, by your leave, I did not think that a continuation of the history of

---

① hysted up his shoulders: 耸了耸肩,动了动肩。
② he ketched Dan'l by the nap of the neck, and hefted him: 他抓住 Daniel 脖子上的皮,掂了掂它的重量。

the enterprising vagabond Jim Smiley would be likely to afford me much information concerning the Rev. Leonidas W. Smiley, and so I started away.

At the door I met the sociable Wheeler returning, and he buttonholed me and recommenced:

"Well, thish-yer Smiley had a yaller① one-eyed cow that didn't have no tail, only just a short stump like a bannanner②, and—"

However, lacking both time and inclination, I did not wait to hear about the afflicted cow, but took my leave.

Questions

1. In Paragraph 3, the writer mentions "its two heroes as men of transcendent genius in finesse". Who are the "two heroes"?

2. What kind of person was the stranger whom Jim Smiley lost the bet to?

3. Do you think "my" experience of being cornered and told stories of Simon Wheeler as a tall tale? Why?

Further Readings

Mark Twain's writing is humorous but sarcastic, spun with tall tales but mirroring the reality. The following are 4 of his frequently read short stories.

1. "The Story of the Bad Little Boy" (《坏小男孩儿的故事》)
2. "The MYM 30,000 Bequest" (《3万美元遗产》)
3. "Journalism in Tennessee" (《田纳西州新闻界》)
4. "The Man That Corrupted Hadleyburg" (《败坏了哈德来堡的人》)

---

① yaller: yellow。
② bannanner: banana。

Unit 13 Hands

About the writer

舍伍德·安德森(Sherwood Anderson, 1876–1941)是20世纪早期美国文学史上第一位现代意义上的小说家,他首先倡导并推进了美国文学由现实主义向现代主义的转变,在美国文学史上具有独特地位和重大影响。安德森的叙述简洁有力,夹杂着口语化的表达,隐藏着晦暗与不安的情绪。这种风格深刻地影响了包括海明威和福克纳在内的其他作家。

安德森1876年出生于俄亥俄州的卡姆登城,父亲是一个马具工匠。安德森没有受过正规教育,很小就做零工补助家用。母亲因辛劳过早离世。安德森成年后在家乡经营小油漆厂,过着稳定富足的中产阶级生活。为芝加哥浓郁的文化氛围所吸引,安德森1912年离开家乡到芝加哥从事文学创作。他深受芝加哥文艺复兴影响,意识到一个作家必须形成自己独特的风格。这期间他创作了大量作品,成为"芝加哥文艺复兴派"的一员。1941年他在前往南美洲的船上因误吞异物不幸感染腹膜炎去世。

安德森的文学成就集中于短篇小说,成名作是短篇小说集《俄亥俄州的温斯堡镇》(*Winesburg, Ohio*, 1919,又译《小镇畸人》)。19世纪末到20世纪初,美国处于从农业社会向工业社会过渡的时期,生长在小镇的安德森既怀恋那淳朴安逸的田园生活,又憎恨与乡村相连的精神贫困和狭隘。他以家乡俄亥俄州克莱德作为原型,虚构出温斯堡这个处在农业文明向工业文明转型的中西部边远小镇,细致地刻画了小镇上各种"奇怪"人物。《俄亥俄州的温斯堡镇》由25个互有联系的短篇小说构成,全书深刻而别具一格地描绘了小镇居民无法适应飞速发展的科学技术所带来的巨大变化,似乎与世隔绝,变成了一批古怪的人。这其中有被恋人抛弃、在苦苦等待中被孤独折磨吞噬的女性,如《冒险》("Adventure")所述;有在情欲与宗教戒律的激烈冲突中苦苦挣扎却在一个裸体女性身上看到了上帝的力量与启示的小城牧师，如《上帝的力量》("Strength of God")所述。

1921年安德森发表了第二部短篇小说集《鸡蛋的胜利及其他》(The Triumph of the Egg and Other Stories, 1921)。这部小说集的取材与风格同《俄亥俄州的温斯堡镇》相近，嘲讽意味更为明显，描写了美国中西部小镇上人们的挫败感和心理失衡。该作使安德森获得国际声望。1933年，安德森发表短篇小说集《林中之死》(Death in the Woods, 1933)。同名短篇小说《林中之死》是安德森最具悲剧性的作品，讲述了一个贫苦的乡下老太婆背着从镇上乞讨来的冷饭，在林中行走，没有到家就倒在树下死去的故事，表达了普通农妇作为弱者的无奈和作为牺牲者的悲哀。

安德森擅长描写人受压抑后产生的精神创伤和变态心理。他抛弃传统的小说结构，采用一种新的短篇小说艺术，凭借敏锐的想象和透视抓住一种气氛、一个地方或是一个人物加以描绘和渲染。他的小说形式多变，不以明显的或者连贯的情节取胜，而是通过某种富有象征意味的形象、某个突然受到启示的片段揭示事物的本质。安德森的小说也很少使用对话，而是用一种信手拈来的语言风格描摹人物精神状态的变化，以及这些变化在行动上的表现。这种信笔写来、似乎故意不讲究风格的特色构成了安德森短篇小说独特的魅力，体现了20世纪二三十年代美国文学中现实主义、乡土主义和心理小说的交汇融合。

About the story

《手》("Hands", 1919)是短篇小说集《俄亥俄州的温斯堡镇》中一个具有奠基性的作品。故事主人公毕德鲍姆是整部小说集中的第一个怪人，他曾是宾夕法尼亚州某所小学的教师，因被家长误认为是同性恋而被逐出学校。作品围绕毕德鲍姆的双手这一意象展开，注重描写人物的内心世界，细腻地表现了主人公复杂的内心情感。

故事开篇读者能看到毕德鲍姆住在小镇附近的幽谷，常常在小木屋破朽的走廊上神经质地来回行走。他总是一副惊惶不定的样子，只有小镇青年乔治·维拉德与他稍有接触。他有一双敏捷的手，摘草莓时速度快得惊人，曾创下当地的记录。日常生活中他的双手还承担着情感表达的功能。毕德鲍姆的原名为阿道夫·迈尔斯，他是一名教师，性格温和，对学生满腔热忱，但他无法用语言表达内心对学生的热爱,只好借助他纤细的手指,通过对孩子们轻柔的抚触表达自己的爱心,消除孩子们的疑团和困惑,帮助他们创造自己的梦想。手取代语言成为毕德鲍姆的情感交流的主要工具。毕德鲍姆的语言不足以充分传递心声,只有借助手指带有节奏感的敲击他才能酣畅淋漓地表达情感。

这双曾经成就毕德鲍姆的手也给他带来了厄运。19世纪中后期,美国中西部乡村仍属清教禁欲思想盛行、传统两性观念根深蒂固的父权社会。毕德鲍姆被误认为是同性恋,险些被群情激奋的家长私刑绞死。在遭到误解、性命攸关的时刻,他仍然无法用语言为自己辩解,狼狈地逃离了那个小镇。他投奔了温斯堡镇的姑妈,改姓更名以做劳工为生。他不明白这厄运突如其来的原因,只记得在他被殴打、被驱逐时,那男孩父亲的吼骂声:"I'll teach you to put your hands on my boy, you beast","Keep your hands to yourself."他猜测出现变故的原因和屈辱的经历与自己的手有关,于是手一夜之间变成了他的耻辱。毕德鲍姆甚至对自己双手的动作惊恐不已,"He wanted to keep them hidden away and looked with amazement at the quiet inexpressive hands of other men who worked beside him in the fields, or passed, driving sleepy teams on country roads."。这种自卑、困惑和惊恐使毕德鲍姆在温斯堡镇生活20多年之后依然处在一种自我隔离状态,无法融入小镇生活,只能孤独终老。

《手》中大量描写了中西部乡村的自然风貌,撒了苜蓿种子的田里长出浓密的、黄灿灿的大片芥草,表明了大自然具有蓬勃的生命力,不受人类控制。毕德鲍姆在夏日午后坐在青草田埂之上,才跟乔治·维拉德敞开心扉回顾往事,暗示只有在自然的恬淡中,毕德鲍姆才能忘记恐惧。恬适宁静的大自然是治愈人们心灵创伤的良药。小说结尾处,夕阳西下,天色黯淡,火车远去,夏夜寂静,毕德鲍姆的双手也安静下来,作者似乎在暗示只有远离尘嚣,方可心归宁静。

小说中安德森通过音韵学、修辞学等语言技巧营造氛围。小说开头,"Upon the half decayed veranda of a small frame house that stood near the edge of a ravine near the town of Winesburg, Ohio, a fat little old man walked nervously up and down."此句中多个长元音、摩擦音和双元音交替,产生一种迟缓、沉闷、压抑和忧伤的情绪,奠定了小说的基调。"Over the long field came a thin girlish voice"一句中双元音、摩擦音和舌边音组合使

人似乎身处空旷的田野之中。安德森还大量使用词语反复表达强烈的情感。短语 up and down 反复被使用了 5 次，生动地描摹了毕德鲍姆紧张、忐忑、恐慌、坐卧不宁的心理。文中 5 次出现 caress，灵活运用其动词词性和名词词性，形象地展现了一个善良、温和、充满梦想和友爱而又倾向于用手的抚触表达内心情感的男性形象。

Hands

Upon the half decayed veranda① of a small frame house that stood near the edge of a ravine near the town of Winesburg, Ohio, a fat little old man walked nervously up and down. Across a long field that had been seeded for clover but that had produced only a dense crop of yellow mustard weeds, he could see the public highway along which went a wagon filled with berry pickers returning from the fields. The berry pickers, youths and maidens, laughed and shouted boisterously. A boy clad in a blue shirt leaped from the wagon and attempted to drag after him one of the maidens, who screamed and protested shrilly. The feet of the boy in the road kicked up a cloud of dust that floated across the face of the departing sun. Over the long field came a thin girlish voice. "Oh, you Wing Biddlebaum, comb your hair; it's falling into your eyes," commanded the voice to the man, who was bald and whose nervous little hands fiddled about the bare white forehead as though arranging a mass of tangled locks②.

Wing Biddlebaum, forever frightened and beset by a ghostly band of doubts, did not think of himself as in any way a part of the life of the town where he had lived for twenty years. Among all the people of Winesburg but one had come close to him. With George Willard, son of Tom Willard, the proprietor③ of the New Willow House, he had formed something like a

---

① the half decayed veranda：朽败的走廊。
② tangled locks：乱作一团的头发。
③ proprietor：酒店老板。

friendship. George Willard was the reporter on *the Winesburg Eagle* and sometimes in the evenings he walked out along the highway to Wing Biddlebaum's house. Now as the old man walked up and down on the veranda, his hands moving nervously about, he was hoping that George Willard would come and spend the evening with him. After the wagon containing the berry pickers had passed, he went across the field through the tall mustard weeds and climbing a rail fence peered anxiously along the road to the town. For a moment he stood thus, rubbing his hands together and looking up and down the road, and then, fear overcoming him, ran back to work again upon the porch on his own house.

In the presence of George Willard, Wing Biddlebaum, for twenty years had been the town mystery, lost something of his timidity, and his shadowy personality, submerged in a sea of doubts, came forth to look at the world①. With the young reporter at his side, he ventured in the light of day into Main Street or strode up and down on the rickety front porch of his own house, talking excitedly. The voice that had been low and trembling became shrill and loud. The bent figure straightened. With a kind of wriggle, like a fish returned to the brook by the fisherman, Biddlebaum, the silent began to talk striving to put into words the ideas that had been accumulated by his mind during long years of silence.

Wing Biddlebaum talked much with his hands. The slender expressive fingers, forever striving to conceal themselves in his pockets or behind his back, came forth and became the piston rods② of his machinery of expression.

The story of Wing Biddlebaum is a story of hands. Their restless activity, like unto the beating of the wings of an imprisoned bird, had given

---

① Wing Biddlebaum, for twenty years had been the town mystery, lost something of his timidity, and his shadowy personality, submerged in a sea of doubts, came forth to look at the world:这位20年来小镇的神秘人物毕德鲍姆的胆怯便会减轻一些,模糊的个性才会浮出怀疑之海,窥视这个世界。

② the piston rods:活塞杆。

him his name. Some obscure poet of the town had thought of it. The hands alarmed their owner. He wanted to keep them hidden away and looked with amazement at the quiet inexpressive hands① of other men who worked beside him in the fields, or passed, driving sleepy teams on country roads.

When he talked to George Willard, Wing Biddlebaum closed his fists and beat with them upon a table or on the walls of his house. The action made him more comfortable. If the desire to talk came to him when the two were walking in the fields, he sought out a stump or the top board of a fence and with his hands pounding busily talked with renewed ease.

The story of Wing Biddlebaum's hands is worth a book in itself. Sympathetically set forth it would tap many strange, beautiful qualities in obscure men②. It is a job for a poet. In Winesburg the hands had attracted attention merely because of their activity. With them Wing Biddlebaum had picked as high as a hundred and forty quarts of strawberries in a day. They became his distinguishing feature, the source of his fame. Also they made more grotesque an already grotesque and elusive individuality③. Winesburg was proud of Banker White's new stone house and Wesley Moyer's bay stallion, Tony Tip, that had won the two-fifteen trot at the fall races in Cleveland.

As for George Willard, he had many times wanted to ask about the hands. At times an almost overwhelming curiosity had taken hold of him. He felt that there must be a reason for their strange activity and their inclination to keep hidden away and only a growing respect for Wing Biddlebaum kept him from-blurting out the questions that were often in his mind.

---

① inexpressive hands: 安静的双手。

② Sympathetically set forth it would tap many strange, beautiful qualities in obscure men: 如果我们怀着怜悯之心去写这本书，一定能够接触到无名小人物们许多奇怪而优秀的品质。

③ Also they made more grotesque an already grotesque and elusive individuality: 这双手还能使原本就古怪、难以捉摸的个性更加怪异。

Once he had been on the point of asking. The two were walking in the fields on a summer afternoon and had stopped to sit upon a grassy bank. All afternoon Wing Biddlebaum had talked as one inspired. By a fence he had stopped and beating like a giant woodpecker upon the top board had shouted at George Willard, condemning his tendency to be too much influenced by the people about him①. "You are destroying yourself," he cried. "You have the inclination to be alone and to dream and you are afraid of dreams. You want to be like others in town here. You hear them talk and you try to imitate them."

On the grassy bank Wing Biddlebaum had tried again to drive his point home②. His voice became soft and reminiscent, and with a sigh of contentment he launched into a long rambling talk, speaking as one lost in a dream.

Out of the dream Wing Biddlebaum made a picture for George Willard. In the picture men lived again in a kind of pastoral golden age. Across a green open country came clean-limbed young men③, some afoot, some mounted upon horses. In crowds the young men came to gather about the feet of an old man who sat beneath a tree in a tiny garden and who talked to them.

Wing Biddlebaum became wholly inspired. For once he forgot the hands. Slowly they stole forth and lay upon George Willard's shoulders④. Something new and bold came into the voice that talked. "You must try to forget what you have learned," said the old man. "You must begin to dream. From this time on you must shut your ears to the roaring of the voices."

Pausing in his speech, Wing Biddlebaum looked long and earnestly at

---

① condemning his tendency to be too much influenced by the people about him: 毕德鲍姆责骂乔治,说他让芸芸众生左右了他的生活。
② drive his point home: 毕德鲍姆设法回到他的老话题上。
③ clean-limbed young men: 阳光少年。
④ Slowly they stole forth and lay upon George Willard's shoulders: 毕德鲍姆的手悄无声息地溜到乔治的肩上。

George Willard. His eyes glowed. Again he raised the hands to caress the boy and then a look of horror swept over his face.

With a convulsive moment of his body, Wing Biddlebaum sprang to his feet and thrust his hands deep into his trousers pockets. Tears came to his eyes. "I must be getting along home. I can talk no more with you." he said nervously.

Without looking back, the old man had hurried down the hillside and cross a meadow, leaving George Willard perplexed and frightened upon the grassy slope. With a shiver of dread the boy arose and went along the road toward town. "I'll not ask him about his hands," he thought, touched by the memory of the terror he had seen in the man's eyes. "There's something wrong, but I don't want to know what it is. His hands have something to do with his fear of me and of everyone."

And George Willard was right. Let us look briefly into the story of the hands. Perhaps our talking of them will arouse the poet who will tell the hidden wonder story of the influence for which the hands were but fluttering pennants of promise.

In his youth Wing Biddlebaum had been a school teacher in a town in Pennsylvania. He was not then known as Wing Biddlebaum, but went by the less euphonic name① Adolph Myers. As Adolph Myers he was much loved by the boys of his school.

Adolph Myers was meant by nature to be a teacher of youth. He was one of those rare, little-understood men who rule by a power so gentle that it passes as a lovable weakness②. In their feeling for the boys under their charge such men are not unlike the finer sort of women in their love of men.③

---

① the less euphonic name: 不怎么悦耳的名字。
② who rule by a power so gentle that it passes as a lovable weakness: 阿道夫的一个讨人喜欢的缺点就是脾性太过温和，他用这种力量来管理学生。
③ In their feeling for the boys under their charge such men are not unlike the finer sort of women in their love of men: 阿道夫对归他管教的孩子们的情感犹如温良女子对自己的爱人一般。

And yet that is but crudely stated.① It needs the poet there. With the boys of his school, Adolph Myers had walked in the evening or had sat talking until dusk upon the schoolhouse steps lost in a kind of dream. Here and there went his hands, caressing the of the boys, playing about the tousled heads. As he talked his voice became soft and musical. There was a caress in that also. In a way the voice and the hands, the stroking of the shoulders and the touching of the hair were a part of the schoolmaster's effort to carry a dream into the young minds. By the caress that was in his fingers he expressed himself. He was one of those men in whom the force that creates life is diffused, not centralized. Under the caress of his hands doubt and disbelief went out of the minds of the boys and they began also to dream.

And then the tragedy. A half-witted boy② of the school became enamored of the young master. In his bed at night he imagined unspeakable things and in the morning went forth to tell his dreams as facts. Strange hideous accusations fell from his loose-hung lips.③ Through the Pennsylvania town went a shiver. Hidden, shadowy doubts that had been in men's minds concerning Adolph Myers were galvanized into beliefs.

The tragedy did not linger. Trembling lads were jerked out of bed and questioned. "He put his arms about me," said one. "His fingers were always playing in my hair," said another.

One afternoon a man of the town, Henry Bradford, who kept a saloon came to the schoolhouse door. Calling Adolph Myers into the school yard he began to beat him with his fists. As his hard knuckles beat down into the frightened face of the school master, his wrath became more and more terrible. Screaming with dismay, the children run here and there like disturbed insects. "I'll teach you to put your hands on my boy, you beast,"

---

① And yet that is but crudely stated:不过这样说未免有些粗鄙。
② half-witted boy:傻乎乎的男孩。
③ Strange hideous accusations fell from his loose-hung lips:他口无遮拦地冒出奇怪的骇人听闻的污蔑之词。

roared the saloon keeper, who tired of beating the master, had begun to kick him about the yard.

Adolph Myers was driven from the Pennsylvania town in the night. With lanterns in their hands a dozen men came to the door of the house where he lived alone and commanded that he dress and come forth. It was raining and one of the men had a rope in his hands. They had intended to hang the schoolmaster, but something in his figure, so small, white, and pitiful, touched their hearts and they let him escape. As he ran away into the darkness they repented of their weakness and ran after him, swearing and throwing sticks and great balls of soft mud at the figure that screamed and ran faster and faster into the darkness.

For twenty years Adolph Myers had lived alone in Winesburg. He was but forty but looked sixty-five. The name of Biddlebaum he got from a box of goods seen at the freight station as he hurried through an eastern Ohio town. He had an aunt in Winesburg, a black-toothed old woman who raised chickens, and with her he lived until she died. He had been ill for a year after the experience in Pennsylvania, and after his recovery worked as a day laborer in the fields, going timidly about and striving to conceal his hands. Although he did not understand what had happened he felt that the hands must be to blame. Again and again the fathers of the boys had talked of the hands. "Keep your hands to yourself," the saloon keeper had roared, dancing with fury in the schoolhouse yard.

Upon the veranda of his house by the ravine, Wing Biddlebaum continued to walk up and down until the sun had disappeared and the road beyond the field was lost in the grey shadows. Going into his house, he cut slices of bread and spread honey upon them. When the rumble of the evening train that took away the express cars loaded with the day's harvest of berries had passed and restored the silence of the summer night, he went again to walk upon the veranda. In the darkness he could not see the hands and they became quiet. Although he still hungered for the presence of the boy, who was the medium through which he expressed his love of man, the hunger became again a part of his loneliness and his waiting. Lighting a lamp, Wing Biddlebaum washed the few dishes soiled by his simple meal and, setting up a folding cot① by the screen door② that led to the porch, prepared to undress for the night. A few stray white bread crumbs lay on the cleanly washed floor by the table; putting the lamp upon a low stool he began to pick up the crumbs, carrying them to his mouth one by one with unbelievable rapidity. In the dense blotch of light beneath the table, the kneeling figure looked like a priest engaged in some service of his church. The nervous expressive fingers, flashing in and out of the light③, might well have been mistaken for the fingers of the devotee going swiftly through decade after decade of his rosary④.

Questions

1. Besides "hands" and "dream", what other images does the author use in this short story? What function do these images play in this story?

2. Why did people give Biddlebaum the nickname "Wing"? What does "wing" symbolize?

Further Readings

Sherwood Anderson's short stories are notable for their naturalistic, emotional and psychological interpretation and their symbolization. The following are some of his important short stories.

1. "I Want to Know Why" (《我想知道这是为什么》)
2. "The Egg" (《鸡蛋》)
3. "I'm a Fool" (《我是个傻瓜》)
4. "Death in the Woods" (《林中之死》)

---

① folding cot: 折叠床。
② screen door: 纱门。
③ flashing in and out of the light: 在亮光中时隐时现。
④ the fingers of the devotee going swiftly through decade after decade of his rosary: 信徒的手指十个一组,敏捷地拨动着念珠。

Unit 14　Dry September

About the writer

威廉·福克纳(William Faulkner,1897 – 1962)是美国文学史上最具影响力的南方作家之一,也是美国意识流文学的代表作家。他一生著作颇丰,共出版19部长篇小说与120多篇短篇小说。福克纳多数作品的故事发生在约克纳帕塔法县(Yoknapatawpha),围绕杰弗逊镇及其郊区若干不同社会阶层的家族展开,被称为"约克纳帕塔法世系"。

福克纳出生于美国南方一个有着悠久历史的家庭,曾祖父威廉·克拉科·福克纳一生成就卓越,既是种植园主,又是军人、作家、政治家。福克纳从小在牛津镇长大,他以牛津镇为原型,虚构出了杰弗逊镇和约克纳帕塔法县。福克纳凭着对美国南方社会的深刻了解,将美国南方的经济发展、生活方式和行为习惯的变更,以及语言的发展统统融入其想象中并加以改造,创造出一个福克纳式的世界。

福克纳的代表作是长篇小说《喧哗与骚动》(*The Sound and the Fury*, 1929),小说讲述了南方没落地主康普生一家数代人的历史。老康普生游手好闲,好吃懒做;妻子自私冷酷,无暇照顾儿女;长子昆丁固守南方的贵族传统不放,认为风流成性的妹妹凯蒂让整个家族蒙耻,他最终选择溺水自杀;次子杰生冷酷贪婪,一心攫取钱财;三子班吉是个白痴,无法独立生活。小说通过三个儿子的内心独白,围绕凯蒂的堕落展开,最后黑人女佣迪尔西的叙述对前三部分的空白提供了补充。小说大量运用多视角叙述方法和意识流叙事手法,反映出人物瞬息万变的心理活动,成为意识流小说乃至整个现代派小说的经典之作。

1930年,福克纳发表了长篇小说《我弥留之际》(*As I Lay Dying*)。小说中,美国南方农民安斯遵守妻子艾迪的承诺,在妻子病故之后带领儿子们将妻子遗体运回家乡安葬,却遭遇了大雨、洪水、大火等重重困难,最终全家人成功将死者安葬。小说由 59 个小节组成,这些小节为安斯一家、众多邻居和相关人员的内心独白。小说使用多视角叙事方法,将意识流手法运用到极致,揭示了安斯一家及周围人的心路历程。

《八月之光》(*Light in August*, 1932)主要围绕黑白混血儿乔·克里斯莫斯悲剧性的一生展开。乔是南方一个白人贵族小姐与一个据说有黑人血统的流浪艺人的私生子。母亲在分娩时去世,父亲被深受种族主义影响的外祖父枪杀。虽然外表上看不出任何黑人的特征,但乔一生都困惑于他的身份,"既不像一个白人也不像一个黑人"。之后,他与一个白人姑娘相爱并同居,对方得知他有黑人血统后提出分手,愤怒之下他失手杀了这位姑娘。几天后,乔自首并被处死。小说运用预叙、闪回、跳跃、更替、时间流逝等手段,追溯了主人公乔的一生,揭示了美国南方根深蒂固的种族主义,以及种族主义给人们带来的伤害。

福克纳创作的"约克纳帕塔法世系"从不同侧面反映了美国南方的风俗人情、种族隔阂和宗教信仰,展现了南方的历史变迁和人们所承受的各种压力。福克纳在作品中经常运用意识流手法和多叙事角度,致力于展示人物复杂的心理变化,揭示社会变迁给人们带来的心理冲击。意识流和多角度叙事使得福克纳的作品呈现出印象主义绘画般的独特审美效果。福克纳许多作品的名称源自《圣经》,如"喧哗与骚动""我弥留之际""押沙龙"等。其作品运用了神话结构,形成与神话的互文,具有丰富的意蕴。

About the story

短篇小说《干旱的九月》("Dry September")发表于 1931 年。故事发生在约克纳帕塔法县的杰弗逊镇,历史背景是美国内战刚刚结束,美国南方正处于社会转型期,许多南方的陈旧观念依然盛行,如"淑女神话""处女情结"、男权至上、黑人种族主义等。

小说中,白人贵族小姐明尼·库伯年轻时曾是镇上最漂亮的姑娘,男人们纷纷向她献殷勤。现在她已经四十多岁,青春已逝,人老珠黄,孑然一身,与母亲和姑妈生活在一起。尽管衣食无忧、生活舒适,她却不甘寂寞。为重新吸引小镇人们的关注,她故意编造出被黑人威尔强奸的谎话。不料,该事在小镇上引起轩然大波。白人理发师霍克肖坚持认为威尔是一个循规蹈矩的黑人，他绝对不可能去侵犯明尼·库伯。他坚持将威尔交给当局调查和处置。但是，以麦克·兰登为首的极端种族主义分子坚信白人小姐不可能说谎，并嘲讽霍克肖关爱黑人，他们最终将威尔私刑处死。

《干旱的九月》反映了美国南方根深蒂固的种族主义。明尼·库伯傲慢虚荣，对黑人的歧视根深蒂固。她处心积虑地利用南方白人贵族男子固有的"处女情结"和白人对黑人的歧视心理，陷害无辜的黑人威尔，以达到引起众人关注的目的。作为一个地位低下的黑人，威尔百口莫辩。镇上的白人们更倾向于相信明尼·库伯的话，而非威尔的辩解。当霍克肖对明尼·库伯捏造的强奸案表示质疑时，麦克·兰登反驳道："that you'd take a nigger's word before a white woman's? Why, you damn niggerloving—"。

小说也反映了种族主义给白人造成的心理异化。明尼·库伯冷酷自私，为一己虚荣，不惜牺牲一个无辜黑人的生命。麦克·兰登残忍、虚伪，表面上似乎很关心白人女性，对威尔的辩解置之不理，深夜率领众人将"罪犯"威尔处以私刑。但是，回到家后，却对自己的妻子异常冷漠，反复责骂她不应该等候自己回家，并且暴躁地用力抓住妻子的肩膀，直至妻子疼痛求饶。霍克肖虽然在刚听到谣言时极力为威尔辩解："Except it wasn't Will Mayes … I know Will Mayes. He's a good nigger. And I know Miss Minnie Cooper, too."然而，他并没有极力阻拦白人对威尔的暴力行为，而是选择中途放弃，默默地看着威尔被处死。

小说中多次运用象征手法，通过环境描写揭示了以小镇为代表的美国南方种族尖锐对立、矛盾一触即发的社会现状。小说开篇便交代了九月的天气炎热干燥，已经连续两个多月没有下雨，人们异常烦躁，此时谣言如火一般极易传播，人们以此为乐。威尔被抓住的那个夜晚，小镇异常寂静，不见人影，不闻虫鸣，四处弥漫着灰尘，连月亮的亮光也被灰尘遮蔽，这喻示着小镇看不到光亮和希望的黑暗社会现状。小说结尾处，死寂黑暗的环境再次被渲染，这表达了作者对美国南方所持有的悲观情绪。在作者看来，被种族主义笼罩的南方没有未来。这其实是一种行动的吁请，呼吁人们行动起来，改变这个现状。《干旱的九月》发表于1931年，在某种程度上讲，它预示了美国60年代如火如荼的黑人民权运动。

Dry September

I

THROUGH the bloody September twilight, aftermath of sixty-two rainless days, it had gone like a fire in dry grass—the rumor, the story, whatever it was. Something about Miss Minnie Cooper and a Negro. Attacked, insulted, frightened: none of them, gathered in the barber shop on that Saturday evening where the ceiling fan stirred, without freshening it, the vitiated air, sending back upon them, in recurrent surges of stale pomade and lotion①, their own stale breath and odors, knew exactly what had happened.

"Except it wasn't Will Mayes," a barber said. He was a man of middle age; a thin, sand-colored man with a mild face, who was shaving a client. "I know Will Mayes. He's a good nigger. And I know Miss Minnie Cooper, too."

"What do you know about her?" a second barber said.

"Who is she?" the client said. "A young girl?"

"No," the barber said. "She's about forty, I reckon. She ain't married. That's why I don't believe—"

"Believe, hell!" a hulking youth in a sweat-stained silk shirt said. "Won't you take a white woman's word before a nigger's?"

"I don't believe Will Mayes did it," the barber said. "I know Will Mayes." "Maybe you know who did it, then. Maybe you already got him out of town, you damn niggerlover."

"I don't believe anybody did anything. I don't believe anything happened. I leave it to you fellows if the ladies that get old without getting

---

① surges of stale pomade and lotion: 变质的润发油和护肤液的气味。

married don't have notions that a man can't—"

"Then you are a hell of a white man," the client said. He moved under the cloth. The youth had sprung to his feet.

"You don't?" he said. "Do you accuse a white woman of lying?"

The barber held the razor poised above the half-risen client. He did not look around.

"It's this durn weather," another said. "It's enough to make a man do anything. Even to her."

Nobody laughed. The barber said in his mild, stubborn tone: "I ain't accusing nobody of nothing. I just know and you fellows know how a woman that never—"

"You damn niggerlover!" the youth said.

"Shut up, Butch," another said. "We'll get the facts in plenty of time to act."①

"Who is? Who's getting them?" the youth said. "Facts, hell! I—"

"You're a fine white man," the client said. "Ain't you?" In his frothy beard he looked like a desert rat in the moving pictures. "You tell them, Jack," he said to the youth. "If there ain't any white men in this town, you can count on me, even if I ain't only a drummer and a stranger."

"That's right, boys," the barber said. "Find out the truth first. I know Will Mayes."

"Well, by God!" the youth shouted. "To think that a white man in this town—"

"Shut up, Butch," the second speaker said. "We got plenty of time."

The client sat up. He looked at the speaker. "Do you claim that anything excuses a nigger attacking a white woman? Do you mean to tell me you are a white man and you'll stand for it? You better go back North where you came from. The South don't want your kind here."

---

① We'll get the facts in plenty of time to act：我们将有充足的时间了解事实的真相。

"North what?" the second said. "I was born and raised in this town."

"Well, by God!" the youth said. He looked about with a strained, baffled gaze, as if he was trying to remember what it was he wanted to say or to do. He drew his sleeve across his sweating face. "Damn if I'm going to let a white woman—"

"You tell them, Jack," the drummer said. "By God, if they—"

The screen door crashed open. A man stood in the floor, his feet apart and his heavy-set body poised easily. His white shirt was open at the throat; he wore a felt hat. His hot, bold glance swept the group.① His name was McLendon. He had commanded troops at the front in France and had been decorated for valor.

"Well," he said, "are you going to sit there and let a black son rape a white woman on the streets of Jefferson?"

Butch sprang up again. The silk of his shirt clung flat to his heavy shoulders. At each armpit was a dark halfmoon. "That's what I been telling them! That's what I—"

"Did it really happen?" a third said. "This ain't the first man scare she ever had, like Hawkshaw says. Wasn't there something about a man on the kitchen roof, watching her undress, about a year ago?"

"What?" the client said. "What's that?" The barber had been slowly forcing him back into the chair; he arrested himself reclining, his head lifted, the barber still pressing him down.

McLendon whirled on the third speaker. "Happen? What the hell difference does it make? Are you going to let the black sons get away with it until one really does it?"

"That's what I'm telling them!" Butch shouted. He cursed, long and steady, pointless.②

---

① His hot, bold glance swept the group:他用愤怒无顾忌的目光扫了一下这群人。
② He cursed, long and steady, pointless:他不停地咒骂,既执拗又无聊。

"Here, here," a fourth said. "Not so loud. Don't talk so loud."

"Sure," McLendon said, "no talking necessary at all. I've done my talking. Who's with me?" He poised on the balls of his feet, roving his gaze.

The barber held the drummer's face down, the razor poised. "Find out the facts first, boys. I know Willy Mayes. It wasn't him. Let's get the sheriff and do this thing right."①

McLendon whirled upon him his furious, rigid face. The barber did not look away. They looked like men of different races. The other barbers had ceased also above their prone clients. "You mean to tell me," McLendon said, "that you'd take a nigger's word before a white woman's? Why, you damn niggerloving—"

The third speaker rose and grasped McLendon's arm; he, too, had been a soldier. "Now, now. Let's figure this thing out. Who knows anything about what really happened?"

"Figure out hell!" McLendon jerked his arm free. "All that're with me get up from there. The ones that ain't—" He roved his gaze, dragging his sleeve across his face.

Three men rose. The drummer in the chair sat up. "Here," he said, jerking at the cloth about his neck; "get this rag off me. I'm with him. I don't live here, but by God, if our mothers and wives and sisters—" He smeared the cloth over his face and flung it to the floor. McLendon stood in the floor and cursed the others. Another rose and moved toward him. The remainder sat uncomfortable, not looking at one another, then one by one they rose and joined him.

The barber picked the cloth from the floor. He began to fold it neatly. "Boys, don't do that. Will Mayes never done it. I know."

"Come on," McLendon said. He whirled. From his hip pocket

---

① Let's get the sheriff and do this thing right：让我们告诉治安官，请求公正地处理这件事。

protruded the butt of a heavy automatic pistol. They went out. The screen door crashed behind them reverberant in the dead air.

The barber wiped the razor carefully and swiftly, and put it away, and ran to the rear, and took his hat from the wall. "I'll be back as soon as I can," he said to the other barbers. "I can't let—" He went out, running. The two other barbers followed him to the door and caught it on the rebound, leaning out and looking up the street after him. The air was flat and dead. It had a metallic taste at the base of the tongue.①

"What can he do?" the first said. The second one was saying "Jees Christ②, Jees Christ" under his breath. "I'd just as life be Will Mayes as Hawk, if he gets McLendon riled."

"Jees Christ, Jees Christ," the second whispered. "You reckon he really done it to her?" the first said.

II

SHE WAS thirty-eight or thirty-nine. She lived in a small frame house with her invalid mother and a thin, sallow, un-flagging③ aunt, where each morning between ten and eleven she would appear on the porch in a lace-trimmed boudoir cap, to sit swinging in the porch swing until noon. After dinner she lay down for a while, until the afternoon began to cool. Then, in one of the three or four new voile dresses which she had each summer, she would go downtown to spend the afternoon in the stores with the other ladies, where they would handle the goods and haggle over the prices in cold, immediate voices④, without any intention of buying.

She was of comfortable people⑤—not the best in Jefferson, but good

---

① The air was flat and dead. It had a metallic taste at the base of the tongues.:空气沉闷而凝滞,有一种金属味道沉在嗓子里。这里形容紧张压抑的气氛。
② Jees Christ, Jees Christ:(口头用语)老天保佑,老天保佑。
③ un-flagging:勤快的。
④ in cold, immediate voices:冷漠而不耐烦的语气。
⑤ She was of comfortable people:她日子过得舒服。

people enough—and she was still on the slender side of ordinary looking, with a bright, faintly haggard manner and dress. When she was young she had had a slender, nervous body and a sort of hard vivacity① which had enabled her for a time to ride upon the crest② of the town's social life as exemplified by the high school party and church social period of her contemporaries while still children enough to be unclassconscious③.

She was the last to realize that she was losing ground④; that those among whom she had been a little brighter and louder flame than any other were beginning to learn the pleasure of snobbery-male—and retaliation—female⑤. That was when her face began to wear that bright, haggard look. She still carried it to parties on shadowy porticoes and summer lawns, like a mask or a flag, with that bafflement of furious repudiation of truth in her eyes⑥. One evening at a party she heard a boy and two girls, all schoolmates, talking. She never accepted another invitation.

She watched the girls with whom she had grown up as they married and got homes and children, but no man ever called on her steadily until the children of the other girls had been calling her "aunty" for several years, the while their mothers told them in bright voices about how popular Aunt Minnie had been as a girl. Then the town began to see her driving on Sunday afternoons with the cashier in the bank. He was a widower of about forty—a high-colored⑦ man, smelling always faintly of the barber shop or of whisky. He owned the first automobile in town, a red runabout; Minnie had the first motoring bonnet and veil the town ever saw. Then the town

---

① she had had a slender, nervous body and a sort of hard vivacity:她身材苗条,有些神经质,非常活泼。
② ride upon the crest:颇出风头。
③ still children enough to be unclassconscious:那时她还是个尚无评判能力的孩子。
④ losing ground:失去年轻的优势。
⑤ snobbery-male—and retaliation—female:男性出于势利的心理,女性出于报复的心理。
⑥ bafflement of furious repudiation of truth in her eyes:否认事实的困惑神情。
⑦ high-colored:深色皮肤的。

began to say: "Poor Minnie." "But she is old enough to take care of herself," others said. That was when she began to ask her old schoolmates that their children call her "cousin" instead of "aunty".

It was twelve years now since she had been relegated into adultery by public opinion, and eight years since the cashier had gone to a Memphis bank, returning for one day each Christmas, which he spent at an annual bachelors' party at a hunting club on the river. From behind their curtains the neighbors would see the party pass, and during the over-the-way Christmas day visiting they would tell her about him, about how well he looked, and how they heard that he was prospering in the city, watching with bright, secret eyes her haggard, bright face. Usually by that hour there would be the scent of whisky on her breath. It was supplied her by a youth, a clerk at the soda fountain: "Sure; I buy it for the old gal. I reckon she's entitled to a little fun.①"

Her mother kept to her room altogether now; the gaunt aunt ran the house. Against that background Minnie's bright dresses, her idle and empty days, had a quality of furious unreality②. She went out in the evenings only with women now, neighbors, to the moving pictures. Each afternoon she dressed in one of the new dresses and went downtown alone, where her young "cousins" were already strolling in the late afternoons with their delicate, silken heads and thin, awk-ward arms and conscious hips, clinging to one another or shrieking and giggling with paired boys in the soda fountain when she passed and went on along the serried store fronts, in the doors of which the sitting and lounging men did not even follow her with their eyes any more.

---

① I reckon she's entitled to a little fun: 我觉得她应该得到点乐趣。
② Against that background Minnie's bright dresses, her idle and empty days, had a quality of furious unreality: 和她的晃眼的服装相比较, 她的懒散空虚的日子有着懊恼、不现实的特点。

III

The barber went swiftly up the street where the sparse lights, insect-swirled, glared in rigid and violent suspension in the lifeless air. The day had died in a pall of dust; above the darkened square, shrouded by the spent dust, the sky was as clear as the inside of a brass bell. Below the cast was a rumor of the twice-waxed moon.

When he overtook them McLendon and three others were getting into a car parked in an alley. McLendon stooped his thick head, peering out beneath the top①. "Changed your mind, did you?" he said. "Damn good thing; by God, tomorrow when this town hears about how you talked tonight—"

"Now, now," the other ex-soldier said. "Hawkshaw's all right. Come on, Hawk; jump in."

"Will Mayes never done it, boys," the barber said. "If anybody done it. Why, you all know well as I do there ain't any town where they got better niggers than us②. And you know how a lady will kind of think things about men when there ain't any reason to, and Miss Minnie anyway—"

"Sure, sure," the soldier said. "We're just going to talk to him a little; that's all."

"Talk hell!" Butch said. "When we're through with the—"

"Shut up, for God's sake!" the soldier said. "Do you want everybody in town—"

"Tell them, by God!" McLendon said. "Tell every one of the sons that'll let a white woman—"

"Let's go; let's go: here's the other car." The second car slid squealing out of a cloud of dust at the alley mouth. McLendon started his car and took

---

① peering out beneath the top: 在车顶下往外瞅。
② you all know well as I do there ain't any town where they got better niggers than us: 你们都像我一样清楚,镇子哪儿都找不到比我们要找的更好的黑人。

the lead. Dust lay like fog in the street. The street lights hung nimbused as in water①. They drove on out of town.

A rutted lane turned at right angles. Dust hung above it too, and above all the land. The dark bulk of the ice plant, where the Negro Mayes was night watchman, rose against the sky. "Better stop here, hadn't we?" the soldier said. McLendon did not reply. He hurled the car up and slammed to a stop, the headlights glaring on the blank wall.

"Listen here, boys," the barber said, "if he's here, don't that prove he never done it? Don't it? If it was him, he would run. Don't you see he would?" The second car came up and stopped. McLendon got down; Butch sprang down beside him. "Listen, boys," the barber said.

"Cut the lights off!" McLendon said. The breathless dark rushed down②. There was no sound in it save their lungs as they sought air in the parched dust in which for two months they had lived; then the diminishing crunch of McLendon's and Butch's feet, and a moment later McLendon's voice:

"Will! ... Will!"

Below the cast the wan hemorrhage of the moon increased. It heaved above the ridge, silvering the air, the dust, so that they seemed to breathe, live, in a bowl of molten lead③. There was no sound of nightbird nor insect, no sound save their breathing and a faint ticking of contracting metal about the cars. Where their bodies touched one another they seemed to sweat dryly, for no more moisture came. "Christ!" a voice said, "let's get out of here."

But they didn't move until vague noises began to grow out of the darkness ahead; then they got out and waited tensely in the breathless dark. There was another sound: a blow, a hissing expulsion of breath and McLendon cursing in

---

① The street lights hung nimbused as in water:街灯悬浮成雨雾状,如同在水里。
② The breathless dark rushed down:漆黑的夜幕骤然罩下。
③ they seemed to breathe, live, in a bowl of molten lead:他们如同在一只熔化了铅的碗里呼吸、生活。

undertone. They stood a moment longer, then they ran forward. They ran in a stumbling clump, as though they were fleeing something. "Kill him, kill the son," a voice whispered. McLendon flung them back.

"Not here," he said. "Get him into the car." "Kill him, kill the black son!" the voice murmured. They dragged the Negro to the car. The barber had waited beside the car. He could feel himself sweating and he knew he was going to be sick at the stomach.

"What is it, captains?" the Negro said. "I ain't done nothing. 'Fore God, Mr. John." Someone produced handcuffs. They worked busily about the Negro as though he were a post, quiet, intent, getting in one another's way①. He submitted to the handcuffs, looking swiftly and constantly from dim face to dim face. "Who's here, captains?" he said, leaning to peer into the faces until they could feel his breath and smell his sweaty reek. He spoke a name or two. "What you all say I done, Mr. John?"

McLendon jerked the car door open. "Get in!" he said.

The Negro did not move. "What you all going to do with me, Mr. John? I ain't done nothing. White folks, captains, I ain't done nothing: I swear 'fore God." He called another name.

"Get in!" McLendon said. He struck the Negro. The others expelled their breath in a dry hissing and struck him with random blows and he whirled and cursed them, and swept his manacled hands across their faces and slashed the barber upon the mouth, and the barber struck him also. "Get him in there," McLendon said. They pushed at him. He ceased struggling and got in and sat quietly as the others took their places. He sat between the barber and the soldier, drawing his limbs in so as not to touch them, his eyes going swiftly and constantly from face to face. Butch clung to the running board. The car moved on. The barber nursed his mouth with his handkerchief.

---

① he were a post, quiet, intent, getting in one another's way: 黑人如柱子一般挡着路，不易降服。

"What's the matter, Hawk?" the soldier said.

"Nothing," the barber said. They regained the highroad and turned away from town. The second car dropped back out of the dust. They went on, gaining speed; the final fringe of houses dropped behind.

"Goddamn, he stinks!" the soldier said.

"We'll fix that," the drummer in front beside McLendon said. On the running board Butch cursed into the hot rush of air. The barber leaned suddenly forward and touched McLendon's arm.

"Let me out, John," he said.

"Jump out, niggerlover," McLendon said without turning his head. He drove swiftly. Behind them the sourceless lights of the second car glared in the dust. Presently McLendon turned into a narrow road. It was rutted with disuse. It led back to an abandoned brick kiln—a series of reddish mounds and weed- and vine-choked vats without bottom. It had been used for pasture once, until one day the owner missed one of his mules. Although he prodded carefully in the vats with a long pole, he could not even find the bottom of them.

"John," the barber said.

"Jump out, then," McLendon said, hurling the car along the ruts. Beside the barber the Negro spoke:

"Mr. Henry."

The barber sat forward. The narrow tunnel of the road rushed up and past. Their motion was like an extinct furnace blast: cooler, but utterly dead. The car bounded from rut to rut.

"Mr. Henry," the Negro said.

The barber began to tug furiously at the door. "Look out, there!" the soldier said, but the barber had already kicked the door open and swung onto the running board. The soldier leaned across the Negro and grasped at him, but he had already jumped. The car went on without checking speed.

The impetus hurled him crashing through dust-sheathed weeds, into the ditch. Dust puffed about him, and in a thin, vicious crackling of sapless stems he lay choking and retching until the second car passed and died away. Then he rose and limped on until he reached the highroad and turned toward town, brushing at his clothes with his hands. The moon was higher, riding high and clear of the dust at last, and after a while the town began to glare beneath the dust. He went on, limping. Presently he heard cars and the glow of them grew in the dust behind him and he left the road and crouched again in the weeds until they passed. McLendon's car came last now. There were four people in it and Butch was not on the running board.

They went on; the dust swallowed them; the glare and the sound died away. The dust of them hung for a while, but soon the eternal dust absorbed it again. The barber climbed back onto the road and limped on toward town.

IV

AS SHE DRESSED for supper on that Saturday evening, her own flesh felt like fever. Her hands trembled among the hooks and eyes, and her eyes had a feverish look, and her hair swirled crisp and crackling under the comb. While she was still dressing the friends called for her and sat while she donned her sheerest underthings and stockings and a new voile dress. "Do you feel strong enough to go out?" they said, their eyes bright too, with a dark glitter. "When you have had time to get over the shock, you must tell us what happened. What he said and did; everything."

In the leafed darkness, as they walked toward the square, she began to breathe deeply, something like a swimmer preparing to dive, until she ceased trembling, the four of them walking slowly because of the terrible heat and out of solicitude for her. But as they neared the square she began to tremble again, walking with her head up her hands clenched at her sides, their voices about her murmurous, also with that feverish, glittering quality of their eyes.

They entered the square, she in the center of the group, fragile in her fresh dress. She was trembling worse. She walked slower and slower, as children eat ice cream, her head up and her eyes bright in the haggard banner of her face, passing the hotel and the coatless drummers in chairs along the curb looking around at her: "That's the one; see? The one in pink in the middle." "Is that her? What did they do with the nigger? Did they—?" "Sure. He's all right." "All right, is he?" "Sure. He went on a little trip." Then the drug store, where even the young men lounging in the door-way tipped their hats and followed with, their eyes the motion of her hips and legs when she passed.

They went on, passing the lifted hats of the gentlemen, the suddenly ceased voices, deferent, protective. "Do you see?" the friends said. Their voices sounded like long, hovering sighs of hissing exultation. "There's not a Negro on the square. Not one."

They reached the picture show. It was like a miniature fairyland with its lighted lobby and colored lithographs of life caught in its terrible and beautiful mutations. Her lips began to tingle. In the dark, when the picture began, it would be all right; she could hold back the laughing so it would not waste away so fast and so soon. So she hurried on before the turning faces, the undertones of low astonishment, and they took their accustomed places where she could see the aisle against the silver glare and the young men and girls coming in two and two against it.

The lights flicked away; the screen glowed silver, and soon life began to unfold, beautiful and passionate and sad, while still the young men and girls entered, scented and sibilant in the half dark, their paired backs in silhouette delicate and sleek, their slim, quick bodies awkward, divinely young, while beyond them the silver dream accumulated, inevitably on and on. She began to laugh. In trying to suppress it, it made more noise than ever; heads began to turn. Still laughing, her friends raised her and led her out, and she stood at the curb, laughing on a high, sustained note, until the taxi came up and they helped her in.

They removed the pink voile and the sheer underthings and the stockings, and put her to bed, and cracked ice for her temples, and sent for the doctor. He was hard to locate, so they ministered to her with hushed ejaculations, renewing the ice and fanning her. While the ice was fresh and cold she stopped laughing and lay still for a time, moaning only a little. But soon the laughing welled again and her voice rose screaming.

"Shhhhhhhhhhh! Shhhhhhhhhhhhh!" they said, freshening the icepack, smoothing her hair, examining it for gray; "poor girl!" Then to one another: "Do you suppose anything really happened?" their eyes darkly aglitter, secret and passionate①. "Shhhhhhhhhh! Poor girl! Poor Minnie!"

V

IT WAS MIDNIGHT when McLendon drove up to his neat new house. It was trim and fresh as a birdcage and almost as small, with its clean, green-and-white paint. He locked the car and mounted the porch and entered. His wife rose from a chair beside the reading lamp. McLendon stopped in the floor and stared at her until she looked down.

"Look at that clock," he said, lifting his arm, pointing. She stood before him, her face lowered, a magazine in her hands. Her face was pale, strained, and weary-looking. "Haven't I told you about sitting up like this, waiting to see when I come in?"

"John," she said. She laid the magazine down. Poised on the balls of his feet, he glared at her with his hot eyes, his sweating face.

"Didn't I tell you?" He went toward her. She looked up then. He caught her shoulder. She stood passive, looking at him.

"Don't, John. I couldn't sleep...The heat; something. Please, John. You're hurting me."

---

① their eyes darkly aglitter, secret and passionate: 她们的眼睛幽幽闪烁，流露出神秘和狂热。

"Didn't I tell you?" He released her and half struck, half flung her across the chair, and she lay there and watched him quietly as he left the room.

He went on through the house, ripping off his shirt, and on the dark, screened porch at the rear he stood and mopped his head and shoulders with the shirt and flung it away. He took the pistol from his hip and laid it on the table beside the bed, and sat on the bed and removed his shoes, and rose and slipped his trousers off. He was sweating again already, and he stooped and hunted furiously for the shirt. At last he found it and wiped his body again, and, with his body pressed against the dusty screen, he stood panting. There was no movement, no sound, not even an insect. The dark world seemed to lie stricken beneath the cold moon and the lidless stars.

Questions

1. What point of view does Faulkner employ in this short story? What role does this point of view play in driving the plot?

2. McLendon is a complex character in the short story. On the one hand, it seems that he is eager to kill Will to safeguard ladies' safety. On the other hand, he is rude to his own wife. He scolded and mistreated her. In your opinion, what kind of person is McLendon?

Further Readings

William Faulkner's short stories are notable for long sentences with complicated structure and multiple themes. The following are some of his important short stories.

1. "That Evening Sun" (《夕阳》)
2. "Barn Burning" (《烧牲口棚》)
3. "A Rose for Emily" (《献给爱米丽的一朵玫瑰花》)

Unit 15　The Killers

About the writer

　　欧内斯特·米勒·海明威(Ernest Miller Hemingway, 1899 –1961)是美国20世纪最著名的小说家之一。1953年,他以《老人与海》(*The Old Man and the Sea*)一书获得普利策奖,次年又获得诺贝尔文学奖。海明威是美国"迷惘的一代"(The Lost Generation)作家中的代表人物之一,他的极简文风对美国文学乃至世界文学产生了重要影响。

　　海明威1899年出生于芝加哥市郊,从小热爱大自然。高中毕业后,海明威到《堪城星报》(*Kansas City Star*)当记者,开始了他的写作生涯。1918年,海明威本打算参军,但因视力不合格,只被派到红十字会担任救护车司机,他在意大利前线目睹了战争的残酷。因运输途中受伤,海明威在米兰一个美国红十字会医院住院养伤。他的早期小说《永别了,武器》(*A Farewell to Arms*, 1929)的创作灵感正源于此。1926年,小说《太阳照常升起》(*The Sun Also Rises*)出版并大获成功。1940年,海明威发表了以西班牙内战为背景的反法西斯的长篇小说《丧钟为谁而鸣》(*For Whom the Bell Tolls*)。1944年,他随同美军去欧洲采访,在一次飞机失事中身受重伤,痊愈后仍深入敌后采访。因身上有多处旧伤,精神忧郁,海明威于1961年用猎枪自杀。

　　长篇小说《太阳照样升起》以1924—1925年的巴黎为背景,美国青年巴恩斯在第一次世界大战后由于脊椎受伤而失去了性能力,之后他与一位英国女子相爱,但两人都清楚这段恋情只能无果而终。小说反映的主题是战争对"迷惘的一代"在生理、心理、伦理等方面所造成的严重伤害,他们所有的信念、梦想、价值观等都被战争摧毁,他们整日酗酒和纵乐,以发泄心中的绝望、悲哀和愤懑。《太阳照常升起》是海明威"冰山创作"原则的起始之作,他运用简洁的对话、简短的句式把事件、景物、人物的语言、心理等呈现在读者眼前。

小说《永别了，武器》主要讲述一位美国青年弗瑞德里克·亨利在第一次大战中受伤，养伤期间与一位英国护士凯瑟琳坠入爱河的故事。伤愈后他重返前线，亲眼看见了战争的各种残酷场面而毅然脱离部队，和凯瑟琳会合后逃往瑞士，结果凯瑟琳在难产中死去。小说通过描述两人的爱情悲剧揭示了战争的荒唐和残酷本质。《永别了，武器》中，情景交融的环境描写、电报般简洁的对话、情感真挚的内心独白、简约隽永的文体等标志着海明威独特创作风格的形成，显示了海明威艺术上的成就。

海明威最著名的代表作为中篇小说《老人与海》(*The Old Man and the Sea*, 1952)。尽管小说中的渔夫是悲剧性的，但他体现了超人般的品质，他沉着勇敢地面对死亡，绝不言败。这种"硬汉子"体现了海明威的人生哲学和道德理想——不向命运低头，永不服输。

海明威提出文学创作的"冰山原则"，认为作家应从繁芜的社会生活中撷取最具代表性的片段，将自己的思想情感隐匿其中，留下大部分空白让读者去阐释。海明威常以最简洁的日常词汇表达复杂的内容，常用简短句式表达具体含义，用有限的语言表达无尽的内涵。他善于用白描的手法写景，寥寥几笔就能勾勒出一幅清爽明了的画面；他的对话简洁，素有"电报风格"之称。海明威的文体特征在于朴素的语言文字、简单的篇章结构、鲜明的人物形象和深刻的主题意蕴。海明威对美国文学乃至世界文学做出了不朽贡献。

About the story

《杀手》("The Killers")创作于1927年，后收录于短篇小说集《没有女人的男人》(*Men Without Women*, 1927)中，是现代美国短篇小说中最优秀的作品之一。该作讲述了一个暗杀未遂的故事：两个杀手受人雇佣来到一家小餐馆，挟持了餐馆的厨师并且布置好暗杀现场，准备枪杀拳击手安德森，结果目标始终未出现，暗杀以失败告终。年轻的餐馆服务生尼克去给安德森报信，却发现安德森对即将到来的杀身之祸无动于衷，并拒绝了尼克主动提供的帮助。震惊之余，尼克回到餐馆并决定离开这个城市。

《杀手》大部分篇幅为人物对话，故事情节通过人物对话逐一展开。海明威巧妙地运用个性化语言使读者能够从中得知不同人物的性格特征。两名杀手在等待安德森出现时与乔治等人的嬉笑言谈，暴露出其凶暴残忍；乔治在整个暗杀行动中与两杀手之间的周旋对话，表现出其沉稳冷静；尼克答应给安德森通风报信，反映出他的善良与乐于助人。

短篇开头有两段精彩的对话：两个人走进餐馆，"'What's yours?' George asked them. 'I don't know,' one of the men said. 'What do you want to eat, Al?' 'I don't know,' said Al. 'I don't know what I want to eat.'" 对话全是简单句，没有形容词，可读者已经从简单明了的对话中领悟到其中的内涵：他们不是来就餐，而是另有所图。描写两个杀手的外貌时，作者仅用几个单句，就把两个自负、冷酷的职业杀手形象惟妙惟肖地展现在读者面前，"He wore a derby hat and a black overcoat buttoned across the chest … He wore a silk muffler and gloves."。另外，海明威还运用独特的比喻形成一种特殊的艺术效果，比如，形容杀手安排凶杀场地时，"He was like a photographer arranging for a group picture"，在照相的欢乐与凶杀的残酷对比中抨击他们的凶狠。

海明威用精练的白描手法，准确生动地勾画出"冰山"的"八分之一"的形象，巧妙地揭示了作品的复杂主题。作者没有让小说主人公尼克发表主观议论，也未细致描写他的心理活动和情感，甚至避免使用带有感情色彩的形容词，只通过三个场景及对话揭示他急剧的心理变化过程。第一个场景中，天真无邪的尼克平生第一次碰到谋杀，这时他没有惊慌，相反，还觉得杀人场面布置新鲜有趣；第二个场景中，这种兴奋很快就随着拳击手安德森的无动于衷化作泡影，随之而起的是内心的困惑和震惊；第三个场景中，在小说结尾他决心要离开这个市镇。小说中写道：

"'I'm going to get out of this town,' Nick said.

'Yes,' said George. 'That's a good thing to do.'

'I can't stand to think about him waiting in the room and knowing he's going to get it. It's too damned awful.'

'Well,' said George, 'you better not think about it.'"

这段对话貌似平淡，实则为整个故事的点睛之笔，因为它点出了作品的主题：一个纯真少年对罪恶世界及法则的失望和抗拒，以及一个见多识广者的淡然和超脱。

该短篇结构简洁、情节明了，既没有扑朔迷离的悬念设置，也没有激烈的打斗场面和血腥描写，但是整个故事跌宕起伏、别开生面、引人入胜。海明威将小说情节淡化至最低限度，只提供了"凶手的杀人准备""受害人的束手无策"和"尼克准备离开此地"三个场面，至于故事的地点、时间和人物，只是在场景的穿插中用寥寥数语予以交代,可谓惜墨如金,体现了海明威别具一格的创作风格。

The Killers

The door of Henry's lunch-room opened and two men came in. They sat down at the counter. "What's yours?" George asked them.

"I don't know," one of the men said. "What do you want to eat, Al?"

"I don't know," said Al. "I don't know what I want to eat."

Outside it was getting dark. The street-light came on outside the window. The two men at the counter read the menu. From the other end of the counter Nick Adams watched them. He had been talking to George when they came in.

"I'll have a roast pork tenderloin with apple sauce and mashed potatoes," the first man said.

"It isn't ready yet."

"What the hell do you put it on the card for?"

"That's the dinner," George explained. "You can get that at six o'clock."

George looked at the clock on the wall behind the counter.

"It's five o'clock."

"The clock says twenty minutes past five," the second man said.

"It's twenty minutes fast."

"Oh, to hell with the clock," the first man said. "What have you got to eat?"

"I can give you any kind of sandwiches," George said. "You can have hamandeggs, bacon and eggs, liver and bacon, or a steak."

"Give me chicken croquettes with green peas and cream sauce and mashed potatoes."

"That's the dinner."

"Everything we want's the dinner, eh? That's the way you work it."

"I can give you ham and eggs, bacon and eggs, liver—"

"I'll take ham and eggs," the man called Al said. He wore a derby hat① and a black overcoat buttoned across the chest. His face was small and white and he had tight lips. He wore a silk muffler and gloves.

"Give me bacon and eggs," said the other man. He was about the same size as Al. Their faces were different, but they were dressed like twins. Both wore overcoats too tight for them. They sat leaning forward, their elbows on the counter.

"Got anything to drink?" Al asked.

"Silver beer, bevo②, ginger-ale," George said.

"I mean you got anything to drink③?"

"Just those I said."

"This is a hot④ town," said the other. "What do they call it?"

"Summit."

"Ever hear of it?" Al asked his friend.

"No," said the friend.

"What do they do here nights?" Al asked.

"They eat the dinner," his friend said. "They all come here and eat the big dinner."

"That's right," George said.

"So you think that's right?" Al asked George.

"Sure."

"You're a pretty bright boy, aren't you?"

"Sure," said George.

"Well, you're not," said the other little man. "Is he, Al?"

---

① derby hat: 常礼帽，一种圆顶、带有窄的弯曲帽檐的硬毡帽。
② bevo: 一种不含酒精的麦芽酒精饮料。
③ drink: 此处指可喝的"烈酒"。
④ hot: （俚语）有生气的，活跃的，繁忙的，危险的。

"He's dumb," said Al. He turned to Nick. "What's your name?"

"Adams."

"Another bright boy," Al said. "Ain't he a bright boy, Max?"

"The town's full of bright boys," Max said.

George put the two platters, one of ham and eggs, the other of bacon and eggs, on the counter. He set down two side-dishes off ried potatoes and closed the wicket into the kitchen.

"Which is yours?" he asked Al.

"Don't you remember?"

"Ham and eggs."

"Just a bright boy," Max said. He leaned forward and took the ham and eggs. Both men ate with their gloves on. George watched them eat.

"What are you looking at?" Max looked at George.

"Nothing."

"The hell you were. You were looking at me."

"Maybe the boy meant it for a joke, Max," Al said.

George laughed.

"You don't have to laugh," Max said to him. "You don't have to laugh at all, see?"

"All right," said George.

"So he thinks it's all right." Max turned to Al. "He thinks it's all right. That's a good one."

"Oh, he's a thinker," Al said. They went on eating.

"What's the bright boy's name down the counter?" Al asked Max.

"Hey, bright boy," Max said to Nick. "You go around on the other side of the counter with your boy friend."

"What's the idea?" Nick asked.

"There isn't any idea."

"You better go around, bright boy," Al said. Nick went around behind the counter.

"What's the idea?" George asked.

"None of your damned business," Al said. "Who's out in the kitchen?"

"The nigger."

"What do you mean the nigger?"

"The nigger that cooks."

"Tell him to come in."

"What's the idea?"

"Tell him to come in."

"Where do you think you are?"

"We know damn well where we are," the man called Max said. "Do we look silly?"

"You talk silly," Al said to him. "What the hell do you argue with this kid for? Listen," he said to George, "tell the nigger to come out here."

"What are you going to do to him?"

"Nothing. Use your head, bright boy. What would we do to a nigger?"

George opened the slit that opened back into the kitchen. "Sam," he called. "Come in here a minute."

The door to the kitchen opened and the nigger came in. "What was it?" he asked. The two men at the counter took a look at him.

"All right, nigger. You stand right there," Al said.

Sam, the nigger, standing in his apron, looked at the two men sitting at the counter. "Yes, sir," he said. Al got down from his stool.

"I'm going back to the kitchen with the nigger and bright boy," he said. "Go on back to the kitchen, nigger. You go with him, bright boy." The little man walked after Nick and Sam, the cook, back into the kitchen. The door shut after them. The man called Max sat at the counter opposite George. He didn't look at George but looked in the mirror that ran along back of the counter. Henry's had been made over from a saloon into a lunch-counter.

"Well, bright boy," Max said, looking into the mirror, "why don't you say something?"

"What's it all about?"

"Hey, Al," Max called, "bright boy wants to know what it's all about."

"Why don't you tell him?" Al's voice came from the kitchen.

"What do you think it's all about?"

"I don't know."

"What do you think?"

Max looked into the mirror all the time he was talking.

"I wouldn't say."

"Hey, Al, bright boy says he wouldn't say what he thinks it's all about."

"I can hear you, all right," Al said from the kitchen. He had propped open the slit that dishes passed through into the kitchen with a catsup bottle. "Listen, bright boy," he said from the kitchen to George. "Stand a little further along the bar. You move a little to the left, Max." He was like a photographer arranging for a group picture.

"Talk to me, bright boy," Max said. "What do you think is going to happen?"

George did not say anything.

"I'll tell you," Max said. "We're going to kill a Swede. Do you know a big Swede named Ole Anderson?"

"Yes."

"He comes here to eat every night, don't he?"

"Sometimes he comes here."

"He comes here at six o'clock, don't he?"

"If he comes."

"We know all that, bright boy," Max said. "Talk about something else. Ever go to the movies?"

"Once in a while."

"You ought to go to the movies more. The movies are fine for a bright boy like you."

"What are you going to kill Ole Anderson for? What did he ever do to you?"

"He never had a chance to do anything to us. He never even seen us."

"And he's only going to see us once," Al said from the kitchen.

"What are you going to kill him for, then?" George asked.

"We're killing him for a friend. Just to oblige a friend, bright boy."

"Shut up," said Al from the kitchen. "You talk too goddamn much."

"Well, I got to keep bright boy amused. Don't I, bright boy?"

"You talk too damn much," Al said. "The nigger and my bright boy are amused by themselves. I got them tied up like a couple of girl friends in the convent."

"I suppose you were in a convent."

"You never know."

"You were in a kosher convent. That's where you were."

George looked up at the clock.

"If anybody comes in you tell them the cook is off, and if they keep after it, you tell them you'll go back and cook yourself. Do you get that, bright boy?"

"All right," George said. "What you going to do with us afterward?"

"That'll depend," Max said. "That's one of those things you never know at the time."

George looked up at the clock. It was a quarter past six. The door from the street opened. A street-car motorman came in.

"Hello, George," he said. "Can I get supper?"

"Sam's gone out," George said. "He'll be back in about half an hour."

"I'd better go up the street," the motorman said. George looked at the clock. It was twenty minutes, past six.

"That was nice, bright boy," Max said. "You're a regular little gentleman."

"He knew I'd blow his head off," Al said from the kitchen.

"No," said Max. "It ain't that. Bright boy is nice. He's a nice boy. I like him."

At six-fifty-five, George said, "He's not coming."

Two other people had been in the lunch-room. Once George had gone out to the kitchen and made a ham-and-egg sandwich "to go" that a man wanted to take with him. Inside the kitchen he saw Al, his derby hat tipped back, sitting on a stool beside the wicket with the muzzle of a sawed-off shotgun resting on the ledge. Nick and the cook were back to back in the corner, a towel tied in each of their mouths. George had cooked the sandwich, wrapped it up in oiled paper, put it in a bag, brought it in, and the man had paid for it and gone out.

"Bright boy can do everything," Max said. "He can cook and do everything. You'd make some girl a nice wife, bright boy."

"Yes?" George said, "Your friend, Ole Anderson, isn't going to come."

"We'll give him ten minutes," Max said.

Max watched the mirror and the clock. The hands of the clock marked seven o'clock, and then five minutes past seven.

"Come on, Al," said Max. "We better go. He's not coming."

"Better give him five minutes," Al said from the kitchen.

In the five minutes a man came in, and George explained that the cook was sick.

"Why the hell don't you get another cook?" the man asked. "Aren't you running a lunch-counter?" He went out.

"Come on, Al," Max said.

"What about the two bright boys and the nigger?"

"They're all right."

"You think so?"

"Sure. We're through with① it."

"I don't like it," said Al. "It's sloppy. You talk too much."

"Oh, what the hell," said Max. "We got to keep amused, haven't we?"

"You talk too much, all the same," Al said. He came out from the kitchen. The cut-off barrels of the shotgun made a slight bulge under the waist of his too tight-fitting overcoat. He straightened his coat with his gloved hands.

"So long, bright boy," he said to George. "You got a lot of luck."

"That's the truth," Max said. "You ought to play the races, bright boy."

The two of them went out the door. George watched them, through the window, pass under the arc-light and across the street. In their tight overcoats and derby hats they looked like a vaudeille team. George went back through the swinging-door into the kitchen and untied Nick and the cook.

"I don't want any more of that," said Sam, the cook. "I don't want any more of that."

Nick stood up. He had never had a towel in his mouth before.

"Say," he said. "What the hell?" He was trying to swagger it off.

"They were going to kill Ole Anderson," George said. "They were going to shoot him when he came in to eat."

"Ole Anderson?"

"Sure."

---

① be through with: 做好、结束（某工作等）；弃绝，厌烦。

The cook felt the corners of his mouth with his thumbs.

"They all gone?" he asked.

"Yeah," said George. "They're gone now."

"I don't like it," said the cook. "I don't like any of it at all"

"Listen," George said to Nick. "You better go see Ole Anderson."

"All right."

"You better not have anything to do with it at all," Sam, the cook, said. "You better stay way out of it."

"Don't go if you don't want to," George said.

"Mixing up in this ain't going to get you anywhere," the cook said. "You stay out of it."

"I'll go see him," Nick said to George. "Where does he live?"

The cook turned away.

"Little boys always know what they want to do," he said.

"He lives up at Hirsch's rooming-house," George said to Nick.

"I'll go up there."

Outside the arc-light shone through the bare branches of a tree. Nick walked up the street beside the car-tracks and turned at the next arc-light down a side-street. Three houses up the street was Hirsch's rooming-house. Nick walked up the two steps and pushed the bell. A woman came to the door.

"Is Ole Anderson here?"

"Do you want to see him?"

"Yes, if he's in."

Nick followed the woman up a flight of stair and back to the end of a corridor. She knocked on the door.

"Who is it?"

"It's somebody to see you, Mr. Anderson," the woman said.

"It's Nick Adams."

"Come in."

Nick opened the door and went into the room. Ole Anderson was lying on the bed with all his clothes on. He had been a heavyweight prizefighter and he was too long for the bed.

He lay with his head on two pillows. He did not look at Nick.

"What was it?" he asked.

"I was up at Henry's," Nick said, "and two fellows came in and tied up me and the cook, and they said they were going to kill you."

It sounded silly when he said it. Ole Anderson said nothing.

"They put us out in the kitchen," Nick went on. "They were going to shoot you when you came in to supper."

Ole Anderson looked at the wall and did not say anything.

"George thought I better come and tell you about it."

"There isn't anything I can do about it," Ole Anderson said.

"I'll tell you what they were like."

"I don't want to know what they were like," Ole Anderson said. He looked at the wall." Thanks for coming to tell me about it."

"That's all right."

Nick looked at the big man lying on the bed.

"Don't you want me to go and see the police?"

"No," Ole Anderson said. "That wouldn't do any good."

"Isn't there something I could do?"

"No. There ain't anything to do."

"Maybe it was just a bluff."

"No. It ain't just a bluff."

Ole Anderson rolled over toward the wall.

"The only thing is," he said, talking toward the wall, "I just can't make up my mind to go out. I been here all day."

"Couldn't you get out of town?"

"No," Ole Anderson said. "I'm through with all that running around."

He looked at the wall.

"There ain't anything to do now."

"Couldn't you fix it up some way?"

"No. I got in wrong①." He talked in the same flat voice. "There ain't anything to do. After a while I'll make up my mind to go out."

"I better go back and see George," Nick said.

"So long," said Ole Anderson. He did not look toward Nick. "Thanks for coming around."

Nick went out. As he shut the door he saw Ole Anderson with all his clothes on, lying on the bed looking at the wall.

"He's been in his room all day," the landlady said downstairs. "I guess he don't feel well. I said to him: 'Mr. Anderson, you ought to go out and take a walk on a nice fall day like this,' but he didn't feel like it."

"He doesn't want to go out."

"I'm sorry he don't feel well," the woman said. "He's an awfully nice man. He was in the ring②, you know."

"I know it."

"You'd never know it except from the way his face is," the woman said.

They stood talking just inside the street door. "He's just as gentle."

"Well, good night, Mrs. Hirsch," Nick said.

"I'm not Mrs. Hirsch," the woman said. "She owns the place. I just look after it for her. I'm Mrs. Bell."

"Well, good night, Mrs. Bell," Nick said.

"Good-night," the woman said.

Nick walked up the dark street to the corner under the arc-light, and then along the car-tracks to Henry's eating-house. George was inside, back of the counter.

"Did you see Ole?"

---

① get in wrong:(美国口语)使某人讨厌、令人陷入困境、失望。
② ring:(用绳子隔开的方形)拳击台。

"Yes," said Nick. "He's in his room and he won't go out."

The cook opened the door from the kitchen when he heard Nick's voice.

"I don't even listen to it," he said and shut the door.

"Did you tell him about it?" George asked.

"Sure. I told him but he knows what it's all about."

"What's he going to do?"

"Nothing."

"They'll kill him."

"I guess they will."

"He must have got mixed up in something in Chicago."

"I guess so," said Nick.

"It's a hell of a thing!"

"It's an awful thing," Nick said.

They did not say anything. George reached down for a towel and wiped the counter.

"I wonder what he did?" Nick said.

"Double-crossed① somebody. That's what they kill them for."

"I'm going to get out of this town," Nick said.

"Yes," said George. "That's a good thing to do."

"I can't stand to think about him waiting in the room and knowing he's going to get it. It's too damned awful."

"Well," said George, "you better not think about it."

---

① double-cross：(口语) 出卖，欺骗。

Questions

1. What is the theme of the story?
2. Discuss the main characters' personalities through the dialogues. Give some examples.
3. How is Hemingway's succinct and lucid prose style reflected in the story?

Further Readings

Hemingway is noted both for the intense masculinity of his writing and for his adventurous and widely publicized life. His succinct and lucid prose style has exerted a powerful influence on American and British fiction in the 20th century. Some of his well-known short stories are as follows.

1. "The Old Man and the Sea" (《老人与海》)
2. "The Snows of Kilimanjaro" (《乞力马扎罗山的雪》)
3. "A Clean, Well-Lighted Place" (《一个干净明亮的地方》)
4. "Hills like White Elephants" (《白象似的群山》)

Unit 16 Christmas

About the writer

俄裔美国作家弗拉基米尔·纳博科夫（Vladimir Vladimirovich Nabokov, 1899–1977）是20世纪世界范围内最著名的作家之一，也是美国后现代主义文学的先驱。1955年，他出版了小说《洛丽塔》(*Lolita*)。1962年，他发表了小说《微暗的火》(*Pale Fire*)。在这两部小说中，纳博科夫进行了叙事实验，揭示了人物丰富复杂、瞬息万变的内心世界。

纳博科夫1899年出生于俄国圣彼得堡一个富裕而显赫的家庭，自幼受到良好教育。1917年俄国二月革命爆发后，纳博科夫一家离开俄国，前往欧洲开始背井离乡的生活。1940年，纳博科夫一家为了逃避德国纳粹，前往美国。在妻子的帮助下，纳博科夫完成了他的重要作品《洛丽塔》。《洛丽塔》获得巨大反响，使纳博科夫不必再为生计奔波。之后，他全身心投入文学创作中，共著有17部长篇小说、50余篇短篇小说、400余首诗歌，还有许多剧本。

小说《洛丽塔》讲述了一个乱伦的故事。法国中年男人亨伯特在少年时爱上了一位14岁的少女，后来女孩由于伤寒去世，这给他留下终生难以愈合的创伤，自此他开始迷恋少女。到美国后，他开始迷恋房东14岁的女儿洛丽塔。为了接近洛丽塔，亨伯特与女孩的母亲结婚，母亲死后他开车带洛丽塔到各地旅行，并和她发生了关系。洛丽塔后来受一位剧作家奎尔蒂的蛊惑，与其私奔。两年后亨伯特找到了她，获悉奎尔蒂曾虐待洛丽塔，亨伯特悲愤不已，他枪杀了奎尔蒂，自己也被捕入狱。尽管小说饱受道德非议，但是小说对亨伯特的精神分裂症和其遭受的恋人早逝的创伤的描写，使得该小说成为反映人性的经典之作。

小说《微暗的火》形式奇特，由虚构的诗人约翰·谢德所创作的999行自传双韵体诗《微暗的火》与学者查尔斯·金博特为该诗所作的包括"前言""评注""索引"等批评文本构成。小说故事的发生地有两个：一个是美国的一所大学，另一个是虚构的岑不拉国。叙述者查尔斯·金博特曾是岑不拉国国王，在一场兵变中被推翻，他流亡到美国，改名换姓在大学里教书。岑不拉国政府派杀手前往美国追杀前国王，却阴差阳错杀死了金博特的同事约翰·谢德。《微暗的火》充满各种文字游戏，典故、双关语、多义词俯拾即是。

1969年，纳博科夫发表了小说《阿达》(Ada, or Ardor: A Family Chronicle)，继续探讨文学和现实的关系。小说描写了主人公伊凡·费恩与堂妹阿达·费恩之间曲折的爱情故事。伊凡到叔父的阿迪斯庄园度假时，爱上了自己的堂妹，这段不伦之恋使得两人异常痛苦。之后，堂妹另嫁他人，丈夫去世后，她排除万难，最终与伊凡走到一起。该作的奇特之处在于，阿迪斯庄园位于与地球相对应的"安迪特拉地球"，这个星球的时间与地球相隔50年。小说凸显了作品塑造的世界与现实世界的差异，再次说明小说的虚构性，作家的任务并不是反映摹写现实世界，而是创造另一种时空、另一种现实。

纳博科夫一生辗转于俄国、西欧、美国三种文化空间，漂泊不定的流亡生活使得他对文学与现实的关系有了深刻而独到的理解。他坚决反对文学能客观地反映现实的模仿论，对文学作品的道德说教功能也不以为然，他认为艺术的本质是虚构，文学创作就是运用各种复杂的技巧进行虚构。他运用多种叙事手法，努力在读者与人物之间拉开一段距离，使读者能够跳出小说之外，更冷静客观地去认识社会、思考人生。

About the story

《圣诞节》讲述的是在原本家庭团圆、充满喜庆的圣诞节前夜，斯列普佐夫却因失去儿子而悲痛万分的故事。他来到儿子生前居住的房间，看着儿子生前用过的物品，忆及儿子过往的点滴，心中万念俱灰，甚至产生了轻生的想法。然而当他看见儿子生前收藏在陶罐里的蚕蛹破茧成蝶的过程，似乎儿子化身为蝶得到重生，这使他又重新燃起对生活的希望。

蝴蝶是小说中的一个重要象征。纳博科夫受父亲影响，对蝴蝶抱有浓厚兴趣，终生都在研究蝴蝶和收集蝴蝶标本。他将对蝴蝶的迷恋融入文学创作之中，赋予蝴蝶多重意义。《圣诞节》中，蝴蝶预示着儿子与父亲之间的浓厚亲情，二人常在夏天外出捕蝶，度过了一段美好时光。小说详细描写了儿子捕蝶时的神态，"Forever-lost laughter plays on his face, under the turned-down brim of a straw hat burned dark by the sun; his hand toys with the chainlet of the leather purse attached to his belt, his dear, smooth, suntanned legs in their serge shorts and soaked sandals assume their usual cheerful widespread stance."另一方面，小说中蝴蝶也象征着重生。儿子死后，斯列普佐夫打开儿子生前收藏蝶茧的陶罐，亲眼看见了硬茧化蝶的过程，内心受到极大震撼。他认为儿子的生命通过这一化蝶过程得到重生，而自己也打消了轻生的念头，准备开启新的生活。作者以细腻的笔法生动描写了破茧成蝶的全过程，"a black, wrinkled creature the size of a mouse was crawling up the wall above the table … with six black furry feet … slowly and miraculously expanding … Gradually the wrinkled tissues … was a great Attacus"。化蝶是小说的高潮部分，暗合了基督教的重生与复活思想。

小说弥漫着浓厚的基督教色彩。故事发生在圣诞前夜，在这个基督教最重要的节日里，喜庆的气氛与主人公悲痛欲绝的心情形成鲜明对比。小说在对村庄的景色描写中凸显了教堂顶上十字架反射出的光芒，"beyond the light silver mist of trees, high above the squat isbas, the sun caught the equanimous radiance of the cross on the church"。小说末尾的化蝶再次提及上帝，"and now they were developed to the limit set for them by God"。作者将蛹化蝶的原因归结于上帝之力，不仅体现了对上帝的虔诚信仰，也反映出主人公希望借上帝之力重获生活希望。

基督教和蝴蝶共同反映了小说关于生与死的主题。基督教文化中，圣诞节是庆祝耶稣诞生的节日，然而主人公却失去了唯一的儿子。痛失爱子使斯列普佐夫万念俱灰。他前往墓地，悼念死去的儿子。回到家中后，他觉得一切都冰冷死寂，罩了白布套的家具暗示着死亡。他来到儿子生前居住的房间，睹物思人，竟产生了死亡的想法："It's Christmas tomorrow … and I'm going to die. Of course. It's so simple. This very night …"这时，一个轻微的响声打破了静寂的氛围，原来是陶罐里的硬茧破壳而出，他看到了化蝶的全过程：由一个不起眼的皱皮生物化为一只绚丽的印度蝴蝶。他为之震撼，惊讶于生命的顽强和绚烂。在斯列普佐夫看来，蝴蝶似乎是儿子生命的延续，同时从硬蛹到蝴蝶的蜕变是斯列普佐夫超脱人生痛苦的隐喻。

叙事方面，纳博科夫擅长细节描写，小说中对村庄景色、主人公心境、化蝶等细致入微的描绘烘托了故事的气氛,揭示了主人公在儿子去世后万念俱灰、悲痛欲绝的心境,以及受化蝶启发重燃生活信心的顿悟体验。小说也描写了主人公的幻觉,在儿子生前的房间徘徊时,他仿佛看到了儿子准备的圣诞树,并责令儿子将圣诞树拿走,儿子却辩解说圣诞节即将来临,圣诞树必不可少。这其实反映了主人公对儿子强烈的思念之情,超现实主义的幻觉描写更凸显了主人公在儿子离世后的绝望心情。

Christmas

AFTER walking back from the village to his manor across the dimming snows, Sleptsov sat down in a corner, on a plush-covered chair which he never remembered using before. It was the kind of thing that happens after some great calamity. Not your brother but a chance acquaintance, a vague country neighbor to whom you never paid much attention, with whom in normal times you exchange scarcely a word, is the one who comforts you wisely and gently, and hands you your dropped hat after the funeral service is over, and you are reeling from grief, your teeth chattering, your eyes blinded by tears. The same can be said of inanimate objects. Any room, even the coziest and the most absurdly small, in the little-used wing of a great country house has an unlived-in corner. And it was such a corner in which Sleptsov sat.

The wing was connected by a wooden gallery, now encumbered with our huge north Russian snowdrifts①, to the master house, used only in summer. There was no need to awaken it, to heat it: the master had come from Petersburg for only a couple of days and had settled in the annex, where it was a simple matter to get the stoves of white Dutch tile② going.

The master sat in his corner, on that plush chair, as in a doctor's waiting room. The room floated in darkness; the dense blue of early

---

① huge north Russian snowdrifts:俄国北方常见的大堆大堆的雪。
② white Dutch tile:荷兰的白瓷砖。

evening filtered through the crystal feathers of frost on the window-pane. Ivan, the quiet, portly valet, who had recently shaved off his mustache and now looked like his late father, the family butler, brought in a kerosene lamp①, all trimmed and brimming with light. He set it on a small table, and noiselessly caged it within its pink silk shade. For an instant a tilted mirror reflected his lit ear and cropped gray hair. Then he withdrew and the door gave a subdued creak.

Sleptsov raised his hand from his knee and slowly examined it. A drop of candle wax had stuck and hardened in the thin fold of skin between two fingers. He spread his fingers and the little white scale cracked.

The following morning, after a night spent in nonsensical, fragmentary dreams totally unrelated to his grief, as Sleptsov stepped out into the cold veranda, a floorboard emitted a merry pistol crack underfoot, and the reflections of the many-colored panes formed paradisal lozenges on the whitewashed cushionless window seats. The outer door resisted at-first, then opened with a luscious crunch, and the dazzling frost hit his face. The reddish sand providently sprinkled on the ice coating the porch steps resembled cinnamon, and thick icicles shot with greenish blue hung from the eaves. The snowdrifts reached all the way to the windows of the annex, tightly gripping the snug little wooden structure in their frosty clutches. The creamy white mounds of what were flower beds in summer swelled slightly above the level snow in front of the porch, and farther off loomed the radiance of the park, where every black branchlet was rimmed with silver, and the firs seemed to draw in their green paws under their bright plump load. Wearing high felt boots and a short fur-lined coat with a karakul collar, Sleptsov strode off slowly along a straight path, the only one cleared of snow, into that blinding distant landscape. He was amazed to be still alive, and able to perceive the brilliance of the snow and feel his front teeth

---

① kerosene lamp：煤油灯。

ache from the cold. He even noticed that a snow-covered bush resembled a fountain and that a dog had left a series of saffron marks① on the slope of a snowdrift, which had burned through its crust. A little farther, the supports of a footbridge stuck out of the snow, and there Sleptsov stopped. Bitterly, angrily, he pushed the thick, fluffy covering off the parapet. He vividly recalled how this bridge looked in summer. There was his son walking along the slippery planks, flecked with aments, and deftly plucking off with his net a butterfly that had settled on the railing. Now the boy sees his father. Forever-lost laughter plays on his face, under the turned-down brim of a straw hat burned dark by the sun; his hand toys with the chainlet of the leather purse attached to his belt, his dear, smooth, suntanned legs in their serge shorts and soaked sandals assume their usual cheerful widespread stance. Just recently, in Petersburg, after having babbled in his delirium about school, about his bicycle, about some great Oriental moth②, he died, and yesterday Sleptsov had taken the coffin—weighed down, it seemed, with an entire lifetime—to the country, into the family vault near the village church.

It was quiet as it can only be on a bright, frosty day. Sleptsov raised his leg high, stepped off the path and, leaving blue pits behind him in the snow, made his way among the trunks of amazingly white trees to the spot where the park dropped off toward the river. Far below, ice blocks sparkled near a hole cut in the smooth expanse of white and, on the opposite bank, very straight columns of pink smoke stood above the snowy roofs of log cabins. Sleptsov took off his karakul cap and leaned against a tree trunk. Somewhere far away peasants were chopping wood—every blow bounced resonantly skyward—and beyond the light silver mist of trees, high above the squat isbas, the sun caught the equanimous radiance of the cross on the

---

① a series of saffron marks: 狗的脚印像藏红花。
② Oriental mot: 黄刺蛾,属鳞翅目、刺蛾科。

church①.

That was where he headed after lunch, in an old sleigh with a high straight back. The cod of the black stallion clacked strongly in the frosty air, the white plumes of low branches glided overhead, and the ruts in front gave off a silvery blue sheen. When he arrived he sat for an hour or so by the grave, resting a heavy, woolen-gloved hand on the iron of the railing that burned his hand through the wool. He came home with a slight sense of disappointment, as if there, in the burial vault, he had been even further removed from his son than here, where the countless summer tracks of his rapid sandals were preserved beneath the snow.

In the evening, overcome by a fit of intense sadness, he had the main house unlocked. When the door swung open with a weighty wail, and a whiff of special, unwintery coolness came from the sonorous non-barred vestibule②, Sleptsov took the lamp with its tin reflector from the watchman's hand and entered the house alone. The parquet floors crackled eerily under his step. Room after room filled with yellow light, and the shrouded furniture seemed unfamiliar; instead of a tinkling chandelier, a soundless bag hung from the ceiling; and Sleptsov's enormous shadow, slowly extending one arm, floated across the wall and the gray squares of curtained paintings. He went into the room which had been his son's study in summer, set the lamp on the window ledge, and, breaking his fingernails as he did so, opened the folding shutters, even though all was darkness outside. In the blue glass the yellow flame of the slightly smoky lamp appeared, and his large, bearded face showed momentarily. He sat down at the bare desk and sternly, from under bent brows, examined the pale wallpaper with its garlands of bluish roses; a narrow officelike cabinet, with

---

① the sun caught the equanimous radiance of the cross on the church: 太阳与教堂上的十字架都发出清冷的光。教堂是基督教的标志性建筑，此处将教堂十字架的光辉与太阳的光芒相比较，凸显出基督徒对上帝的虔诚信仰。

② a whiff of special, unwintery coolness came from the sonorous non-barred vestibule: 房间里面飘出了一股独特的冷气，不像冬天的严寒。

sliding drawers from top to bottom; the couch and armchairs under slipcovers; and suddenly, dropping his head onto the desk, he started to shake, passionately, noisily, pressing first his lips, then his wet cheek, to the cold, dusty wood and clutching at its far corners.

In the desk he found a notebook, spreading boards, supplies of black pins, and an English biscuit tin that contained a large exotic cocoon① which had cost three rubles. It was papery to the touch and seemed made of a brown folded leaf. His son had remembered it during his sickness, regretting that he had left it behind, but consoling himself with the thought that the chrysalid inside was probably dead. He also found a torn net: a tarlatan bag on a collapsible hoop (and the muslin still smelled of summer and sun-hot grass).

Then, bending lower and lower and sobbing with his whole body, he began pulling out one by one the glass-topped drawers of the cabinet. In the dim lamplight the even files of specimens shone silklike under the glass. Here, in this room, on that very desk, his son had spread the wings of his captures. He would first pin the carefully killed insect in the cork-bottomed groove of the setting board, between the adjustable strips of wood, and fasten down flat with pinned strips of paper the still fresh, soft wings. They had now dried long ago and been transferred to the cabinet—those spectacular Swallowtails②, those dazzling Coppers and Blues③, and the various Fritillaries④, some mounted in a supine position to display the mother-of-pearl undersides. His son used to pronounce their Latin names with a moan of triumph or in an arch aside of disdain. And the moths, the moths, the first Aspen Hawk⑤ of five summers ago!

The night was smoke-blue and moonlit; thin clouds were scattered

---

① a large exotic cocoon:一只大蛹茧。
② Swallowtails:燕尾凤蝶。
③ dazzling Coppers and Blues:黄蓝斑纹蝶。
④ Fritillaries:豹纹蝶。
⑤ Aspen Hawk:蛾子的拉丁学名。

about the sky but did not touch the delicate, icy moon. The trees, masses of gray frost, cast dark shadows on the drifts, which scintillated here and there with metallic sparks. In the plush-upholstered, well-heated room of the annex Ivan had placed a two-foot fir tree in a clay pot on the table, and was just attaching a candle to its cruciform tip when Sleptsov returned from the main house, chilled, red-eyed, with gray dust smears on his cheek, carrying a wooden case under his arm. Seeing the Christmas tree on the table, he asked absently: "What's that?"

Relieving him of the case, Ivan answered in a low, mellow voice: "There's a holiday coming up tomorrow."

"No, take it away," said Sleptsov with a frown, while thinking. Can this be Christmas Eve? How could I have forgotten? Ivan gently insisted: "It's nice and green. Let it stand for a while."

"Please take it away," repeated Sleptsov, and bent over the case he had brought. In it he had gathered his son's belongings—the folding butterfly net, the biscuit tin with the pear-shaped cocoon, the spreading board, the pins in their lacquered box, the blue notebook. Half of the first page had been torn out, and its remaining fragment contained part of a French dictation. There followed daily entries, names of captured butterflies, and other notes: "*Walked across the bog as far as Borovichi*①..."

"Raining today. Played checkers with Father, then read Goncharov's *Frigate*②, a deadly bore."

"Marvelous hot day. Rode my bike in the evening. A midge got in my rye. Deliberately rode by her dacha twice, but didn't see her."

Sleptsov raised his head, swallowed something hot and huge. Of whom was his son writing?

---

① Borovichi：博罗维奇村。

② Goncharov's Frigate：冈察格夫《环球航海游记》讲述了作者在欧洲、非洲和亚洲的见闻与感触。作为19世纪中叶俄国第一位到过中国内陆的批判现实主义作家，冈察洛夫用严谨的态度将1852—1855年旅途中的所见所闻著成了一部长篇游记，文中对中国香港与上海进行了生动描写。

"Rode my bike as usual," he read on, "Our eyes nearly met. My darling, my love ..." "This is unthinkable," whispered Sleptsov. "I'll never know ..."

He bent over again, avidly deciphering the childish handwriting that slanted up then curved down in the margin.

"Saw a fresh specimen of the Camberwell Beauty① today. That means autumn is here. Rain in the evening. She has probably left, and we didn't even get acquainted. Farewell, my darling. I feel terribly sad ..."

"He never said anything to me ..." Sleptsov tried to remember, rubbing his forehead with his palm.

On the last page there was an ink drawing: the hind view of an elephant—two thick pillars, the corners of two ears, and a tiny tail.

Sleptsov got up. He shook his head, restraining yet another onrush of hideous sobs.

"I—can't—bear—it—any—longer," he drawled between groans, repeating even more slowly, "I—can't—bear—it—any—longer ..."

"It's Christmas tomorrow," came the abrupt reminder, "and I'm going to die. Of course. It's so simple. This very night ..."

He pulled out a handkerchief and dried his eyes, his beard, his cheeks. Dark streaks remained on the handkerchief. "... death," Sleptsov said softly, as if concluding a long sentence.

The clock ticked. Frost patterns overlapped on the blue glass of the window②. The open notebook shone radiantly on the table; next to it the light went through the muslin of the butterfly net, and glistened on a corner of the open tin. Sleptsov pressed his eyes shut, and had a fleeting sensation that earthly life lay before him, totally bared and comprehensible—and ghastly in its sadness, humiliatingly pointless, sterile, devoid of miracles ...

---

① Camberwell Beauty:在英格兰称为"坎伯韦尔美人蝶",也称作"蛱蝶"。
② Frost patterns overlapped on the blue glass of the window:蓝莹莹的窗玻璃上面结满了窗花。

At that instant there was a sudden snap—a thin sound like that of an overstretched rubber band breaking. Sleptsov opened his eyes. The cocoon in the biscuit tin had burst at its tip, and a black, wrinkled creature the size of a mouse was crawling up the wall above the table. It stopped, holding on to the surface with six black furry feet, and started palpitating strangely. It had emerged from the chrysalid because a man overcome with grief① had transferred a tin box to his warm room, and the warmth had penetrated its taut leaf-and-silk envelope②; it had awaited this moment so long, had collected its strength so tensely, and now, having broken out, it was slowly and miraculously expanding. Gradually the wrinkled tissues, the velvety fringes, unfurled; the fan-pleated veins grew firmer as they filled with air③. It became a winged thing imperceptibly, as a maturing face imperceptibly becomes beautiful④. And its wings—still feeble, still moist—kept growing and unfolding, and now they were developed to the limit set for them by God⑤, and there, on the wall, instead of a little lump of life, instead of a dark mouse, was a great Attacus moth⑥ like those that fly, birdlike, around lamps in the Indian dusk.

And then those thick black wings, with a glazy eyespot on each and a purplish bloom dusting their hooked foretips, took a full breath under the impulse of tender, ravishing, almost human happiness.

---

① a man overcome with grief:这里指主人公 Sleptsov。
② taut leaf-and-silk envelope:枯叶一般的丝茧壳。
③ fan-pleated veins grew firmer as they filled with air:扇形的翅膀随着空气的充入越来越坚实。
④ a maturing face imperceptibly becomes beautiful:犹如一张日益成熟的脸不知不觉中变得漂亮了一样。
⑤ now they were developed to the limit set for them by God:眼看着就长成了上帝为他们设计的尺寸。
⑥ Attacus moth:皇蛾,又称"蛇头蛾"。

Questions

1. What does the ending imply?
2. Nabokov is good at detailed descriptions of natural scenes and characters' psychology. While describing these realistic details, he also adds some other factors, such as hallucinations and dreams in modernism and postmodernism in order to portray the characters vividly. In this short story, how does Nabokov combine realism, modernism and postmodernism together to show the psychological state of the protagonist?

Further Readings

Nabokov's works are famous for their detailed psychological profile of the characters. The following are some of his important short stories.

1. "Signs and Symbols" (《符号与象征》)
2. "A Russian Beauty" (《俄罗斯美女》)
3. "Spring in Fialta" (《菲雅尔塔的春天》)
4. "Cloud, Castle, Lake" (《云·堡·湖》)

Unit 17　The Chrysanthemums

About the writer

约翰·斯坦贝克（John Steinbeck, 1902 – 1968）是美国现实主义小说家，因忠实地记录和再现了经济大萧条时期美国农民与季节工人的凄惨遭遇，创造了"斯坦贝克式的英雄"形象，他被称为"红色 30 年代"的代言人。

斯坦贝克 1902 年出生于加利福尼亚州中部山谷小城塞利纳斯（Salinas）的一个中产阶级家庭，他在那里生活了 30 多年，对那里的自然环境与劳动生活十分熟悉，为日后创作积累了丰富的素材。1919—1924 年，斯坦贝克就读于斯坦福大学，其间他从事了大量体力劳动，对社会底层的农民和农业工人的生活有深入了解。1937 年和 1947 年斯坦贝克两次访问北欧和苏联，接触了马克思主义和无产阶级文学。1968 年他因心脏病在纽约去世。

斯坦贝克近 30 年的小说创作生涯大致分为 3 个时期。第一个时期是 20 世纪 30 年代前后。斯坦贝克对美国经济大萧条所导致的农业工人的破产与贫困给予了极大关注。长篇小说《胜负未决》（In Dubious Battle, 1936）尝试从阶级对立角度表现农业工人问题，斯坦贝克认为，工人的罢工只能是一场胜负未决的战斗。在中篇寓言性小说《人鼠之间》（Of Mice and Men, 1937）中，他描写了两个季节性农业工人乔治与雷尼的虚幻理想与现实命运，表达了梦想、友谊和寂寞的主题。作品中多次出现失去了窝和被捏死的田鼠意象，表明如同生物界被捉弄、被毁灭的弱小生命，在现代资本主义社会农业工人的梦想必然会破灭。1940 年，《人鼠之间》被斯坦贝克改编成同名戏剧并获成功。

斯坦贝克最有影响的作品是长篇小说《愤怒的葡萄》（The Grapes of Wrath, 1939）。小说以 20 世纪 30 年代的经济大萧条为背景，真实地描写了破产农民向西迁徙的悲惨历程及他们的愤慨和斗争，反映了经济危机年代美国的社会现实和重大变动,揭露了美国社会的积弊,在一定程度上促进了社会改革。《愤怒的葡萄》中丰富的社会生活画面、深厚的象征意蕴、丰富绚烂的想象等使其获得1940年普利策奖,斯坦贝克也因该作获得1962年的诺贝尔文学奖。

20世纪40年代是斯坦贝克创作的第二个时期。第二次世界大战中他以战地记者身份到欧洲采访,这段前线经历为他提供了新的创作素材。中篇小说《月落》(*The Moon is Down*, 1942)描写了德国人占领时期挪威人民的抵抗运动,他因此获得挪威的自由十字勋章。《罐头厂街》(*Cannery Row*, 1945)反映二战结束后人们的迷惘和困惑,批判了金钱至上、罔顾伦理道德的社会风气。

20世纪50年代是斯坦贝克创作的第三个时期。长篇小说《伊甸之东》(*East of Eden*, 1952)具有一定自传成分。他将自己对赛利纳斯谷地的生活印象再现于当代生活场景中,借用该隐杀兄后蛰居伊甸以东的圣经故事赋予现实生活以超验意义——人的生存意志和在"善与恶"之间的抉择。

斯坦贝克的作品多以加利福尼亚州为背景,蕴含强烈的乡土文化价值观,通过以现实主义为主,同时融合浪漫主义、自然主义和象征主义的艺术风格,表达作者对劳动人民的同情、对大自然的热爱和对资本主义现实的愤懑。斯坦贝克的作品对之后的美国文学尤其是西部文学的发展产生了深远影响。

About the story

《菊花》("The Chrysanthemums")是斯坦贝克最优秀的短篇小说之一,1937年在《竖琴师杂志》(*Harper's Magazine*)上发表,后收录于短篇小说集《长谷》(*The Long Valley*, 1938)。该短篇是斯坦贝克一生中少有的以女性为主题的作品,小说因质朴的风格和细腻的人物刻画广受赞誉。

《菊花》的故事情节十分简单,讲述了加利福尼亚州塞利纳斯山谷一位家庭主妇伊莱莎的生活片段。伊莱莎和丈夫亨利过着平淡如水的生活,像所有传统美国农场的女主人那样,她关爱家庭、关心丈夫、埋头于各种家务,最大的特长和爱好是照料摆弄菊花。一天,有位流浪补锅匠来到伊莱莎的农庄,其自由逍遥的生活激发了伊莱莎深埋心底的对外界的好奇和向往,在补锅匠的误导诱哄之下她不仅给补锅匠提供了工作机会,还把珍爱的菊花送给他。伊莱莎最后发现补锅匠半途将菊花丢弃,这让她异常伤心。

小说伊始，作者描绘了加利福尼亚州塞利纳斯山谷的景色，这是一个笼罩着浓厚冬雾的山谷，大雾就像一个锅盖压在山上。山谷像一个严丝合缝的大铁罐，与世隔绝。十二月的冬日，山谷里没有阳光，只有微薄清冷的微风。这段景物描写为故事结尾伊莱莎由于对男人世界的极度失望而表现出的强烈悲愤埋下伏笔，预示伊莱莎的梦想注定要失败，奠定了小说的悲剧基调。

接下来，读者看到一个草料割好码放整齐、果园田地犁好只待雨水浸润、山坡上牛群皮毛丰厚可以安度寒冬的农场。妻子伊莱莎在整理花圃，丈夫亨利在院子另一头和两位衣帽整齐的男人说话，她时不时朝他们望去。在 looked down, watched them for a moment, looked down toward, cast another glance toward 中，"瞧""看""瞥"一系列动词的使用，把一个生活在男权社会里以家庭为人生舞台，过着单调乏味的生活，对男人世界充满好奇和向往，却又无法参与其中，内心里幻想与现实、渴望与压抑激烈斗争的年轻女人形象栩栩如生地展现在读者面前。伊莱莎是一位能干的主妇，她把家打理得井井有条、纤尘不染。

封闭单一的农场生活并不能限制伊莱莎对外部世界的向往和憧憬。她羡慕补锅匠自由惬意的生活，希望自己也能这样不再拘囿于农场樊笼之中而自由地生活。伊莱莎最初对补锅匠保持了谨慎的提防态度，连番拒绝他提出的磨剪子、补锅的请求。当狡猾的补锅匠心怀戒备，并将话题转到菊花上时，伊莱莎烦躁、冰冷的神情瞬间从脸上消融，变得健谈起来。伊莱莎不仅给补锅匠提供了工作机会，还将补锅匠编造出的爱花女士当作知音，并请补锅匠把菊花带给那位女士。她找来一个漂亮的新花盆移栽菊花，仔细地培土，装好花苗，并详细交代了种植注意事项。当发现送出的菊苗被漫不经心地抛在路边时，她受到极大打击，仿佛自己遭到践踏和侮辱一般，对虚伪的男性世界的失望和愤懑难以抑制。

菊花作为贯穿全文的主题，代表着自然的清纯和美丽，菊花和女主人公的紧密联系也象征着中年女性的美好。菊花被补锅匠扔在路边，象征了男权社会中女性的从属地位，出于经济、文化、社会等诸种原因，女性可能被男性利用、忽视、丢弃。此外，斯坦贝克也给小说中许多其他事物象征意义，他多次运用词语重复和过度词化的手法突显这些事物的象征意义，如 fence 一词反复出现 8 次，见证了伊莱莎平静抑郁、意识觉醒、满怀希望、愤懑屈服的心路历程。

The Chrysanthemums

The high grey-flannel fog of winter closed off the Salinas① Valley from the sky and from all the rest of the world. On every side it sat like a lid on the mountains and made of the great valley a closed pot. On the broad, level land floor the gang plows bit deep and left the black earth shining like metal where the shares had cut. On the foothill ranches across the Salinas River, the yellow stubble fields② seemed to be bathed in pale cold sunshine, but there was no sunshine in the valley now in December. The thick willow scrub along the river flamed with sharp and positive yellow leaves.

It was a time of quiet and of waiting. The air was cold and tender. A light wind blew up from the southwest so that the farmers were mildly hopeful of a good rain before long; but fog and rain did not go together.

Across the river, on Henry Allen's foothill ranch there was little work to be done, for the hay was cut and stored and the orchards were plowed up to receive the rain deeply when it should come. The cattle on the higher slopes were becoming shaggy and rough-coated.

Elisa Allen, working in her flower garden, looked down across the yard and saw Henry, her husband, talking to two men in business suits. The three of them stood by the tractor shed, each man with one foot on the side of the little Fordson③. They smoked cigarettes and studied the machine as they talked.

Elisa watched them for a moment and then went back to her work. She was thirty-five. Her face was lean and strong and her eyes were as clear as

---

① Salinas: 塞利纳斯,位于美国加利福尼亚中部,临近太平洋,周围土地肥沃,气候温和,阳光充足,物产丰富,农业发达。
② stubble fields: 收割后只剩茬儿的庄稼地。
③ Fordson: 福特发动机公司制造的一款拖拉机。

water. Her figure looked blocked and heavy in her gardening costume, a man's black hat pulled low down over her eyes, clod-hopper shoes, a figured print dress almost completely covered by a big corduroy apron① with four big pockets to hold the snips, the trowel and scratcher, the seeds and the knife she worked with. She wore heavy leather gloves to protect her hands while she worked.

She was cutting down the old year's chrysanthemum stalks with a pair of short and powerful scissors. She looked down toward the men by the tractor shed now and then. Her face was eager and mature and handsome; even her work with the scissors was over-eager, over-powerful. The chrysanthemum stems seemed too small and easy for her energy.

She brushed a cloud of hair out of her eyes with the back of her glove, and left a smudge of earth on her cheek in doing it. Behind her stood the neat white farm house with red geraniums close-banked around it as high as the windows. It was a hard-swept looking little house, with hard-polished windows②, and a clean mud-mat on the front steps.

Elisa cast another glance toward the tractor shed. The strangers were getting into their Ford coupe③. She took off a glove and put her strong fingers down into the forest of new green chrysanthemum sprouts that were growing around the old roots. She spread the leaves and looked down among the close-growing stems. No aphids were there, no sowbugs or snails or cutworms.④ Her terrier fingers destroyed such pests before they could get started.

Elisa started at the sound of her husband's voice. He had come near quietly, and he leaned over the wire fence that protected her flower garden

---

① corduroy apron: 灯芯绒围裙。
② hard-swept: 费力清扫过的; hard-polished: 费力擦亮的。说明伊莱莎打理房屋非常仔细。
③ Ford coupe: 福特(斜背双门)汽车。
④ No aphids were there, no sowbugs or snails or cutworms: 没有蚜虫、土鳖、蜗牛和夜盗蛾。

from cattle and dogs and chickens.

"At it again," he said. "You've got a strong new crop coming."

Elisa straightened her back and pulled on the gardening glove again. "Yes. They'll be strong this coming year." In her tone and on her face there was a little smugness.

"You've got a gift with things," Henry observed. "Some of those yellow chrysanthemums you had this year were ten inches across. I wish you'd work out in the orchard and raise some apples that big."

Her eyes sharpened. "Maybe I could do it, too. I've a gift with things, all right. My mother had it. She could stick anything in the ground and make it grow. She said it was having planters' hands that knew how to do it."

"Well, it sure works with flowers," he said.

"Henry, who were those men you were talking to?"

"Why, sure, that's what I came to tell you. They were from the Western Meat Company. I sold those thirty head of three-year-old steers. Got nearly my own price, too."

"Good," she said. "Good for you."

"And I thought," he continued, "I thought how it's Saturday afternoon, and we might go into Salinas for dinner at a restaurant, and then to a picture show—to celebrate, you see."

"Good," she repeated. "Oh, yes. That will be good."

Henry put on his joking tone. "There's fights tonight. How'd you like to go to the fights?"

"Oh, no," she said breathlessly. "No, I wouldn't like fights."

"Just fooling, Elisa. We'll go to a movie. Let's see. It's two now. I'm going to take Scotty and bring down those steers from the hill. It'll take us maybe two hours. We'll go in town about five and have dinner at the Cominos Hotel. Like that?"

"Of course I'll like it. It's good to eat away from home."

"All right, then. I'll go get up a couple of horses."

She said, "I'll have plenty of time to transplant some of these sets, I guess."

She heard her husband calling Scotty down by the barn. And a little later she saw the two men ride up the pale yellow hillside in search of the steers.

There was a little square sandy bed kept for rooting the chrysanthemums. With her trowel she turned the soil over and over, and smoothed it and patted it firm. Then she dug ten parallel trenches to receive the sets. Back at the chrysanthemum bed she pulled out the little crisp shoots, trimmed off the leaves of each one with her scissors and laid it on a small orderly pile.

A squeak of wheels and plod of hoofs① came from the road. Elisa looked up. The country road ran along the dense bank of willows and cotton-woods that bordered the river, and up this road came a curious vehicle, curiously drawn②. It was an old spring-wagon, with a round canvas top on it like the cover of a prairie schooner.③ It was drawn by an old bay horse and a little grey-and-white burro. A big stubble-bearded man sat between the cover flaps and drove the crawling team. Underneath the wagon, between the hind wheels, a lean and rangy mongrel dog walked sedately. Words were painted on the canvas in clumsy, crooked letters. "Pots, pans, knives, sisors, lawn mores④, Fixed." Two rows of articles, and the triumphantly definitive "Fixed" below. The black paint had run down in little sharp points beneath each letter.

Elisa, squatting on the ground, watched to see the crazy, loose-jointed wagon pass by. But it didn't pass. It turned into the farm road in front of her

---

① a squeak of wheels and plod of hoofs：吱哑作响的车轮声和嗒嗒的马蹄声。

② a curious vehicle, curiously drawn：怪模怪样的牲口拉着的怪模怪样的车。

③ It was an old spring-wagon, with a round canvas top on it like the cover of a prairie schooner：一辆破旧的弹簧马车，有类似草原上扎篷的四轮马车那样的圆形帆布顶篷。

④ sisors, lawn mores：补锅匠的招牌上单词拼写错误，应为 scissors, lawn mower。

house, crooked old wheels skirling and squeaking. The rangy dog darted from between the wheels and ran ahead. Instantly the two ranch shepherds flew out at him. Then all three stopped, and with stiff and quivering tails, with taut straight legs, with ambassadorial dignity, they slowly circled, sniffing daintily.① The caravan pulled up to Elisa's wire fence and stopped. Now the newcomer dog, feeling outnumbered, lowered his tail and retired under the wagon with raised hackles and bared teeth.

The man on the wagon seat called out, "That's a bad dog in a fight when he gets started."

Elisa laughed. "I see he is. How soon does he generally get started?"

The man caught up her laughter and echoed it heartily. "Sometimes not for weeks and weeks," he said. He climbed stiffly down, over the wheel. The horse and the donkey drooped like unwatered flowers.

Elisa saw that he was a very big man. Although his hair and beard were graying, he did not look old. His worn black suit was wrinkled and spotted with grease. The laughter had disappeared from his face and eyes the moment his laughing voice ceased. His eyes were dark, and they were full of the brooding that gets in the eyes of teamsters and of sailors. The calloused hands he rested on the wire fence were cracked, and every crack was a black line. He took off his battered hat.

"I'm off my general road, ma'am," he said. "Does this dirt road cut over across the river to the Los Angeles highway?"

Elisa stood up and shoved the thick scissors in her apron pocket. "Well, yes, it does, but it winds around and then fords the river. I don't think your team could pull through the sand."

He replied with some asperity, "It might surprise you what them beasts

---

① Then all three stopped, and with stiff and quivering tails, with taut straight legs, with ambassadorial dignity, they slowly circled, sniffing daintily: 三条狗都停了下来, 晃动着僵硬的尾巴, 四条腿紧蹬地面, 不慌不忙、神气十足地绕起了圈子, 并用鼻子郑重地嗅着对方。

can pull through."

"When they get started?" she asked.

He smiled for a second. "Yes. When they get started."

"Well," said Elisa, "I think you'll save time if you go back to the Salinas road and pick up the highway there."

He drew a big finger down the chicken wire and made it sing. "I ain't in any hurry, ma'am. I go from Seattle to San Diego and back every year. Takes all my time. About six months each way. I aim to follow nice weather."

Elisa took off her gloves and stuffed them in the apron pocket with the scissors. She touched the under edge of her man's hat, searching for fugitive hairs①. "That sounds like a nice kind of a way to live," she said.

He leaned confidentially over the fence. "Maybe you noticed the writing on my wagon. I mend pots and sharpen knives and scissors. You got any of them things to do?"

"Oh, no," she said quickly. "Nothing like that." Her eyes hardened with resistance.

"Scissors is the worst thing," he explained. "Most people just ruin scissors trying to sharpen 'em, but I know how. I got a special tool. It's a little bobbit kind of thing, and patented. But it sure does the trick.②"

"No. My scissors are all sharp."

"All right, then. Take a pot," he continued earnestly, "a bent pot, or a pot with a hole. I can make it like new so you don't have to buy no new ones. That's a saving for you."

"No," she said shortly. "I tell you I have nothing like that for you to do."

His face fell to an exaggerated sadness. His voice took on a whining

---

① fugitive hairs: 散落出的头发。
② It's a little bobbit kind of thing, and patented. But it sure does the trick.: bobbit 应为 habit; 这工具不大, 但是我的拿手戏。这里面有窍门。

undertone. "I ain't had a thing to do today. Maybe I won't have no supper tonight. You see I'm off my regular road. I know folks on the highway clear from Seattle to San Diego. They save their things for me to sharpen up because they know I do it so good and save them money."

"I'm sorry," Elisa said irritably. "I haven't anything for you to do."

His eyes left her face and fell to searching the ground. They roamed about until they came to the chrysanthemum bed where she had been working. "What's them plants, ma'am?"

The irritation and resistance melted from Elisa's face. "Oh, those are chrysanthemums, giant whites and yellows. I raise them every year, bigger than anybody around here."

"Kind of a long-stemmed flower? Looks like a quick puff of colored smoke?" he asked.

"That's it. What a nice way to describe them."

"They smell kind of nasty till you get used to them," he said.

"It's a good bitter smell," she retorted, "not nasty at all."

He changed his tone quickly. "I like the smell myself."

"I had ten-inch blooms this year," she said.

The man leaned farther over the fence. "Look. I know a lady down the road a piece, has got the nicest garden you ever seen. Got nearly every kind of flower but no chrysanthemums. Last time I was mending a copper-bottom washtub for her(that's a hard job but I do it good), she said to me, 'If you ever run acrost① some nice chrysanthemums I wish you'd try to get me a few seeds.' That's what she told me."

Elisa's eyes grew alert and eager. "She couldn't have known much about chrysanthemums. You can raise them from seed, but it's much easier to root the little sprouts you see there."

"Oh," he said. "I s'pose② I can't take none to her, then."

---

① acrost: 应为 across。
② s'pose: suppose 的缩写形式。

"Why yes you can," Elisa cried. "I can put some in damp sand, and you can carry them right along with you. They'll take root in the pot if you keep them damp. And then she can transplant them."

"She'd sure like to have some, ma'am. You say they're nice ones?"

"Beautiful," she said. "Oh, beautiful." Her eyes shone. She tore off the battered hat and shook out her dark pretty hair. "I'll put them in a flower pot, and you can take them right with you. Come into the yard."

While the man came through the picket fence Elisa ran excitedly along the geranium-bordered path to the back of the house. And she returned carrying a big red flower pot. The gloves were forgotten now. She knelt on the ground by the starting bed and dug up the sandy soil with her fingers and scooped it into the bright new flower pot. Then she picked up the little pile of shoots she had prepared. With her strong fingers she pressed them into the sand and tamped around them with her knuckles. The man stood over her. "I'll tell you what to do," she said. "You remember so you can tell the lady."

"Yes, I'll try to remember."

"Well, look. These will take root in about a month. Then she must set them out, about a foot apart in good rich earth like this, see?" She lifted a handful of dark soil for him to look at. "They'll grow fast and tall. Now remember this. In July tell her to cut them down, about eight inches from the ground."

"Before they bloom?" he asked.

"Yes, before they bloom." Her face was tight with eagerness. "They'll grow right up again. About the last of September the buds will start."

She stopped and seemed perplexed. "It's the budding that takes the most care," she said hesitantly. "I don't know how to tell you." She looked deep into his eyes, searchingly. Her mouth opened a little, and she seemed to be listening. "I'll try to tell you," she said. "Did you ever hear of planting hands?"

"Can't say I have, ma'am."

"Well, I can only tell you what it feels like. It's when you're picking off the buds you don't want. Everything goes right down into your fingertips. You watch your fingers work. They do it themselves. You can feel how it is. They pick and pick the buds. They never make a mistake. They're with the plant. Do you see? Your fingers and the plant. You can feel that, right up your arm. They know. They never make a mistake. You can feel it. When you're like that you can't do anything wrong. Do you see that? Can you understand that?"

She was kneeling on the ground looking up at him. Her breast swelled passionately.

The man's eyes narrowed. He looked away self-consciously. "Maybe I know," he said. "Sometimes in the night in the wagon there—"

Elisa's voice grew husky. She broke in on him. "I've never lived as you do, but I know what you mean. When the night is dark—why, the stars are sharp-pointed, and there's quiet. Why, you rise up and up! Every pointed star gets driven into your body. It's like that. Hot and sharp and—lovely."

Kneeling there, her hand went out toward his legs in the greasy black trousers. Her hesitant fingers almost touched the cloth. Then her hand dropped to the ground. She crouched low like a fawning dog.

He said, "It's nice, just like you say. Only when you don't have no dinner, it ain't."

She stood up then, very straight, and her face was ashamed. She held the flower pot out to him and placed it gently in his arms. "Here. Put it in your wagon, on the seat, where you can watch it. Maybe I can find something for you to do."

At the back of the house she dug in the can pile and found two old and battered aluminum saucepans. She carried them back and gave them to him. "Here, maybe you can fix these."

His manner changed. He became professional. "Good as new I can fix them." At the back of his wagon he set a little anvil, and out of an oily tool box dug a small machine hammer. Elisa came through the gate to watch him while he pounded out the dents in the kettles. His mouth grew sure and knowing. At a difficult part of the work he sucked his under-lip.

"You sleep right in the wagon?" Elisa asked.

"Right in the wagon, ma'am. Rain or shine I'm dry as a cow in there."

"It must be nice," she said. "It must be very nice. I wish women could do such things."

"It ain't the right kind of a life for a woman."

Her upper lip raised a little, showing her teeth. "How do you know? How can you tell?" she said.

"I don't know, ma'am," he protested. "Of course I don't know. Now here's your kettles, done. You don't have to buy no new ones."

"How much?"

"Oh, fifty cents'll do. I keep my prices down and my work good. That's why I have all them satisfied customers up and down the highway."

Elisa brought him a fifty-cent piece from the house and dropped it in his hand. "You might be surprised to have a rival some time. I can sharpen scissors, too. And I can beat the dents out of little pots. I could show you what a woman might do."

He put his hammer back in the oily box and shoved the little anvil out of sight. "It would be a lonely life for a woman, ma'am, and a scarey① life, too, with animals creeping under the wagon all night." He climbed over the singletree②, steadying himself with a hand on the burro's white rump. He settled himself in the seat, picked up the lines. "Thank you kindly, ma'am," he said. "I'll do like you told me; I'll go back and catch the Salinas road."

"Mind," she called, "if you're long in getting there, keep the sand

---

① scarey: scary。
② singletree: 车辕。

damp."

"Sand, ma'am? ... Sand? Oh, sure. You mean around the chrysanthemums. Sure I will." He clucked his tongue. The beasts leaned luxuriously into their collars. The mongrel dog took his place between the back wheels. The wagon turned and crawled out the entrance road and back the way it had come, along the river.

Elisa stood in front of her wire fence watching the slow progress of the caravan. Her shoulders were straight, her head thrown back, her eyes half-closed, so that the scene came vaguely into them. Her lips moved silently, forming the words "Goodbye—good-bye". Then she whispered, "That's a bright direction. There's a glowing there." The sound of her whisper startled her. She shook herself free and looked about to see whether anyone had been listening. Only the dogs had heard. They lifted their heads toward her from their sleeping in the dust, and then stretched out their chins and settled asleep again. Elisa turned and ran hurriedly into the house.

In the kitchen she reached behind the stove and felt the water tank. It was full of hot water from the noonday cooking. In the bathroom she tore off her soiled clothes and flung them into the corner. And then she scrubbed herself with a little block of pumice, legs and thighs, loins and chest and arms, until her skin was scratched and red. When she had dried herself she stood in front of a mirror in her bedroom and looked at her body. She tightened her stomach and threw out her chest. She turned and looked over her shoulder at her back.

After a while she began to dress, slowly. She put on her newest underclothing and her nicest stockings and the dress which was the symbol of her prettiness. She worked carefully on her hair, pencilled her eyebrows and rouged her lips.

Before she was finished she heard the little thunder of hoofs and the shouts of Henry and his helper as they drove the red steers into the corral. She heard the gate bang shut and set herself for Henry's arrival.

His step sounded on the porch. He entered the house calling, "Elisa, where are you?"

"In my room, dressing. I'm not ready. There's hot water for your bath. Hurry up. It's getting late."

When she heard him splashing in the tub, Elisa laid his dark suit on the bed, and shirt and socks and tie beside it. She stood his polished shoes on the floor beside the bed. Then she went to the porch and sat primly and stiffly down. She looked toward the river road where the willow-line was still yellow with frosted leaves so that under the high grey fog they seemed a thin band of sunshine. This was the only color in the grey afternoon. She sat unmoving for a long time. Her eyes blinked rarely.

Henry came banging out of the door, shoving his tie inside his vest as he came. Elisa stiffened and her face grew tight. Henry stopped short and looked at her. "Why—why, Elisa. You look so nice!"

"Nice? You think I look nice? What do you mean by 'nice'?"

Henry blundered on. "I don't know. I mean you look different, strong and happy."

"I am strong? Yes, strong. What do you mean 'strong'?"

He looked bewildered. "You're playing some kind of a game," he said helplessly. "It's a kind of a play. You look strong enough to break a calf over your knee, happy enough to eat it like a watermelon."

For a second she lost her rigidity. "Henry! Don't talk like that. You didn't know what you said." She grew complete again. "I'm strong," she boasted. "I never knew before how strong."

Henry looked down toward the tractor shed, and when he brought his eyes back to her, they were his own again. "I'll get out the car. You can put on your coat while I'm starting."

Elisa went into the house. She heard him drive to the gate and idle down his motor, and then she took a long time to put on her hat. She pulled it here and pressed it there. When Henry turned the motor off she slipped into her coat and went out.

The little roadster bounced along on the dirt road by the river, raising the birds and driving the rabbits into the brush. Two cranes flapped heavily over the willow-line and dropped into the river-bed.

Far ahead on the road Elisa saw a dark speck. She knew.

She tried not to look as they passed it, but her eyes would not obey. She whispered to herself sadly, "He might have thrown them off the road. That wouldn't have been much trouble, not very much. But he kept the pot," she explained. "He had to keep the pot. That's why he couldn't get them off the road."

The roadster turned a bend and she saw the caravan ahead. She swung full around toward her husband so she could not see the little covered wagon and the mismatched team as the car passed them.

In a moment it was over. The thing was done. She did not look back.

She said loudly, to be heard above the motor, "It will be good, tonight, a good dinner."

"Now you're changed again," Henry complained. He took one hand from the wheel and patted her knee. "I ought to take you in to dinner oftener. It would be good for both of us. We get so heavy out on the ranch."

"Henry," she asked, "could we have wine at dinner?"

"Sure we could. Say! That will be fine."

She was silent for a while; then she said, "Henry, at those prize fights, do the men hurt each other very much?"

"Sometimes a little, not often. Why?"

"Well, I've read how they break noses, and blood runs down their chests. I've read how the fighting gloves get heavy and soggy with blood."

He looked around at her. "What's the matter, Elisa? I didn't know you read things like that." He brought the car to a stop, then turned to the right over the Salinas River bridge.

"Do any women ever go to the fights?" she asked.

"Oh, sure, some. What's the matter, Elisa? Do you want to go? I don't think you'd like it, but I'll take you if you really want to go."

She relaxed limply in the seat. "Oh, no. No. I don't want to go. I'm sure I don't." Her face was turned away from him. "It will be enough if we can have wine. It will be plenty." She turned up her coat collar so he could not see that she was crying weakly—like an old woman.

Questions

1. Many words and phrases such as *fence*, *good*, *nice*, *strong* and *fight* are repeated in the short story. Please find them out and analyze the functions of these repetitions in shaping Elisa's image and emotion.

2. Chrysanthemum is a symbol of Elisa. Are there other symbolic images in this story? If so, what do they symbolize separately?

3. How do you think of the tinker in this story?

Further Readings

John Steinbeck's short stories are typical for dramatic landscapes and symbolic meanings. The following are some of his important short stories.

1. "The Murder" (《谋杀》)
2. "Flight" (《逃亡》)
3. "The Leader of the People" (《人民的领袖》)
4. "The Red Pony" (《小红马》)

Unit 18　A Good Man Is Hard to Find

About the writer

弗兰纳里·奥康纳(Flannery O'Conner, 1925–1964)是美国著名小说家,被认为是继福克纳之后美国南方最杰出的作家以及二战后美国最伟大的短篇小说家。奥康纳共创作了 2 部长篇小说、32 个短篇小说以及大量的评论文章。

奥康纳 1925 年出生于美国南方佐治亚州的萨凡纳(Savannah)一个具有浓厚宗教氛围的家庭,祖辈是 19 世纪移民美国的爱尔兰天主教徒。1942 年,奥康纳入读佐治亚州女子学院,1945 年获社会学与文学学士学位。1950 年,奥康纳正致力于第一部长篇小说《智血》(Wise Blood)的创作,却意外发现自己身患红斑狼疮,正是这种疾病在多年前夺去她父亲的生命。从此,奥康纳开始了与病魔的顽强搏斗,她在母亲的农场里一边疗养一边写作。1964 年奥康纳病逝,年仅 39 岁。

1955 年出版的短篇小说集《好人难寻及其他故事》(A Good Man Is Hard to Find and Other Stories)奠定了奥康纳在美国文坛的地位。这部小说集收录了 10 个短篇故事,其中包括《好人难寻》("A Good Man Is Hard to Find")、《救人如救己》("The Life You Save May Be Your Own")、《善良的乡下人》("Good Country People")、《难民》("The Displaced Person")等多个名篇。

第二部短篇小说集《上升的一切必然汇合》(Every Thing Rises Must Converge, 1965)在奥康纳逝世后面世,共收录了 9 个短篇故事,其中包括《上升的一切必然汇合》("Every Thing Rises Must Converge")、《绿叶》("Greenleaf")、《启示》("Revelation")3 篇欧·亨利短篇小说奖获奖作品。

1971 年出版的奥康纳《短篇小说全集》(The Complete Stories)收录了 31 个短篇,次年该小说集荣获美国国家图书奖。1988 年,著名的"美国文库系列丛书"(The Library of America Series)出版了《奥康纳集》(*Flannery O'Connor: Collected Works*),其中收录了奥康纳的第 32 个短篇小说《林中午后》("An Afternoon in the Woods")。

奥康纳的小说常被视为南方哥特式小说,一般以美国南方乡村为背景,描写南方社会中的普通人,并大量运用南方方言、俚语、黑色幽默等,具有典型的南方性。小说中经常出现有肢体残疾的人物,如《救人如救己》中仅有半截左胳膊的流浪汉、《圣灵所宿之处》("A Temple of the Holy Ghost")中的阴阳人等。就情节而言,故事中反复出现溺水、猝死、车祸等不幸事件,以及抢劫、残杀等暴力事件。对此,奥康纳认为,具有基督教信仰的小说家目光最为锐利,可以识别当下怪异、堕落和不可接受的东西,更易发现现代生活中令其厌恶的扭曲。无论畸形与怪异抑或暴力与死亡,均是作家震撼读者并唤醒其宗教意识的一种手段。奥康纳将这种写作风格称为"天主教现实主义"。

奥康纳的小说多数围绕穷人生活展开,描写了穷人遭受的各种折磨。奥康纳尝试从基督教信仰入手分析他们的遭遇,对她而言,生活的意义集中于基督对人类的救赎,她"在世界与救赎的关系上来看待世界"。耶路撒冷的圣西里尔曾指出,人们在前往灵魂之父的路上必须要经过蹲在路边的巨龙。奥康纳的小说关心的正是这趟神秘的旅程,无论龙以什么形式出现,人们都不得不经过它。这在《好人难寻》等故事中得到充分体现。

About the story

《好人难寻》选自奥康纳的第一部短篇小说集《好人难寻及其他故事》。该短篇可以分为两个部分。第一部分叙述老祖母一家人的旅行。老祖母不愿意去佛罗里达州,她想去东田纳西州探望亲友。因此,她以佛罗里达州有一名逃犯在流窜为由,说服儿子带着一家老小驱车前往东田纳西州。途中,老祖母忽然想去重访她年轻时参观过的一个古老的种植园,儿子不得不更改行程,在母亲的指挥下掉头驶上了一条坑坑洼洼的土道。没过多久,老祖母意识到自己记错了地方。窘迫间她不小心碰翻了装着猫咪的旅行袋,猫咪窜出来跳上了儿子的肩膀,一场车祸随即发生。第二部分讲述了老祖母一家人与三个逃犯的故事。一家人幸好只受了点轻伤。这时一辆车朝他们缓缓驶来,当他们请求对方协助修车时,老祖母突然发现其中一人竟是报纸上登载的越狱逃犯,并脱口道出了逃犯的绰号"格格不入"(The Misfit)。老祖母试图劝说"格格不入"不要乱开杀戒。与此同时,另外两名逃犯将老祖母的家人一个接一个带到树林里并将其杀害。最终,老祖母自己也死在"格格不入"的手下。在第一部分中,作者以轻松幽默的语调与夸张的戏剧性描写叙述日常琐事,使读者以为故事会平淡地发展下去。随着逃犯出现在车祸现场,第二部分的叙述笔调突转,出现了触目惊心的转折,故事最终以暴力与死亡结尾。

老祖母显然是故事的主角,但"格格不入"也是故事中一个至关重要的人物。读者能够从其自述中了解他大致的人生经历。"格格不入"出生在一个笃信基督教的家庭,母亲在他眼中是上帝造出的最好的女人,父亲有一颗如金子般宝贵的心灵。他从小就和其他兄弟姐妹不一样,对生活总爱问个究竟。他在教堂唱过福音;在陆军和海军服过兵役;有过两段婚姻……他并不认为自己是坏人,至今也没弄清楚自己为何会进监狱,只听监狱里的医生说过他的罪名是杀死了亲生父亲,可实际上他的父亲是死于1919年的大流感。世界的荒诞与法律的不公使他背离了宗教信仰,最终丧失了人性。

故事结尾处,老祖母称"格格不入"为自己的孩子,并伸手去抚摸他的肩膀。此时此刻,在老祖母清醒的意识中,"格格不入"不再是一个逃犯、一个陌生人,而是一个能够被上帝的恩泽拯救的同胞。面对老祖母这突如其来的异常举动,"格格不入"像是被蛇咬了一口似的猛然闪开,向老祖母的胸口连开三枪。半躺半坐在血泊之中的老祖母像孩子一样盘着腿,面朝着万里无云的晴空,脸上挂着一丝微笑去接受上帝的恩典。

在小说最后一段,"格格不入"告诉波比·李,人生没有真正的乐趣。然而,仅仅在不久之前,他还声称人生唯一的乐趣就是干点坏事。这种转变暗示着他同样获得了某种程度上的恩典。在奥康纳看来,要唤起人们的宗教意识、拯救这个缺乏信仰的社会,仅仅靠讲道和说教是行不通的。只有"格格不入"这类畸形人以暴力的手段引起强有力的破坏,才能使人获得宗教救赎,而死亡则是暴力的终结,是通往神圣之爱与宗教救赎的途径。小说充分体现了奥康纳对天主教的信仰及其宗教哲理——上帝会恩宠每一个人,即便是那些可憎可恶的。

除了宗教这个最重要的主题外,这篇作品还涉及对南方往昔的怀旧之情。作品的标题"好人难寻"出自故事中加油站兼餐厅老板瑞德·萨米的一句话。萨米与老祖母一起回忆起过去的美好时光,那时人们出门可以不锁大门,孩子们对家乡、父母及其他一切都充满谦恭,如今这一切已荡然无存。小说反映了主人公对古老南方的浓厚怀旧之情。

A Good Man Is Hard to Find

The grandmother didn't want to go to Florida. She wanted to visit some of her connections in east Tennessee and she was seizing at every chance to change Bailey's mind. Bailey was the son she lived with, her only boy. He was sitting on the edge of his chair at the table, bent over the orange sports section of the Journal. "Now look here, Bailey," she said, "see here, read this," and she stood with one hand on her thin hip and the other rattling the newspaper at his bald head. "Here this fellow that calls himself The Misfit is aloose from the Federal Pen① and headed toward Florida and you read here what it says he did to these people. Just you read it. I wouldn't take my children in any direction with a criminal like that aloose in it. I couldn't answer to my conscience if I did."

Bailey didn't look up from his reading so she wheeled around then and faced the children's mother, a young woman in slacks, whose face was as broad and innocent as a cabbage and was tied around with a green headkerchief that had two points on the top like rabbit's ears. She was sitting on the sofa, feeding the baby his apricots out of a jar. "The children have been to Florida before," the old lady said. "You all ought to take them somewhere else for a change so they would see different parts of the world and be broad②. They never have been to east Tennessee."

The children's mother didn't seem to hear her but the eight-year-old boy, John Wesley, a stocky child with glasses, said, "If you don't want to go to Florida, why dontcha③ stay at home?" He and the little girl, June Star, were reading the funny papers on the floor.

"She wouldn't stay at home to be queen for a day," June Star said

---

① aloose from the Federal Pen: 从联邦监狱里逃出。Pen 为 Penitentiary 的缩写。
② be broad: 开阔眼界。
③ dontcha: don't you。

without raising her yellow head.

"Yes and what would you do if this fellow, The Misfit, caught you?" the grandmother asked. "I'd smack his face," John Wesley said.

"She wouldn't stay at home for a million bucks," June Star said. "Afraid she'd miss something. She has to go everywhere we go."

"All right, Miss," the grandmother said. "Just remember that the next time you want me to curl your hair."

June Star said her hair was naturally curly.

The next morning the grandmother was the first one in the car, ready to go. She had her big black valise that looked like the head of a hippopotamus in one corner, and underneath it she was hiding a basket with Pitty Sing①, the cat, in it. She didn't intend for the cat to be left alone in the house for three days because he would miss her too much and she was afraid he might brush against one of her gas burners and accidentally asphyxiate himself. Her son, Bailey, didn't like to arrive at a motel with a cat.

She sat in the middle of the back seat with John Wesley and June Star on either side of her. Bailey and the children's mother and the baby sat in front and they left Atlanta at eight forty-five with the mileage on the car at 55,890. The grandmother wrote this down because she thought it would be interesting to say how many miles they had been when they got back. It took them twenty minutes to reach the outskirts of the city.

The old lady settled herself comfortably, removing her white cotton gloves and putting them up with her purse on the shelf in front of the back window. The children's mother still had on slacks and still had her head tied up in a green kerchief, but the grandmother had on a navy blue straw sailor hat with a bunch of white violets on the brim and a navy blue dress with a

---

① Pitty Sing：原为吉尔伯特(W. S. Gilbert)与沙利文(Sir Arthur Sullivan)创作的歌剧《日本天皇》(*The Mikado*, 1885)中的一个角色。老奶奶用这个角色的名字为她的猫咪命名。

small white dot in the print. Her collars and cuffs were white organdy trimmed with lace and at her neckline she had pinned a purple spray of cloth violets containing a sachet. In case of an accident, anyone seeing her dead on the highway would know at once that she was a lady.

She said she thought it was going to be a good day for driving, neither too hot nor too cold, and she cautioned Bailey that the speed limit was fifty-five miles an hour and that the patrolmen hid themselves behind billboards and small clumps of trees and sped out after you before you had a chance to slow down. She pointed out interesting details of the scenery: Stone Mountain①; the blue granite that in some places came up to both sides of the highway; the brilliant red clay banks slightly streaked with purple; and the various crops that made rows of green lace-work on the ground. The trees were full of silver-white sunlight and the meanest of them sparkled. The children were reading comic magazines and their mother had gone back to sleep.

"Let's go through Georgia fast so we won't have to look at it much," John Wesley said.

"If I were a little boy," said the grandmother, "I wouldn't talk about my native state that way. Tennessee has the mountains and Georgia has the hills."

"Tennessee is just a hillbilly dumping ground②," John Wesley said, "and Georgia is a lousy state too."

"You said it," June Star said.

"In my time," said the grandmother, folding her thin veined fingers, "children were more respectful of their native states and their parents and everything else. People did right then. Oh, look at the cute little

---

① Stone Mountain:石头山。位于亚特兰大市东郊,山上刻有南北战争时期南方邦联"总统"杰斐逊·戴维斯(Jefferson Davis)、南方军将领罗伯特·李(Robert E. Lee)和杰克逊(Stonewall Jackson)三人的巨型浮雕。

② a hillbilly dumping ground:一个乡下人住的鬼地方。

pickaninny①!" she said and pointed to a Negro child standing in the door of a shack. "Wouldn't that make a picture, now?" she asked and they all turned and looked at the little Negro out of the back window. He waved.

"He didn't have any britches② on," June Star said.

"He probably didn't have any," the grandmother explained. "Little riggers in the country don't have things like we do. If I could paint, I'd paint that picture," she said.

The children exchanged comic books.

The grandmother offered to hold the baby and the children's mother passed him over the front seat to her. She set him on her knee and bounced him and told him about the things they were passing. She rolled her eyes and screwed up her mouth and stuck her leathery thin face into his smooth bland one. Occasionally he gave her a faraway smile. They passed a large cotton field with five or six graves fenced in the middle of it, like a small island. "Look at the graveyard!" the grandmother said, pointing it out. "That was the old family burying ground. That belonged to the plantation."

"Where's the plantation?" John Wesley asked.

"Gone With the Wind③," said the grandmother. "Ha. Ha."

When the children finished all the comic books they had brought, they opened the lunch and ate it. The grandmother ate a peanut butter sandwich and an olive and would not let the children throw the box and the paper napkins out the window. When there was nothing else to do they played a game by choosing a cloud and making the other two guess what shape it suggested. John Wesley took one the shape of a cow and June Star guessed a cow and John Wesley said, no, an automobile, and June Star said he didn't play fair, and they began to slap each other over the grandmother.

---

① pickaninny:piccaninny,小黑鬼。
② britches:breeches,(裤脚束于膝下的)半长裤,马裤。
③ Gone With the Wind:随风飘走了。此为双关语,暗指美国作家玛格丽特·米切尔(Margret Mitchell,1990-1949)的小说《飘》(*Gone with the Wind*)。这是一部关于南北战争的小说。

The grandmother said she would tell them a story if they would keep quiet. When she told a story, she rolled her eyes and waved her head and was very dramatic. She said once when she was a maiden lady she had been courted by a Mr. Edgar Atkins Teagarden from Jasper, Georgia. She said he was a very good-looking man and a gentleman and that he brought her a watermelon every Saturday afternoon with his initials cut in it, E. A. T. Well, one Saturday, she said, Mr. Teagarden brought the watermelon and there was nobody at home and he left it on the front porch and returned in his buggy to Jasper, but she never got the watermelon, she said, because a nigger boy ate it when he saw the initials, E. A. T. ! This story tickled John Wesley's funny bone① and he giggled and giggled but June Star didn't think it was any good. She said she wouldn't marry a man that just brought her a watermelon on Saturday. The grandmother said she would have done well to marry Mr. Teagarden because he was a gentle man and had bought Coca-Cola stock when it first came out and that he had died only a few years ago, a very wealthy man.

They stopped at The Tower for barbecued sandwiches. The Tower was a part stucco and part wood filling station and dance hall set in a clearing outside of Timothy. A fat man named Red Sammy Butts ran it and there were signs stuck here and there on the building and for miles up and down the highway saying, TRY RED SAMMY'S FAMOUS BARBECUE. NONE LIKE FAMOUS RED SAMMY'S! RED SAM! THE FAT BOY WITH THE HAPPY LAUGH. A VETERAN! RED SAMMY'S YOUR MAN!

Red Sammy was lying on the bare ground outside The Tower with his head under a truck while a gray monkey about a foot high, chained to a small chinaberry tree, chattered nearby. The monkey sprang back into the tree and got on the highest limb as soon as he saw the children jump out of the car and run toward him.

---

① tickled John Wesley's funny bone:把约翰·韦斯利逗得咯咯直笑。

Inside, The Tower was a long dark room with a counter at one end and tables at the other and dancing space in the middle. They all sat down at a board table next to the nickelodeon① and Red Sam's wife, a tall burnt-brown woman with hair and eyes lighter than her skin, came and took their order. The children's mother put a dime in the machine and played "The Tennessee Waltz", and the grandmother said that tune always made her want to dance. She asked Bailey if he would like to dance but he only glared at her. He didn't have a naturally sunny disposition like she did and trips made him nervous. The grandmother's brown eyes were very bright. She swayed her head from side to side and pretended she was dancing in her chair. June Star said play something she could tap to so the children's mother put in another dime and played a fast number and June Star stepped out onto the dance floor and did her tap routine.

"Ain't she cute?" Red Sam's wife said, leaning over the counter. "Would you like to come be my little girl?"

"No I certainly wouldn't," June Star said. "I wouldn't live in a broken-down place like this for a million bucks!" and she ran back to the table.

"Ain't she cute?" the woman repeated, stretching her mouth politely.

"Arn't you ashamed?" hissed the grandmother.

Red Sam came in and told his wife to quit lounging on the counter and hurry up with these people's order. His khaki trousers reached just to his hip bones and his stomach hung over them like a sack of meal swaying under his shirt. He came over and sat down at a table nearby and let out a combination sigh and yodel. "You can't win," he said. "You can't win," and he wiped his sweating red face off with a gray handkerchief. "These days you don't know who to trust," he said. "Ain't that the truth?"

"People are certainly not nice like they used to be," said the grandmother.

---

① nickelodeon: 一种旧式自动点唱机。

"Two fellers① come in here last week," Red Sammy said, "driving a Chrysler. It was an old beat-up car but it was a good one and these boys looked all right to me. Said they worked at the mill and you know I let them fellers charge the gas they bought? Now why did I do that?" "Because you're a good man!" the grandmother said at once.

"Yes'm②, I suppose so," Red Sam said as if he were struck with this answer.

His wife brought the orders, carrying the five plates all at once without a tray, two in each hand and one balanced on her arm. "It isn't a soul③ in this green world④ of God's that you can trust," she said. "And I don't count nobody out of that, not nobody⑤," she repeated, looking at Red Sammy. "Did you read about that criminal, The Misfit, that's escaped?" asked the grandmother.

"I wouldn't be a bit surprised if he didn't attack this place right here," said the woman. "If he hears about it being here, I wouldn't be none surprised to see him. If he hears it's two cent⑥ in the cash register, I wouldn't be a tall⑦ surprised if he …"

"That'll do," Red Sam said. "Go bring these people their Co'-Colas," and the woman went off to get the rest of the order.

"A good man is hard to find," Red Sammy said. "Everything is getting terrible. I remember the day you could go off and leave your screen door unlatched. Not no more.⑧"

He and the grandmother discussed better times. The old lady said that in her opinion Europe was entirely to blame for the way things were now.

---

① fellers: fellows。
② Yes'm: Yes, madame。
③ It isn't a soul: There isn't a soul。
④ green world: good world。
⑤ not nobody: not anybody。
⑥ it's two cent: there are two cents。
⑦ a tall: at all。
⑧ Not no more: Not any more。

She said the way Europe acted you would think we were made of money and Red Sam said it was no use talking about it, she was exactly right. The children ran outside into the white sunlight and looked at the monkey in the lacy chinaberry tree. He was busy catching fleas on himself and biting each one carefully between his teeth as if it were a delicacy.

They drove off again into the hot afternoon. The grandmother took cat naps and woke up every few minutes with her own snoring. Outside of Toombsboro she woke up and recalled an old plantation that she had visited in this neighborhood once when she was a young lady. She said the house had six white columns across the front and that there was an avenue of oaks leading up to it and two little wooden trellis arbors on either side in front where you sat down with your suitor after a stroll in the garden. She recalled exactly which road to turn off to get to it. She knew that Bailey would not be willing to lose any time looking at an old house, but the more she talked about it, the more she wanted to see it once again and find out if the little twin arbors were still standing. "There was a secret panel in this house," she said craftily, not telling the truth but wishing that she were, "and the story went that all the family silver was hidden in it when Sherman① came through but it was never found …"

"Hey!" John Wesley said. "Let's go see it! We'll find it! We'll poke all the woodwork and find it! Who lives there? Where do you turn off at? Hey Pop, can't we turn off there?"

"We never have seen a house with a secret panel!" June Star shrieked. "Let's go to the house with the secret panel! Hey Pop, can't we go see the house with the secret panel!"

"It's not far from here, I know," the grandmother said. "It wouldn't take over twenty minutes." Bailey was looking straight ahead. His jaw was as rigid as a horseshoe. "No," he said.

---

① Sherman: 谢尔曼(William Tecumseh Sherman, 1820 – 1891), 南北战争中的北方军将领。在著名的"向海洋进军"途中, 他的军队穿越佐治亚州, 并沿途大肆劫掠。

The children began to yell and scream that they wanted to see the house with the secret panel. John Wesley kicked the back of the front seat and June Star hung over her mother's shoulder and whined desperately into her ear that they never had any fun even on their vacation, that they could never do what THEY wanted to do. The baby began to scream and John Wesley kicked the back of the seat so hard that his father could feel the blows in his kidney.

"All right!" he shouted and drew the car to a stop at the side of the road. "Will you all shut up? Will you all just shut up for one second? If you don't shut up, we won't go anywhere."

"It would be very educational for them," the grandmother murmured.

"All right," Bailey said, "but get this: this is the only time we're going to stop for anything like this. This is the one and only time."

"The dirt road that you have to turn down is about a mile back," the grandmother directed. "I marked it when we passed."

"A dirt road," Bailey groaned.

After they had turned around and were headed toward the dirt road, the grandmother recalled other points about the house, the beautiful glass over the front doorway and the candle-lamp in the hall. John Wesley said that the secret panel was probably in the fireplace.

"You can't go inside this house," Bailey said. "You don't know who lives there."

"While you all talk to the people in front, I'll run around behind and get in a window," John Wesley suggested.

"We'll all stay in the car," his mother said.

They turned onto the dirt road and the car raced roughly along in a swirl of pink dust. The grandmother recalled the times when there were no paved roads and thirty miles was a day's journey. The dirt road was hilly and there were sudden washes in it and sharp curves on dangerous embankments. All at once they would be on a hill, looking down over the blue tops of trees for miles around, then the next minute, they would be in a red depression with the dust-coated trees looking down on them.

"This place had better turn up in a minute," Bailey said, "or I'm going to turn around."

The road looked as if no one had traveled on it in months.

"It's not much farther," the grandmother said and just as she said it, a horrible thought came to her. The thought was so embarrassing that she turned red in the face and her eyes dilated and her feet jumped up, upsetting her valise in the corner. The instant the valise moved, the newspaper top she had over the basket under it rose with a snarl and Pitty Sing, the cat, sprang onto Bailey's shoulder.

The children were thrown to the floor and their mother, clutching the baby, was thrown out the door onto the ground; the old lady was thrown into the front seat. The car turned over once and landed right-side-up in a gulch off the side of the road. Bailey remained in the driver's seat with the cat—gray-striped with a broad white face and an orange nose—clinging to his neck like a caterpillar.

As soon as the children saw they could move their arms and legs, they scrambled out of the car, shouting, "We've had an ACCIDENT!" The grandmother was curled up under the dashboard, hoping she was injured so that Bailey's wrath would not come down on her all at once. The horrible thought she had had before the accident was that the house she had remembered so vividly was not in Georgia but in Tennessee.

Bailey removed the cat from his neck with both hands and flung it out the window against the side of a pine tree. Then he got out of the car and started looking for the children's mother. She was sitting against the side of the red gutted ditch, holding the screaming baby, but she only had a cut down her face and a broken shoulder. "We've had an ACCIDENT!" the children screamed in a frenzy of delight.

"But nobody's killed," June Star said with disappointment as the grandmother limped out of the car, her hat still pinned to her head but the broken front brim standing up at a jaunty angle and the violet spray hanging off the side. They all sat down in the ditch, except the children, to recover from the shock. They were all shaking.

"Maybe a car will come along," said the children's mother hoarsely.

"I believe I have injured an organ," said the grandmother, pressing her side, but no one answered her. Bailey's teeth were clattering. He had on a yellow sport shirt with bright blue parrots designed in it and his face was as yellow as the shirt. The grandmother decided that she would not mention that the house was in Tennessee.

The road was about ten feet above and they could see only the tops of the trees on the other side of it. Behind the ditch they were sitting in there were more woods, tall and dark and deep. In a few minutes they saw a car some distance away on top of a hill, coming slowly as if the occupants were watching them. The grandmother stood up and waved both arms dramatically to attract their attention. The car continued to come on slowly, disappeared around a bend and appeared again, moving even slower, on top of the hill they had gone over. It was a big black battered hearse-like automobile. There were three men in it.

It came to a stop just over them and for some minutes, the driver looked down with a steady expressionless gaze to where they were sitting, and didn't speak. Then he turned his head and muttered something to the other two and they got out. One was a fat boy in black trousers and a red sweat shirt with a silver stallion embossed on the front of it. He moved around on the right side of them and stood staring, his mouth partly open in a kind of loose grin. The other had on khaki pants and a blue striped coat and a gray hat pulled down very low, hiding most of his face. He came around slowly on the left side. Neither spoke.

The driver got out of the car and stood by the side of it, looking down at them. He was an older man than the other two. His hair was just beginning to gray and he wore silver-rimmed spectacles that gave him a scholarly look. He had a long creased face and didn't have on any shirt or undershirt. He had on blue jeans that were too tight for him and was holding a black hat and a gun. The two boys also had guns.

"We've had an ACCIDENT!" the children screamed.

The grandmother had the peculiar feeling that the bespectacled man was someone she knew. His face was as familiar to her as if she had known him all her life but she could not recall who he was. He moved away from the car and began to come down the embankment, placing his feet carefully so that he wouldn't slip. He had on tan and white shoes and no socks, and his ankles were red and thin. "Good afternoon," he said. "I see you all had you a little spill."

"We turned over twice!" said the grandmother.

"Oncet"①, he corrected. "We seen it happen. Try their car and see will it run, Hiram," he said quietly to the boy with the gray hat.

"What you got that gun for?" John Wesley asked. "Whatcha gonna do with that gun?"

"Lady," the man said to the children's mother, "would you mind calling them children to sit down by you? Children make me nervous. I want all you all to sit down right together there where you're at."

"What are you telling US what to do for?" June Star asked.

Behind them the line of woods gaped like a dark open mouth. "Come here," said their mother.

"Look here now," Bailey began suddenly, "We're in a predicament! We're in …"

The grandmother shrieked. She scrambled to her feet and stood staring. "You're The Misfit!" she said. "I recognized you at once!"

"Yes'm," the man said, smiling slightly as if he were pleased in spite

---

① Oncet: Once。

of himself to be known, "but it would have been better for all of you, lady, if you hadn't of reckernized me①."

Bailey turned his head sharply and said something to his mother that shocked even the children. The old lady began to cry and The Misfit reddened.

"Lady," he said, "don't you get upset. Sometimes a man says things he don't mean. I don't reckon he meant to talk to you thataway②."

"You wouldn't shoot a lady, would you?" the grandmother said and removed a clean handkerchief from her cuff and began to slap at her eyes with it.

The Misfit pointed the toe of his shoe into the ground and made a little hole and then covered it up again. "I would hate to have to," he said.

"Listen," the grandmother almost screamed, "I know you're a good man. You don't look a bit like you have common blood. I know you must come from nice people!"

"Yes mam," he said, "finest people in the world." When he smiled he showed a row of strong white teeth. "God never made a finer woman than my mother and my daddy's heart was pure gold," he said. The boy with the red sweat shirt had come around behind them and was standing with his gun at his hip. The Misfit squatted down on the ground. "Watch them children, Bobby Lee," he said. "You know they make me nervous." He looked at the six of them huddled together in front of him and he seemed to be embarrassed as if he couldn't think of anything to say. "Ain't a cloud in the sky," he remarked, looking up at it. "Don't see no sun but don't see no cloud neither."

"Yes, it's a beautiful day," said the grandmother. "Listen," she said, "you shouldn't call yourself The Misfit because I know you're a good man at heart. I can just look at you and tell." "Hush!" Bailey yelled. "Hush!

---

① if you hadn't of reckernized me: if you hadn't recognized me。
② thataway: that way。

Everybody shut up and let me handle this!" He was squatting in the position of a runner about to sprint forward but he didn't move.

"I pre-chate① that, lady," The Misfit said and drew a little circle in the ground with the butt of his gun.

"It'll take a half a hour to fix this here car," Hiram called, looking over the raised hood of it. "Well, first you and Bobby Lee get him and that little boy to step over yonder with you," The Misfit said, pointing to Bailey and John Wesley. "The boys want to ask you something," he said to Bailey. "Would you mind stepping back in them woods there with them?"

"Listen," Bailey began, "we're in a terrible predicament! Nobody realizes what this is," and his voice cracked. His eyes were as blue and intense as the parrots in his shirt and he remained perfectly still.

The grandmother reached up to adjust her hat brim as if she were going to the woods with him but it came off in her hand. She stood staring at it and after a second she let it fall on the ground. Hiram pulled Bailey up by the arm as if he were assisting an old man. John Wesley caught hold of his father's hand and Bobby Lee followed. They went off toward the woods and just as they reached the dark edge, Bailey turned and supporting himself against a gray naked pine trunk, he shouted, "I'll be back in a minute, Mamma, wait on me②!"

"Come back this instant!" his mother shrilled but they all disappeared into the woods. "Bailey Boy!" the grandmother called in a tragic voice but she found she was looking at The Misfit squatting on the ground in front of her. "I just know you're a good man," she said desperately. "You're not a bit common!"

"Nome③, I ain't a good man," The Misfit said after a second as if he had considered her statement carefully, "but I ain't the worst in the world

---

① pre-chate: appreciate。
② wait on me: wait for me。
③ Nome: No。

neither. My daddy said I was a different breed of dog from my brothers and sisters. 'You know,' Daddy said, 'it's some that can live their whole life out without asking about it and it's others has to know why it is①, and this boy is one of the latters. He's going to be into everything!'" He put on his black hat and looked up suddenly and then away deep into the woods as if he were embarrassed again. "I'm sorry I don't have on a shirt before you ladies," he said, hunching his shoulders slightly. "We buried our clothes that we had on when we escaped and we're just making do② until we can get better. We borrowed these from some folks we met," he explained.

"That's perfectly all right," the grandmother said. "Maybe Bailey has an extra shirt in his suitcase."

"I'll look and see terrectly③," The Misfit said.

"Where are they taking him?" the children's mother screamed.

"Daddy was a card himself," The Misfit said. "You couldn't put anything over on him.④ He never got in trouble with the Authorities though. Just had the knack of handling them."

"You could be honest too if you'd only try," said the grandmother. "Think how wonderful it would be to settle down and live a comfortable life and not have to think about somebody chasing you all the time."

The Misfit kept scratching in the ground with the butt of his gun as if he were thinking about it. "Yes'm, somebody is always after you," he murmured.

The grandmother noticed how thin his shoulder blades were just behind his hat because she was standing up looking down on him. "Do you every pray?" she asked.

---

① it's some that can live their whole life out without asking about it and it's others has to know why it is: 有些人活一辈子却对生活提不出一个问题, 而另一些人总想要知道生活为何如此。
② we're just making do: 我们只好凑合着。
③ terrectly: directly。
④ You couldn't put anything over on him: 你什么都瞒不过他。

He shook his head. All she saw was the black hat wiggle between his shoulder blades. "Nome," he said.

There was a pistol shot from the woods, followed closely by another. Then silence. The old lady's head jerked around. She could hear the wind move through the tree tops like a long satisfied insuck of breath. "Bailey Boy!" she called.

"I was a gospel singer for a while," The Misfit said. "I been most everything①. Been in the arm service, both land and sea, at home and abroad, been twict② married, been an undertaker, been with the railroads, plowed Mother Earth, been in a tornado, seen a man burnt alive oncet," and he looked up at the children's mother and the little girl who were sitting close together, their faces white and their eyes glassy; "I even seen a woman flogged," he said.

"Pray, pray," the grandmother began, "pray, pray …"

"I never was a bad boy that I remember of," The Misfit said in an almost dreamy voice, "but somewheres③ along the line I done④ something wrong and got sent to the penitentiary. I was buried alive," and he looked up and held her attention to him by a steady stare.

"That's when you should have started to pray," she said. "What did you do to get sent to the penitentiary that first time?"

"Turn to the right, it was a wall," The Misfit said, looking up again at the cloudless sky. "Turn to the left, it was a wall. Look up it was a ceiling; look down it was a floor. I forget what I done, lady. I set⑤ there and set there, trying to remember what it was I done and I ain't recalled it to this day. Oncet in a while, I would think it was coming to me, but it never come."

"Maybe they put you in by mistake," the old lady said vaguely.

---

① I been most everything:我几乎什么活都干过。
② twict:twice。
③ somewheres:somewhere。
④ done:did。
⑤ set:sat。

"Nome," he said. "It wasn't no mistake. They had the papers on me."

"You must have stolen something," she said.

The Misfit sneered slightly. "Nobody had nothing I wanted," he said. "It was a head-doctor at the penitentiary said what I had done was kill my daddy but I known that for a lie. My daddy died in nineteen ought nineteen of the epidemic flu① and I never had a thing to do with it. He was buried in the Mount Hopewell Baptist churchyard and you can go there and see for yourself."

"If you would pray," the old lady said, "Jesus would help you."

"That's right," The Misfit said.

"Well then, why don't you pray?" she asked trembling with delight suddenly.

"I don't want no hep②," he said. "I'm doing all right by myself."

Bobby Lee and Hiram came ambling back from the woods. Bobby Lee was dragging a yellow shirt with bright blue parrots in it.

"Thow③ me that shirt, Bobby Lee," The Misfit said. The shirt came flying at him and landed on his shoulder and he put it on. The grandmother couldn't name what the shirt reminded her of. "No, lady," The Misfit said while he was buttoning it up, "I found out the crime don't matter. You can do one thing or you can do another, kill a man or take a tire off his car, because sooner or later you're going to forget what it was you done and just be punished for it."

The children's mother had begun to make heaving noises as if she couldn't get her breath. "Lady," he asked, "would you and that little girl like to step off yonder with Bobby Lee and Hiram and join your husband?"

"Yes, thank you," the mother said faintly. Her left arm dangled

---

① nineteen ought nineteen of the epidemic flu: 1919 年的大流感。
② I don't want no hep: I don't want any help。
③ Thow: Throw。

helplessly and she was holding the baby, who had gone to sleep, in the other. "Hep that lady up, Hiram," The Misfit said as she struggled to climb out of the ditch, "and Bobby Lee, you hold onto that little girl's hand."

"I don't want to hold hands with him," June Star said. "He reminds me of a pig."

The fat boy blushed and laughed and caught her by the arm and pulled her off into the woods after Hiram and her mother.

Alone with The Misfit, the grandmother found that she had lost her voice. There was not a cloud in the sky nor any sun. There was nothing around her but woods. She wanted to tell him that he must pray. She opened and closed her mouth several times before anything came out. Finally she found herself saying, "Jesus. Jesus," meaning, Jesus will help you, but the way she was saying it, it sounded as if she might be cursing.

"Yes'm," The Misfit said as if he agreed. "Jesus thown everything off balance. It was the same case with Him as with me except He hadn't committed any crime and they could prove I had committed one because they had the papers on me. Of course," he said, "they never shown me my papers. That's why I sign myself now.① I said long ago, you get you a signature and sign everything you do and keep a copy of it. Then you'll know what you done and you can hold up the crime to the punishment② and see do they match and in the end you'll have something to prove you ain't been treated right. I call myself The Misfit," he said, "because I can't make what all I done wrong fit what all I gone through in punishment."

There was a piercing scream from the woods, followed closely by a pistol report. "Does it seem right to you, lady, that one is punished a heap③ and another ain't punished at all?"

---

① That's why I sign myself now:所以我现在自己来签字(指通过杀人来证明自己有罪)。
② you can hold up the crime to the punishment:你可以把罪行和惩罚加以对照。
③ a heap:a lot。

"Jesus!" the old lady cried. "You've got good blood! I know you wouldn't shoot a lady! I know you come from nice people! Pray! Jesus, you ought not to shoot a lady. I'll give you all the money I've got!"

"Lady," The Misfit said, looking beyond her far into the woods, "there never was a body that give the undertaker a tip."

There were two more pistol reports and the grandmother raised her head like a parched old turkey hen crying for water and called, "Bailey Boy, Bailey Boy!" as if her heart would break. "Jesus was the only One that ever raised the dead①," The Misfit continued, "and He shouldn't have done it. He thown everything off balance. If He did what He said, then it's nothing for you to do but thow away everything and follow Him, and if He didn't, then it's nothing for you to do but enjoy the few minutes you got left the best way you can by killing somebody or burning down his house or doing some other meanness to him. No pleasure but meanness," he said and his voice had become almost a snarl.

"Maybe He didn't raise the dead," the old lady mumbled, not knowing what she was saying and feeling so dizzy that she sank down in the ditch with her legs twisted under her.

"I wasn't there so I can't say He didn't," The Misfit said. "I wisht I had of been there②," he said, hitting the ground with his fist. "It ain't right I wasn't there because if I had of been there I would of known③. Listen lady," he said in a high voice, "if I had of been there I would of known and I wouldn't be like I am now." His voice seemed about to crack and the grandmother's head cleared for an instant. She saw the man's face twisted close to her own as if he were going to cry and she murmured, "Why you're one of my babies. You're one of my own children!" She reached out and touched him on the shoulder. The Misfit sprang back as if a snake had

---

① Jesus was the only One that ever raised the dead：耶稣是唯一能使死人复活的人。
② I wisht I had of been there：I wished I had been there。
③ I would of known：I would have known。

bitten him and shot her three times through the chest. Then he put his gun down on the ground and took off his glasses and began to clean them.

Hiram and Bobby Lee returned from the woods and stood over the ditch, looking down at the grandmother who half sat and half lay in a puddle of blood with her legs crossed under her like a child's and her face smiling up at the cloudless sky.

Without his glasses, The Misfit's eyes were red-rimmed and pale and defenseless-looking. "Take her off and thow her where you thown the others," he said, picking up the cat that was rubbing itself against his leg.

"She was a talker, wasn't she?" Bobby Lee said, sliding down the ditch with a yodel.

"She would of been a good woman," The Misfit said, "if it had been somebody there to shoot her every minute of her life."

"Some fun!" Bobby Lee said.

"Shut up, Bobby Lee," The Misfit said. "It's no real pleasure in life."

Questions

1. How would you characterize the grandmother in the story?
2. What does the author seem to imply through the story?

Further Readings

Flannery O'Connor's works, usually set in the rural American South, concern the relationship between the individual and God. The following are some of her important short stories.

1. "The Life You Save May Be Your Own" (《救人如救己》)
2. "Good Country People" (《善良的乡下人》)
3. "A Temple of the Holy Ghost" (《圣灵所宿之处》)